UNEASY CASTLES

Also by Myra King:

Cyber Rules, Certys UK, 2012
City Paddock, Ginninderra Press, Adelaide, 2010, reprinted 2016
The Journey of Velvet Brown, Ginninderra Press, Adelaide, 2015
The Diaries of Velvet Brown, Ginninderra Press, Adelaide, 2017

Uneasy Castles

MYRA KING

MacGregor House

First Printing 2017

ISBN 978 0 6480740 2 1

_MH_

MacGregor House Publishing
South Australia

Foreword

After the wake, standing in my sister's spare room, we look down at what is left of my mother's belongings. A small cardboard box filled mostly with paper memories. Pictures in frames, photo albums and lettercards I had sent when I lived too far away to visit regularly. Mum was never a hoarder, never a collector.

I started collecting with my writing. Over thirty-five years ago. In the beginning it was my published articles, saved in scrapbooks before the art of scrapping was popular.

For some years now it has been things which have connections with these following stories and poems. A Bushells Tea Caddy, a Lucky Strike cigarette tin, a golden sunned pendant. My original birth certificate with Myron as my first name. And bespoke by a good friend with talented mind and nimble fingers, ten thousand kilometres away, a blue bird and a soft felt horse. Also on my computer-table's ledge there's a piece of beach coral, intricate wormholes of calcium in impossible patterns, collected mid-sunrise pause on a grey early morning jog, and a shattered red-gum fragment from a broken cleat on a century old steamboat.

Uneasy Castles, written over some years, is a collection of my stories and poems.

CONTENTS

Little Sisters
e-fiction USA

We're three little sisters; we're all nice and new,
there's Mar-gar-et and Ros-lyn Rat
and My-ron Eskimo...

Myron is a boy's name, but that's what it says on my birth certificate: Myron May MacDonald.

In a role reversal of A Boy Named Sue, I am a girl named Myron. But when my big sister, Margaret, made up this sister solidarity song, I had no idea of genders or anything outside the fish pond of poverty that was my motherless existence. And when she explained what an Eskimo was I'd argued that I wasn't, until she told me how my feet, when pressed up against her at night in the bed we often shared, were as cold as an igloo. 'And your nose isn't much better,' she'd said, tweaking it.

Only six years older than me but wise beyond many adults, Margaret held us together when our father died and we'd ended up in one foster home after another.

'Why is Rozzie a rat?' I'd said. 'She's nice.'

It was true to a point, the point being how to sharpen the word *nice*. If *nice* was quiet and shy with a voice to match and rarely heard, then my sister, Roslyn, was nice.

Margaret had looked up with a face which showed she was tired of explaining, tired of carrying two little sisters on her back. But all she'd said was, 'That way it has better cadence,' and then left it there, hanging, with yet another word I didn't understand but felt I ought to.

I'll be ninety tomorrow, ninety candles on my cake, if I choose to have one that is.

No one, when they are young, really believes that they'll get old. Old is for other people who have arrived there somehow, from some parallel universe.

Youth plays lip service to old age, as if talking about it will prevent it from happening in the same way one might try and ward off something bad by bringing it to mind, or voice... *I want to live till eighty-five, that's enough. I don't want to get to a hundred, that's far too old... when I reach retirement I'll be a recluse with a house full of cats...*

Some try to demystify it, confront it but they never *really* believe in growing old anymore than they do in the death-fairy.

But reality has a way of creeping up on you like the dusk. Like a thief in the night - I think that's from the bible. Something about the second coming and I guess if you want to satirise, old age creeps up in seconds, it's all seconds coming together that makes a life. And what you fit into it.

My father, who was a blacksmith, always said life is how you shape it.

'Myron,' he would say, 'you have to make the shoe fit the horse, not the horse fit the shoe.' And with that metaphor going way over my four-year-old head I would watch, eyes wide, reflecting the flame of the forge, while he banged and fitted and banged and fitted.

In between the shaping, the draught horse he was shoeing would drop his hoof with a thud and snort puffs of thin morning breath. No competition for the hissing steam which rose in plumes when father plunged the glowing shoe into the bucket of water.

Father would disappear behind that steam.

Then the anvil would ring out once again, as the next shoe had to be shaped and fitted.

Later, Margaret would say I could not have remembered this. I would have been too young, she'd say.

But I do remember. She would have been surprised by what I remember.

It's been a month now since I broke my hip and two weeks since the pneumonia set in. Today is the best I've felt; last week I wouldn't have given you a smile for my chances of seeing my ninetieth. But this improvement I know happens sometimes. The patient rallies just before they pass away, sending all the relatives into shock: *But he looked so well yesterday. He was even sitting up in bed watching TV.*

Thank goodness I have no one left to mourn me.

The nurses are good to me here. I was a nurse once and I think they respect the fact that I know how the system works and are relieved they don't have to explain every procedure to me. It's not much fun being on the other end of it all, though. Much easier being on their side, I tell them. They laugh, prop up my pillows, smooth my sheets and say, 'You don't have to worry about anything, Mrs Mac.' (Everyone calls me Mrs Mac, even though I've never been married). 'You just concentrate on getting better.'

And I feel I *am* improving, my lungs seem to be clearing and my sense of smell has come back, reminding me how much I hate the smell of hospitals. Funny when you think of how I spent fifty years of my life working in them. The last time I was a patient though, was after the fire which killed my father. Margaret and I both had smoke inhalation and were admitted. Roslyn was fine, she managed to escape the house before it was engulfed by flames or smoke.

There is a young girl, of about fifteen, in the bed opposite to me. She is only just embarking on the realities of life. She had to face the starkest one this morning when the patient in the bed next to hers passed away.

Now this girl sits staring at a dinner gone as cold as poor Mrs Claire, the old lady who died.

I know when she went too. It was at two am, the time I cannot sleep. I heard *that* breath. When you'd been a nurse for as long as I had, you got to know the signs and sounds.

I look at the girl until she sees me.

'Eat up your dinner,' I say to her stare. 'Life goes on. Mrs Claire was over eighty, she had a good innings.' Platitudes, I know, but they are all I can think of at the moment.

The girl's eyes lift into mine.

'I didn't even speak to her,' she whispers. I can barely hear her but being a little deaf has made me a good lip reader. And then as if trying to make up for the fact she hadn't spoken to me either, she opens her voice and tells me her name, Amy, and why she is here. Placenta Previa. When she starts to explain what that is, I tell her, I know. I was a nurse once. Still am, in my mind, but I don't tell her that.

Amy picks up a piece of bread and looks at it as if it's a foreign object. She takes a nibble but when she speaks her mouth is empty.

'That poor old lady. I heard her moaning through the night. And, Mrs Mac, they only gave her Panadol.'

Her voice is hushed like she is telling me a secret.

I lean forward, seeming to join in the conspiracy. 'I think she had a stroke,' I say. 'There was no way the doctors could have known until they did a scan.'

'I know, she was going to have one this afternoon.' Amy looks at her watch. And takes a shuddering breath. 'Now, actually.'

I can feel her guilt like a palpable thing. Her reluctance to connect and the knowing she could have been the last one to talk to the old lady if she had. Perhaps offer some words of comfort.

In the world of guilt hers is only a small island. But no less real for that.

I fall back on the pillows and push my tray forward a little to stop it from slipping off. I haven't managed to eat anything and I feel

4

ashamed of my wastefulness. Even the cutlery is still in its paper wrapper. I can see the ice-cream melting, pooling up the jelly like a miniature green mountain.

It's the end of visiting time. No one has come to our room. If my sisters were alive they would have insisted on being here with me all day.

I raise my voice above those fading in the corridor. 'Mrs Claire talked to me yesterday. Just before you were brought in.'

Amy nods, and I continue. 'She told me how much she hoped her son would visit her. "But," she said, "he's so busy. And it's his golfing day and he deserves a break."'

Amy's eyes show a light of hope as if one guilt might negate another, soften it somehow.

And I wonder if Mrs Claire's son even feels guilty.

My guilt has lived with me almost every day of my life.

The girl begins to cry. I don't try and stop her; sometimes tears are what we need.

My sister, Margaret, used to cry every morning at two am. Before the house fire I could have slept through a bomb but Margaret's crying reset my internal clock and made my sleep as fragile as hers. That's when she'd sing the song like a lullaby.

We're three little sisters; we're all nice and new...

Father had always wanted boys. I was his last hope. And apart from giving me a boy's name he carried it further with the toys he bought me and the games he played. Plastic army soldiers and toy trucks, and the killing fields of the garden.

'Come with me Myron,' he'd said to me on a Saturday when the wind was messing about with the sulky sun, blowing hot afternoon breath, even though it was only morning.

He gave me a bucket and told me to collect all the caterpillars I could find.

5

I was only four years old and these little creatures still held the fascination of life for me; I'd often kept them as pets in jam jars.

I hurried around, plucked them from the bushes and the fleshy undersides of plants, and wondered what my father could want with them. He was out of my vision and I didn't see him dig the pit, with its dark sides square and deep.

And so, with all the horror of my innocence, I watched as he placed my gatherings of caterpillars, their furry coats glowing gold in the sun, in their grave and then, as they tried climbing out, picked them off one by one with a slingshot. My protests held no power to stop him.

I'd run to Margaret, I knew Roslyn would offer no comfort.

That day marked the full stop to any attention from my father. Some things like female daughters could not be shaped.

A short time after, I found the kitten he'd given me for my birthday, drowned in our little blow-up swimming pool. The one with the fish going nowhere forever, around its plastic rim. For the rest of that summer I would not go in that pool no matter how hot it got.

After that, Father's attention turned to my sister Roslyn, but he didn't try and make her a boy. Later, with the sickening wisdom of hindsight, I knew it was more of a woman he was trying to shape.

'They tell me I have to stay in hospital until the baby is born,' Amy says, her voice sounding washed from the crying.

'Yes, you could haemorrhage if the placenta detaches itself. Bed rest is best.'

Echo words of my nursing days. A little bit of poetic licence, really it's: Breast is Best.

'My boyfriend, Trevor,' Amy says, 'was coming to see me today, but he didn't turn up.'

I can see now there was more to the crying than her guilt. I wonder how old Trevor could be; this girl barely looks old enough to conceive.

I smile at her and she continues, bringing out all the words held back in shyness from the day before. Parading them as the future set in hope. She tells me how she really wants this baby and how she would do anything to keep from losing it. Trevor feels the same and she is not so young at sixteen. Her mother was not much older.

My gasp at her age brings her head up.

'I know I look younger and I guess it *is* really young to be having a baby. But I did that course, like, at school, with the dolls. You know the ones that are programmed to act like real babies? And Mrs Mac, I was top of my class. Lots of the other kids' babies died. Not really of course, but they can tell what you've done to them by the data.'

I start to tell her it's a bit different with reality but I stop my words. She needs encouragement not defeat.

I think about my own mother in her last days. The waiting, the hoping, probably for a boy. I wonder if she even had a girl's name picked out for me. I try to harden myself against her with this thought. But a cold numbness is the closest I get.

The doctors wanted my mother to have an abortion. But she couldn't do it even though the odds were against her carrying full term.

Her choice let me live while she perished. A life for a life.

I know I shouldn't feel guilty but knowing does not make it so.

There's Mar-ga-ret and Ros-lyn Rat and My-ron Eskimo.

Father always had work but there never seemed to be enough money. Never enough for shoes or clothes although always enough for beer and cigarettes.

When he was killed in the fire and we lost all our possessions, as few as they were, I didn't grieve for those or him but for the life I wished I could have had. And the foster homes offered no reprieve; we were never long enough in any one of them to form bonds of attachment. We became known as the Jonas kids. Things always seemed to happen to the families which took us in. Their pets ran away. Their children got sick. Things broke down. Nothing was ever traced directly to us, we three sisters would close up like a pact. But in the end only the children's home would take us.

I hear arguing in the corridor. A man's voice pleading, another more authoritative voice stating that visiting times were over. The voices soften. Foot-shuffles and a young man steps through the door carrying a balloon with the words, 'I love you' shining around it like a banner.

He does not see me; I am past the age of notice by a man of such youth.

His eyes are for the waif-like girl. 'Hey Amy, I bought you this.' The balloon passes between them like an exchange of vows. She takes the string and before he relinquishes it they are joined by a hands touch.

'This is Mrs Mac.' The girl indicates with her free hand but the boy doesn't turn around. It's only when I say pleased to meet you, Trevor, that he acknowledges me with a half cheek and nod.

I leave them to themselves; it is a young person's world. Although we three little sisters never knew it.

But we learned that guilt shapes many faces: the fleeting one of slight regret, the furrowed remorse of survival, or the guilt screwed to hatred as ugly as our childhood.

Roslyn was never happy in the foster homes. And as I grew older I learned about her, knew what she was capable of.

When I wake it is to a semi-darkness once so familiar to me on night shift, the not quite dark, not quite light of the early hours. I think of Margaret waking forever at 2 am, reliving the fire which killed our father and erased our childhood. Took all the remnants of a mother I never knew.

Another memory, framed through our bedroom window, of Roslyn running from our house, candle clutched in her hand like a sword. The fire's glow casting shadows that lengthened down the tracks of my mind. I know Margaret had seen her, she was looking out of the window with me, while the house cracked and burned and pushed seemingly impossible heat against our backs.

It was never talked about and our sister trinity held as strong as faith for all the following years of Margaret's and Roslyn's life.

And we never married. I pledged myself to relieve the suffering of others while Margaret gave her life to care for Roslyn.

I hear myself coughing and then the murmuring voices of comfort. Familiar voices.

I sink back in the pillows, close my eyes, listen to those words, our three little sisters song once more played to the tune of my memories and the faltering rhythm of my breath.

Running Away

Valley Review Magazine, Massachusetts, USA

Mitchell hunched forward in his seat on the train and looked down at his riding boots. They'd been a gift from his father for his thirteenth birthday almost two years ago, but they'd been too big for him then and they didn't quite fit him now. Still too loose.

He could feel through his soles the vibration of the wheels over the rails, running him away from home, kilometre by kilometre. His stomach felt as tight as it did when he had to visit the dentist or on those nights his stepfather came home late with drunken fists.

When the train stalled, his old school bag, tucked under the seat, jolted forward into the back of his legs. He drew it out, held it between his feet and slipped the zip. The money, holding accusation in its crumpled-ness, spilled out. He counted it again. There was more than enough for his trip Up North. His new life. It would take days to get there. Australia was a big place.

The cash smelt of his mother's tea-caddy, tea leaves, sweet-mown, although the container had not held tea for a long time.

Five years' savings. His mother's getting-away-from-it-all money. Now his. But he knew he would pay it back, or pay for his mother to join him. If she would come.

Mitchell looked past his shadowed reflection, through the train's window grime, to the sidewalls of the railway tracks. A gallery of graffiti. The passengers, captive viewers. Mandatory scenery for everyone. Unless you closed your eyes.

He read the scrawl: *Power To Us All*, screaming statically in letters over a metre tall. Paint blacker than his skin.

An old woman, hair receding in grease, unfolded her body into the seat opposite, grunting an apology as her ancient bag caught his knees. Her unshod feet, flat-lined-cracked from years of walking the streets, stuck out duck-like from beneath tired clothes.

"Wot you got there, lad? Looks like you's headed off campin', hey?" She directed a thumbnail with its groove of black at Mitchell's swag.

He nodded, ran a finger along the straps, feeling the coolness of the buckles holding taut the green canvas roll that smelled of tents and summer.

The woman uncoiled and sucked her gums. "Looks pretty new. Like them boots. Where you's goin'? Hey! wanna lolly?"

She brought out a paper bag soggy at the top with strawberry stain. It fell open like an overripe flower.

Mitchell shook his head and drew the swag onto his lap, folding his arms across it, almost an embrace. He looked down at his boots once more.

Then his voice caught his words. "I'm heading Up...North to meet my dad... he's working on a cattle station." He wondered why he was telling a stranger this. What if his mother and stepfather sent the police looking?

But he knew they wouldn't. Somehow that felt a whole lot worse.

The old woman indicated the side of her cheek and looked him in the eyes. "Wot happened there?"

Mitchell touched his face in a mirrored reaction and winced, he hadn't thought the bruise would show above the colour of his skin. He could feel the swelling and the broken dryness of the abrasion where his stepfather's knuckles, factory hardened, had connected. His hand felt stuck to his face. He turned away without answering.

The train pulled up in a grease-steeled screech at their first stop. People got off but more got on.

11

Mitchell noticed no one took up the offer of an empty seat next to him or the woman. And he could see by their faces it was not just her that made their choice to stand more desirable.

Alone, he and she were together in separateness.

The old woman told Mitchell her name was Pearl. He didn't tell her his but he did tell her about where he was heading. Anna Creek Station, over five million acres, the biggest cattle station in the world. He'd marvelled when his dad wrote and told him this. And about the horses and the Brahma bulls. The note had come, two years ago, with the riding boots and an IOU to learn to ride. *Come up for the holidays* was scratched as a postscript.

He hadn't gone then, too scared of going on such a long journey by himself and he knew, without asking, his mother wouldn't take him, not newly re-married with a baby on the way.

"So this dad of yours, he's a stockman or sumthin'?" Pearl withdrew some sweets from the bag, stuffed them into her mouth and started chewing. The movement of her gums reminded Mitchell of a house-cow they'd once owned.

"He's a ringer. A drover. He flies the helicopter they use to find the herds. He used to ride horses. Now they round up most of the cattle with motorbikes."

"So you's gunna fly up there? Long way, hey."

Mitchell looked at Pearl's face. He'd never felt like this before. Safe in anything he said. "No. I mean I'm flying to Adelaide but then I'm taking the train. Where are you going, Pearl?"

"Long way." Mitchell wasn't sure if she meant that's where she was heading, or if she was just repeating what she'd said. Or maybe the distance she had already travelled.

He knew *his* journey, had been living the route in his mind and dreams for weeks before he was even sure he would be going. But what had happened at school decided it.

Pearl began talking again. "You know, I used to have a pair of boots like that. R. M. Williamses. Boyfriend bought em for me when I was seventeen. Didn't expect anythin' for em. Which was good, cos he wouldn't have got anythin'." Pearl laughed and for a moment Mitchell wondered what she meant. Then he felt his face warming.

"My dad's going to teach me to ride," Mitchell said. "There's a muster coming up. The Great Outback Cattle Ride. Mostly for tourists. But anyone can go."

Pearl nodded, chewing gummily. Her face bovinely placid.

Mitchell hesitated. "Dad doesn't know I'm coming yet."

Pearl's expression didn't change. Then, between mouthfuls, she continued like he hadn't spoken. "I grew up on a dairy. Bloody hard work. Had to get the cows in real early every mornin'. I had a little roan pony. Bubbles." Pearl snorted a laugh. "He was always fartin'."

Mitchell laughed and placed his swag on the seat next to him again. The train took a bend and, in the aisle, people swayed and their knuckles whitened as they gripped the tops of the seats. But they kept their faces averted.

"Anyway, I learned to ride bareback. Couldn't be blowed saddlin' up. I got to be a pretty good rider. Betteren any of the boys in the district."

"Is it hard? Riding, I mean."

Pearl narrowed her eyes at him. "I reckon you'll be fine. It's in your blud. Best stockmen alive, the aborigines."

Mitchell sat up a little straighter. He saw one of the standing passengers looking at him. He tried to meet his eyes but the man turned away.

Pearl moved her bulk and squished the empty lolly bag into her pocket.

She leaned back and stretched.

"One thing you gotta remember, lad, is a horse'll pick up on yer fear. But don't ya worry bout that, just pretend you *is* brave. Like Joan of Arc said, if you think yerself brave that's the most important thing."

Mitchell had heard of Joan of Arc but for a moment he mixed her up with Lady Godiva riding through the streets naked, with only her hair to cover her modesty. He felt his face heating again, pulled his swag over his lap and looked up at Pearl. She had her eyes shut, but seemed to know he was looking and opened them.

"I'm not brave, Pearl," he said to her pale stare.

She raised eyebrows and nodded almost imperceptibly.

"Ah lad, there's brave an then there's foolhardy, s'not the same at all. I'll tell you sumthin', cos you look like a kid that's goin' places and not just Up North." Pearl laughed and shifted her large frame again, then, finding comfort in putting her feet up on the seat next to Mitchell, she closed her eyes and added in a clear voice, "Just afta I got them R.M. Williamses, Jack, the old horse trader from down the road got in another load of Brumbies." Pearl paused then pre-empted Mitchell's next question. "Yeah, probly from Up North. Wild buggers they was and also some roughies too. Supposedly dropouts from the Rodeo. So old Jack was tellin' us. We kids was always goin' to old Jack's on weekends. Tryin' to outdo each other, flank ropin' the horses with binder twine to make em buck, fightin' over who was first goin' ride the unbroken colts."

Mitchell opened his eyes wide and leaned forward over his swag. "Did you ever do that, Pearl. I mean did you ever break in a horse yourself?" The last words a rush.

"Yes, I sure as hell did lad, but that's not what this story is about." Pearl went quiet for several seconds, then continued. "Well on this day old Jack had gone off to town and we kids was hangin' over the rails and lookin' at the mob. When one of the boys, but older than meself, said, 'Look at that grey there. Jack said that under no circumstances was we to ride him. Buckjumper and dirty with it, too. Parrently if you come off he's just as likely to stomp on your head like some of them rodeo bulls.'"

Mitchell said that he'd heard of bulls like that, and how the rodeo clowns had to try and keep them away from the fallen riders.

"Yes, well, that's how mean this horse was supposed to be. But I couldn't keep my mouth shut, could I? I said to Barry, that was the boy's name. He was always diggin' at me for just bein' a girl. I said,

'Why don't *you* ride him, Bazza?' An then as fast as spit he says 'Why don't you, Oyster?'"

"Oyster?" Mitchell said. He looked up and noticed most of the commuters were staring at them now with different looks on their faces. Then some young woman giggled and Mitchell understood. Oyster – Pearl.

"Anyways I was sunk then wasn' I? I hadn't no choice."

"Weren't you scared, Pearl? I mean, was he a big horse?"

"Yeah, he was, but that don't matter, them little buggers can throw you off just as hard, maybe not so far to fall. But..."

Someone coughed in the aisle and Mitchell saw that people seemed to be leaning towards them now in a connected sway. One of them removed his iPod earphone. And the guy whose mobile had just rung turned it off and put it back in his jacket.

The train rumbled on and on, and for a moment the silence floated above the track like a palpable entity.

The lull dragged Mitchell's thoughts back to last Friday, after school, the kids ganging up on him with sticks. Hiding down the road where the houses had been demolished and where only a disbanded factory site, a gangly steel monster, loomed around and over them like empty prison walls. They were yelling at him like they hated him but he couldn't think of a single thing he'd done wrong. Screaming at him and calling him 'Boong' and 'Black Bastard'. Then the hiatus of quiet before the blows began.

Mitchell hugged his swag closer and said, "Go on Pearl, what happened when you rode the horse?"

Pearl rolled her eyes and face past her audience. "Kids," she said, addressing no one. "Always in a blurry rush. Well lad, I saddled that horse. No one helped me of course, the word got around our little town faster than the shits an soon I had every kid in the neighbourhood watchin'. I was really bloody scared then. Scared of comin' off, scared of what the grey'd do to me if I did come off, but most of all, scared of makin' a fool of meself in front of everyone."

Mitchell stopped breathing for a moment, held tight, as he was, in the clutches of Pearl's recollection. His own fear forgotten.

"But do you know what happened next, lad? Nothin'. That's what. That grey trotted off quiet as a milkman's horse. Then I kicked him up and hung onto the monkey strap. Now, I never did that before cos that leather strap across the pommel is only for the beginner riders and sissies. But I could see on everyone's faces, no one was begrudgin' me of it."

"So, did he buck then, Pearl?"

"That's the funny thing, lad, no, he didn't." Pearl took a deep breath and laughed loudly. "Nothin', not even a pigroot. Just broke into a canter like the minister's little cart pony on Sundy. And off I went round and around that paddock faster and faster. Then I pulled him up from a gallop in a slide to the fence right up in front of Barry. And someone shouted at me, 'Good one Pearl!' It was me boyfriend, you know, the one who bought me R.M. Williamses."

"But why, Pearl? The horse didn't do anything."

"No, lad. But I did. I did sumthin'. That's what I mean. I was shittin' meself but I still got on the horse believin' he was an outlaw. That's it. Doin' what scares yer. Thinkin' yerself brave. Just like you's doin'. Goin' all that way Up North. On yer own."

"What about Barry, the boy who was mean to you?"

"He never said nothin' more to me on that day, or about that day, but he stopped teasin' me. So's that was worth it, too, I reckon."

Mitchell stared down at his boots over the roundness of his swag. He hunched forward, his voice muffled. "These guys bashed me when I was going home from school. I fought back. But I couldn't do much, there was too many of them."

"Is that how you got that?" Pearl indicated Mitchell's cheek again.

"No. My stepfather gave me a hiding when he found out I'd been fighting."

Pearl nodded, and Mitchell was sure he heard a collective breath from those standing.

Pearl leaned over and touched his arm. "But you's tried, lad. If that horse had thrown me would I have been any less brave? Feelin' no fear isn't brave. It's the feelin' of it and doing sumthin' anyways."

Mitchell looked up and was surprised to see the man closest to them, the one who had switched off his phone, nodding. But then he saw Mitchell looking and turned away.

"My stop," said Pearl suddenly.

The people started murmuring again but softer now, almost reverent. A woman smiled at Mitchell and asked if he minded if she sat next to him.

Then, as the doors opened they all parted and one man leaned over, held Pearl's elbow, kept her steady as she left the train.

The One Fine Thing

I have seen the persona, or should I say the non-persona, of Death. Not a speaking-in-capitals Terry Pratchett Death, nor even the classic Grim Reaper ready to scythe down the unwary like human skittles. This Death was a grey-padded voiceover: *Dying is harder than living*, it echoed. I still feel its claustrophobic pull as I drag myself back to consciousness and survey the paddock around me. Then, shaking my head to clear my vision, I see the mild devastation of another earthquake and the reason for my near meeting with the unmaker.

I rub my belly and gasp relief, as the growing life within me wriggles against my hand like a fluttering moth. This is the second earthquake in as many days. Yesterday, when the first one struck I'd been heading back from town, my station-wagon full of groceries and sheep drench. At first I thought I'd hit a bad stretch of road. I pulled over, but when the shaking didn't stop, I raced home where a still quivering railing veranda confirmed my suspicions.

At least today's quake doesn't seem as bad. I live as isolated as an island, two hundred kilometres from Perth and Albany, in Western Australia, on a sheep farm which I ran with my husband until his departure five months ago, three months after I got pregnant. I'm not entirely alone, I have my Kelpies, my tireless working dogs, Penzance and Caribbean (Penza and Beanie for short) and then of course there is my little in-utero one, whom I've taken to calling Pirate.

The minute before today's near Death encounter I was cleaning the sheep troughs, scrubbing out the green slime, while at the same time hoping the ballcock on the self-waterer would still work when I released the twine holding back the flow. When I saw the water shimmy and felt the earth shake, I realised again what was happening. Luckily, because of my bulge, I was kneeling so I didn't fall far when the quake hit, but now I see why I blacked out. A branch from a red gum had snapped off, the decay in the jagged piece as obvious as the lump now forming on the back of my head.

The ground seems to sway as I try to rise. I call out to Penza and Beanie, who come running, tongues flapping from the sides of their mouths like errant flags. They sniff around the trough, tousle each other then dash off again in puffs of claw-driven dust. "Penza... Beanie." My voice threads around them with years of training, gathers them up and draws them back. They sit at my feet, eyes locking mine.

For a moment I think of doing a Lassie and sending them home for help but I know this won't work for two reasons: they'd never leave me, and there's no one at the farmhouse to come and find me. I take a deep breath and look across the cracked bleakness that is my land.

'Sheep farm' is an optimistic notion - though the acres are many, the holding capacity's almost nil. The few sheep I have, I keep for their superior breeding and the fact they are coloured. No bias on my farm. There's a good market for black, brown and grey wool. I supplement my income with agistment (some local girls lease a ten-acre paddock for their horses). And I write plays. When I first met my husband, Ian, I told him I was a drama queen. He'd laughed, and it soon became the standard joke whenever he introduced me to one of his colleagues or friends. As time went by though, we both stopped laughing.

Penza nuzzles my arm and closes his mouth, almost forgetting to withdraw his tongue. Beanie nudges into his side as if he thought it was funny. I'm still holding my stomach, praying that I feel no more than I have for the last eight months. Pirate moves again. I touch the bump of his foot, it's my second pregnancy in nineteen years, I'm nearing the end of my trimester and the walls of my womb are thin. I slide to my knees in the dust, hang over the trough, undo the twine and watch in hypnotic fascination as the water trickles to a flow that sends bubbles up from the pooling greenness like a miniature fountain. It will have to do, I can't finish it. The sheep have drunk worse.

I pull away the fallen log and sit down, holding my head. Its throbbing staccato reminds me of the boom box in my teenager Mick's car. He and his best mate, Robbie, who boarded with us, have matching hotted-up cars. Mick has gone off to university now. Robbie I haven't seen for months.

I think of the play growing on my computer back at the farmstead. It's about a couple whose relationship has reached its use-by-date and then the freshness of infidelity comes on offer. I've been toying with the idea of bringing in yet another character. You have to be careful how many players you have in a small production, same as the set. This one's in the bedroom: Scene sets theme.

I try to stand, succeed at half-mast and hobble to my station wagon. The dogs beat me through the door and scramble into the back, heads staring forward, tails drumming the cracked upholstery in a mismatched beat. The air conditioner whirrs to life as I turn the key. I breathe deeply, shift the stick into gear. That's when I feel a pain like hot blown glass, but I know what it really is, even though my last confinement was so long ago. This sort of pain is instantly memorable. I grip the wheel hard.

When I stop to open the gate to the dam paddock another spasm hits me, seems to go on forever. I lean on the steel railing - Penza has followed me and jumps up on my leg. I swear at him and at all male-dom. He just looks at me with a silly grin creasing his lips. Maybe I'll make this play a homicidal one, or something to do with castration. If the heroine wants to keep her hands clean she can use a sheep marking ring. He'd never be able to get one of those things off.

Another pain brings my face to the steering wheel as I try to restart my car. I realise I've flooded it, so I slump back and wait, stare out across the paddock. The sun laughs on the shoulders of the dam, sparking prisms that flicker colour change like cut diamonds. I close my eyes. I wake twenty minutes later to what feels like a wet towel repeatedly wiping my cheeks but in reality is Penza licking my face like a demented kid with a lollipop. My headache's gone and so have my contractions, although I sit for many minutes still holding the kind of dread you have at the dentist's, waiting to have a tooth pulled. And this one's an extraction that will be far bigger.

I wind down a window to release the fumes of hot doggy breath, feeling relief at my pain-free state as refreshing as the cool evening breeze that's drawing itself in like a vacuum. I notice something near the dam; it looks like a round, soft tangle of grey weed. Then it moves and I see it's one of my ewes. It seems like she's stuck in the glutinous sludge that makes up the edges of the watering hole. A bundle of sheep stand nearby with a few of the wethers, last year's offspring, still nuzzling optimistically at their mother's underbellies. I turn to my dogs and put my hand up, palm outwards. "Stay here you two." From behind the seat I drag a plastic-handled tray containing my sheep-keeping stuff. At least there'll be no need for the lambing paraphernalia. None of my ewes have been joined. One confinement's more than enough for me to deal with this year. I've pimped Shakespeare, my ram, out to my neighbour, which helps offset the loss. He's also promised me some of his progeny – Shakespeare's lambs that is, not my neighbour's.

I waddle across the landscape, watching out for snakes - difficult to do when you can't see your feet - remembering evening is their favourite time.

21

Then I open my eyes to a scene of disbelief. It's Ophelia, one of my oldest ewes and either she's growing another head or is in the last strains of lambing. I wrestle the lamb's legs forward and pull with the contractions. I still can't understand how this has happened.

As the lamb slips into life, Ophelia gives a grunt, her sides heave and then she expires. Completely. "Oh, you poor old girl," I murmur. After her last lambing I'd made a mental note to retire Ophelia. She'd only just made it that time. This time she wasn't so lucky. I feel the cold claw of guilt gouging my memory. Hadn't I made all the ram lambs into wethers? I must have left one entire. I stroke my conscience with the thought that maybe the ring had broken.

I scan the bunch of wethers bar one. But which one? Hard to see in this light. I nuzzle the little wet lamb to Ophelia's wrinkled udder. Its swollen pink mouth grasps the teat with a surprisingly strong suction, while it drinks the all important, first milk. I squat kneeling in the dust with the ewes, wethers and one hidden adolescent ram circling around me, heads down, curious looks on their woolly faces. It's then I realise with a shudder that all the ewes, even the recently shorn ones, look in very good condition for so late in the season. I slump forward, supporting myself by my arms, my shoulders shaking, watch the hot dry earth soak up my tears like blotting paper.

Sometime later I pull myself up and, cradling the lamb under one arm and my tray under the other, return to my car. The gloom has descended, making for a murky visibility, and I'm praying that the heavy footfalls of one pregnant woman with lamb will persuade any snakes to keep out of the way. As I rattle over the cattle grid leading to my driveway, I notice a familiar car near the house. It belongs to Ian, my dearly, almost departed husband. Just when I think he's gone for good up he pops, bearing some excuse about sorting out paperwork, or collecting something he'd forgotten. I let the dogs out, wrap Horatio the lamb (I named him that on the way home) in old baby blankets, and place him in a large cardboard box. A little later I have Horatio in situ in my kitchen and the stove packed to burning. My husband's nowhere in sight. I recall seeing a shadow glimpse of him scuffling in the back of the garage when I locked up the car. I make myself a cup of tea and a bottle for the lamb. I contemplate breast feeding - not Horatio of course - Pirate. So much easier. No sterilisation. Speaking of sterilisation, I think again of the Un-wether. I need to deal with him as soon as possible. I also sigh resignation that, if I don't want any more orphan lambs, I'll have to set up some sort of night-time watch. Depressing stuff, involving alarm clocks and lots of torchlight vigils.

I'm leaning over, holding the bottle for Horatio, when I'm creased in half again by a gripping pain. This one bursts my bubble of denial with its finality of broken waters. At that moment Ian walks in. "This is Horatio," I say, pointing the bottle teatwards towards the bleating lamb. Then, unable to deny the spreading stain on the wooden floorboards, I add, "I think the baby's coming."

"I thought you weren't having any more lambs this year?"

I almost say I'm not, it's a bloody baby, you idiot. But then I see the realisation in Ian's widening eyes, bringing to light the second part of my statement.

"Oh my god, Angie. Really?"

He takes over the feeding and stuffs Horatio into silence with a well-aimed bottle.

I slide myself backwards onto my chair and feel the contraction recede like a hot tide. I decide I may as well answer his first question. "I thought I'd marked them all last year, but I must have missed one. It looks like the little bugger has got them all in lamb."

"Not so little, Angie. Old enough. A teenager in sheep years." He looks at me with slanted eyes.

I shiver. "So it seems."

"Anyway, you look a bit better now. Are you sure the baby's really coming?"

Ian follows my glance to the floor. Where my broken waters colour the floorboards red. "Oh," he says.

I watch his strong back as he ambles over to the phone. I hear his voice, low tones, explaining how to get to our place. He covers the mouthpiece, "How far apart are the contractions?"

Another pain girdles my stomach like barbed wire, renders me speechless. I hold up four fingers.

Ian comes to me, touches my shoulder. "The ambulance is on its way. Can I get you something?"

Another life, I think to myself and wonder if dying would really be so hard. Perhaps I'd die like Ophelia, in birthing. Another thing we'd have in common. Ophelia was certainly old enough to be the Un-wether's mother. I shudder and Ian goes over to the stove and stokes it up. He opens a cupboard.

"You feeling hungry..?" The question stops abruptly. I know I am glaring at him and I feel all sorts of awful. He doesn't deserve this. Never has. And still I can't believe I've let this happen. But looking down, I see the bulging proof and feel the pain of its reality.

I see Ian fixing me another cup of tea. The light catches the side of his face and makes him look youthful. It draws me back twenty years, to when we first came here. I was pregnant then, too.

As if reading my mind, Ian says, "Angie, remember our first year together? How excited you were to be moving here from the city. How you said this was our new beginning? Not long after that it was Mick's beginning. Remember?"

I laugh. "Yeah, I wanted a home birth and no intervention."

Ian is silent for many minutes. Then I realise what he may be thinking - that I might get my wish, albeit nineteen years late.

Back then, I had complications which put me into hospital for the last few weeks of my pregnancy. Ian was there for the birth. Afterwards he told me it was the most amazing experience of his life. Ian and Mick have always been close. I constantly felt they had a secret understanding to which I could never hold the key.

I put it down to the fact they were both blokes, doing all the things father and son do together, hallmark moments of fishing and shooting, and all things automobilian.

I saw even less of Ian when Robbie, Mick's mate from high school, moved in. The three of them were forever working on those damn cars.

Ian is watching me. He draws up a chair and slides it directly opposite.

He takes my hand. "You know, Angie, you never told me why it happened. Sometimes I think this is just some nightmare and I'll wake up and find everything back the way it was."

The way it was. A flashback of black-and-white, the four of us sitting at this table - Ian. Mick. Robbie. Me.

Another memory rips it away with stark fecundity: Robbie's eyes, blue electric, staring into mine. It's evening and we are alone.

The remembered touches, accidental at first, the denial on my part. *God, I'm old enough to be his mother. I'm his best mate's mum, and his landlady, for Christ's sake.* Then the relinquishing of reason, the tangling of limbs, the soft and the hard. Sheets stained forever.

I look at Ian, squeeze his hand. "I don't know. Really, Ian, I don't. It just... happened."

I want to tell him I'd been drinking, want to say it was because of our fight that morning. Want to explain how I yearned for excitement in this godforsaken, boring, dry and desolate place. But he's held too much blame already. And none of this is his fault. I was the one who wanted to move here. I was the one who...

And my body had come up with the punishment. Had stolen my marriage, my future. But I didn't blame my little Pirate. As the pregnancy grew so had my love.

I confessed to Ian and told him to leave. I could see no other way and it seemed fitting, the one fine thing, seeing I'd brought this on myself, that I face it on my own.

Lately though, it feels like I'm in one of my own plays, a soliloquy, acting out roles of everyday living, but where real life is standing still.

The contractions are running into each other with the ferocity of road train collisions. My grip on Ian's hand becomes continual. He makes murmurings of *Not long now* and *Hang in there.*

For some reason I keep thinking of Ophelia alone, waiting until I came and delivered her of her lamb and her last breath. I glance at the cardboard box, see Horatio's tiny head peeping, nose up, over the edge. Life after death.

I hear the ambulance, its sirens lifting the night air to high vibration. I look up into Ian's face as they stretcher me out. He is still holding my hand.

"I'll stay with you, Angie," he says. "You won't be alone." But the flicker of a frown crossing his brow tells me it's only for now, only for the delivery.

Uneasy Castles

Their names were Dorothy and Dashiell. Dot and Dash.

To their friends they were The Morse Code, like some sort of enigma.

Dashiell was Dash-yell to his mother, in deference to boy-mindedness and how she thought the name, being a French one, would be pronounced.

Dorothy grew up in London, next-door to Dashiell. Her mother had called her Dot from the start, when downy head bobbed on breast and Dot's tiny hand, surprisingly strong for a newborn, gripped her finger, as if letting go would mean falling away to oblivion.

Dot and Dash shared birthdays and backyard adventures. Cricket on the streets. A wooden fruit box for the stumps.

Destined to end together, Dot and Dash like sea and sand. Dot was the sea, deep and beautiful, craggy peaked one day, calm to rippling another. Dash was the sand on which she shifted, making uneasy castles in the sky.

As teens, dreams danced alive and horizons seemed never too high to breach. All things possible.

But when war arrived, it was Save Our Souls, Save Our Ships - SOS knows no acronym. And the Blitz knew no boundaries.

Too Rich or Too Thin

The Valley Review - Massachusetts - USA

"A carton of Skinny Milk, Janet", I said to the shopkeeper of our little town's service station.

Funny that, Skinny Milk, like it's been on a diet or something, then again it is pretty thin. I know the French say you can't be too rich or too thin, but surely there must be limits.

Milk brings thoughts of my schooldays, the highlight of our mornings, drinking the cream off our mini-milks. Now, I see Monica Mornington with snot candling down to her mouth, loose-lip seal around the rim of her bottle, and I have to turn around my mind before I turn off my stomach. I mean, I'm on my break; I've been mowing people's lawns. I deserve a rest, not a gut churning. Damn milk would become butter if there was any cream left in it.

"You want anything else, Kat?" Janet plumps the carton of milk on top of my paper, it topples over, narrowly missing my pie.

There is a short-bell sound and we both look out of the glass windows of the servo. See a black BMW pull up near the petrol pumps. A man gets out, stretches and umbilicals his car to the premium.

"Nah, that's all. Diet again," I say, yawning.

When I leave the shop I'm as invisible as the wind to Mr BMW man but I can't help noticing his wife, who is looking at me kind of wistful like. Gold shackles her wrists and earlobes, glints, draws my gaze to her hands and face.

Mr BMW man stands on the pedal and I become a dust cloud, invisibly inverted, can't even see Janet, who's standing next to me, sluicing off the petrol he'd spilt.

"Heck, he's in a hurry," she says. "Must be from the city or something."

She means it as a revelation.

I'm in need of a humour fix. I think of my friend, Gemmy, my main supplier.

I seatbelt myself to my old station wagon and pilot it through the serpentine lanes, out past paddocks of languid cattle and dusty horses, to Gemma's farm.

I have to be careful not to let out a calf and two lambs, which come bunting and baaing as I fold back the wire gate.

"Feeding time?" I say, spying Gemma carrying a bucket with something that slops. She's wearing overalls and Wellingtons which are at least two sizes too big.

"Always feeding time around here. If it's not orphans it's mama horse by three or..." She waves her hand in a loop, indicating her two hundred acre backyard. Her Border Collies are rounding up hens, and a fat drake enjoying some afternoon delight squashes a duck into the mud. They both have that resigned look I've seen on old married couples.

Gem follows my eyes. "Oh God," she says. "I've left the hose on."

She rushes off behind a tank where I can hear a motor dredging up sub-artesian.

"Righto," she says. "That's enough for today. Let's have a cuppa. Mind you don't let Gemma and James One and Two in. The kids accidentally let them in this morning."

"You've named the calf and the lambs after you and James?"

Gem stops mid pull of a recalcitrant boot, I see now she has on two pairs of socks, all mismatched. Then she straightens. "Well, James named the calf after me, said it has my eyes. So I thought it was only fair that I named the lambs. He's not too pleased though, cause they're ewes."

I think of something but Gem brakes it with her hand. "No you ewe jokes, you," she says.

I wedge myself past the orphans and squish the door shut. I see she wasn't joking about them getting in earlier. She'd made some attempt to clean up. That's what's in the bucket. She disappears for a second and comes back with a mop.

"Sorry about the mess."

"That's okay," I say, and get up to put on the kettle. I find it tented in paper work.

"How's the farm going?"

"You don't want to know, Kat."

She smears more water around. I hear the metal of the mop nail-scratching the tiles, and scrunch my shoulders.

"Oh, yeah," Gem says, "Old Garretson's place has been sold. Met the new owners at the auction."

"What are they like?" I watch Gemma the calf licking the glass door. Marvel at her blue tongue.

"City."

"Oh. Farm charmed. Is he married?"

"I knew you'd ask that, Kat. Yes, he is. Drives a flashy car."

I look up. "Not a BMW by any chance?"

"Yeah. You seen them, then?"

"I think I might have. Black car? Shell-shocked wife?"

Gemma taps her temple. "Electrics gone in that one." She gets up and rummages in her cupboard. "You want something to eat?"

"Nah, I bought a pie at the servo, ate it on the way here."

"Thought you were on a diet." Gemma drops some bread on the floor but doesn't seem to notice.

"I bought skinny milk," I say.

Gemma pulls a sarcastic face. "Oh, righto. Seven hundred calories for the pie, but only fifty for the drink. That makes it okay, then."

"Heck, Gem, you the diet police all of a sudden? Anyway, I think she looks quite nice. I felt a bit sorry for her. Didn't like *him*, though. He seems a right mongrel."

"Yeah," says Gem, not losing the thread. "Well, that figures, then. That's why she's a spark plug short of a mower."

"Hey," I say, "you, farm jokes, me, mower jokes." I look out at my rusty mower bent double in the back of my station-wagon.

Gemma raises her brows. "*She* certainly doesn't need to diet. Scrawny. Covering it up though. Baggy clothes. My sheep are like that. Look quite good till you take the wool off." I look out to the bone-cracked paddocks surrounding the house. Say nothing.

Gemma follows my gaze. "Everyone's doing it tough," she says, gripping the back of her chair. "I'm not the only one. Can't blame the Garretsons for selling up. Place went for a song. Less than it would have ten years ago. You'd cry if you didn't mind wasting the water." She sits down but pushes away her plate.

I get up and rub her arm as I pass. Pick up the slice of bread from the floor and toss it out of the window. A goose gaggles it down. All the chooks start running like a starter pistol has been fired. No more wins. The bread is long gone.

"I wonder if they need anyone to mow for them," I say, "I'm running short of clients. Only got the ones with bores. Not too many house blocks with those."

"You could ask. Lawns looked okay at the auction. They could afford you."

I hate this bloody drought, I think, as I pull up at my house. I never thought anything could get Gemma down like this.

I slip beneath a longer than short shower. Feel guilt rise but flatten it. My water usage was low last month.

I pull on moleskins and a clean blue shirt. Brush my hair and slap on some more sunscreen. I should buy shares.

One good thing about drought, I muse as I point my keys, is that you have an excuse for not washing your car.

31

The road to the Garretson's is unsealed, I take a corner too fast, my wagon fishtails, I feel my heart tattooing my ribs. I steer the car back, pray no one is coming in the opposite direction.

Prayer goes unanswered. I narrowly miss the BMW before I manage to gain control. I see his face, a blood orange, mouth working around obscenities that don't require lip reading. I'm glad that he's going the other way and that his wife isn't with him.

I drive over the cattle grid, note the absence of stock, feel disappointment grip as, in the distance, someone atop a mower swathes wide lines in a fine green lawn. Weeping willows and oaks have a circle of pre-mow under them.

I wonder if I should even bother, but curiosity drives me forward and parks me parallel to the front gate.

Mr BMW man's wife answers the door. She's pale, hollow faced, hair dragged back. Dressed in a loose T shirt and stripe-sided track pants.

I hold out my hand and launch into speech before she can say anything. I don't know how much time I have before her husband gets back.

"Hi, I'm Kat, Katrina. I was wondering if you needed any mowing done. Oh... and I know you've just moved in, so, welcome, too."

She glances past me to where the mowing guy is hanging a three-sixty. The smell of chopped grass plays my nostrils like a well known tune.

"I'm Mrs Audrey Holbridge," she says.

I wait, the silence stretches. She tightens it with her next words, soft, talc on tongue, accentuated.

"I saw you outside the service station in town? It was you, wasn't it?" She doesn't wait for an answer. "My husband takes care of the outside work. But I do need someone to do housekeeping. Would you be interested in that, perhaps?"

"It would have to be weekends if that's okay," I say.

32

The following Saturday I arrive at nine-thirty, half an hour early. Audrey's wearing thick makeup, tightly folded arms, and breathing like she's trying to suck into herself.

"Hi Katrina, come in. Don't mind me. I've had a heavy night," she says.

I know the signs. I had lots of heavy nights too, before my husband got off and left.

Her hand trembles as she gives me a list. I read three aubergines, balsamic vinegar, and 'Bruise Away'-anti-thrombotic-cream, before she hurriedly swaps it for another more neatly printed page. Standard stuff this one: Housekeeper's things to do.

Audrey's gone all morning and thankfully I haven't bumped into her husband, whose name, I've learned from collecting the mail, is Bernard.

Amazing what else you learn about people when you clean their houses. While I'm vacuuming I find cigarettes under the bed, behind the bed-head post. It's on the right side so I figure it's his hidden stash. I remember reading somewhere that over seventy percent of women prefer sleeping on the left. I also remove empty whisky bottles from the dining room. Take them outside to the mountain of uncountable.

Audrey gets home just before noon. She calls me into the kitchen for coffee and chocolate éclairs. My eyes open wide as I watch her hoeing into them.

She stops mid bite. Eyes meet mine. "I know what you're thinking," she says. "No, I don't have an eating disorder. No, I'm not going to barf this all up afterwards. I've always been this thin. I'm just really lucky." Her hand shakes as she adjusts the dark sunglasses she is still wearing. She finishes the éclair and picks up another.

On Friday I'm down with some bug. Gemma, on transit to the stock agents, pops in.

"I stopped off at the Holbridges, like you asked, Kat," she says. "I told her you'd been trying to get in touch. Home phone's out of order. Here's her mobile number. She sends best wishes by the way."

I start to get up off the lounge. Gemma pushes me down. "Stay right there. I had the same thing a few weeks ago. Really lays you low. Feel like a cuppa?"

"You never told me you were sick…" Gemma cuts me off with a joke delivered in technicolour. I laugh so much I forget how bad I feel until I stop.

"That Audrey woman doesn't have a sense of humour."

"Oh God, Gemma, you didn't tell her that one, did you?"

Gemma rubs her nose and half covers her mouth. "Nah, Kat. Some people you just know. Mind you, that husband, Bernard?"

I nod, and she continues. "Well, he's a bit of a joke himself, isn't he? I heard him going on like a demented clown as I was coming up to the house."

"Gee, Gem," I say. "You heard them fighting but you still went up?"

"Yeah, not my problem. Anyway, I had to tell them you wouldn't be coming. Audrey answered the door. I couldn't see him. Must have disappeared when he heard the knocking."

For the next week I run hot and cold like a faulty tap. Feel like I'm going through early menopause or something.

Saturday morning I wake in a cold sweat, realise that it's not just the flu but from something I've forgotten to do. I sit up in bed, glance at the luminous numbers of my clock and remember that I need to tell Audrey I'm not coming this week either.

I drag my carcass out to the lounge room and search the coffee table for the slip of paper bearing Audrey's mobile number. I find it stuck to the back of a coaster.

Falling back on the chair, I dial. Audrey answers as I say hi.

"Oh... damn it," she says, and the line goes dead.

Charming, I think. I redial. This time I get androgenous electronics informing me that the person you have called is not answering, or has turned off their mobile. *Well,* I think, as I fold arms and legs back into bed, *I did try.*

As I drift off, Audrey's words echo. Later they are replaced by sirens as my dreams turn to smoke-dust and bushfires.

When I wake, Gemma is shaking me. I open my eyes into her face, centimetres from mine. She stands back.

"Gemma? What...what are you doing here?" I rub knuckles over my eyes and squint. The blind is up and sunshine finds me like a spotlight.

She moves to the window. "Well, Kat," she says, gathering the curtains into pleats. "You won't be cleaning the Holbridges ever again."

I prop up on my elbow. "What do you mean? What's happened?"

"I had a little visitor this morning. Audrey. She'd come over the bush paddock way."

I sit up and lean forward.

"What do you mean? She walked? Heck, her farm is at least six kilometres from yours."

"Yeah. I don't know why she didn't go to Dennis's place. It's closer."

I grab Gemma's arm. "Damn it Gemma. Tell me what's happened!"

"Fire. Homestead burnt down. Audrey just managed to get out in time. I had the police at my place after the fire brigade got it under control. They took her statement."

"Gee, Gem, is she okay?"

"Yeah, Kat, she is. Actually more okay than the last time I saw her. Funny that. Anyway, I did hear what happened. She said she couldn't sleep so she got up and had a cigarette."

I put up my hand. "Don't tell me, Gem. She was smoking in bed and dozed off?"

"Yep. When she woke up later, the bedclothes were on fire. Said she couldn't wake Bernard. She escaped from the house, walked to my place and I rang the fire brigade."

"That's strange. I didn't think she smoked. Where is she now?"

"They took her to hospital."

I raise my eyebrows. "Did they find Bernard?"

"He's in hospital too," Gemma says. "In the morgue. They found him in the bedroom. Head out of the window. Body stuck. He didn't die straight away, apparently. Most people in fires die of smoke inhalation before they burn. Unluckily for Bernard he had access to fresh air. It was some time before Audrey got to my place. The fireman said if they'd got the call earlier, they might've saved him."

"Why didn't she ring them on her mobile?

"She told them she'd lost it a week ago."

I scrunch up my face. "What time did the fire start?"

"About eight o'clock this morning, Kat. Would have taken Audrey at least an hour to arrive at my place. Nine o'clock News was on."

"Well," I say, "Audrey had her mobile this morning, when I rang around eight thirty to tell her that I couldn't make it today. She answered. It was definitely her. She said damn it, then hung up. Her mobile was disconnected after that."

I go quiet for a moment. Gemma looks at me, wide-eyed. "When you rang she would have been on her way to my place. So why didn't she ring the fire brigade?"

We both sit quietly for a few minutes.

I rub my eyes, "Anyway, you didn't tell me, Gem, how *did* Audrey get out? Through the door?"

Gemma shakes her head. "No. Actually she managed to get through the window."

"Really? Are you sure? Those are the type that wind out on a bike-chain thingy. I had a hard time cleaning them. They can't open very far."

"I know, Kat, that's how Bernard got stuck. But think about how thin Audrey is."

I pull the blind down on the day and shepherd Gemma to the kitchen.

You can't be too rich or too thin. The French may be right after all.

Wild Swimming

Eye to eye with a cormorant
in this iced water
temperature in single figures
feels like freezing
body in varying degrees of numb
but for me only temporary

this morning, my wheelchair hero's email
one by one, the letters jabbed in jest
mad woman!
his sense of humour
still moving me to laughter
as I swim
I carry him
in my thoughts
and my struggle, sans wet-suit in winter
becomes nothing harder than mind

my arms raise, hands dip and lift
the tear drop bubbles
from my finger tips
its moments of standing still
touching
like this
the water surface and beyond

crystalline clear
today, I and he will make it to the shore
of this salt sea lake
wild swimming.

Boston Literary Magazine USA

(For my brave friend, Sid James, who triumphs over quadriplegia. And my crazy pledge to him to swim all winter without a wetsuit!)

Photogenic Lens

Bohemyth magazine - Ireland

Josie was happy to look after Christopher's child. But not on her own.

He'd said, "Back soon, Josie girl. Two hours, tops." But that was years ago, and she hasn't heard from him since.

She'd had no children of her own and this one was only a freckle past a newborn when he presented him to her, wrapped in a dirty blue bunny rug. Josie knew nothing about babies, her life had been hollow of them and so many other things until she met Christopher.

The baby was called Cabbage. She laughed at the time Christopher told her, but didn't ask if this was his real name, and the baby had no words to tell her otherwise.

Cabbage has grown like his namesake but that is where any connection ends, everything else is as normal, as much as she would know. Except he stopped talking at the same time that Christopher left, and she is too far from help to ask for it.

He's not well, Josie thinks. She wishes Christopher was here, for what does she know about childhood illnesses?

Cabby, as she calls him, is not outside chasing the chickens or playing with his dog, Sherpie, the little white terrier he loves so much. She sees him sitting on the armchair, the one with the flock coat that's balding in places like an old man's head.

Josie warms some milk on the stove, taking care that it doesn't heat so much as to spill over the pan. She pours it into Cabby's favourite mug, cradles it in her hands, feels the warmth ease the stiffness in her fingers. *"Here you are lovely boy, milk to make you feel better."*

But Cabby is no longer in the chair. Placing the mug on the table, she shouts from the back door: "Cab, Cabby.' She smiles, it seems like she's calling an errant taxi. She brings her hands to her face then snatches them forward to focus. They look like her grandmother's. She touches one hand with the other, traces the wrinkles, frowns. She was only twenty-five when Christopher brought Cabby to her.

Josie walks out into the farmyard. Everything looks the same but the trees have grown tall and the ducks and chickens have gone. Stolen, she thinks. Or taken by dingos. She squints towards the horizon, sees that the night is coming, wonders if she should set some traps. Her gaze draws around the fence-line, stopping at the old magnolia tree which, in contrast to everything else, is blooming. Soft apricot flowers like coupling butterflies are tip-massing on branches otherwise as barren as the earth. A breeze tickles her hair, sending it to cover her eyes, but she pushes back its greyness with fingers thinner than her memory.

Who was she calling? She feels the residue of something not right, something to which she cannot put a thought. Her stomach feels tight and her hands are shaking. Josie calls again, but this time not a name.

"Come on, come on now."

A black cat with a white smudge on its nose stretches out from under a rusting car-body wreck, its claws driving the sand before them. It yawns, and walks a crooked path to her. She knows this cat, but she cannot remember what to call it. It follows her into the house and begins to scratch the old armchair in a rhythmic pawing. Josie takes the cup of milk and pours it into a bowl near the front door. She sits down, wraps herself in her arms and watches the cat drinking. Tiny flicks of milk spatter the floor like dandruff.

The pictures are clearer if she shuts her eyes, but then there is always the threat of sleep from which she fears she will never wake.

41

She rises and takes the cup to the sink, sees a note stuck on the fridge with a purple magnet. *The cat's name is Bobby*, the note says, in a scrawl that is only decipherable by its size.

"Bob-by.' She tries the name; her voice sounds empty, the syllables robotic, like a child learning to read. The cat looks up from the plate, there is milk on its whiskers and its eyes are staring. Josie turns away, reaches into the sink and sluices water through the mug, watching it swirl down the plug hole. She sees the greasy kitchen curtain, the edge of its faltering hem stuttering in the draught. The window behind is dirty and someone has written something in the grime. She lifts the curtain and reads: *Turn off the stove.* She stretches a bony finger and writes her name next to it: *Josie.* She leans back and stares. The writing is the same.

Then she writes: *Christopher.*

She closes her eyes and sees an image clearer than life.

"Josie girl, you have a photogenic memory," he once told her. She recalls laughing. "Don't you mean a photographic memory?" "No," he said. "Photogenic, you remember the past more beautiful than it really is. Even the dark you turn grey."

When she met Christopher she was attracted to him in a way she found hard to set to words. He was freedom and promise wrapped in a package. But she'd stopped trying to peel back the layers when she found nothing holding the structure.

Josie wipes tears from her eyes with the back of her arm and notices she is wearing her nightdress and dressing-gown. She wonders if it is morning and she has just got up. She rummages in the drawer until she finds what she is looking for. She pulls at the material on her sleeve. She wants to write: *Go and get dressed* but the fabric slips and the pen only writes the first word: *Go.*

Christopher was the man at the corner store. She saw him every time she went there with eggs to sell or cheques to cash. She has no eggs now and a woman brings meals to her house and puts them in her freezer. She reminds Josie of her chickens. She makes funny noises in the back of her throat. The last time she came, she kept shaking her head as well.

Then people came in two cars. Josie saw them coming. She hid in the bush-scrub surrounding her farm and waited, crouched like a dingo, swirling her fingers in the red dust, making circles that spiralled to nothing.

It was dark by the time she got home, and they had gone.

Where was Sherpie? Cabby loved that little dog, he was always taking it for walks, she remembers. Maybe he's gone for a walk with it now.

But no, Sherpie is dead. She closes her eyes and sees a picture of the terrier, its white turned red with blood.

Then she sees Cabby standing over the body. She quickly opens her eyes and sees him again in the chair. He is not well. That is why she made him the milk. *Milk to make you feel better, my lovely boy.*

It's been so good since Cabby came, Josie thinks. The wonder of childhood is hers now.

He reminds her of Christopher. He looks like him, with his blue-green eyes and pale skin. His hair is as fair as Christopher's was, with the same under-streaks like tiger's stripes.

But now Cabby is gone again.

"Come out, my lovely boy. It's too late to play." She hears an old voice, wonders how it's hers.

He was always a good boy, always happy, never making a fuss. But he's been too quiet since his father left.

Christopher told her he'd adopted Cabby. It was a year after their wedding, not long after she'd been told she couldn't bear children. She loved children, she said, when the doctor told her she couldn't *bear* them. Doctor Willits had opened his eyes wide and gone silent, but Christopher had smiled at her. He knew her ways. He was the only one who ever had. And when he brought Cabby home she hadn't

43

questioned why she didn't have to sign any papers. Why it had been so easy.

And when Cabby had grown more like Christopher every day, she'd laughed and said that's what she'd heard, that adopted children often grew to look like the people who adopted them.

She recalls one day, when Cabby was just beginning to walk, an elegant lady came knocking on the door. Her breath smelled of alcohol and her fingers shook. She also had no manners, for she barged past Josie and demanded to see Christopher.

"Christopher's at work," Josie said.

"Not that one," the elegant lady said. "The baby, Christopher."

"My baby's name's Cabbage, but I call him Cabby." Josie recalls saying.

The lady had collapsed onto the old chair; her shoulders were shaking and her face was red. Her hand was clutching her mouth and when she brought it away there was lipstick smudging her knuckles like blood.

"Christopher did say you were a bit simple. He told you the nickname I'd given the baby because he was growing like one. A cabbage that is. He couldn't tell you the baby's real name, I suppose."

Josie was still trying to fathom why the lady thought she was simple. Simple meant easy. Her mother had told her 'easy' women were ladies of the night, but she hated the dark.

The lady continued. "I need to see my baby. I made a mistake saying I didn't want him. Where did Christopher tell you the boy came from? The cabbage patch?" Once more the lady fell back into the chair. But this time her laughter took her to coughing until Josie went to her and banged her on her back. Then the lady looked at her strangely. "Perhaps..," she said, "Perhaps..." Then she nodded to herself as if she was affirming an unspoken question.

Josie can't remember how it ended that day. Maybe she'd got her gun, the one she uses for the dingos, and threatened the lady with it if she didn't leave. Perhaps they had hugged and she'd let the lady see the baby.

Cabby had slept through it all. That much Josie does remember.

Josie lowers herself into the old chair. She strokes the soft fabric of the armrest, watches as the pile flattens this way and that. Her eyes close and the pictures come once again but she hears the words first.

Cabby's words. Is he speaking to her again? But these words she's heard before. They are not from today. How could she have forgotten them? They were the start of crying words, for Cabby and for Christopher.

"Mommy, Sherpie has blood on him, and he's not moving."

Josie had gone outside and found the little dog lying still, by the old magnolia tree. There was blood on him. Cabby was standing near him holding an axe.

"What have you done?" That was her voice.

"There was a dingo, mommy. I tried to get him. He ran over there." She saw Cabby pointing, followed the line of his finger. Saw a tawny shape in the distance. There were two others matching it, and feathers scattered like snow, leading a trail back to the hen-runs. Then she saw the axe was clean.

Josie opens her eyes, pulls her dressing-gown around her and rises stiffly from the chair. There is something she wants to see. Outside, the moon is bright and the stars light a path that is strewn with potholes but Josie finds her way to the old magnolia tree. There, beneath its branches, blending with the fence, is a little cross. She remembers Christopher made that cross from a loose paling, and marked Sherpie on it with a burning twig. Now it's as faded as her eyesight.

Cabby is crying. His sobs punctuate her mind in stabs. Then she hears Christopher's voice. Josie closes her eyes to see his face. "Poor little bugger," he says. "He really loved that dog."

She tries to stop her answer but it comes like a flood. "Chris, why don't you take him for a drive in the car? I'll give him a drink of warm milk before you go. It'll make him feel better."

45

Now she hears the car doors slam. "Back soon, Josie girl, two hours, tops."

She drops to the ground and once more the pictures come, but these have no words. Josie sees the police car with its flashing blue light, sees the policemen walking towards her. Sees herself, a young self, climbing into the car.

Then in a room full of whiteness, a man and a child lying together in death.

When Josie enters the house she walks on slow feet to the kitchen. There's the note on the fridge. Her voice comes softly: "The cat's name is Bobby," she says. Then she glances at the kitchen window, the curtain is still drawn back: "Turn off the stove," she says to her scribble, her words. Then she looks at her sleeve. *Go*, she reads. Go where, she wonders.

Josie finds her bedroom, sees the sheets pulled back, sees an impression of a body in the mattress. She climbs into it, being careful to match its form with hers. Then she pulls up the blanket and stares at the wall. She closes her eyes, lets the dreams come but shapes them to her memory with its photogenic lens. Even if she sleeps forever, she thinks, better asleep than this awake. And in the morning the sun will scrawl its shine, write its pictures of brighter days across her mind, lift the darkness to a paler shade of grey.

Heather and Gorse

The Pages UK

The wind is catching itself, turning and touching my face from different directions. It isn't helping me find my bearings.

"Here, Jolly." My voice draws across the paddock and drops a lonely line into the distance, where there is a break of trees.

I hear him scuffling through the dry grass, smell the wet bogginess of him long before he bumps against my leg, all hair and wiggles and doggy joy.

I run fingers along his neck, slip on his harness, adjust the strap and feel him lose tension like a storm that has run its course. He straightens, all business-like and ready for work.

"Oh Jol, you've been in that damn dam again." I laugh at my words and hear again the solitude in the echo. I stand and face what I think is the direction of home but because of the wind change I am no longer sure.

"It's great here, isn't it Jolly?" I shouldn't really be chatting with him; he's a working dog once his harness is put on. I've told so many well-intentioned people over the years. "Please don't pat or talk to the dog. He's working and it may distract him." Some have walked off with a "Pff!", others apologise so profusely I can feel my face burn. Some say nothing at all.

Jolly's name, when I was paired with him at the Guide Dog School, was Roger. I call him Jolly, as in Jolly Roger. It suits him far better. And he made the transition to me from his trainer and the name as seamless as silk.

The wind has weakened and I feel a spatter of rain warm against my face, it runs over my cheek like a tear. I brush it away and take a deep breath.

David has gone away again, back to college. He said I could still let Jolly have his run though every day on his farm.

I remember him ruffling Jol's coat just before he left on the bus. "Can't let you go without, old boy. You look after Nettie Pot when I'm gone." Then I felt him touch my hair too. He'd held my face in his hands and kissed me lightly.

"You'll be fine, Nettie Pot." He'd called me this ever since he'd seen something on an Oprah episode.

My voice was tight as I'd said, "You know I hate that. It's Antoinette or Nettie. Not some nasal device thing."

He'd hugged me and said, "Sorry", then he'd touched my lips with a finger as light as a snowflake. "It won't be long. I'll be home for the holidays before you know it."

That had been almost a year ago. He hadn't made it back midterm. Too busy, he'd told me on the phone. "Really, Nettie Pot, I've been doing too much socialising and not enough swatting. I'm getting behind in all my assignments. I'll really need to get stuck into it these hols." He'd laughed round and loud but the bottom dropped out of it and the sound had run away to nothing.

Thunder grumbles around me. I can feel it in my chest and I shiver despite the warmth. I can smell the ozone, and sense the fizz of lightning upturning the hairs on my arms. My heart seems to beat inside my ears.

There are only two things that really scare me: spiders and storms.

Thank goodness Jolly doesn't share my fears.

I can feel him leaning into his harness, wanting to get going, sensing the danger with every hair of canine intuition. I grasp the harness handle and let the leash flop on his back. My fingers scratch through his coat, feel his life force, his heart beating a steady mantra. Come on, come on, let's go, let's go, it seems to be saying.

"Forward. Home, Jolly."

We are off at a fast pace. There are rumbles of thunder overhead, like boulders tumbling backwards and forwards in some giant cement mixer.

Jolly is pulling hard, his Labrador wiggle now replaced by a determined walk.

I pull back, a slight leash correction, nothing more than squeeze and release. He drops a pace in response and I imagine him looking at me apologetically.

I'm breathing fast, I don't know which track we've taken, but it seems to be the homeward bound one. And I trust Jolly, he's the best guide dog I've ever had.

"This is like when we first met David, isn't it, boy?" My voice seems far off. The rain is soaking into my skin. I'm only dressed in a tee-shirt and shorts. This storm was not forecast until tonight and it's been so hot for the past week.

We reach a gate, Jolly sidles up so I can slip over the catch, it's one of those chain and socket things, you have to line it up just right or the steel hasp won't slide over.

My hands are slippery with rain, and dam water from Jolly's coat. I fumble, and Jolly moves just as I almost manoeuvre the hasp into position.

I resist the urge to swear. My whole life has been about patience. And steady as you go. I don't feel so steady at the moment.

I've never had sight. I'm glad of that. Not ever seeing, I think, is better than having sight and losing it.

"What does it feel like, Nettie?" my best friend and flat mate, Kayla, had once said. I'd reacted by asking, "What does it feel like to see?" We both had no answers. She never asked me again.

Sometimes I try and imagine colours. I know my skin is black, like my vision, but all of my friends are colour blind. They wouldn't be my friends if they weren't.

I think I have the shapes okay, I know the smoothness of round and the sharpness of corners. The long and the short of everything in its place. Then there are all those numbers held in memory. How many paces here, how many steps there. Sequence of method in all I do. Safety in tidiness.

I finally get the gate open and it swings away as we pass through. The wind picks up, a gust of terminal velocity that wrenches it from my hand.

I follow along the gate's length and pull it back to post, dragging Jolly behind me.

A tree splinters nearby. Creaks a crack like a drawn-out gunshot. Suddenly, Jolly is gone. Now I feel him in front of me, pushing me backwards with his nose, leaning against me with all his weight. I stagger back several steps then drop to my knees. Thunder travels though the ground like a train crash. The tree has come down. I feel the wet-leaf-fingers of a branch glance my face. Feel the leaves bounce a-swish and then lay still. My body is trembling and my hands won't stop tingling.

Even though my breath is snatching away, I manage to steady my voice: "Hell, that was close wasn't it, Jol? That almost fell on us."

I bury my face in his wet coat, let him lick me over and over. Tell him what a clever, clever boy he is. How he's saved us both.

Eventually my heart slows its tattoo, my breathing less audible. I swallow heavily and pull myself to standing.

I think that the tree may be blocking our path but now more than anything I just want to go home. Jolly comes to my hand without words, I lean down and reposition the harness, grasp the handle. Force my voice calm: "Forward, Jolly."

He goes straight a few steps then turns. I know this is the wrong direction but it seems so familiar I flow with him.

Soon I sense hollowness all around us, I know it hasn't stopped raining but I can't feel it or hear the patter. Neither can I feel the wind.

"Jolly?" That one word resonates, doubles and trebles and in an instant I know where we are. I reach out to the side of me, find the cold stone of the walled tunnel and breathe a long sigh.

This was where we first met David. I had been with Kayla and Jolly that day and we were making our way though this underpass. I remember saying how strange it was not to hear the rumble of the traffic, until Kayla had told me how far down we were.

David had been approaching from the opposite direction.

"Hi girls," he said, and then added, "I know I'm not meant to talk to your dog. My cousin is blind. He's got a guide dog too."

I loved his directness. No hint of embarrassment. I slipped off Jolly's harness. "He's not working now," I said.

Jolly had been all over David like a tick.

It had rained that day as well, not like this, but enough to keep us tunnel-bound for an hour. By the time it had stopped, David had invited us to his farm. I probably wouldn't have gone if Kayla had not been with me. But I might have.

I trust Jol's judgement.

It wasn't long before I felt the same way. I never let on of course. But I loved the times when Jolly was running free and David would take my right arm and lead me through his paddocks, handing me pieces of flora, letting me see the thorniness of the gorse or the paper softness of the heather.

Jolly is sniffing the air, the trouble with Labs is the fact they are always hungry. I couldn't smell anything, but that didn't mean there was nothing to eat. What Jol would have thought edible anyway.

"Leave it." A half dozen *'leave its'* echo, reinforcing the reprimand, but still Jol is sniffing and now he is wiggling and wagging, his tail wet-slapping my leg.

Then I hear footsteps. Someone is coming.

"David?" I whisper.

Kayla's voice reverberates, "Nettie. Nettie! Is that you? God, it's so dark in here." Now Jolly is wriggling fit to burst his skin.

"Here," I say, trying not to sound too disappointed.

"Oh, Nettie, thank goodness you're okay. I was so worried. Hi there, Jol, old lad."

I hear her ruffling Jolly's coat.

"We're fine." I decide not to tell her about our tree episode. She worries about me too much already.

"Bloody weather forecasters, they couldn't get it right if they looked out of the window," Kayla says.

For a moment I wonder what that would be like. Windows are square, the glass hard and transparent. My mind won't stretch at that. The concept of seeing through something solid is beyond me.

"Jolly has been so good. You know what I'm like in storms."

Kayla touches my shoulder. "God, Nettie, you're wet through. Let's get home. I've parked just down the road."

She stops for a second after we leave the tunnel. I hear her rattling in her bag. "Guess what?" she says. "David is back. He rang me just as I was going out to look for you. Told me he'd come over. I'll give him a call. Let him know you're fine and we're on our way."

Jolly shakes himself obligingly before we climb into the car. He stretches out on his blanket in the back seat, panting hot happy doggy breath in my direction but I don't mind at all.

I settle in and peel over my seatbelt. Turn my face towards Kayla.

"Kayla, what does David look like?" I've never asked her this before.

There is a small silence before she answers.

"Oh, you know... like any man really. He's got blonde hair, kinda streaky. Tall, but you'd know that." Her words are coming directly at me.

"Watch the road, Kayla."

Her voice has a grimace in it, "I don't know how you do that. How did you know I wasn't looking?"

"Lucky guess." I smile and feel the tension drop. Wonder for a moment why my intuition seems to be on high alert. And not just about Kayla's lack of attention.

"I have to tell you something, Nettie."

Coldness washes me like a tide.

"David has brought someone home with him," Kayla says. She's turning the car now and I know we are nearly at our apartment.

"Oh." My voice is cracked, I try to mend it, tack it to other words. "Who is it? Are they staying?"

She doesn't answer but stops the car and says, "I didn't ask. Look, they're here already. I guess we'll find out soon."

I don't care what David looks like, one thing about being blind is you can't judge any book by its cover, pardon the old analogy. But to be honest I do go for a nice voice and an intelligent mind, so I have my own terms of judgement, I suppose.

But right now I'm feeling vulnerable, and wet, and tired. I know my hands are still shaking and not from being cold, although I'm that as well. I really don't feel up to meeting anyone.

Jolly leans against me as I tighten his harness. I can hear Kayla in the distance saying "Hello". I can also make out David's voice, low and sensuous. I stretch my ears but I can't hear anyone else.

"Nettie Pot!" David's arms are around me like a wrap. I feel his muscles bulging hard into my back.

"Welcome back, David," I say. "Have you been working out?" I sound strong and relaxed. Think to myself I should take up acting.

"Yeah, I have actually. You look well, Nettie..." David holds me at arms' length and then leans down. "How's my best boy?"

I'm breaking all the rules letting Jolly go to him with his harness still on. But what the heck, I feel too flat to worry. I stand with my arms hanging by my side, waiting for the wild-flurry that is Jolly to subside. It takes a full three minutes. I know, I am counting.

I seize his harness. I can't hold back any longer. "Kayla tells me you have a friend with you," I say.

David's voice is moving away. "Yeah, come and meet him."

53

"Him!" My mind sings a happy song but not gay. David doesn't play that tune.

Cameron turns out to be David's roommate. He seems nice. I think of Kayla. She and her last boyfriend have been split for nearly a year now. Suddenly I feel energy like a power surge.

"How about you two stay for dinner? Kayla's a great cook and I make a mean salad." I lean down towards Jolly, who wriggles as if on cue. "Look, even he wants you to stay."

David laughs. "Well, we can't turn down an invitation like that. Although what's he going to serve us? I've seen what he eats sometimes. And it ain't a pretty sight."

I think of David's paddocks, of his two ponies. "Hors d'oeuvres," I say, deliberately mispronouncing it. Everyone laughs. It warms me like sunshine.

I snap open my watch and touch the time. "It's nearly six o'clock; if you two head off and get some wine we'll make a start."

"So," says Kayla after the men have left. "What do you think of Cameron?"

"Too soon to tell. Seems nice." I'm washing lettuce and trying to find the salad dressing I made last night.

"You really have it bad for David, don't you? You should have seen your face when I said he was bringing home someone else. To tell you the truth I thought it might have been a woman, too."

"Do you think this needs a little more mustard?" I hold out the spoon with what I hope is a tincture of tartar on the end.

"You're not going to answer me, are you? But look, Antoinette, I've known you... how long now? I don't want you to get hurt again. I'm really not sure about David."

I'd first met Kayla at a Guide Dogs' fundraiser. Well, Jolly had found her really. I wanted to know where I had to register. I had a few items for the auction: my old Braille typewriter (I have a computer with a speech synthesizer now) and a harness that didn't fit Jolly anymore. That was my fault. Too much good food.

I didn't even know she was sighted at first. She treated me so normally. And Jolly loved her. I could tell. His wiggle had increased by ten.

It wasn't long before she'd moved in with us (I'd been looking for a new flatmate and she'd been looking for somewhere to live) and after a few hiccups of the housekeeping kind we worked together like a good partnership. It's paid dividends ever since. Jolly knows how to pick them.

I set the table and open the wine to let it breathe. It smells divine. An expensive one. I sit down, my chair is closest to the kitchen door.

Kayla comes in and I hear her putting down the men's plates. Then mine.

"Nettie, fish is at twelve o'clock. Chips at six o'clock. You know where you put your salad and the bread is in front of you."

Cameron's voice sweeps the table like a broom. "Gee, Kayla you're good with her. I get it, she knows six o'clock is..."

David cuts his words in a snap, "Cameron, *she* has a name and is sitting right here with us."

"Oh, sorry, Nettie." His voice is loud enough to hear in the next room.

"And she's not deaf, either."

I stand up, almost bringing the tablecloth and my plate onto my lap. "That's enough, David. I can fight my own battles... anyway, Cameron doesn't know. Lots of people make the same mistakes." I sound more charitable than I feel.

I head out to the kitchen. Mutter something about the salt. Jolly's paws tip-scratch the floor behind me.

I run water in the sink, lean against it with stiff arms, take a few deep breaths.

Cameron is effusive when I return. I tell myself this is normal too.

The wine is good and soon the conversation turns to the guys and their studies.

55

David is doing a degree in English Literature, and Cameron one in Fine Arts. They talk about their tutors and Cameron makes us laugh with an anecdote involving one of their nude models. Finishing with, "so this prudish, and not too bright, student says to him, if god had wanted us to parade around with no clothes on we would have been born naked."

After dinner we throw tea towels at the men, who take the hint good naturedly and Kayla and I head off to the video store for a DVD.

Just as we are pulling out of the driveway I remember I haven't let Jolly out for his ablutions.

"You stay home, I'll go," Kayla says, as she lets us out. "Jolly takes ages at night sniffing around before he gets down to business. I know what we want anyway."

I take Jol around the back and let him loose. "Go quick quicks," I say, rather optimistically. Kayla is right, he always does seem to take longer in the evening.

The weather has warmed and the air has a fresh-washed smell like clean linen.

I wander along the side of the apartment, feel the gravel scuffling away under my feet. Rosemary essence wafts up to meet me and I know I am directly beneath the kitchen window where it is growing. When I want to use the herb for cooking I only have to reach out and break off a sprig. Kayla calls it Nettie's shortcuts to good house-keeping. She says I should write a self-help book. These thoughts are pleasantly jangling my mind when I hear my name mentioned and realise the window is open.

Jolly comes sniffing up to me, snuffles my hand once and when I don't react, disappears again.

David's voice is as clear as if he were standing next to me, which in a way I suppose he is.

"Antoinette is such a great girl. I haven't got the heart to tell her."

Antoinette even, I think, feeling the cold tide again. Then Cameron's voice: "Well, man, don't say anything. You don't need to. I

56

mean, you say there's nothing to it. Between you and Kayla, that is. So let it lie. In both senses of the word."

I feel certain they can hear my breathing. I am struggling to make sense of their conversation. But part of me knows already.

David's voice again: "It's just that Kayla's been ringing me all the time and texting. Asking me when I'm coming back. She's been so pushy. It's one of the reasons I didn't come home at mid-term."

"How come you're here now then, man?" David doesn't answer this and I hear Kayla's car pulling up in the drive.

My face is burning and my heart is a tight ache in my chest.

No wonder she'd told me she wasn't sure about David. She wanted me to forget about him so she could have a go. And was David being completely honest? What didn't he want to tell me? There must have been something between them for Kayla to be acting like this.

I feel like I don't know the world anymore. My truth is turning as dark as my skin.

Jolly comes up to me and bumps against my leg. I speak harshly to him, he sits down, completely still, even his panting has stopped, and immediately I feel all kinds of awful. He forgives me with a wash of his tongue and thump of his tail. It sounds dull, like my heartbeat, and I just want to get to bed and curl up on the day like a possum. Dogs don't have to worry, their life is one straight line of predictability.

I scratch his head. "Come on Jolly, I suppose we better go in."

Kayla meets me at the door, her voice light with anticipation, "They had one copy left, Nettie. But I just about had to wrestle it from another customer."

I try to get interested in the movie but my thoughts are unravelling, leaving tangled knots of disbelief. There is no way I can concentrate.

I start to get up out of my seat.

"Aren't you going to watch the movie?" Cameron says, then his words trip over themselves. "Oh, god... I'm so sorry.... I didn't mean to say watch...You know what I mean don't you, Nettie?" His voice is still too loud. This time David says nothing.

"It's okay, Cameron, to say look and see, and watch, for that matter," I say. "I do all those things in my own way. Gee, if I let that worry me."

Then Kayla says, "I never worry about what I say to you, do I, Nettie?"

No, I think, and not what you're doing either, it seems.

I stretch and yawn. "I'm really tired guys, I'm going to give the movie a miss. Will you be out tomorrow, David? We'll be at the paddock at the usual time."

When I wake the next day I feel normal, until I recall last night. I know I should confront Kayla with it. But if I do, I will have to disclose how I really feel. And I'm not ready for that. Not yet anyway.

My last lover, Michael, had left me after two years. He'd wanted someone to look after and thought that a blind girl would fit his needs. He'd fought my independence until he'd lost so many bouts that one day he left and found someone who'd back up his corner.

It had hurt like fire and I'm not sure when I'll be able to give myself like that again.

It's a long walk to David's farm and the road is greasy with mud. Twice I slip and I am glad I have the harness handle to steady me.

Jolly is living up to his name, his wiggle has a wag in it too, this morning.

We arrive at Jolly's favourite paddock, I let him go free and take up my post on a fallen log. I keep my hands on my knees and try not to think about the creepy things inherent to the countryside, especially spiders.

Suddenly I feel a tickle at the nape of my neck. I scream and stand upright. Jolly is bounding around me and I realise we are not alone.

"David! You mongrel!"

"Spider on you," he says. Despite myself I gasp again and then brush away his hand.

Before I know it, words flow like lava. "I'm cross with you at the moment, David."

"Oh come on, it's just a little joke, Nettie Pot." He catches hold of my hand but I thrust it away.

"I'm not talking about now," I say. "I'm talking about you and Cameron, your conversation last night while you were doing the dishes."

There is a silence vacuum. It seems even the birds have gone quiet.

David takes my arm and this time I don't resist. "Come with me Nettie." We walk swiftly in the direction of his homestead. Jolly is running away and then bounding back, barking once or twice before skidding off again.

"There's a blanket here," David says. "Sit." The one word like a command. I do as I'm told, feeling as listless as a sigh.

"I'm a bit surprised, Antoinette," he says, "I never thought of you as an eavesdropper." I explain to him about Jolly and why I happened to be outside the kitchen window. But I still feel my face warming.

I hear David stretching his long body out beside me. I pick up a corner of the rug, rubbing it between my fingers, feeling the contrast of the wool lining and plastic backing. Then I feel his hand over mine.

He takes an indrawn breath, it seems an age before he lets it out.

"Look, Nettie. I have to be honest with you. You give so many mixed signals I don't know if the bus is running or not."

I laugh. "Gee, I can see your course is paying off. That's not a bad metaphor."

David's hand lifts from mine. "See," he says, "that's what I mean. Nothing is serious with you."

Jolly takes this moment to come up and shake dam water over both of us. The droplets prick little cold needles over my bare skin that don't seem to dry.

David is scuffling in a bag. I can smell the raw meatiness of a bone.

"Here you go, old boy." Jolly brushes past me and the smell is stronger. Soon I hear him padding away, his panting containing something solid.

"So, David." I take out a handkerchief and wipe my arm. "What is it between you and Kayla?"

"You tell me? She's your friend, not mine."

I clench my fists and thump the blanket. "Don't play semantics with me now, David. I'm the one who doesn't know what the hell is going on. For instance what didn't you have the heart to tell me about?"

"I think Kayla may have the hots for me."

"So? Why shouldn't she? What does that have to do with me? Is your ego so big that you think all women want you? Including me?"

I know I have gone too far.

David's voice is quiet, a temporary lull before a gust makes it billow once more. "I know what trust means to you, Nettie. I thought, the way Kayla was acting... Oh, what the hell. You think you don't have a chip, but you do. Just like any of us. The meaning of life according to Nettie. Well, have a good one."

I sit still for what seems to be a long time. I know I am alone. In some ways I am thankful. But the numbness is lifting and now I can't even think about what I've said. I cover my mind in a blanket of denial.

I call out to Jolly and in minutes, it seems, we are home although I can't recall how we got here.

As soon as I enter the apartment, I can hear that David is there too. He and Kayla are laughing. I start to turn around but Kayla stops me. "There you are, Nettie," she says. "Come and have a nice cuppa tea, and we've saved a sticky bun for you, too."

I can't believe her audacity.

David steers me gently to a chair. "Cuppa's near your right hand," he says. "Sticky bun on your left. And seeing I seem to be good at getting other things arse about, I'm going to let Kayla do the talking."

Kayla's hand is on my shoulder, I feel her warmth through the thin fabric of my shirt.

"I'm not going to beat around the bush with this, Nettie. The reason I've been phoning David is that I could see what it was doing to you, him being away, I mean. I knew you wouldn't do anything about it. And I was pretty sure David didn't know how you felt. I wanted him to come here so I could tell him. I wasn't certain if he felt the same way about you."

Kayla stops for a moment. I start to say something, but her hand squeezes my shoulder hard, so I let her continue. "You two are both so bloody minded, that I knew if I didn't intervene it would go nowhere. Now take this picnic basket and go, get lost... together."

I feel my wicker basket being thrust into my hands; feel the promise of food in the weight of it and, for the second time that day, I do as I'm told.

My Friend Meredith
Bohemyth Ireland

The almost garden of the house that my friend Meredith wanted to break into, was one dying bush, a dirty rock and two pot plants with spider ferns crawling up their sides. I knew they were spider ferns because our gardener grows them behind his cottage but he grows them in an old tub, one of those claw types although it's not so old. Anyway, my friend Meredith didn't even lift one of the pots because she says that's too obvious a place for keys and poor people don't like to look too obvious whereas rich people don't think of it either way.

After we knocked on the door and no one answered, I lifted them both up just in case. As usual, Meredith was right. She always knows about these things. She's fourteen and much smarter than I am.

We found the key under the windowsill at the back of the house, in fact the key found us, because we stepped on a loose porch-board and it hit the sill and the key popped out and we nearly missed it because it was rusted the colour of the house. Meredith told me she didn't want to use a key anyway because then it wouldn't be bona fide 'break and enter', so she put it back.

There was an empty house next door where we didn't need a key, we just walked through a wall or where a wall would have been if it hadn't fallen down with neglect. Some people are so neglectful.

We waited there watching the house, for what seemed like too long but of course time drags too much when you just wait and have nothing to do and Meredith made me be quiet, by placing a finger over her mouth every time I started to speak and then by putting her hand over my mouth when I kept on talking.

A man soon came along pushing a wheelbarrow with a large sack of potatoes and two cabbages perched on top. He went behind the house with the spider ferns, propped up the wheelbarrow and opened the door. I saw Meredith's eyes narrow when he didn't even use the key. She had pushed the key so far back it had fallen through and under the house but he didn't look for it because the door had been unlocked all along. The man was wearing denims with knee worn holes and a dirty shirt. Maybe he was one of the dirty men Meredith's mother warned us about. Although I know it's not that kind of dirty but maybe the dirty dirt shows the other kind of dirty. He also had tattoos like sailors have, but I couldn't see if they were of naked mermaids or not. Meredith's eyes opened wide but of course she wasn't scared. Meredith's not scared of anything.

The man came back out, tossed the bag of potatoes over his shoulder, and we could see how he got dirty, because the bag puffed out dirt, kind of like smoke and the dirt went all over his shirt and down his back. He picked up one of the cabbages in his other hand and went back inside his house. Some people always eat cabbage. And they often smell like cabbage. An old man who sat next to us on the train smelled like cabbages.

Here's what happened next. Meredith ran out and grabbed the other cabbage, she tossed it to me and kept running, but I dropped it. I could see Meredith's eyes going as black as her clothes, her eyes always go black when she's cross with me so I snatched up the cabbage and tossed it back over to her. She ran around the side of the house where we'd been hiding and threw it as far as she could into the backyard, which was all weeds and rubbish, then she grabbed my hand and dragged me into the empty house.

The man came outside again and looked at the wheelbarrow for ages, kind of like he thought the cabbage would rematerialize. If he'd started shaking his head we wouldn't have been able to hold back our laughter, it would have all been just too ghastly, but then he walked over to where we were hiding. I ducked down but Meredith just kept standing and staring. I wondered if she was going to use her little-girl voice but she didn't.

"Hey you. There," the man said, lifting his hand in half a wave. "Do you know you're trespassing?" Meredith and I exchanged a glance which said of course we do but then Meredith did go very little-girl. "No, please, mister. We thought nobody lived here anymore."

"Well," the man said, "that may be by the by. But folks don't always live where they own. And someone owns this house." Meredith grabbed at my hand; kind of grazed it, not held on and I followed her out. She stood in front of the man, with her hands behind her back, eyes lowered and her head tilted sideways and one of her feet hooked back over her other ankle.

The man was having none of it. "Go and get that cabbage you threw away," he said, his hand doing a wide arc across the yard. We both took a short breath and looked over at his house; he must have seen us from his window.

"If you knew I had thrown it why did you stare at the wheelbarrow then, like you thought the cabbage was coming back?" said Meredith. That's how Meredith is. Now she didn't have her little-girl voice; she sounded like her mother, all vowels and sniff nosed.

The man shook his head; he looked at me and then at Meredith. Longer at her because of how gorgeous she is. I'm used to folks doing this between me and her. Then he turned away and strode over to the yard and came back out of the long grass carrying the cabbage. He plucked a slug from it, flicked the slug to the ground and went back into his house without looking at us. Meredith followed and I followed her. That's how we have fun talking to these people. Although we've never gone into their houses to talk to them and maybe that's what Meredith meant about 'doing a house,' not just stealing. Anyway, the man couldn't be dangerous if he didn't even kill slugs; our gardener puts all the snails and slugs into buckets of salt and they shrivel up like they're burning alive and he doesn't give a toss.

The man had gone into another room and didn't see us come into his house and we walked like we do when we're trying not to wake everyone up when Meredith sleeps over and we sneak out for midnight feasts in the park. He had the ball game going but his television was inside and we didn't see any beer.

Meredith put her finger to her lips again as the man went back outside and we watched him pass by the window and go down the street, pushing the wheelbarrow. The little grocery store was a ten minute walk so we figured we had time to look around, but there was nothing interesting and everything smelled like cabbage even the potatoes cooking in a huge pot on the stove. It was quietly bubbling, Cook calls that simmering and sometimes she boils up bones like that for father's hunting dogs. Meredith poked through the drawers in the kitchen and held up a leaflet: Help The Homeless, it said. Saturday Soup Kitchen 6 pm. There was an address circled in red ink, of course we had never heard of it and of course Meredith wanted to go. I had to remind her we had to be at the station at 5 o'clock to meet her mother, but she said her mother was always late which was true. I had never known her mother to be on time but then we were never on time either so we really didn't know if she *was* late because she was always there waiting. Anyway it was only 2 o'clock, so we had lots of time and then we saw the man coming back.

His wheelbarrow was full of wooden slatted boxes, the kind Cook uses for kindling; they were stacked on top of each other but balanced so they toppled a little bit to one side. The man kept stopping and straightening them, we could see this from the window but soon he was at the backdoor. This is how Meredith is; she hurried over and locked the backdoor from the inside, there was this little slide-across bolt the kind they have in public toilets sometimes, especially here in this part of town.

65

We held our breaths and watched the door. We could hear the man twisting the knob and pushing on the door, it rattled the bolt but the door held, and then after he'd done it lots of times Meredith opened the door and the man fell inwards nearly knocking into her. But I'd jumped back and hidden behind the other door and pushed my fist into my mouth to stop from laughing aloud, it was all just too ghastly.

The man did a strange thing, he didn't yell at Meredith, like I thought he would but spun around, shut the backdoor and pulled the bolt across and then he took out a key; it was a different key from the one Meredith had lost. This was a shiny key but he didn't use it, he just stood with his back braced up against the door like someone was trying to get in from the outside. Meredith, this is how fun she is, said "Please mister I've come about the Soup Kitchen. My friend's gone home but I want to help." He nodded kind of slow and smiled and instead of arguing like I thought he would, said, "Sure, sure you do." And went over to the huge pot cooking on the stove and stirred the potatoes with a long handled spoon. I thought it was a bit strange he hadn't got cross because he seemed crosser when we were just trespassing in the deserted house next-door. And it was kind of like we *had* broken in to *his* house but Meredith said, you have to break something like a door or a window to actually break in, so maybe that's why.

Meredith half looked at me hiding behind the door and touched her lips with her finger, she went over to the sink and started to chop up the cabbage with a large wooden handled knife. The man came over and told her to do it this way. "Just like this," he said, his voice low and different. His arms went around her from behind and he directed her hands. Then Meredith turned on the faucet and washed the cabbage. The water spluttered and the pipes whined and rattled and screeched like someone trying to get out.

Without Consent

BuzzWords Magazine UK

You never thought you were capable of rape.

Before fifteen, life is footy, friends and nothing worse than the occasional whiff of tobacco shared behind the shelter shed, its rusted roof and bowed gutters giving little shelter to you or your friends who huddle, crooked backed, hands curved in defence against a wind which threatens to extinguish the glow before it's even your turn.

You frantically search for lexicon loopholes but find only confirmation of your shame.

It's there in black on white: **Rape - The act of taking anything by force.**

Your mother flutters by and smiles, her thoughts as translucent as the fragile pages you turn in desperation. *My boy is studying hard looking up words in the dictionary.*

Your guilt becomes a living thing, gnawing at the corners of your life, tearing chunks from satisfaction gained in kicking goals, and snatching pride from boldly underlined 'A's gained on essays.

You taunt fate to get you if it dares.

You dare. And win. Each success diminishes you. Unfairness tips unbalanced scales until they touch the ground and go no further.

Years rush and faded memory becomes a Monet painting of the past which only comes into focus when you stand back. And you never stand back.

You think, *I was so young then.*

Now your computer has mail with a request from the class of 66.

Grey words on your screen, grey thoughts in your mind, grey skies above a landscape you don't deserve.

Your wife reads over your shoulder.

"Danny, you should go. It would be fun. Catching up."

It is fitting punishment. Flaying yourself with let's play remembering. *"Remember all the good times Danny, all the games we won Danny. Remember Brother Leaver? He was a dirty bugger wasn't he, Danny?"*

You think, *He never molested me.* In an intro-perverted way you wonder why and suddenly wished he had. To even the score.

"You remember Maggie, Danny?"

You shake your head, half yes, half no.

"Sure you do. You went out with her. Remember, Danny?"

Margaret McGuire. Maggie. Beautiful, sweet, and pure as youth. Hair which channelled the sun in fire filaments of red gold. You remember the day you met, the day you took her home, the night you saw Dr Zhivago together. How she quavered when you first held her hand, and, when you went to let go, how she caught it up and held it tight until the end of the movie.

Mam always says she's so glad I'm going out with you Danny. Says she knows her little girl is safe with Danny Sullivan. He's such a nice boy she tells my pa. Why are parents always like that Danny? Don't they know I'm not a baby anymore?

You think of your children, how even now, with children of their own, they are still your kids.

Even the smell of your alma mater, despite the renovation of the years, is the same.

You know there is a name for recollection by aroma. But you can't recall it.

You do remember hers. 'Attar of Roses'.

You are glad the perfume was not a common one. Now, no one wears it.

"Maggie was the one with the big tits. You never did tell me, Danny, did you get to touch them? Did you get to first base?"

You turn away from your friend and look at the honour board. It brings no joy to see your name in every list. The letters etched in brass which only fire can destroy.   Milestones with mindless epitaphs of false words: BEST and FAIREST.

The year book is turned to your page. *Most likely to succeed* is the heading. You look at the photo into eyes that are as old as yours.

You cannot breathe. You escape through familiar doors to a quadrangle you cannot remember.

You turn the corner and a cold breeze lifts leaves and dust in tiny maelstroms of activity.   The light of the moon glints off the shelter shed's new roof. But that is all that has changed. You walk in hushed feet towards the place where the shed joins the main building. The blind spot.

Danny, we can't do it here!
It's night, no one will see us. Did you bring the blanket?
I took the old grey blanket from the spare room. Mam won't miss it then.

You are sure you can see the depression where you both lay. But the night was darker than this.

I'm cold Danny.
Here, have my coat.
Thanks Danny.

How does that feel?
Oh Danny, that's so nice.
You like that?

Your face is burning despite the breeze.

You have taken an antique from its original wrapping. Now you see its true colours, feel its real texture. But any worth is ruined.

What are you doing? We have to stop now. Danny please stop. Please stop! I don't want to do it now. Please, Danny, please! You're hurting me...

You kick the shed. You don't care if anyone hears. You hope they do. Then you will tell them, Yes! I raped a girl here, on this very spot. She wanted me to stop but I wouldn't.   "Maggie I'm so sorry. I am so bloody sorry!"

You realise you are screaming.

Someone touches your back. You turn around. A middle aged woman is standing there. Her hair is grey but her perfume is familiar. Attar of Roses.

"Danny? Jack said you were out here."

"Maggie?" You don't wait for an answer. You start to say something but speech has burned to bile in your throat. Tears stream down your face and you are glad of them.

Proof of your remorse.

You see that you are not the only one who is crying.

"Are you really sorry, Danny? Are you? Can you say honestly you've given me any thought over all these years? And leaving straight after, like you did. I felt like sex was the only thing you really wanted."

The strokes of memory become a stark picture. You see yourself running until you collapse, until your sobs match those of the girl you left behind on the old grey blanket,   curled like a question mark, with your coat draped over her.

The sluice is opened. Words tumble from you. You tell her how self imposed penitence has turned your life to living monochrome. How you wish you could change that night to frame a different image. And how truly sorry you are, not for what you have missed but for what you have taken.

Maggie tells you her story. Of self blame, of sadness, of isolation. Then of empowerment and marriage and children.

Finally strong arms encircle, you feel the warmth of forgiveness without further words being spoken.

Your wife was right. Reunions are all about catching up.

On Train and Boat

On train and boat,
cousins both
by breath of steam
a century rocked
in waves and sleepers
across the land and sea

They forged the country
cleaved the rivers
carried man further than call
now the aged at their beck on rail and deck
but good hands all

The train whistles back
steel shrouded black
in clouds of cinders coal
the boat in paddles rushing, hissing,
warning, warning I am passing
to toll its bell in tunes of old

My First Husband

My first husband worked on the railways
in a shotgun town, a railway cottage thrown in
to pay the wage and to even the deal
afternoon night shift and a shunting yard
ten feet behind the back door

if you closed your eyes
sometimes sleep shut your ears
while rusted couplings clanged
in points against your marriage
and your first husband changed the gauge
but your babies learned early
to go all night, with the noise

And some years later my first husband
who was now a train driver
ran over a teenaged boy and mate-brimmed car
all playing chicken, with only his Learner's
for protection
the brake-slide stopping time of trains
never matching that
of random traffic

crushed steel left aside bloodied sleepers

and now
in long guilt
redundant nights
my first husband shuts his eyes
but the noise still plays out behind closed lids.

San Pedro River Review - California - USA

Where the Kookaburras Laugh

First prize in UK Global short story competition

There's a different feel to the air in the cemetery when the evening cools and calls. A cloistered breeze touches the stones, wafts across the fenced-in plots of blood-rust steel and bone-coloured cement. Somewhere near, a crow caws its bawdy ballad, the last note a drawn lament. But the kookaburras too, have their song.

A little boy, Danny, walks alone along the rows, stopping in front of one particular gravestone where the inscription has eroded to undecipherable scratches. His head moves from side to side, his lips soundless, mouthing words that cannot be read.

Danny lives nearby with his mam, his gran and his uncle, the brother of his father who died in the Great War. Danny's mam got the telegram the day Danny was born. For her, his father died in childbirth.

Danny stoops and stretches an arm as pale as a robber's promise through the steel pikes, feels the rust rub his skin, leave a mark like ochre. Like war-paint.

His fingers touch the top of an imbedded flower container. There is an earthen ping, then his treasure (a small lead horse, hand-painted and unmounted by harness or rider) becomes as irretrievable as rain.

'Danny, lad, where are you, boy?' His uncle's voice seems not to echo here.

Danny doesn't answer but crouches at the side of the grave. He listens as the sound descends on him with the impending dark.

'There you are. What are you doing?'

'Nothing, Uncle Don.'

'Well get up, lad and dust yourself off. Your mam's had your dinner ready for an hour now. She's fit to burst. Come-a-long, quick.'

His uncle turns around and heads off without waiting.

Danny pulls himself up using the grave-fence for support, rubs rust-powdered hands over his knees and the tops of his shorts. He smiles, strangely satisfied at the result.

He puts his hand in his pocket, feels the carrot nestled there like a fifth finger, and quickens his pace.

The moon is up already, even though the sun has just sat down on the horizon. The cemetery seems to breathe Danny gone, trails behind him so that he is too scared to look back.

He stumbles on the rocky track that leads back to his house. Ghost gum branches spider-web the evening sky, ensnare the light but speed his step. Soon he is at the horse paddock and Major, their carthorse, snickers softly, an almost human sound. Danny hears the horse before he comes into dusk-focus, grey silhouette on grey, the familiar smell of horse sweat and dirt as comforting as a hug.

Soft but bristled lips nuzzle his hand; he opens it, keeping the palm flat, and the carrot is whisked away in a disappearing act. There are sounds of crunching, then the big head comes back, nose tucks under Danny's empty hand and flicks it upwards.

'Hey, Major. There's no more, boy.' Danny laughs as the horse quivers back his lips, white teeth visible in the moonshine, almost a smile.

He climbs up the fence and slips a leg over Major's broad back. Major shakes his head as if in mock amusement and begins to amble back towards the farmhouse, his footfalls cuffing his huge feet in dust haloes.

Sliding from Major's back, Danny stands staring at his home. It looks oddly like the cemetery in this light. The fence of steel and picket demarcates the house from paddock and track. The front door is shut, the black form of the knocker hangs there like a decaying tooth.

The door opens; he sees his mam, hand shading her eyes as if scanning the sun. She stares at him, sight unseeing.

He comes forward into the thin light streaming about her. Her hand, as fast as a snake, snatches him to her side.

'Where have you been? And look at the state you're in.' Rough fingers streak down his front and the blood-rust is smeared. He notices her hands are wearing it now.

There is a gust of wind, Danny shivers, sees his uncle standing behind his mam with the horse whip held upright, his eyes look tired but his grip is firm. 'I'm sorry my lad, but your mam is right. You can't keep going off when it's getting dark. It worries her. And it pains me to be the one to have to put it right.'

Major neighs for his dinner, the noise follows Danny into the house but the door is shut behind him and the sound is cut mute. We'll both go hungry tonight, he thinks, but at least Major will miss out on the flogging.

Some time later, Danny hears a soft tap on his bedroom door; he rolls over from his stomach and sits up slowly. The door opens and Gran Sarah, his father's mother, creeps bent to his bed, balanced by a candle in one hand and a plate of sandwiches in the other.

'Hush there now, lad. I couldn't be letting you go without supper. Eat quiet like and slip the plate under the bed when you're finished with it. I'll collect it myself in the morning.'

'Why does me mam hate me so, Gran?'

'Ah, she's always been under a drop that one, never bonnie like your aunt Rosie. And like I've said before, lad, when she got the news of your da, in the midst of her birthing, she tied the blame to you. I don't think she understands it herself but there it is and no denying.'

Danny takes the plate. The gloom has parted slightly and he watches as his gran shuffles on leaden feet from the room. He lies back on the bed but sleep darts from behind his lids. Images and voices of snatched conversations are caught in his mind: *Selling up...moving...*

Danny has lived here all his life. His gran came from Ireland sixty years ago when she was just a lass and freshly wed. And when Danny's grandpa died, his mam and his da moved in to help his uncle Don run the farm. After the war ended it began receding year by year, fifty acres sold off here, ten there, until now there is just the oasis of the horse paddock left. The working dogs are growing lazy and Major only has the cart to pull, the horse-drawn harvester has gone the way of the Stump-Jump-Plough. Sold to the highest bidder at their farm auction two weeks ago.

Danny's mam ignores him when he comes for breakfast the next morning. She's talking to his uncle Don, her voice as light as a thread.

'So, you did order the green one? The one I saw advertised in the catalogue?'

Uncle Don tousles Danny's hair, last night's beating forgotten with the dawn. 'Just like a woman,' he says. 'To be worrying about an incidental thing like a colour. I know what you want to hear, Danny. Ah, my lad, it truly is a wonderful thing to see. A Buick - a touring car. All six cylinders, four-speed gear box, and rear wheel drive of her. Dozens of horses under her bonnet, makes a mockery of old Major out there.'

He cocks his thumb towards the paddock. Danny is pleased to see someone has fed the horse. Major stands in a circle of hay. Strands of golden raffia cascade from his mouth and reflect the silver in his coat. He snorts the dust and stomps the flies. It seems to Danny the earth tremors beneath those hooves. No car could ever match that.

His mam scoops tea leaves from the Bushells tea-caddy. Danny can see the kangaroo and koala, soft grey embossed. He tries to find the kookaburra but the tin is facing the wrong way. 'Should be a treat to drive on the good roads when we move back to town,' his mam says.

Danny's gran is in one of her talking moods, she sits, perpetually cold despite the weather, in her favourite chair, with a rug over her knees. She only has Danny for an audience. But his ears are as forward as old Major's are when the dogs are howling at the moon.

'I just wish I had my boy back here in the place where he was birthed. Not buried in some far-flung country which I can never visit. I think it would have helped your mam too, Danny. Although I still have my Don. Nothing like my Adrian though, but I'd never say it to him. Your da loved horses, like you. He had no time for the automobiles.'

Danny sits closer, plucks at a stray thread on the side of the old chair, feels it flake and disintegrate beneath his fingers.

'I have somewhere I go to visit my da.' His voice is low and his gran cups her ear and leans towards him.

'I have somewhere I go,' he says, so loudly that she withdraws as if she's been shot.

'No need to yell, boy. I'm not deaf. What's that? You have someone you know?'

Danny folds his arms around his legs, drawing them close to his chest. He rests his chin in the dip between his knees. 'Tell me again. About my da,' he says.

Later, with her story still sounding in his mind, Danny leaves his sleeping gran and runs to the horse paddock.

Major sees the bridle he's carrying and skitters away like a colt. But then he stops, wheels around, takes a few steps towards Danny and lowers his head. Danny approaches slowly, all soft-voiced words and promised treats. He slips on the bridle and fastens the strap. With thin strong hands he grabs a hunk of mane at the horse's withers and as deftly as a jockey, vaults onto his back.

'GO.'

He screams it like a battle cry. Major accelerates, his large bulk a catapult, but Danny is ready. He leans forward along the horse's neck, his bare heels batter Major's sides like tiny fists. He can feel his own heart and the strong pulse of living force beneath him. All around, those of the Twelfth Light Horse Regiment are galloping in a mad headlong dash, some to oblivion, some to live to die another day. *The horses by the hands of the ones they trusted. Can't let the Turks have them.*

He whispers in Major's ear, it flickers back, listening. 'We can do it this time, boy.'

Danny sees the fence approaching, sees the top wire, a tightrope of tiny razors stringing across it.

'To the wells of Beersheba,' he yells. The fence is in front of them, larger now by its closeness.

'Over!'

The one word like a spur. He digs in his heels, loosens the reins and lifts with the leap. For one suspended moment both are flying.

'We've done it boy! We've jumped the trenches. We've saved the troops.'

Danny lets the horse stretch out under him, feels the smoothness of the gallop, watches over Major's shoulder for pitfalls in the unravelling terrain. Moves his hands, steers him safe. Horse and rider saving each other. His breath gasps and grasps his chest. He smells the acridity of fear and death. He hears the battle, the shots, the screams, the thuds of fallen men and horses. Knows his father is one amongst them. Danny lets out his breath, a long sigh that seems like it will never end.

Soon he reins Major to slow, loosens his grip once more as the graveyard comes into focus. It is different in the daylight. He only goes there in the dark. In the light it would be too hard to pretend. He thinks of his father, of the gravestone with the make-believe words, thinks of the little lead horse, of town, wonders if the kookaburras will laugh there.

Mercury Rising

First place 'Gone Fishing' Flash Fiction competition - New York

I live downtown next door to an extreme cleaner. OCD, not commercial. Sadie Badenoch. Sadbad we called her at school but she wasn't bad and before the gunman came she was cat sleek beautiful.

My rental-room looks into her kitchen. Six a.m. I see her cleaning to Queen's music. Mercury rising. Her house gleams like the stars.

Ten a.m., safe behind my impenetrable screen, I watch her prepare for outside. Living in the real world.

Keys jangle. Her hands dart round, up and down her front door's frame. Her ritual protection. Takes two hours before she leaves.

Wish I could.

Breasts by Candlelight

She steps out of
going-away clothes
like a dainty dancer
white waxed thighs,
meet in shadow's flickering
vertical line
to a promised entry.
Curves carve the darkness
a silhouette
worthy of the greatest sculptor.

Wedding day's froth and ritual
gone
lost in love light's flame
for, before life
sped her on her way,
the always serious friend
showed a different face,
pressed a candle, thin
in its golden holder,
into her hand.

Take this,
she'd whispered,

and give him
a night
to remember.

In a Woman's Voice - Silver City New Mexico

Jonathon's Gulls
Fiction Shelf - UK

I'd put off reading my grandfather's journals for months. His death had been too raw for me to pick up the sentences of his past or maybe I was afraid of what I would find, that the man in the pages would not live up to the grand-poppy of my boyhood.

I'd been named after him and we had once been close.

The first page entry was his last:

This is the final entry of Christopher H Johnston.

Please note that the starred entries are the ones worth reading. You will also see that they are few and far between. "Such is life," as that infamous Australian, Ned Kelly, was supposed to have said, before he went to the place where I am now headed, be that up or down.

Also, corresponding to each entry in these journals is a photo of myself, taken on the last Sunday of every month since I left home at the age of seventeen. They carry on my father's work. Together with those photos he took, which I include with these journals, you will see that they number almost all my eighty-nine years by twelve. The only hiatus was the three years during which I was abroad.

"Abroad" was grand-poppy's way of describing his years in the British Army, before he married an Aussie girl and emigrated to

Australia. And the portrait photos of himself had indeed begun when his own father, a keen but amateur photographer, started with a monthly snap of his newborn and, as it turned out, only son.

As regular as the calendar, Poppy had never missed a month and in a way I thought, even though the earlier photos were Box-Brownie faded, it was time-lapse photography before that was generally heard of. And of 'Selfies' too.

There were nine journals. One photo for each entry. Over a thousand pictures painting the words.

In the later photos, if you scanned across them, you could see my grand-poppy crinkling with age, in contrast to the pictures as they grew crisper with technology.

I sat and shuffled through the years, trying to match the faces of my childhood Poppy with those on the bed before me. One decade coalesced like sunlight; these were the years of my holiday stays before he moved so far away that seeing him became almost impossible.

After I'd spread the photos over the bed, I checked the dates on their backs, scanned them into sequence with the journal, and the time we'd shared became as lucid as a movie.

One photo stood out like a plea. Taken in the same chair, and in the same stance as all the others, this one seemed brighter but less focused. I remembered the last time I saw it. I was there the day it was taken and seeing it again now, my childhood peeled away like a shell.

This photo, however, wasn't the one I had ruined. I was fourteen and that was the last time I was to see my Poppy. I am thirty now. I never managed to find the money for the trip to visit him in between.

Poppy seldom tolerated fools gladly. I'd sensed this from the earliest age and was always at pains not to disappoint him. He wasn't a stereotypical grandparent; I have no recollection of fishing, football, or hallmark moments. Ours were of the darkroom and the bright sky-lit hills, the watery, dusk-gloamed creeks and coppery fields in walking closeness to his cottage. The motionless kangaroos before their bounding flight, the koalas curled in their grey-green eucalypts.

Poppy taught me about bulb setting, shutter speed, background, backlighting, and the all important balance of the shot. How you could frame the picture with branches gnarling the edge of a pond, or the canopy of a tree uplifting the sky. Framing was important, he said.

Since Grandma's death though, he seemed to be a step out of time with the Australian landscape, and started talking about the Marsh Harriers of his English country childhood in the Norfolk Broads or borrowing the wind to sail the rivers.

"So, Chris," he'd said that autumn morning, sixteen years ago, at my arrival. "Just in time to help me with The Frog."

The Frog was his nickname for his old wooden rowboat. Its outer coat of green the only legacy of its name that I could see. The Frog was sluggish when you rowed. Poppy never knew this. He'd had an outboard motor fitted when he'd bought it.

Both his arms had limited movement, courtesy of having some of 'the war' lodged in his spine. Over the years, the paralysis worsened and I often marvelled at his ability to function so well on his own, and at his dexterity in what was known as his 'Light-tight' room, its only illumination a filter-fitted safelight.

Poppy carried on the self-portrait photos, taken every month, in obligation to his father's tradition. And kept up his own journal with its stars highlighting his best days. But his real love, and indeed his profession, was photographing the wild, although he went for the commonplace rather than the exotic. "All nature is miraculous, Chris," he'd say, his eyes lighting up his smile.

This new autumn morning, I'd arrived buzzing with excitement. It was March 1995 and the first digital camera had not long been out. I'd received one for Christmas and couldn't wait to tell Poppy about it. But he had other ideas and as soon as I'd unpacked he had me rowing out to his favourite spot. The outboard on The Frog had died a few weeks before and he hadn't had time to fix it.

"Jonathon's gulls are back, Chris. I heard them screeching over the house last night. I know where they'll be heading. We had fishermen down here last weekend. One of those tour groups from the city. Left lots of bait and dead carp by the old pier."

Five years before, when holidaying at the coast, Poppy had found an abandoned baby seagull and had taken it home and raised it. He'd named the bird Jonathon, as in Jonathon Livingston Seagull, one of his favourite books.

Poppy lived in the high country of Australia. The mountains pushed their rounded peaks into the sky, and before Jonathon, gulls never came that far inland.

I was there the day he'd released him into the valley where the ghost gums struggled with the drought and the cliff tops arched over them like god's hands. Jonathon and his flock of seagulls had come back every year after that, but this time they were early. I'd had the long weekend planned since Christmas, although I hadn't expected to see the gulls. They usually didn't appear until spring.

"Going to be a bad winter, I reckon, Chris," Poppy said, as I pulled the oars, heading inland. Uncomfortable position facing backwards. No way of seeing where I was going.

The Frog's hull snagged the reeds and the river's outbound flow slowed our progress. My city arms ached and soon I had to stop. The boat swung sideways as Poppy cursed.

"Keep it moving boy. If you don't keep moving forward you lose your steering."

He only ever called me 'boy' when he was getting irritated. I started rowing again.

I remember that Poppy had grown quiet after saying this. At the time I'd thought it was his anger rising in silence, but now I am not so sure.

Soon I'd nudged the endorphin threshold and had my second wind, but my muscles would be on fire the following day. It was always like this. Even when the outboard was operational Poppy had me rowing. Secretly I think he hated using the 'oil', as he called it. And I had to admit that gliding down the river with the breeze for song, accompanied by the dip drip of the oars, was the best way to photograph wildlife before it departed for bush or sky.

Poppy leaned over, keeping hold of the tiller, and dragged his kitbag towards himself. He opened the clip, took out his latest camera with its telescopic lens, and a large bag of broken bread and rolls.

"The gulls will be hungry after such a long journey. I've been saving these scraps for ages. Kept them in the fridge. Poor old hens have had to go light." He gave a gruff laugh. I just nodded. I needed all my breath for the rowing.

"Stop at the first bend before the pier, Chris. I don't want to spook them. We'll moor at the old log and walk up along the track."

When we got to the pier there was no sight of the flock. Poppy made his seagull sound, a sort of shrill whistle, then scattered some crumbs across the river. I watched as the lazy current swirled them outwards then inwards, snaring a few pieces on the tree roots sucking at the river's edge.

When Poppy grabbed my arm I froze. A casual flapping sound crossed overhead. A seagull slapped the water and rose upwards with some of the bread clamped in its beak. Poppy shook his head. "Not Jonathon," he murmured. He covered his eyes with a broad hand and looked skywards. A squawking rose from the trees and then, as if one, the flock descended. Impressive in white and orange beak trim. Some birds landed to float in the water, some along the river bank. One gull alighted on the pier, as dainty as a ballerina. It took a step towards Poppy, snatched the bread scrap from his fingers and took off to a high branch above our heads.

"That's him Chris! That's Jonathon."

I couldn't tell. They all looked the same to me.

And then it happened. Another bird came close and took a piece of bread right from my hand. I picked up a chunk of roll and another gull swooped and snatched. Poppy picked up pieces of bread too. The air swirled wings around us. Gulls dipped and skimmed and dived for the offerings from our trembling fingers. For a moment it seemed as if we had become one with them, threaded, part of the flock.

When the food was finished they all took off. We watched the phalanx veer to the left, a half circle and then, in a shimmering grey white flash framing the sun, they were gone.

Poppy still held his camera and I wondered if he had caught any of it on film. But I knew nothing could capture our feelings.

Silence held us together as we climbed aboard The Frog. I lifted the oars like a half salute and let the river's flow take us back home. Later, when Poppy still hadn't spoken, I knew to leave him alone. I remember hoping it wasn't anything I'd done. I spent the rest of that afternoon fooling around with my digital camera and laptop, and wishing I'd had the camera with me when we'd fed the flock.

When it was getting dark I began looking for him. First calling and then searching through the house. As I opened a back bedroom door Poppy shouted, "Bloody hell, boy. I'm working in here. Clear off!" It was not his Light-tight room, I knew better than to go in there unasked, but as soon as the door had opened I'd seen this room was as dark as a blackout too.

I retreated to my bedroom and waited. Watching my door like a chased hare. He stormed in some minutes later.

"The best bloody shot I've ever had. And you ruined it. Didn't your damn mother teach you to knock?"

I pulled back, unable to answer. I was tingling down to my fingertips with the unfairness of it all. How was I supposed to know he'd made up another darkroom?

That evening, he said he'd forgiven me. But the rest of the weekend I was on my own. A month after that, Poppy left to go back to England, for good, to the place he was born. He wrote to me saying he had lost his steering, that he had to go back to go forward. And he sent me photos of Marsh Harriers and The Broads, and of white sails riding through flat paddocks, the water in the rivers hidden behind whispering reeds.

For me though, photography had lost its appeal.

But here, sitting on my bed, sixteen years later, reading the corresponding journal entry to the photo that I held in my hand, I finally understood.

Poppy wrote of his oneness with the gulls that day. Watching them heading off home, to the water so far away, had made him see what he really wanted. And my messing up the photo of Jonathon's flock, that total glimpse of freedom, had made him recognise something which had been tugging at his soul. He needed to go back to his home country. He also wrote that he hoped I would forgive him one day.

I traced my fingers around the star at the top of the entry, closed my eyes and, in my mind, tightened the grip on the picture of my Poppy.

His other faces, time snaps, merged and folded when I shifted my position, like waves of still memories. Now, perfectly framed.

Little Red

Tuck Magazine UK

When Papa is slaughtering the chickens I keep my hands over Ben's ears. He keeps his eyes shut himself.

Papa insists we help. He told Mama we needed to know about the Realities Of Life. I've known about them for five years now. Since we moved here in '52.

I was four like Ben is now, when I first had to watch. But I didn't have no big sister to block out the noise. Our place is up in the hills, it's a long way from town. We don't have to go to school. Mama does that for us. The teaching.

She still has all her books from when she grew up in the big city, from before she met Papa.

We have one of the biggest chicken farms around and every three months is the slaughtering. Mama says there would be no chickens bred in our farm if it were not for the slaughtering. Cause, she says, why would anyone breed chickens for just being chickens? Daft chickens are, like you kids, she says.

I did have a pet chicken once that I called Little Red, from the story, The Little Red Hen. It was one of the books that Mama has. I can read that one better than Mama now. But Papa says what is all this learning going to do for us kids. Better to learn how to pluck and dress the chickens.

I know how to do that. It's the boiling water you have to be careful of. And I told Ben that too, not to get too close to the overflowing.

I was just six when I first got burned and Mama put butter on it and told me to stop with the crying. She pulled open her shirt and showed me the scald-scar running down the middle of her chest like red lava. She said she hadn't needed no doctor and I wasn't going to need no doctor either.

That night when I was crying, Papa came in with the strap and then, when the bed springs creaked, as he climbed back in with Mama, I heard him laugh as he told Mama how that had shut me up. When I saw the strap.

But Mama and Papa they don't know, but it was biting down on my fist that stopped the crying noise. I still had tears that wouldn't stop. But you can't hear tears, I suppose.

Mama and Papa didn't know about Little Red. I kept her a secret and took her scraps that Mama didn't see was left over from my dinner. Little Red would come to me in the pen, jostling away the other chickens to feed out of my hand. I knew which was her, cause she was the one with the floppy comb, like a large red petal.

One night I sneaked Little Red over to one of the breeding cages. But Papa saw her the next day and Mama got in trouble for getting the mix up. Breeding hens is different from killers. I was too scared to tell that I was the one who put her there.

At the next slaughtering I saw Little Red's comb in amongst all the other heads that was in the barrel we toss out to the pigs.

I didn't want no more pets after that.

The chickens, they know what's coming. I know they do. I can't stand that noise. The squawking that sounds like screaming. Different from normal chicken noise. It starts after the first one is killed. I think they can smell it. The smell of the singed blood on the neck where the head used to be. And the boiled feathers like the sheets Mama once left in the copper overnight.

I have to take out all the innards and put them back later, in little bags. But you never get the same chicken to put them back into. Bag Of Giblets, it says that on the labels Ben will be putting on today. His job.

I know the worst is yet to come. Tomorrow I have to help with the slaughtering. But for now I hope no one looks over and sees me closing off Ben's ears. And see that his eyes are shut.

Sometimes I just wish there was someone here to cover mine.

The Black Horse

Shortlisted - Glass Woman Prize - USA

The playing cards are scattered across the pavement in the Mall, some showing their numbers, others backs of contrasting pictures. Two packs, thinks the woman.

One card, the Joker, grins up at her and she wonders if the cards are a sign to stop her from going. The woman treads on the Joker's face with a stab of heel and swirl of toe. Her shoe loses traction and she leaves a fractal footprint that obliterates the picture and ends in a point. It's aimed in the same direction to where she is travelling tomorrow. Alone. Some places no one else can visit.

A magpie swoops then swipes at a card and discovers it's not to eat. It ascends clapped-beaked to a sheltered cove among the eaves of one of the many shops. The smells of quick snacks and fresh specials drift in the air. Dresses on outside racks flap seasonal price-cuts and clang their hangers, silver on chrome, as if trying to escape. Some of the cards are shuffled upright by the same breeze.

The woman wonders how the cards have come to be here. She knows the Mall is frequented at night by the homeless, the lost – only the Muzak deters the hip-youth from being added to that list.

She closes her eyes, sees two old men squatting by the light of the street lamp, fags drooping Clint Eastwood-like from slitted mouths. Her mind provides their voices, the throated gruffness of the over drinker. The picture runs fast forward in stereotype, right down to the thin cracked belts holding up their trousers.

94

Cursing, one man stands and flings the cards in the air. They spread in a random pattern, descend to the ground, and hold the slow-mo dance of the woman's imagination.

She can't stop her hand from drawing the image in the air.

The cards lie where they have fallen.

As she pauses, people flow past her, staring, and suddenly she feels as directionless as a changing wind. And when the overhead speakers sing: *A horse with no name,* her mind whirs up an image of her mother and father and a childhood so small, the only horse in it was an imaginary one. Her horse with no name.

Later, the tram carries her to a house saddened by age and neglect, propped against similar houses in a crooked street in Melbourne. She shares the rent with a teenage girl, Katrina.

The woman draws her thin coat—only her makeup she wears in layers—around equally thin shoulders. Her body is fine, her features chiselled Asian but with the round-eyed look of her European mother. A white leather bag slung around her neck holds the few items she bought at the Mall. But still it is heavy.

When she enters the house, the cold, lined by the voice of her housemate, Katrina, greets her.

'So, big trip tomorrow, mate. Long time since you've been back. You never talk about it. It's gotta be a big deal.' Katrina flicks ash from her cigarette towards the tray but misses. She rubs at it with the sleeve of her denim jacket, smearing it to an almost indiscernible smudge on the coffee table. Then she tilts forward, leans her elbow on her knee for a prop and takes a deep drag.

The woman shakes her head. She sees Katrina's face, soft as youth, eyes closed, lips a hard line. Hair catching the light of the failing evening, the shadows dampening its golden highlights.

Then Katrina stubs out her cigarette and continues, the words hissing through her teeth in a stream of smoke: 'What was it like growing up in such a little town? Does everyone really know all your business? Wasn't it safe? Is that why you always carry your bag with you everywhere you go?'

The woman shrugs, turns her back on the questions, goes over to the heater and looks for the wood basket. She sees it, empty as usual, near the back door.

When she returns, with the basket full, Katrina has left the room. The woman can hear her talking on her mobile, her voice trailing away as she walks down the hall.

'Yeah,' Katrina's saying, 'come over this weekend. I've got the place all to myself. Yeah, should be a blast.'

She hears laughter then nothing more as the door to Katrina's bedroom closes.

The woman knows her parents will not be greeting her as she steps down off the train. And the rest of the town? They won't even remember who she is. It's been thirty-five years since she walked the main street or visited her old home. She was eight when she left for good...bad...the latter word jabs her hard with memories she believed had long ago lost their point.

The woman has written home every month since she was eleven. She doesn't watch the calendar but times her letter writing with her period, which is as regular as night. Except once when she was fifteen and the bleeding didn't come.

The last letter is waiting on the mantel. But she knows it word for word without re-reading it.

Dear Mama and Papa,

I am coming home this Saturday. I am sorry it has been so long since I visited. But you know how hard it is for me to travel. I am bringing you a present.

Love as always from me.

The woman knows she will not send the letter, that it should have been posted days ago if it were to arrive before she did.

She doesn't have to pack; everything she needs is in her bag. It's the sturdy one of her early childhood years, a white leather bag with a black horse tattooed on one side, sketched by her when she was just learning to draw and paint. She could do much better now but finds the familiarity comforting.

The lines askew near the horse's mouth bleed the colour into the edges. Crazed, but softened by the years.

The bag was a present from her father when he returned home from diplomatic work—for ever. Only no one knew that then.

She enters her bedroom, locks the door and looks up at the ceiling, sees her latest painting brushing across it like a Michelangelo. Babies on black, winged horses, fleeing across a blue-streaked sky. She'd touched up the last of it that morning, couldn't stand to leave it in an unfinished state.

The woman moves the ladder away from the corner of the room where she'd last been working and props a canvas onto its lower rung. Fixing a clip to hold it tight, she fights the urge to start painting. If she does, she knows she won't stop. And tomorrow is the only day she *can* go back home.

She slumps down on a chair, picks up her bag, feels the weight of its contents; they rumble to one side and then the other until she balances the bag flat on the floor.

Now the horse is facing her.

Her mind skips a beat as she remembers doing the drawing all those years ago. It had been hard going. Pen and ink. The nib bending, the black lines becoming scratches as she struggled to trace her pencilled sketch.

She hears the words she said to her father when she showed him.

'Look, Papa. I did this horse. Look, he's smiling.'

'So he is. You know, darling, that's a really good drawing.' Her father had lifted her onto his lap. The woman remembers the bag covered her like a stiff rug.

'You know where I got this?' Her father held up the bag; it unfolded and now the horse was laughing.

She shook her head.

He told her the bag had come from one of the conferences he'd attended. The woman cannot remember which. It didn't strike her as strange that he'd been happy she'd drawn on his gift. He'd encouraged her love of art since as far back as walking.

Her father had continued in a low voice, 'I said to myself, Baby-girl would love this bag. She could draw a picture of a horse on it.'

He swung the bag with one hand and the horse was flying.

She recalls stretching back in his lap and giggling like she'd been tickled. 'No, Papa. You didn't say that. You didn't know what I was going to draw.'

Her father laughed then knotted his brow in a mock frown. 'So, Baby-girl,' he said. 'What are you going to call this horse, it should have a name, you know.'

'It's just a picture, Papa.'

'Ah, but darling, all great pictures have a name. Remember when we went to the London Gallery? If you are going to be a famous artist you have to come up with good names for your paintings.' He'd hugged her, then took her off his lap and hung the bag around her neck. 'You sleep on it, okay? Tell me what you've decided in the morning.'

Then her mother had come in with milk for her and a glass of wine for her father, her eyes brighter than the sparklers on Guy Fawke's Night.

Her mother kissed her on the top of her head. The woman can still feel the fingers sweeping back her hair, the soft touch of her mother's lips.

'Drink this, sweetie. And then off to bed. Big day tomorrow.'

Later that night, she listened to her parents' bed banging on the wall. With life's hindsight the woman knows that's what lovers do. It is a hard thought to mind.

The woman settles in her chair, stares about her room, realises the dusk has crept up unseen.

Without the light, the colours of her painting are black and grey shadows, the lines thin as ice's edge.

The last words her mother said all those years ago repeat without sound.

The woman wraps an old blanket about her shoulders, and nods.

Yes, Mama, big day tomorrow.

The song from the Mall keeps playing through her mind and images of herself astride her black horse ride across her dreams.

The next day arrives with a sun so bright it burns doubts to ash.

The woman stretches, gets up from the chair and runs a brush through her hair. She washes her face and replaces her make up, making sure her eyes carry the weight of it. She puts on her coat of the seventies, black suede, blue patterned edging and yellowed wool trim. She still has her pale blue flares but they have grown too large for her over the last few years.

The first part of her journey will be the worst. The railway station where something happened. Twenty-eight years will make no difference.

The woman catches the tram and stands with the bag slung from her neck. She is used to the stares.

When she arrives at the station it is as familiar as breathing. It was night the last time she was here. And late. Very late. She was fifteen, a runaway, alone, but not by herself. A sinew of teenagers was drawn to her fear, its allure strong as their lust.

Dear Papa and Mama,

I'm sorry for not writing for so long. I hope you won't be too cross when I tell you I have decided to leave school. My art teacher, Mrs Clemens, said I should stay and go on to University to further my talent. But I don't want to. I am still living at the same place. I tried to leave but something happened. You are not to worry. I am fine now. And I can write again every month. I can't tell you about it. But the man at the hospital told me that I should write everything down. So that is what I have done. I am still painting.

Your Baby-girl.

She had felt the boys behind her even though their feet were sneakered and their tread was light.

And laughter came with young hands to shuffle her destiny. A card game. Joker the trump. Winner to have her first. Then the losers, ripping her apart, taking her in every way but out. Until familiar guilt overrode and so she welcomed the agony they inflicted, in the way a pregnant woman welcomes the pain of her first contraction.

In the half light of that deserted platform they uncovered nothing. She'd been hollow long before they had got to her.

The train skims the rails, the sound of steel on steel.

The woman draws pictures on the carriage window, blowing steamed breath first to create a base. Then she swipes them away before anyone can see them.

Each wheel rotation takes her away from where it happened to where it began. The beginning and the end of her life as she'd known it. She's been living the past ever since. The layers of her life keep peeling back like a painting left in the elements.

When she read the newspaper article about her home town and the new planning development, the highway which was to cut a swathe through the only childhood she remembered, she knew she must go back. She needed to see her home one more time.

The woman dozes on the train, her bag still around her neck, her hands resting on its curve. The leather is ingrained with thirty-five years of living. People had tried to take it from her as she was growing up. 'Give it to me,' they'd say, 'I'll just give it a clean and bring it right back. There's a good girl'. But they soon stopped trying.

When she was twelve, a man in a suit in a quiet room asked her why the bag was so important. He held a board and pen but he wasn't an artist. She had no words to give him, none he would have accepted. She couldn't tell him it was because the horse had no name. And it only had her. If it was lost who would know where it belonged?

The woman hears the song again in her mind's ear, hums aloud, opens her eyes briefly, sees the other travellers looking at her and closes them again. Her black horse is kneeling and she climbs astride. He throws his head up and ascends. The clouds crowd around them; his mane tangles in her fingers and she feels the pulse of borrowed force beneath her carrying her on.

Her eighth birthday, the big day, had come, but not the one planned of duck feeding, gallery hunting, scribbled drawings and watercolour paintings with her Mama and Papa. For the woman, her eighth birthday came with whiteness and vomiting and never again home or parents. When she did wake, it was to a strange bed, stranger than the hospital one, and to brothers and sisters not her own. No one told her what had happened until two weeks after the event. Later, she hated gas fires.

Dear Mama and Papa,

Thank you for this writing paper and the envelopes with the little blue flowers on them. It is a good present for my eighth birthday but I wish you could have given them to me yourselves. I promise to keep writing letters to you. I am looking after the bag you gave me Papa. I keep all my toys in it. The other day foster-sister, Tessa, took it from me when I was sleeping and then I got mad and hit her. Foster Father smacked me really hard with his leather belt. I screamed at him that you would tell him off when you came back. He said you would never be coming back. But you are Papa, aren't you? When you get back from Heaven will you bring me another present? Is Mama all right? Is Heaven like when you were a diplomat in Romania? Where it was hard to post a letter. I will wait until you have time to go to a Post Office.

Then I will show the letter to Foster Father. I am trying to be brave but I don't like it here.

Love from your Baby-girl.

The woman stirs when she hears that they have reached their destination. She leaves the train and notices she is the only one to do so. Her home town looks different, seems smaller even though it has spread out. There are trees where none were before and houses have grown up from fields that once had only cattle and sheep for residents. She walks the main street, sees ahead the loud signs of progress, of promised speed and easy access. Bulldozers and excavators sit like bloated dragons. Waiting. Her old footpath is waves of corrugated dryness. She stumbles but doesn't look down, her focus is fixed like a sight on the white-brick house with the green fence at the end of the road.

Both her parents had died in their sleep. *'There's the mercy, child, don't cry now, they wouldn't have felt nothing.'*

A faulty gas heater, the coroner said in his report. The woman found the truth in the Melbourne library archives, when she was twelve. *Gone to heaven*, was all she had been told about their passing.

And now she stands near the house of her lost dreams. In the garden there are flowers she can't remember, sprouting colours unattainable even in her pallette of many. The willow tree that she planted with her father is gone. There is a new carport tacked to the side of the house like an afterthought. And gravel where a lawn once grew.

She lifts the bag from around her neck and carries it swinging to the front door. No one is there, the houses all around look as abandoned as death. She doesn't feel alone. She recalls her Papa and her Mama and her seven-year-old self from a gallery of memories. Superimposed on reality, they walk hand in hand to the side of the house. Her father lifts a loose vent and points. Words as distant as seagull cries echo in her mind. 'This is where we've hidden the spare key, Baby-girl. You may be locked out one day.' And then: 'Not on purpose, silly. Only by accident.'

And so it has been. By accident. But this is the first time she's wanted to get in. The key is still there, buried beneath the dust of decades. The woman rubs the rust off, sees a glint of silver as she slides it into the lock. Her old home opens to her, looking as different as the town. For a moment she wonders if she has the right place. She walks on slow feet to the kitchen. The pantry door is ajar, the inside of it has not been repainted. She sees her growth, in pencilled degrees, a figure eight, drawn neatly, at the top. She recalls her Mama saying she was not eight yet. *But nearly, Mama. I nearly am.*

When she was nearly eighteen, before she left the care of the state, the woman saw the man in the quiet room once more.

He told her of survivor guilt, how sufferers feel guilty that they survived a terrible event. Or sometimes they feel they could have, in some way, prevented it from happening.

She had sat staring across the room, seeing her horse. She'd begun to trace his outline in the air. The man watched her, stopped talking. His words held no help. But the little blue pills he gave her did.

She waited until he'd written her prescription for life.

Dear Papa and Mama,

You will be pleased to know I have found a nice house to rent. It is a long way from where my foster parents live. They told me that they never want to see me again. I am glad about that. The man I told you about before, the one who said for me to write everything down, is only going to see me once a year now. He said I could have the injections. But you know I have always been scared of them. I take a little blue pill every morning after I have read the paper. That's how I remember to take my pill and I still remember, Papa, you telling me how important it is to keep up with what is happening in the world that's why I get the paper everyday. Mama, I still bake those biscuits you taught me to make and I remember to put in the spices, but not too much because you said that would spoil them (I tried it once and you were right, it does)

Love, from me.

Now the woman lies on the wooden floor of her old bedroom, closes her eyes and sucks her thumb. Later, her voice curls her up as she sings the lines from A Horse With No Name.

She remembers not being able to sleep that last night in this house. She had almost gone to her parents' room, like she had done so many times before, to cuddle up in the comfort of their bed, to feel their warmth around her like a hug. But she'd felt silly that she hadn't thought of a name yet, for her drawing. Her Papa had said, *If you are going to be a famous artist, Baby-girl, you have to come up with good names for your paintings.*

The woman thinks, as she has so many times before, I should have gone. I could have saved them. Could have yelled at them to wake up and get out. I was awake as they were dying.

Soon, she stretches away from the pain, walks out of the door and around to the front of the house.

She stands back and sees the proportions materialising, the shadowed depths of light and dark. Then she opens her bag and takes out the tins of paint she bought yesterday at the Mall. There are four of each but only two colours, black and white.

The woman takes out her brushes and begins to paint. She doesn't stop until the light is too faded for her to see her strokes, then she returns to her room and sleeps.

The next day, on her way back to the city, she tries to scrape the paint from her hands. She finds the black is the hardest. But she has always known it would be.

Monday's paper comes, translucent from the morning's frost. She opens it out to let it dry in front of the wood fire. Katrina is still in bed and the traffic's chorus is humming its carbon impact to the world.

The woman sees the headlines of the middle section: 'Black horse painting a mystery.'

She folds out the page carefully, sees her black horse, looks down at her fingers with their nails of paint. She begins to read: *On an entire front wall of one of the houses in Glenford, marked for demolition later today, an unknown artist has painted a black horse. The painting was reported by one of the council workers. The overseer says it is not being viewed as a protest to the highway going ahead. Work is continuing as scheduled.*

Mrs Rathburn, curator of the local Art Gallery, told us: 'This was definitely the work of a professional. The brush strokes are bold, the subject matter stark. There's a vibrancy about it. But the style is not familiar to me so I have no idea who the work is by. And this name is no help. It may all just be a ploy by the artist to get some publicity.'

The woman brings the paper closer to focus, pulls tight her brows at the words that she'd painted like a caption beneath the horse's flying hoofs: *And my name is...*

She reaches out to the horse with a finger touch as soft as the leather of her bag, her face relaxes in a whisper, *that's his name papa,* and she smiles as she traces the name she has written.

The woman folds and refolds the newspaper into a neat square, picks up her bottle of little blue pills and opens the lid.

On That Day

There wasn't much blood. Later, we all agreed on that. After the gunshot only a sharp red stream, thin as a laser, and that hushed silence like the retort had sucked all the noise from our world as fast as it had taken the light from my best mate's eyes.

The five of us were friends and although I was the youngest, my ability on the skateboard brought me acceptance. And being part of the group made me even more daring, as if I had to prove their faith in me was not misplaced. I took the chances and it usually paid off. But most times I think it was just dumb luck.

There was me and Dell, Mackie and Ross, and my big brother, Cassidy. Cassidy because of his gammy knee and slight limp.

I was the only one who was called by my Christian name, Tom, although even this was, most times, Tommo or Tom-Thumb, because I was the shortest. Cassidy injured his knee two years before I joined the gang, trying to do the Barrel Kick Flip and Roll. Not the exact term for it, but we had our own language, our own challenges. It was in the eighties, skateboard parks had not long come in, and as our dirt poor neighbourhood - in a town not even big enough for McDonalds - had nothing else going for it, there were lots of kids with rollerblades or BMX's, crowding and cramping our style. That's why we made ourselves the main attraction. When we rolled up, the other kids got off and stood like silent witnesses to our ever increasingly difficult stunts. Some picked favourites. I even had two or three groupies, snot-nosed kids from the fourth grade. I was in the ninth so I guess I was grown up to them. But it was the girls who watched the others, especially Cassidy. His limp seemed to give him a kind of appeal like James Dean, damaged sort of but still out there, facing it, doing it.

I'm sitting here, midnight, watching this video, I've not seen for over twenty years, of the morning on that day, and there's Cassidy, in grainy footage, jumping and board-sliding, turning and landing, his board seemingly glued to his feet. His best mate, Ross, rolls down into the frame, tries to emulate Cassidy, and crashes heavily; you can hear his grunt, the wind knocked from him, the crowd of kids taking it up with their inward gasp. He gets to his feet as neat as any ballerina and shrugs it off. But, and I hadn't noticed this before, he slants a nasty-eyed look over his shoulder Cassidy's way.

Dry land surfers we were, without the relative softness of water to cushion our mistakes. Riding the concrete waves of the skate park. We never wore protective clothing, no helmets or anything like that. "Makes you soft," Mackie used to say, "Doesn't hurt to skin off some bark and we've all got hard heads, haven't we?"

Our teachers told us this often enough, not in what they said, but in a glazed eye why-am-I-bothering with this no-hoper-kid sort of look, when handing back our assignments or reports. Our parents gave us the same look but didn't hold back with the words. "What the hell do you think you'll end up doing, with grades like these? Your mother and I work our guts out and this is the best you can do?" Later mum used to say, "You don't want to end up like your old man do you?"

We lived in a mining town so far from the coast lots of kids had never seen the ocean. All around, red dirt like rust and manmade mountains of slag. Nothing beautiful about it. Nothing that would make you want to take a picture. Most of us couldn't wait to get away, but few of us did. I was one of the lucky ones. Now I own a townhouse by the sea. White light sands, hard greyed pebble beach.

When the mine downsized in 91, Dad lost his job and took up drinking full time. Cassidy moved out of home soon after, concrete-surfed away the mornings and went spotlighting rabbits at night, for their skins. Making a bit of extra money for grass. Ross used to go with him in his old ute; the others came too, sometimes. I didn't have the stomach for it, the blood, the guts, but still tagged along. Cassidy never minded.

Once, in a quiet moment when it was just the two of us, he said to me, "Tommo, don't be like me. I'm going nowhere. I'm like dad, behind the eight-ball. Snookered. You've got the ability to get somewhere. So just go out and do it." Something in the way he said it, made me take notice. Sitting there, spliff firm in his fingers, the way he looked staring into distance, to a place I couldn't see and didn't want to follow.

My grades began to improve after that. He was my best mate as well as my brother.

In the shed in the evening on that day, the skins of a dozen rabbits drying behind us, we'd been talking about nothing, until Ross suddenly held the gun he'd been cleaning to Cassidy's head, and said, "I'm going to shoot you." Just like that. Of course we'd laughed and, although I'm not sure if my memory's right, Cassidy smiled. He didn't turn away, he didn't say don't be so stupid. He just sat there like the rabbits they'd been hunting with their Twenty-Two's. Sat in the spotlight. And then the gunshot.

For a split second we thought we'd all imagined it. That maybe Ross had yelled bang or something, even though we knew he hadn't.

I leaned over and put my finger in the hole, marvelling how it seemed a perfect fit and how the blood stopped. I didn't want to take my finger away. Thought somehow I could hold it back. Fix it, like the little Dutch kid did with the dyke. Everything would be okay. The flood wouldn't wipe out the town. I wanted to believe that, even though I knew it was nonsense, utter crap, nothing so small could stop something so big from happening. Then and now.

Ross had waved the gun at my head minutes before but without the bullet discharging and without the threat. I'd brushed away the muzzle as the hammer clicked. The bullet lodged in the breech. The bullet Ross told the police he was sure was not there. He swore he'd emptied the gun.

In the end it was Russian Roulette, Ross held the chances but I held the luck.

And now here's me on the video, in thirteen year-old invincibility, ready to tackle it, the big one, the Barrel Kick Flip and Roll. Everyone quiet. I'm carving up the concrete wave, you can hear the whirr of the wheels going faster and faster, the clunk as I hit the top and then I do it. I nail it! On the video age has blurred the cheers into white noise static. But I remember it was loud and clear and the loudest cheer was from Cassidy. I know that Ross is behind the video camera now. It was a huge thing, had a strap over his shoulder like the sling of a gun. I hear him say, "You lucky little bastard, Tommo. Just like your brother, Cassidy." There's no camaraderie in his voice, he spits it out like venom.

I snatch up a breath. I hadn't heard this on that day, or the last time I'd watched the video so long ago on the evening of the shooting. He zooms in on my face and I see my smile, my eyes mirroring the bright morning and then he pans over the crowd, on their feet cheering like I'd won The Melbourne Cup or something.

My father had a gun too, a Smith and Wesson. A remnant of the war. Inherited from my grandfather. One afternoon, when my mother was at work, he came home from the pub and shot a hole in the lounge room floorboards. It's still there. One neat drill of lead. In the nineties the veneer of polished wooden floors were fashionable. After it happened my mother covered up the hole with a mat.

On that day Cassidy died it was deemed friendly fire. Misadventure, the inquest called it. A prank gone wrong.

When the video finishes I stare long and hard at the blank screen, listening to the whirring of the emptiness. Finally I get up, eject the old cassette and slip it along with my memories, into the darkness of its cover. Outside the waves crash their voices against the shore, polishing the pebbles of doubt to light but from the distance they mute to whispering shadows.

Tomorrow I'll watch it again.

The Music

2nd place The Cambridge Fiction Awards - UK

My neighbour. She keeps playing it. The Music. She hears its beauty, all I hear is death.

I ask her to turn it off, but she is young and does not understand, does not know my past. The old country. The salute and strident tones of history. The Final Solution.

Association, my psychologist says, when I tell him of The Music. Just as a scent can bring a scene unbidden from the past, he says, so can a song, or tune, bring back what has gone before.

I don't want to remember. I have my tattoos for that. Or what is left of them. A laser removed the numbers, but the scars are still embedded. Indelible.

When she plays The Music I can still see them in my mind's ear. Hear them. The voices of my mother, my older sister, my baby sister. I was the middle one. Now the only one.

It's not Chamber Music, although some would say it is. Wagner's Ring Cycle, Hitler used like spin. My neighbour plays it uncut. The full fifteen hours. Maybe she needs to. And so I face it, The Music. Penance. The guilt of survival.

111

Red Vinyl and Debt

1966
in the heat
Father's new Holden smells of red vinyl and debt
Mother's
weekend work
and late night shifts
holding the family together

Sunday afternoon father with cigarette
and nicotine fingers the paper
job search ads
sweat dripping from his brow
turning the pages
the only work he's done
in the last few months

heading to Outer Harbour
wind blows you all there
while traffic follows ice cream dreams
and castles of sand to be washed away
with the incoming tide
the neap predicted early this day

parking first in Commercial Street
soon-to-be-wed sister confirms

her bridal hire
her age difference of ten years
held between you like competition
but still you are excited for her escape

buying the car has seen to your father's pride
and your family never looks as poor as it is
but there are ice creams in the backseat
and at the beach your father finds an easy park
the other families
having gone home already,
while you stay and face the cold wind change
blowing in all directions
your hair caught up and wild on your sticky cheeks
missing the sandcastle dreams.

Collecting Writers Ginninderra Press AUS

Yesterday, Today and Tomorrow

Celapene Press Australia - Short and Twisted; also Foundling Review USA under the title: Brunfelsia Americana.

Yesterday, Today and Tomorrow. That's what they call this shrub, no taller than I am, struggling in my old front yard. It seems as if it hasn't grown at all in the twenty years since last I saw it. Since I was last here.

A fragile bush, its flowers fade and change so at any one time it can display three different coloured blossoms. If it were more robust it would look beautiful.

My mother used to say that about me, when I was little.

You are not a strong girl, Kindra. Not like your sister. A strong girl like your sister is a beautiful one. And she will find the husband. But you, I am not so sure. Men want a woman who will work hard. Like I do. Not a girl who lies in bed all day.

My younger sister was my father's favourite too; he never had much time for me. And my sister never let me forget it. *No wonder he hates you. You are stupid and weak,* she would say with the same look that my mother gave me. A slight turn up of the upper lip like she was smelling something disagreeable.

Later, Mother thought that there was something wrong with my heart and that was why I was so fragile: *Maybe it has the hole.*

The only one with that deficiency, as far as I could see, was her. She never got over the loss of my father.

It happened when I was eleven, and my sister was nine, two years after we moved here. That was over twenty years ago.

Mother would say to me, *No, Kindra I have never got over the losing of him,* in the same voice and tone she used to tell me when it was time to go to bed: *Brush teeth, wash face and go to the bed.*

I had given up long ago trying to make her speak correctly. I guess it was a little like me with my punctuation. I could never get the full stops or commas in the right place.

Mrs Callington used to tell me, "Just put them in when you need a rest".

But that never worked; maybe I rested at different times than the other kids. I don't know. You take it slow when you feel so tired.

Perhaps it was my mother's fault for bringing me here to another country. But then I was sure it was harder for her than me.

Today: two women in a kitchen

I can see the Yesterday, Today and Tomorrow bush, through the open front window of what used to be our parlour, and also the little path wending to the letterbox. Only it's a different letterbox. And the path that used to be white gravel is asphalt, sticky as my sun-screened skin and steel grey like my thoughts. The sweet scent of the shrub has drawn the past as clearly as a photograph.

This woman, Mrs Thomas, owns my old house now and when I told her I used to live here, she was kind enough to let me in to have a look. I had walked around the block three times, winding up my nerve enough to lend me the courage to knock on the door and face her.

Now the tension is loosening from the words tumbling over my tongue.

"I'm sorry, Mrs Thomas, for talking so much. Mrs Callington always said I talked too much."

I lean over and take a biscuit which, I see, is really two biscuits jammed together. The red oozes out and smells of strawberries and the past.

"Mrs Callington was my teacher. She'd be dead now."

I look into Mrs Thomas's eyes, which have opened wide. She sits still, brows slightly raised but says nothing. Then she picks up the teapot.

"No. No thanks. I don't want anymore, thanks." I brush crumbs from my black skirt, being careful not to snag it with my jewellery. Diamonds flicker. "I should explain about my…"

Mrs Thomas holds up her hand, shakes her head and pours me more tea in a fresh cup.

She hasn't spoken, apart from telling me her surname but then I haven't given her much of a chance.

"That bush out there, do you know what it's called?"

She nods and smiles. Her hand is pale with freckles, dappled like the rocking horse given to me one Christmas.

Yesterday

I couldn't believe my aunt had sent me the horse. Nothing I ever got was new.

When my sister saw it, she narrowed her eyes and stamped her feet: *You don't deserve this rocking horse. I was the one who did well in the exams. You are so stupid you can't even spell your own name. I'm going to go and tell Daddy that it isn't fair.*

I was surprised my mother had sided with me against my father. I wasn't sure exactly what was said as by then I had forgotten much of the old language. But in the end it all turned out the same.

The rocking horse was moved to my sister's room and I didn't even get the doll my aunt had bought her in return.

Today

I stare at my cup, my hands encircling it, my long nails shining from their professional manicure, tiny stars sparkling over cuticle moons.

I gesture towards the window. "Its botanical name is Brunfelsia Americana. It's not the common variety."

Mrs Thomas lifts her eyebrows. "Brunfelsia Americana. I didn't know that." Her voice barely raises a whisper, a soft chord in a wind chime. There's familiarity in the tune.

I take a bite of the biscuit and then cover my mouth as I speak. Mrs Thomas asks me to repeat my question. I swallow and reiterate, "How long have you lived in this house?"

My voice sounds as dry as my mother's. And I am not sure why I'm asking this. I know when she moved here - six months ago.

I had known when the place went on the market, about eighteen months back. It took a year to sell.

I'd seen Mrs Thomas on open day. I hadn't gone into the house to have a look but I'd noticed her getting out of her battered old car as I rolled past, hoping she wouldn't see me in my Mercedes. No sign of a husband. For a while I wondered if she could afford the property. But something told me she would find the funds. She had that hungry set like a dog gets, narrow-eyeing off another dog's dinner. It was a familiar look.

Yesterday

I can remember the morning when my mother planted the Brunfelsia. But then she had to dig it up that evening, as soon as my father got home.

You've put it too far in the earth, stupid woman. It will get collar rot and die just like the roses did.

That's what killed my father, my mother said. Collar rot.

A blue collar worker, he went off to work one day and never came home. My mother told me he had to be put in the earth.

Because I never got to see the grave, I wondered, at the time, if they put him too far in as well.

My sister disappeared from my life soon after we lost our dad. She went off to summer camp and I didn't see her again until a year later. On a TV news flash.

I was alone, we had moved from this house by then, living in a one-bedroom unit. Mother was away working, cleaning other people's houses. *We need the money to make hen's meat*, she used to say.

Ends meet, Mother, *ends meet*, fell on deaf protests.

I say it how I hear it, she would counter.

I gave up in the end and then, in a kind of solidarity, fell in with her. So it became: *a walk in the dark, too many cooks spoil the child, can't see the forest for the disease.*

The news flash was about an airline strike. A panned-over waiting room showed my sister, among other yawning commuters, reading a magazine. She looked up, blinked briefly like a camera lens into the reporter's one and quickly hid her face away behind the pages. But I had seen her. Then a man came up holding out a paper cup of something. Even with his back to the camera he was familiar to me. The black hair, the stride.

It did not seem possible but I was as sure as my youth that it was him. My father. Our father... *who art not in heaven.*

Today

"Can I see my old bedroom?"

Once again Mrs Thomas doesn't answer. But she gets up and takes her cup to the sink. Then, without looking back, heads over to the stairwell.

Everything appears smaller than I remember and the colours are all wrong. Perhaps there is more light now. I look up expecting to see a skylight but find only the ceiling, but even this has changed; the rose has gone from its centre.

There is one thing that is the same. A small crack in the corner of the landing. That was where, cartoon like, I pretended that my little friend lived.

Yesterday

The times I spent feeding my little friend, protecting him from my mother's traps and telling him all my childhood woes, comes back on yesterday's memories like the sunbeams streaming though the side window. I recall saying how I would never end up like my mother, working so hard. And that one day I would have all the beautiful things like my sister had, even if I never got married.

There must be easier ways to make money, I had told him.

Today

Mrs Thomas waits; her hand pauses over the doorknob of the closed door. I am not surprised that she seems to know which room was mine.

I nod and she opens the door slowly, as if unveiling a statue or great work of art.

It looks like any bedroom. Except there in the corner is the rocking horse. The rocking horse of my childhood standing there, as faded as a memory, in my old room.

Mrs Thomas looks at me, she smiles, our eyes meet like a truce and I see that she knows who I am. I already know who she is.

It seems that we have both been good at pretending. My sister and I.

Tomorrow there will be plenty of time for talking. Plenty of time for explanations. But at this moment all my words are as taken as my breath.

I walk over to the horse and gently push on its pale neck. What's left of its mane tangles in my fingers, the rocker squeaks a rusty sound like a sad apology, dipping my arm forward with its movement. My sister starts to come towards me but I shake my head and she stops mid-step and sits down on the bed.

Going to the window I stare down at the Brunfelsia; it looks as sparse as a bad haircut. But on its crest, only viewable from this aspect, I can see the ragged blossoms of the three colours which give it its other name. *Yesterday, Today and Tomorrow.*

And I remember how I used to open this window and breathe in its scent wafting up on the evening's warming.

My mother was right, there is something wrong with my heart, and I still *lie* in bed at all hours. But she was wrong about me being as fragile as this plant.

It and I do have one thing in common. High class.

Brunfelsia Americana is also known as Lady of the Night.

That's when its fragrance is most powerful.

Conjugation

The Valley Review - Massachusetts - USA

Jem is a poet. "Some people should be edited and written again" is one of her lines. To me Jem has always been my inspiration. Not for writing, but for life.

You know how you see things but don't see them? Like that white painted bench at the cemetery. Your eyes are so filled with the sights of graves, and the sentiment of their words, your mind doesn't have time to reference the mundane. Sometimes you'd swear that something must have been put up overnight. Surely it wasn't there all the time? But then, someone points out the patina of age and you know it has been there probably longer than you have been alive.

"Mert," Jem said to me the other day. Jem calls me Mert, after her favourite tree, the Laurel Myrtle. The Bay Laurel in California and the Myrtle in Oregon is the same tree. Jem's paying job is at the local garden centre. "Mert," she said, "come and see the new plants we got in the other day. Could change your mind about gardening."

I have no time for gardens, not the ones that produce pretty flowers. Anyway, Jem's green thumb only extends as far as the pots full of herbs that grudgingly grow, despite their purported hardiness, on her kitchen window. She is far more the poet, growing her words. And when we are together, when she feels energised by my presence, she writes her best pieces.

I wish I had been there when she first met Stinger, not his real name of course, because then maybe I would have heard his side of the story.

But a week later when I was with Jem, at the café, watching her picking guilt in the form of crumbs from her choc-chip banana muffin, she suddenly hissed through clenched teeth, "Don't look now, but that's Stinger out there." I stared through the café window, trying to ignore two buzzing copulating flies and saw a rather stringy-muscled man with beach blond hair, climbing out of what looked like a golf buggy. He was wearing faded blue knee-cut jeans, no tee-shirt. We live in a coastal town, so this sort of undress is not surprising. What did surprise me though, in view of all Jem's negative comments about him, was the fact that this Stinger guy actually looked quite pleasant.

Jem stiffened in her chair, her knees scraping the table support as she stretched out her legs. She didn't open her mouth, but I knew what she was thinking: *"Oh, God, no! He's coming in."*

As Stinger entered the shop, the now uncoupled flies escaped to the great outdoors to start a family, and a sea breeze, laden with the smell of seaweed and salt, filtered through the aroma of the coffee that was sending out its presence like an invitation.

At the counter, Stinger waved an old lady ahead to be served first, picked up a newspaper and dropped his coins into the honesty box. Engrossed in what he was reading, he didn't even see Jem as he pushed open the door and headed back to his car.

People don't know Jem like I do, but then my existence is because of her, so I owe her that acknowledgement. To know *her*. And no one knows me like she does.

Funny thing the word, 'know'. That hidden letter, 'k', it's there but what does it do? Confuse kids learning to read and write? A silent letter. For what purpose? I am silent too, silent, unless I am talking to Jem. She hears me like no one else can. I have been her companion since teenage-hood and nothing she does can deter me.

She has chosen my name well, the Laurel Myrtle has an intoxicating perfume but its roots can be invasive.

I am not always with her. I disappear when she is doing drugs, both illegal and prescription, but I am always *there* for her, and now she accepts me. Accepts my help.

"Anyway," I said, "what's the deal with this Stinger?"

"Can't talk here," she whispered, eyeing off the people in the café. The real-estate honcho, pseudo important in his pinstripe suit. The single mum wiping dribbled ice-cream from her two-year-old still strapped in his pusher. The teenage lovers huddled in the corner sipping with straws from one milkshake, its coldness just beginning to show from the moisture forming droplets on the retro-blue of its holder. And I knew they would all start staring if Jem started talking. People always did.

So soon, there she was sitting on a bench beside the ocean, slanted seagulls with one hopeful eye on her as they dipped past, and people walking by, glancing, then turning their heads as she began to talk.

In the open, people ignore Jem more easily than in a place like a café.

"Well, Mert," Jem said, "Stinger supplies all the herbal medicines, you know, in that new range we have. And homeopathic stuff. Boss said we had to branch out. His idea of extending while still keeping with the garden theme. Still botanic, you know?"

That's the thing with Jem, she sounds like everyone else. But she is a simile, or a word like 'patient', a noun or adjective. Or sometimes both. For there is Latin to Jem. A conjugation.

I am invisible though. I see it in the half turned stares of the passers-by until Jem herself finally sees it and we walk along the beach, to keep three or four strides ahead of judgement.

Along the esplanade the river meets the sea in a tidal exchange, on the surface all looks calm, but underneath are contrasting currents, powerful, yet invisible. One is trying to escape, but the other converges on it unseen, and turns the fresh water to salt.

I have been called a muse. Her doctors have another name.

"Stinger told me, Mert, that I should try some of the herbal remedies... you know, for my..."

Her words stopped, faltered then picked up like a breeze that has renewed its strength. "I mean, I know you're not... real."

I realised then that she was talking about me, wanted me to have this benefit. The benefit of the pharmaceuticals. The help of others.

And I saw why she was so scared of this guy, this Stinger. It was for me she feared.

My annihilator, her saviour... perhaps.

One Grey Day

Monochrome like an old time movie
the tides breathe a lap, a lap
like a becalming sail,
going nowhere
my footsteps sink
lightly in the sand
being careful of hidden rocks
without my direction

black the washed up seaweed
curled so foetal
I'd swear a body lay there
and then the sea and sky
the same grey
part a cloud and sunlight
washes the colour green across it
like an old time movie
when they try to bring it back
the way it was
but still
it seems unreal

published in San Pedro River Review - California - USA

Beloved, my Bess

Fields of Gold anthology - AUS

Apples are related to roses. And apple trees and rose bushes can live for more than a hundred years. The island state of Tasmania in Australia is renowned for both.

Let's cast a sweeping look across this Apple Isle and see in a valley, little known to the mainland, a garden gnarled like old man's hands behind a crumbling house of red and ochre brick. Only two chimneys stand upright now, in testament to its builders long gone to ash and dust. And yes, there's an orchard of rosy apples still falling to ground, but coddled in moth and never making the cider.

Behind this you will see, if you take the path overgrown but discernable to the end, an ancient rose bush, and behind that a gravestone of pale cement with nail-dragged words: Beloved, my Bess.

There are pebbles outlining a broken rectangle too small to be an adult's. But it is not a child's grave. And beneath the soil nothing now remains of leather collar and favourite blanket.

Who of us knows the answer to the question of the soul? And who can say whether the rose grown and tangled over this stone and binding upright, the pickets of the fallen fence, holds in its bush-climbing tenacity the spirit of the one laid to rest there, so long ago?

Beloved, my Bess.

The rose bush flowers with the seasons and carries on despite the sheep, which use the cottage walls as shelter. They do a good job in the pruning and it has grown deep roots, drought-tough. These sheep are descendents of those she drove. My Bess, never needing more than a pat and a feed for all her work.

This year the foragers have nibbled away all but one of the rose's blooms. Almost black velvet with lights of dew retrieving the sun in its ragged petals. No one but you will see it. A rose that would never win best in show. But more perfect now, than that, for all its loyal struggle.

A rose bush behind an apple orchard. An ancient grave in pale cement, broken pebbles and words.

Beloved, my Bess.

Nothing About Love

Highly Commended in Ouen Press short story competition and published in Ouen Press's collection, Last Call, UK

Joe swung his horse around and swore. "Get behind there, you useless mongrel." The words cut through the valley and lined the hills with a blue echo: *useless mongrel, useless bloody...* He caught a glimpse of his dog, an Australian red heeler, hiding behind a clump of Kangaroo grass. The cattle were twitching and looking over their shoulders, more afraid now than before, when at least they could see their predator.

Joe stood up in his stirrups, then sat down heavily and leant back. He had to move this mob before the weather changed. They were a young bunch and in this paddock he knew the fences would never be up to any storm-driven stampede. For a long moment and not for the first time, he wished he could be anywhere but here.

The dog, named Sunshine, had been given to him by Old Tom from the adjoining property. She was the runt of the litter, but as far from a mongrel as you could get. The rest had all sold months before and, as Old Tom had said, it would have been a shame to knock her on the head. 'Those bloodlines are as long as both me arms,' he'd told Joe.

'I'll give her a try,' was as committed as Joe could be when he took the binding twine lead from the old man's hand. When he saw the cowering animal at the end of the line, his stomach clenched as he thought, Looks like I'll be doing the job for Old Tom myself.

128

Today's mustering seemed to be proving that premonition right.

Joe's horse snorted and tossed her head. He shortened his reins and spoke, his voice soft as mist. "Easy there, Girl. We'll be home soon." But the thought of the farmhouse with its wide verandas and sprawling jasmine brought him no comfort, now that Beth, his beloved Beth, was no longer there. It felt like she'd been gone forever.

He squinted across to the south. The backdrop of roiling clouds was bearing down on them, sucking up what little light was left from the day.

When Joe nudged the mare forward, he didn't need to use much leg, the horse was already too willing, but over the ridge she stumbled and would have gone right down had it not been for Joe's quick action with his weight and reins. When she stood up again, he could see he wouldn't be riding her any further today.

As he dismounted he cursed, but quieter this time.

He glanced back the way they'd come. He could just make out Old Tom's farmstead left of the pine plantation. No lights on, but that didn't mean Old Tom wasn't up. He was of the old school. Saving on everything.

Joe slipped the reins over the mare's head to lead her. She took a step forward, heavily favouring her nearside foreleg. He ran farm-roughened hands over her fetlock, could feel the heat already swelling the joint. Then, when he turned, he almost fell over Sunshine and the dog leapt back like she'd been whipped. Instead of running away though, she hunkered down, and despite the irritation rising in him like an unreachable itch, Joe stretched out a hand and stroked her nose.

The cattle had dropped their heads to grazing, but every few moments one of them would dart away only to return to the herd like a shot, when he saw his companions weren't following. Joe noted the dog always looked up and started when this happened, as if she would go after the renegade, but then that glaze of confusion seemed to cloud her courage and she hunkered down again.

Joe squatted next to her. "Great trio we make, hey Sunny," he said. "Useless working dog and lame horse." He knew he should have added 'misfit farmer' to make up the three, but he couldn't bring this thought to voice.

He stood up, tugged the reins, started walking. The mare took a toe step forward without heel, and followed him. Sunshine did likewise, but feet flat, belly slunk, making sure she cut a wide berth of the herd. The cattle bunched together, rumps to rain, and the dark clouds descended light into night even though it was barely eight o'clock.

When he got to Old Tom's place, Joe found no amount of knocking seemed to rouse the old man. He entered the farmhouse, called loudly, "Tom. Are you there?"

He found Old Tom slumped in front of a thirty-year-pre-plasma TV, a bottle of Jack Daniels on the ring-stained coffee table next to him but no drinking glass. The bottle was more than half empty.

Joe touched Old Tom's shoulder and Tom cracked open an eye. He didn't seem surprised to see Joe standing there in front of him, dripping rain all over the floorboards. He sat up, pushed past Joe's arm and grabbed the bottle by the neck, like choking a chicken, lifting it to loose lips. Then he passed his hand across his mouth.

"What's life all about anyway, Joe?" he rasped. "In the end there's just bloody memories. And what the hell does anyone do with those?"

Joe knew what Old Tom meant. He wondered if he'd ever be ready to face his memories. His Beth coloured memories. At the moment he kept them hazy, like a badly faded watercolour or a Monet, which only came into focus if you stood back. And he never stood back.

He'd only seen Old Tom like this once before, when Tom's wife, Meg, had passed away. A tough winter too, in more ways than fighting the elements.

Old Tom held up the bottle in a kind of salute. "Here's to me anniversary. We would've been married sixty years. Today. What's that? Gold? Platinum?" He coughed and cleared his throat. "Meg would've known."

Joe said nothing. He pulled a chair closer, dragged the bottle from Tom's stiff-fingered grasp and took a swig. A little less for the old man to get drunk on.

Tom nodded slowly, like the liquor held all the answers, then took back the bottle.

Sunshine crept across the floor, looked at Joe with half-turned head and flattened ears and slunk behind the sofa.

"I've never cared much for the finer things. You know that, Joe," Old Tom said. "Meg was always one for remembering birthdays and anniversaries. And always helping others. But you know when I married her, Joe, I was as wet and as green as that young pup." Tom pointed the nearly empty bottle at the sofa. Squinted an eye. "I see you hiding behind there. Bloody little half pint. Should've drowned you as soon as you popped out." But as he asked, "How's she doing Joe?" his eyes softened. "Lots of cow in that breed. Best working dogs." He sucked the bottle dry and retrieved another from a cracked glass dresser. Everything had its patina of dust. He swiped the bottle across his chest, read the label, grunted and unscrewed the cap. "And," he said, "I knew nothing back then. Nothing about love."

You and me also, thought Joe.

Lightning ignited the silence before a thunder boom made Joe jump. Old Tom didn't flinch. "Well, that's right overhead," Tom said through barely opened lips. "Didn't even need to count the seconds." He laughed and started choking until Joe reached over and patted him between the shoulder blades.

Widening his eyes like he'd just woken up, he spluttered. "What the hell are you doing here anyway, Joe?" Not waiting for a reply, he said, "Oh, you got caught up in this." He waved the bottle ceiling-wards. The tin roof resonated rain like hail. "Did you manage to get your mob in?"

131

Joe told him. About the mare going lame and how he couldn't move the herd. How he had just made it here before the worst of the storm. He made no mention of the dog. Her poor performance. That the only thing bright about her was her name.

Tom stretched back, took a long draught and held out the whiskey. "Here, help yourself. Good evening for it. Bloody rain. There. I bet you never thought I'd ever say that."

Joe took the bottle. Grinned a little, but didn't answer.

"You know, Meg loved the sound of the rain on the roof, " Old Tom said. "Not much of that before she died though. God, I wish I could have done more for her. You know she was always doing little things for me. Romantic things. Like leaving me notes saying she loved me, that sort of fluff."

"She knew you loved her, Tom," Joe said, leaning down to rub Sunshine behind the ears. When he stopped, the dog thrust her damp head in an upward motion, jolting his hand and Joe began rubbing again. She smelt like wet dirty socks.

"Yeah, you're probably right." Old Tom gave a ghost smile, sat up a little straighter, then stared at the dog. "Could never understand that little mutt. How she doing anyway? You never said?"

Joe got up and hung his coat over the back of a chair, closer to the fire. When he turned around he saw Tom had closed his eyes. Sunshine was by the old man and looking up at him with a kind of intensity Joe had not seen in any of Tom's other working dogs. And when Old Tom sat up suddenly, the dog didn't run away, but came closer.

Old Tom's eyes softened again. "Meg would have loved a house dog." He pointed towards Sunshine with the bottle again. "But me, always too bloody practical. Veggies instead of rose gardens. And I always said, the only good dogs were working ones. Not bloody useless little pan lickers."

Joe took the bottle once again from Tom's hand and swigged. Felt the liquid warming his insides.

"How's the painting going?" Old Tom asked, reaching down for the dog. "When are you having that exhibition? God, Meg was always going on about you being a famous artist one day. She loved that one you did of her."

Joe said the painting was going fine, but that was a lie, he hadn't picked up a brush since Beth walked out on him four months ago. It seemed now his life was as blank as that canvas he had sitting in his studio, at the back of his farmhouse. Anyway, he was a farmer wasn't he? Not an artist. As financially insecure as farming was, the world of art was a whole lot harder. He'd put off having an exhibition for years. And there was security in doing what you knew, even if you hated it.

Beth, although she tried so hard for five years, had never taken to farming life. Hell, he could understand that. Bloody drought. Prices crashing. Bush fires. But hadn't he been born to it, like Sunshine? Three generations of farmers on this exact land. All leaving their marks of improvement. The extra dams. The scrub blocks cleared. They had found their place and left him with farming bloodlines, as long and as strong as Sunshine's.

His father had never approved of his art. 'Damn waste of time,' was the nicest thing he'd ever said about it.

But, if nothing else, Joe knew at least his painting had helped him find Beth. They had met at an art gallery. She'd asked, with a glint of challenge firing her voice, "What do you think of the Pre-Raphaelites?" as they stood in front of a Rossetti. And it went on from there to dinners, theatre and finally, her moving in. Sharing the cooking and watching 'The Farmer Wants a Wife' on TV, every week like religion. Joking about how that could be them. But Beth hadn't really wanted a farmer, was not cut out for the loneliness and the penny-pinching reality of being asset rich, but cash poor. Hated the brutality of it. The castrations. The branding. The unpredictability of Market days. "How can you stand it, Joe?" she'd asked, turning her head away, her words coming out tight. And he questioned it again himself then, too, had been tired of it for so long. Tired of the uncertainty, the ongoing hardship, the blood and guts of it all. Sometimes he wondered if he'd been adopted. For wasn't it supposed to come out in the bloodlines, like Tom said about his red heelers?

Joe looked at Sunshine, with Old Tom scratching her wet woolly head, and wondered.

"Be okay if I borrow the Bedford to get home?" Joe said, handing back the empty bottle of whiskey.

"Sure," Old Tom said, fumbling the keys from his pocket. "And you can leave Sunshine here with me, if you like." His eyes half closed, hiding, what Joe was sure, the lie in Tom's following words. "Just for tonight, mind."

Later, back in his studio, Joe picked up a brush. Began painting. The background colours. And the memories of Beth came surging like an inward tide. Beth there every night in his bed. The long walks and longer conversations. Her smile pooling the little dimple in her right cheek. The flash of her hair in the sunlight, like alchemy. Beth leaning over him as he painted, her firm breasts pushing into his back, her compliments warming him like the whiskey he'd had at Old Tom's.

There is another life, she'd said, after she had told him how good an artist she thought he was. It's not too late to find your place, she said.

And then later, her parting words. Not forever goodbye words. Never those. She'd asked him to think about what he really wanted. Make up his mind. What really mattered.

And now, as Joe lifted his brush, touched the canvas and stroked her face to life, he knew.

Of Flies and Friends

commended in Tabor Creative Writing Awards AUS

Flies love chocolate. Cadbury Flake is their favourite. The tiny pieces stick neatly on the end of their proboscis. I watch with a giant's fascination as a fly tap-dances amongst my fallen crumbs. 'He won't eat much' comes as a line from a distant thought and it is true. To me it seems there is just as much chocolate left when he finishes as when he started.

There is tenacity to a fly, it keeps going from speck to speck as if trying to find the perfect fit.

Nature is the same wherever you turn, just in different degrees and sizes.

No one size fits all.

I remember the silence vacuum, the hiatus of a hurried departure. A note of expectation written in the air. A willing of a 'return to me' sign or 'a don't go' gesture.

A husband leaving. Nothing unusual about that. Nothing at all except the unexpected finality. And it continues throughout the week, the only things constant are the tiny summer flies. But it is only autumn and winter will be here soon.

I know that flies live an average of seventy-two hours. Three days in which to eat, mate and stretch their wings. That is unless I wield my fly swat, the one in the shape of a hand.

I hold the power of life or death the power to let the flies reach their cosmo-potential or die impotent with scant flight hours beneath their wings.

My friend, Viv, peers at me, eyes dark with pity, or sadness, or guilt. The blackness of it a stain on our friendship, a friendship which is receding like a tide.

I fight the resistance to face an avalanche of facts which crash my thoughts. Double betrayal and more.

"So will you take him back, Andrea?" she says, a nervous twitch to her voice.

I look into her eyes, trying to find the truth there. They remind me of a fly's, myriad faceted, but depthless.

I focus again on the coffee she has made me, like thousands of coffees before, over more than two decades of sharing.

I wonder how she justifies it. Wonder that I did not see it coming. I recall her past relationship and how it had ended in the same way.

But that was her other best friend at another time, it was not me.

I address my own shallowness. I recall how I save beetles from drowning in the dog's water bowl, but not the black conglomeration of tiny bugs, each smaller than a pin prick. As if size matters to worth.

How much then the weight of a soul? But my friend can't grasp the gravity of anything heavier than the burden of day to day living. She takes and complains and lives.

Suddenly, she looks sad. I ask what's wrong and fear the answer.

It doesn't come. Nothing to which I can put a question.

Her tears push forth in gushes of self sympathy. I wonder if any will be left for me.

"It's just that I've known you guys for so long. I hate to see you breaking up. I haven't been able to sleep or eat."

Viv's eyes open wide as I ask why ever not?

Her twisting shrug, as she collects her deceit, tells me more than any confirmation by words.

With a shaking hand she brushes her hair from her face even though it has not fallen away. The gesture unmistakable as a nervous tic.

I continue staring until she turns her back on me, and asks if I want more cake. She opens the door to the cupboard, the one with only plates. Even I know where she keeps her cake.

"I will have more, Viv," I say as she wavers with her thumb in her mouth, staring at the stacked plates. "And some chocolate too, Cadbury Flake, if you have any."

Chocolate is supposed to have similar chemicals to those the brain produces when you fall in love. My mind stretches to accommodate this thought, to wrap it around my friend and my husband. Binding them together with something more honourable than lust.

Are they in love?

But the thought is viced in its frame of wrongness. The glass veneer of trust shattered.

Viv at last finds the right cupboard. I take two pieces of chocolate and eat them, drink my coffee and think of a poisonous chalice and how it could be delivered. So many ways. So many ways to die, to kill.

And I do it every year in the name of hygiene and living. Trillions of germs, thousands of insects, dozens of animals.

I bend my environment, distort time and rush over travel. Arrive at my destination yesterday, even as the crow flies, for time is altered by distance.

I recall my last plane trip. There was a fly sitting on my window rim. They were all window seats on this plane.

This fly seemed to have a flying phobia. He was agitated, washing his eyes cat like, over and over, with his arms. I wondered if they had lubricant or if the surface of his many lenses were being flayed with tiny scratches. That soon he would be blind as well as being afraid.

Strange paradox, I thought, a fly afraid to fly.

But then there were those living, afraid to live. Afraid to push the envelope, afraid to branch out, afraid to take the road less travelled, afraid of the many other platitudes which came to mind as easily as I could have squashed this fly with my thumb.

No one would condemn me. But *I* would.

And he was flying faster than any other fly on earth.

But between us I alone held the concept of speed and the focal point, or lack thereof, which makes it seem as if we are either racing along or cruising leisurely.

This fly was real to me, as real as the woman across the aisle with the paper bag held to her mouth, as real as the child draped across his mother's shoulder with his grubby fingers sleep-gripped to her back, as real as the sky, milk white with the clouds we seemed to be drifting through.

My friend is speaking far too quickly.

"So, Andrea, you didn't answer my question. Will you have him back?"

I realize she wants to know for her sake. To save waiting until I am ready. In that instant I know that my husband would still choose me over her if I wanted it so.

"I am not sure, Viv. The time he's given me to decide isn't up yet."

She stops stirring her tea and looks at me crookedly.

"Surely three more days won't make any difference."

It is not a question and I detect a glint of hope in her eyes.

A fly settles near her hand. She squashes it without thought and then grimaces at the mess. The carnage of its tiny body, the viscous entrails splattered in a red dot.

"Damn flies," she says, getting some paper towel to clean the mess.

I watch as she washes the blood from her hands.
I opted for my flies to die of old age.
In the morning they were gone.
Three days can make a difference.

Last Man Standing

The Valley Review - Massachusetts - USA

Jason's words echoed in my mind like a voiceover in a movie.

'All you'll ever do, Cassandra, is live your sad little life like everyone else with their sad little dreams, nothing more, nothing less.'

Don't get me wrong. Jason is a great mate, more loyal than a puppy is my friend Jason. But sometimes, like this grey afternoon when our dreams were as dead as our idealism, he could write me up the facts in one uncut sentence.

I've had friends who've stabbed me in the back with something that familiarity has bred, or something I've told them in a moment of trust. But Jason stabbed you in the face and paid compliments behind your back. And often you wouldn't discover he'd said anything nice about you until years after he'd said it. Like that morning when I had, literally, run into a mutual acquaintance.

It was during my five kilometre jog, at the time of day when I usually only have mist for company. I had my iPod on full enough to pop my hearing and my head down, eyes scanning the immediate ground in front of me, while at the same time wishing I had a torch instead of my water bottle. It was so damn foggy it was like running on clouds.

'Cassy... is that... you? Geez, how long has it been?'

An apparition had grabbed me by my shoulders and was shaking sweat beads in my face, gasping words.

I stopped, leaned forward on my legs. I'd been nearing the end of my run and fright and exhaustion robbed my breath. 'Hell... Robbie?... I can't believe it's you. You scared the shit out of me.'

'Yeah, me too,' he said, and drew a lungful before letting it out in a whistle. 'Hey, whatta you know? Jason was right... How'd you manage it?'

I looked up, wiped my face with a back hand and, glad now of the water bottle, took a swig.

Two women walking dogs at high power blew past us, the dogs panting fit. They were followed closely by a man in a tummy-sagging T shirt, panting unfit. The morning was speeding up.

I hadn't needed to ask what this compliment was from Jason. I knew already. Last time Robbie saw me I had been big enough for two.

'About seven years ago. At the Year Twelve Formal,' I muttered, answering Robbie's first question of how long.

Robbie slowed our jog to a walk-talk. 'Hey Cassy. Do you remember that farm with the blue fence and all the chooks? You know, the one we walked past every day on our way to school?' When I didn't answer, he added. 'You and Jason wanted to grow organic vegetables and sell free range eggs. Did you ever buy it?'

I'd forgotten all about that farm. Jason and I were going to be partners, make our fortune. The farm was up for sale now, actually.

'No.' My answer had the finality ring to it. 'I run a little shop in Main Street.'

'Not Caz's Café?'

I nodded and he continued. 'I saw it as I drove in. I've come back for a few days. Staying at the pub.'

I stopped in front of my car, suddenly feeling ashamed of its faded duco and dented bottom. I made my voice sound cheery. 'Well, that's me finished on the exercise front. Maybe I'll catch you tomorrow.'

That afternoon, Jason and I were discussing Gay rights. He said he was all for equality within reason and then added how only extremists seemed to get things changed.

'Well then,' I'd said, 'aren't you contradicting yourself, Jason? I mean, if we need radicals to get things happening.'

Jason stopped sipping his tea and put the cup back in its saucer with the precision of a surgeon. 'It doesn't follow that I like extremists, Caz.'

I had to head off as another customer had come into the shop, so I didn't answer. It was as Jason was leaving that he made his revelation about my sad little life. He could talk, he had grown to hate his enterprise as much as I hated working at the café. But seeing that running into Robbie that morning had been the highlight of my week, how could I disagree?

Now, after watching the door close behind Jason with his words reverberating in my mind, I felt an overwhelming tiredness far heavier than any marathon.

The thing is, he was right, more right than he supposed. I hadn't even got around to telling him about my break-up with Troy Erickson, or Trick as everyone in our small town called him. He'd find out soon enough and about Robbie's return to Bunduburra. The three of them had been friends from way back.

For a moment I felt like one of the heroines in a Thomas Hardy novel except that those women often had three men running after them. The men in my life seemed to be running away, or into me, as in Robbie's case.

It was all so much simpler when we were kids.

Growing up with only brothers, I found I preferred male friends and it wasn't long before I, Trick, Robbie and Jason were known around Bunduburra as the Fearsome Foursome, although we never did anything worse than put dog shit in the letterbox of a teacher we hated.

Our friendship was purely platonic, but I do recall a 'show and not tell' after Jason had stated that there wasn't much difference between boys and girls. Even back then he was bloody argumentative.

I felt my face warming as I shut up shop and counted out the till.

Outside held the air of desertion. It smelt like petrol fumes and Friday night fish and chips. Bunduburra was not big enough for KFC.

My car was waiting around the corner parked at an angle only I could achieve. I patted its side and inserted my key.

Thinking back, I saw how I'd let providence take me along for its fateful ride. Both Robbie and Jason had left Bunduburra after high-school, only Trick remained, as an apprentice jockey for the local racing stables. We didn't start 'going out', we just didn't stop seeing each other, a continuum of our childhood friendship. And, although it was Trick who had taken it further, I'd always felt it was just that he was the last man standing. This thought seemed to justify Jason's statement and I shrugged into myself. Was I an outline so sad that I believed not one of them could have really wanted me?

And what now, with Trick going off to the city?

It's no good, Cass-lass. Long distance relationships never work.

I hadn't even argued or pleaded.

When Jason came back four years after leaving and set up his IT business, Trick was so happy I hadn't seen him for a full week. 'Catching up, Cass-Lass,' he'd said, like Jas had been living on the moon not just an hour's drive away. Now Trick was the one moving, and this time interstate – they'd probably never speak to each other again. And they say women are hard to understand.

Trick had been okay as a boyfriend though. After the Year Twelve Formal debacle he had accompanied me on my weight loss journey, more of a damn trek really. But I had 'reached my destination' in two years and dropped four dress sizes, not that I ever wore dresses.

Being a jockey Trick also knew all about fighting weight. He was never fat but he was 'over' weight sometimes and that meant not being able to ride.

'No ride, no eat, Cass-Lass. So it may as well be no eat, then ride, then eat.' He'd often carry on semantics like this until I'd have to tell him to stop messing with my head.

And I never took to his harsh way of dropping the kilos either. Sweating it out in a sauna and starving was not my idea of any sort of sustainable weight loss. It was different for Trick, he was thin as a sigh already. But then he was always there for me in the mornings to get me up for my run and, if I complained, reminding me that not everyone had the luxury of sleeping till six. How could I argue with that when he'd been up since four, galloping horses on the track?

When I arrived home it looked as it had that morning, although in the evening's gloom the hydrangea standing near the front door seemed almost alive and the paint work not so accusing.

Running a café had worried me at first. Wouldn't I want to eat all the leftovers? But I got so sick of preparing junk food all day it had the opposite effect. At night I found I had to force myself to cook and it had to be healthy.

I scurried around with broccoli and a piece of salmon. Its pink was the same hue as a certain jacket I owned.

I wondered if Robbie would remember the last time he'd seen me. I hoped not, even now the mind-pictures I recalled had to be once removed, so I could bring them into view without cringing. Anyway I *was* a different person back then.

The phone rang and, as if superimposing on my thoughts, it was Robbie.

'Oh, Cassy. I really need to talk. About that last time I saw you.'

It may be harder for The Beautiful People to lose their looks. But even though I never had any to misplace, at the Year Twelve Formal my self-image couldn't have been more torn if it had been put through a shredder.

I had been on my diet for about six weeks, hoping to fit into the salmon outfit in time. My trio of guys persuaded me to go for it;

144

Robbie had been the most vociferous. And so, that night seven years ago, the night of Saturday the 19th of September, cool and cloudy, I had taken up my courage like a heavy bag and rocked up at Bunduburra's only recreation hall. The RSL.

I only got as far as trying to sit down.

In hindsight I realised why the chair I'd chosen had been pushed over to the side, close to the band, but at the time I figured it was the last one and I was thankful for it, my legs were shaking. This gratefulness only lasted as long as the chair did. The crash splintered over the sound system and screeched protests from the amplifier. As all heads turned in my direction only the laughter was louder.

I gripped the receiver and held it away from my ear, peering at it as if I could conjure Robbie up through the wires. I knew my voice would be muted. 'That was a long time ago, Robbie. Don't worry about it.'

'I need to come over. Tell you to your face. Please, Cassy.'

The memory rolled like a tired rerun. Me escaping from the RSL hall, Robbie near the door in peripheral. His face contorted. Mobile to his ear.

Then and now.

'Okay. Come over. You want some dinner? How's salmon grab you?'

In the fifteen minutes he took to get to my place I had defrosted another fillet and had it sizzling. Its companion waited on the heating plate.

Robbie had left Bunduburra a week after the Formal without coming to see me to say goodbye, and now here he was wanting to get all chummy. I flipped the salmon and pressed down on it hard with the spatula.

He looked good. His aftershave had a musky smell to it that I couldn't remember and his shirt was neatly pressed. The bottle of wine looked good too.

After dinner we sat out on the landing, the hills fencing the fields in blue dusk.

I held up my glass.

Robbie rattled his into it.

'You really have no idea do you, Cassy?'

I turned my glass and toasted the fields.

'Nope. Never have. But what I'd really like to know, Robbie, is why you didn't come after me that night. I mean I can understand you laughing, but hell. You were the one who insisted I should go to the damn Formal.'

Robbie sat quietly for a moment. His voice was barely above a whisper and I found I had to turn my head to hear him.

'I encouraged you to go because I was hoping you'd meet someone.' He rubbed his brow. 'And, Cassy, I don't expect you to believe me but I never knew what happened to you that night. I only found out about it yesterday, when I talked to Jason.'

I held my breath but words escaped like an opened valve.

'I saw you, Robbie.'

'I don't know what you saw. But what was happening was I was being dumped. I was on my mobile, coming in as you were leaving, Cassy. I hadn't seen anything.'

'Dumped? By whom? You weren't seeing any women.'

My voice sounded straight, but my mind was churning circles.

'You're right about that.'

A sharp intake of breath was my only answer. Robbie got up without meeting my eyes and took the glasses back into the kitchen. I couldn't believe it. Robbie? Gay? When I came in several minutes later he was leaning stiff-armed over the breakfast bar.

I rubbed his shoulder and he flinched. 'Who was it, Robbie? Do I know him?'

He nodded. 'That's why I had to get away. Start all over.'

My mind caught its tail and stopped the circling. The guy who'd dumped Robbie had to be Jason. That would make sense. Jason had never had a girlfriend. And all that talk about Gay rights. He and Robbie had left Bunduburra at the same time too, in opposite directions.

What happened to me at the Formal faded into its reality of insignificance.

'I had to leave. We were attracting attention,' Robbie said. 'And you know what a small town Bunduburra is.'

I knew he wasn't talking about its dimensions.

'God, I see Jason every day, you'd think I'd have picked it.'

Robbie turned towards me. 'That's because it's not Jason.' He looked me straight in the eyes. 'It's Trick.'

I felt hysterical laughter rising in me like the day they buried the postmistress and someone said the coffin made her look slim.

'Quit kidding, Robbie. I've been going out with Trick for the past seven years.'

Robbie's voice was pencil thin again. 'I know.'

I slumped down in the kitchen chair and poured myself another drink.

Robbie turned away. 'Why do you think I couldn't see you to say goodbye? You were Trick's plan to see if he could go straight.'

My hands were shaking so much the glass couldn't reach my lips. I set it down with a thump and some of the wine spilled over the cloth. Fuck the stain.

'Christ, Robbie, are you telling me I've been some sort of experiment for all these years? And you were so jealous you couldn't even face me?' I threw the glass in the sink and it shattered into myriad pieces. I grabbed his arm, spinning him around and spat my words. For some reason I remembered his sweat beads spraying my face that morning and I slanted a queer smile. 'Well, Robbie. I can tell you it worked. His cock worked.'

His shoulders slumped and I wondered what he expected of me. At the same instant I hated them all, even Jason. He must have known. Why hadn't he told me? I pushed Robbie towards the door.

'Piss off. You've ruined everything. You shouldn't have come back. You should've stayed away. Trick's leaving now, going off to the city. That should tell you something.' Suddenly I wanted to hurt Robbie even more. 'I hear the Gay movement's pretty big there.'

147

Robbie's face was calm, but readable. It stopped my words. Instantly I felt all sorts of awful. And I knew, with a certainty as strong as life, that Robbie wasn't going to the city alone. Trick would be going with him. In that moment I was sorry and angry for us all.

After Robbie left, his aftershave lingered like a sad reminder. I watched his car back out of my drive and slink away.

How could I have been so wrong about the three of them all these years?

My hands were still shaking when I rang Jason. He didn't seem surprised to hear from me.

'Jason,' I said in a voice that was as strong as my conviction. 'Consider yourself just an acquaintance from now on. My sad little life might just be that but it's not sad enough to have you three in it.'

I couldn't hear his reaction. His answer was as faint as our connection. Then his voice became louder, more insistent.

'Christ, it's not what you think, Cass. I argued with Robbie and Trick that night. Said it was a bloody terrible idea. But Trick was so convincing. I think he really wanted to believe it himself.'

I played for time, not able to release him. 'When I saw you this afternoon, Jas, you didn't even tell me Robbie was back in town.'

'Nor did you.'

'You knew first,' I said, knowing I sounded like Trick with his semantics. I suddenly realised I wasn't going to miss those.

'Seriously, Cass, I didn't say anything about that night at the Formal because I knew it would hurt you. And after you and Trick had been going out for so long, I thought you were a real couple. I never stopped hoping though. You, me?'

For many moments the line held a silence stronger than any words.

'See you tomorrow then, at the café? Cass?'

'Sure,' I said, 'And Jas?'

'Yeah, Cass?'

I took a deep breath. 'I'm thinking of not renewing my lease on the cafe'. I have an eye on that little farm just out of town. You know the one. It's just come up for sale, actually.'

I let out a slow exhalation and then, as I hung up the phone, I looked down and saw that my hands were no longer shaking.

Hacking River

Where tributaries flow
Kangaroo and Muddy
and the river lives
in creek
sometimes a drought trickle
of itself
reaches down to Port Hacking
reminisces a drowned valley
where water is still clean
for all things aquatic
but where Middens
gone now in the greed
of white need
dreamtime echoes the buildings of the city

In the mid-19th century, many aboriginal middens were destroyed from the Port Hacking catchment in the need for lime, to be used in the construction of Sydney.

Meusepress AUS

Thanks For The Mammory

I'm not a murderer. Well, I don't consider myself one anyway. I mean what I killed was human, I'll concede that. But there's human and 'human' if you get my drift.

'Drift is right,' my husband, Howard, would say. 'Maureen,' he'd say, 'you're always going off on a bloody tangent. You start talking sunsets and finish up with your friend's bloody choice in knickers. A man has no bloody idea what you're on about.'

And when I stated that I was going for a job on a mobile van, he'd asked, one rheumy eye a glitter of hope, was it to get away from him?

I'd shaken my head, but after twenty-eight years of marriage we weren't fooling anyone.

Lately, it had become worse; he, the recently retired, littering my life and routine with garden boots and boozy mates, and me, still insisting (and why shouldn't I!) on my Girls' Afternoon, twice weekly, and interrupting his footy, cricket, golf - you name the sport of the season - watching.

'Get away' was only partly true though, this van came to our town every two years and stayed in situ for just three months, in our local council offices' car park. So, if I got the job, I would only be 'getting away' from him, and he from me, on a biennially, quarterly basis. And it was only a few days a week. His eye lost its gleam when I told him that.

The van hailed from the city three hundred kilometres away, and while the radiographers were happy to stay at hotels for the duration, their regular receptionists weren't. An ad had appeared in our local rag: *Four receptionists wanted. On the job training provided. Limited office experience necessary. People handling skills preferred.*

I could do that. Hadn't I always handled my Howard? And he was a 'people' wasn't he? I don't mean that as a question, I've got nothing against the old guy, except he's always underfoot, misunderstood (loudly according to him) and under my roof. Forget all this bullshit about it being a man's castle, a woman's house is *her* domain, he has his damn man-cave-shed for being the lord of.

The long and the curly of it is, I got the job. Me and three others, and we spent the next few weeks learning all about consent forms, regulations, and how the computers worked, or how to troubleshoot when they didn't. It turned out my age was an asset, as I was around the same vintage as those coming for mammograms. Therefore, as the reasoning went, I would be less intimidating (than what, I never asked) and more understanding. Did I mention mammograms? Well, that's what happens in a BSMU: Breast Screen Mobile Unit Van.

We also did role playing, to shine up our communication and handling skills. Literally. Some of the patients needed help, verbal encouragement and hands on, getting up and down the steps of the van, they could be pretty frail. The patients that is, the twelve-metre van was robust enough. And that plastic plate-vice thing, that captured and compressed the breast, was indestructible too. I'd seen it before, on TV, on those women's health programmes. It didn't look too healthy to me. It was one of the reasons I'd never got a mammogram. Well, not until I got this job. And then I sort of had to, didn't I? I mean, otherwise, it's like a salesman not buying his own product, or a tradesman not endorsing his own skills. What made my transition from un-mammogramed to mammogramed easier, was that my best mate, Elspeth, was one of the others who'd got the job. She held my hand, so to speak, while the radiographer compressed and cajoled my reluctant breasts into positions they'd never thought possible. Actually it wasn't as bad as I'd imagined, but all the same I was over the moon pleased when it was finished. Then it was Elspeth's turn. Not her first. She'd had many an encounter with the plastic vice, and her breasts flattened easily to positions of squish and squash without a squeak of protest. Still, I know I was grimacing watching it, almost as much as I had when the damn thing had mine in its superior grip.

Elspeth and I had been mates for over thirty years, she was ten years my senior, but a childish sense of life had her almost the same age as me. And would have, if I didn't have the same outlook. She always called me Mo, instead of Maureen, and she never missed any of my Girls' Afternoons, commonly known as Maureen's Feast Fests.

The thing I love more than eating, is creating things to eat. Master Chef was my 'must watch' and the morning after would find me supermarket bound, trailing a shopping list with hand drooled scrawl of ingredients to bake. Most of that stuff is pretty fattening, which is why my other friends, Cynthia, Nancy, and Debbie had been declining lately, in lieu of jogging and gym. Getting ready for summer. But I knew they'd be back as soon as autumn withdrew its daylight saving.

So, it was just the two of us, me and Elspeth, on our RDO: Rostered Day Off, that Monday afternoon, five days ago.

'Hi Mo. How's Howard?' Elspeth said, drawing out the *how's* and beginning a giggle which I picked up and turned into a laugh.

'Oh, that's very droll, that is.' Howard's voice echoed from somewhere down the hallway. 'You two couldn't get any more predictable if you tried.' The front door slammed sending shock waves of wind to rattle the kitchen window.

I cocked my head. 'He's off to Roger's,' I said, 'reckons it's quieter there with Roger's seven kids, and five Rotties, than here with us two.' I looked at Elspeth and we crumpled into a full blown chuckle attack. When we finished we wiped our eyes and I flapped my apron up to my face. It was then I noticed Elspeth had a funny look. Sure, her face was flushed too, from the laughing, but her eyes held something I hadn't seen for a very long time.

When a tear tracked a line down one cheek, I flashed her a glance and fast footed it to the kitchen. I came back balancing a chocolate cake I'd made that morning, triple layered and dripping icing like a melting glacier. No Master Chef recipe, this one's mine.

Elspeth brushed a closed fist down one side of her face and smiled, although it didn't reach her lines.

I cut a large slice and put it in front of her.

'Okay, El, out with it. I haven't seen you this upset since that time you thought Jack wasn't going to propose.'

That had been over twenty years ago. Elspeth is one of those eternal optimists. You know, the sort who always says, Isn't this downpour/deluge/flood lovely, so good for the flowers. I mean, she was always happy. And why not? Jack was a great husband. She had a lovely daughter who brought her little gifts all the time, and took her shopping every week. A 'House and Garden' worthy cottage, replete with show winning roses and a Jacuzzi. And recently she'd bloomed into a poet. I mean she's always been a ham and when I'd convinced her to enter a poetry slam, she'd aced it! Even beaten some of the top contenders from the other states. Much to their snotty surprise.

If I had to be honest, I'd have to admit I was a little envious of Elspeth, her wonderful relationship with Jack The Perfect (he was everything Howard wasn't) and her great life.

Elspeth's eyes opened wide. 'It *is* about Jack, actually.' She sounded almost formal, but then she dissolved into long sobs and a sniffy nose. I reached behind me without looking, and grabbed a handful of tissues from the tissue box.

It was several minutes before my ears made sense of her words.

Her husband Jack, big goofy loyal Jack, was having an affair. Midlife crisis and all that. Maybe Elspeth and I were not the only ones who were predictable. Although I never thought Jack would ever do anything like that.

'Who is she?' I pushed Elspeth's plate closer and filled her coffee cup. 'Do I know her?'

Elspeth blew her nose hard. She stuffed the tissues down her blouse, between her ample breasts. I marvelled how well they'd bounced back from the mammograming. Mine hadn't, but then mine had always been flat.

'You do, actually. Remember that first poetry reading we went to?' Her voice came out cracked, like a boy on the verge of teenager.

I nodded, gathered a recollection and raised an eyebrow. 'Not that skinny little blonde woman with the Botox face?'

It's not that I have anything against Botox, but this had been poorly done. Eyebrows peaked to her hairline, so she looked like the devil. Pretty right in this case because it turned out it was her. Jack's love diversion, Sylvia Petron Waters.

Elspeth had seen them in a head-bent canoodle over a Slushie in Maccas. Two straws, one Slushie. The connotations were obvious. And it *was* Jack all right, he was wearing the reindeer jumper Elspeth had knitted for him last Christmas. 'No one else has a jumper like that,' Elspeth said. I had to agree.

Sylvia was one of the slam poets from interstate whom Elspeth had beaten. Now she had moved here. To the poshy part. The opposite side of town from where we lived.

Her face might be horrendous, but Jack was a tit man, which is why he'd first been attracted to Elspeth all those years ago. And Sylvia Petron Waters had breasts to die for. And a cleavage which would rival some of my cracked puddings, when I've had the oven too hot. Okay, I'm exaggerating, but you get my drift.

She was a top notch slam poet too. Ode To My Leftover Ovary was pretty damn decent, I hate to say. But blatant honesty is another of my failings, according to Howard.

155

Her money was eye turning as well. The Aston Martin Sylvia drove was sleek and black, and had all the bells and grunt any man on the brink of midlife self-destruction could crave. And she lived in a house which took up two blocks. The old style quarter acre ones.

I didn't know what else to do but keep up a steady flow of cake, until there was only a sliver of a slice left for Howard. Elspeth was still on her first piece.

'Mo, I can't go to the next poetry slam now. She'll be there. I'll want to kill her.' Elspeth pulled out a crumpled piece of paper from her pocket. 'Look!' She thrust it under my nose. I pulled back. It smelt of sweat and angst.

'This is the sort of think I've been writing.' She actually said 'think' instead of thing. Freudian slip at its finest.

I took it, scanned the page and drew a breath. A cake crumb caught, but I swallowed down the tickle.

She tossed me a knowing look. 'See, I can't read that out. They'd lock me up.'

I cleared my throat, curled up a smile, which I hoped looked supportive, and nodded. 'Most cathartic, I'm sure.' I leaned forward, scraped up Howard's slice. He didn't need it. He and Roger would be scoffing chips and grog all afternoon.

'Hell, Mo. Could you stop eating and listen. This is serious.' Elspeth started sniffing again.

I waved a napkin over my mouth. 'I am listening, El. But really. Jack? He's not going to do anything stupid. It's Jack we're talking about here.'

Elspeth shook her head, tried to talk but her words just squeaked. She took out more pages, so dishevelled I couldn't have wiped my arse on them.

'Look at these emails from her to him. And him to her. I printed them out.' She waved the pages over her head and brought them back to eye focus, holding them tightly with both hands.

'He calls her Sylvia Sweetie.' She flipped to the second email. Her voice dipped to sarcastic. 'And she calls him, Jack The Bodice Ripper.'

Jack The Bodice Ripper? I stifled a giggle and bit my bottom lip.

A squeal of protesting brakes heralded the postman. With my face turned away, I held up my hand like an apology and raced out to the letterbox.

For several moments I stood, back to the screen door, breathing slowly, caught midway between laughing and crying. It was as if the world had somersaulted into paradox.

Loyal, decent Jack, having his head turned by that cheap - yeah, I know she has lots of money, but you know what I mean - floozy, and Elspeth so upset. I'd never seen her brought so low. My never say anything's rotten Elspeth had disappeared like sunlight in a thunderstorm.

Two magpies were loudly copulating on the lawn, while another looked on from the eaves. I glanced up and caught its slanted eye. 'Don't worry, mate, your turn next.'

I directed my gaze to the fluffed up one on the bottom. 'Sylvia,' I hissed. Its head turned and, I swear by the cosmos, for a microsecond its dark-shadowed eye met mine in recognition. I shuddered and was instantly transported to the day of the poetry slam. The one Elspeth had aced.

Sylvia Petron Waters, poured perfectly into a white gown, her eyes smoky lidded in eye-shadow. A cape of gold draped her shoulders and, minutely visible, a black bra, which lacily hitched high her cleavage, to all vantages.

She wore the look of someone sure of their own mythology, sure they would win the five hundred dollars and have their name etched forever, in first place, on the Galore Poetry Slam Cup.

Unable to frown, she looked almost comical when she came in second. But it was unmistakable how she felt.

I took the letters from the box, opened one with tight lips and held breath, then smiled and walked slowly back into the house.

Elspeth had not moved, she lifted her head from the table, but narrowed her eyes when they met mine.

'Mo, you're smiling. I can't believe it! What the hell's so funny?'

'Not funny. I'm just relieved,' I said. I opened the letter again and held it out for her.

The results from my mammogram.

She swallowed. 'No signs of breast cancer detected,' she read, her voice subdued. 'That's good.'

'You'll probably get yours today too, El. We had them done at the same time.'

'I know that.' Her lips clamped shut, shortening the last word to a snap.

I didn't like this Elspeth. I wanted my nice, happy Elspeth back.

She picked up the email printouts again. 'Sylvia *forwarded* these to me, you know. Put 'IMPORTANT' in the subject title.'

I lowered myself onto my chair, it took me with a faint wheeze of protest.

Sylvia had sent these emails, these incriminating emails, to Elspeth? The world *had* gone mad. Or maybe Elspeth had lost it.

'Oh, come on, El. Why would she do that?' My voice leaked hysteria like a deflating soufflé.

Elspeth's next words came out measured with the strength of someone who was very, very angry. And someone who was fast losing patience with me, for not keeping up. Not getting it.

'She wants to rattle my cage, Mo. Stop me doing well at the Strathdurie Poetry Slam. And wants to get back at me for beating her at the last one.'

I almost said that was the Galore Poetry Slam. But one look at her stopped me. Now was not the time to be pedantic.

'But...what if...you confronted Jack? Or went to her house and beat her up. She was taking a risk to send it to you. It just doesn't make sense.'

'Don't forget how she got so bloody rich, Mo. Suing Westlinks for a too hot curry that burned her lips. She'd love me to have a swing at her. She'd sue the pants off our backs.' I itched to say something to that, but sucked on my tongue.

Then I cleared my throat. 'I still don't think Jack would really *do* anything, El. I mean sharing a Slushie. That's pretty lame on the infidelity scale.'

Elspeth leaned back in her chair, then lurched forward and straightened the printouts.

Now she sounded like someone talking to a three-year-old. A mentally challenged one.

'Mo, you should know *me* by now. Of course I didn't go off at the Slushie thing. I made all sorts of excuses for Jack doing that.' She paused, sipped her coffee. For a minute I wondered what the hell she could have thought up. But it's Elspeth we're talking about.

I lifted my brows and swept my hand in a 'go on' gesture.

She turned one of the printouts over and slid it across the table to me. When I finished reading, I couldn't speak. Once again the world was upside down.

In the email Sylvia had suggested a rendezvous next Saturday night, at a certain hotel known for such things. Her final words were: *Let's make your name come true, my darling man.*

'Jack The Bodice Ripper,' I murmured.

Elspeth's face screwed up, sadly triumphant. 'Exactly,' she said.

Elspeth rang me in my lunch-break, two days later.

'I can't come into work today,' she said. 'Could *you* take my afternoon shift, Mo?' Her voice sounded as flat as my boobs.

'Oh god, is it Jack? Is he leaving you?' It had to be something bad. Elspeth loved working on the van. Even more than I did. There was a prolonged silence on the phone and for a second I thought we'd been cut off.

'No, no, nothing like that.' I heard a faint sigh down the line. 'I got my results this morning.'

For another second I felt adrift. Results? Results? Must mean her mammogram ones. But why hadn't she got them on Monday, when I got mine? Why had they taken so long to send hers. Then the coin slipped into the slot.

'I'm coming right over, El,' I said, and hung up.

As I drove to Elspeth's place I cursed Sylvia. Sylvia with her teenage-like breasts. No, she wouldn't get cancer. Not, that selfish, conniving, man-stealing, money-grubbing bitch. I gripped the steering wheel, feeling my fingernails indent the leather cover, like that would give me more of a grip on the situation. I had to think clearly. Didn't we tell all our patients that if they got a positive result (funny how a positive can be a negative) it didn't mean it was cancer? Most lumps or bumps proved to be benign. Elspeth would be fine.

'I'm not telling Jack,' Elspeth said, mid bite of my Apple Tarte Tatin Cake.

A doctor had been seen and a biopsy scheduled.

'You have to,' I said. 'He needs to know.'

Elspeth lifted her eyes slowly to mine. 'I don't want him staying with me out of duty, Mo. That was the main reason I didn't confront him with the rendezvous thing.'

The rendezvous was coming up in three days. Saturday. The day before the Strathdurie Poetry Slam. I sighed. Talk about arranged timing. I imagined Sylvia gloated up with conquest, and poor Elspeth a shivering puddle of self doubt.

Poetry slamming was all about confidence and conviction, both of which would be lost for Elspeth.

Not lost. Taken. My stomach churned bile like a volcano. Hatred was curdling me into action I could not fathom. I mean what the hell could *I* do? (Give her Howard as a replacement? No, I couldn't do *that* to anyone.) And poor trusting Elspeth, normally as happy as a bucketful of puppies and just as loyal. She didn't deserve this. Possible breast cancer. A cheating husband. And her other love snatched from her too. Her poetry. The more I thought about it the angrier I became. Even Howard noticed. Every night baked beans on toast. And no fancy desserts. I think he put it down to The Change. You know, The Change Of Life. And in some ways, except the obvious, he was right. Topsy turvy change didn't come into it. What had though, was bitchy and curvy: Sylvia Bloody Petron Waters.

The next morning, Elspeth resigned her position. I didn't blame her. But it meant an extra day each week which I, and the two other receptionists, had to fill in. Four days a week I was on now. Howard was overjoyed. Smiling all over the place and singing silly little tunes. When I confronted his exuberance he put it down to the extra cash I'd be making. But he wasn't fooling me. Not with the Tour de France running. Or should I say rolling. Before I left every morning, he was already watching the previous nights' recording, ensconced in front of the wide-screen, a packet of crisps on his lap and a beer coasting on the coffee-table beside his right hand.

Elspeth's job had been handling the mammogram appointments. Making sure people were able to come on their allotted days. No patient had a choice, but if someone had real problems they did make allowances. Elspeth was a whizz at juggling times. And being so nice, others didn't mind changing their appointments to accommodate those others who could only make it on certain days. The van was not open on weekends, which made it hard for those who worked weekdays.

I didn't have Elspeth's charm and loveliness, but I did my best.

Friday, I was scanning the computer spreadsheets for the upcoming appointments. Pages of names and details passed by in a blurred monotony of black on white.

Suddenly my eyes braked hard. Her name stood out like Mastiff's balls on a Chihuahua.

Sylvia Petron Evelyn Waters. *Evelyn?* For a micro-blink I smirked at the acronym.

Then it was like lava flowing, my mind red hot with thoughts and plans and possibilities. I could do this. I would do this. For Elspeth.

All it took was one phone call. To Sylvia. One call to say could she move her appointment? Would she mind terribly coming tomorrow morning instead of Monday?

She did ask how we could do it on a Saturday, but when I explained that the radiographer was willing to work in the morning, she agreed. Although I could almost hear her lips pouting as she assented.

That night I tossed so much, Howard got up and went to sleep in the spare room. He did ask me if there was anything he could get me first. He'd been extra nice to me lately, which further teetered my world to unbalanced.

Saturday, I dressed in my black pants and white top. I brushed my hair into a bun. I slathered on so much makeup, Howard took a step back, like a badly balanced dancer, when he glimpsed me in the bathroom.

'Where the hell are you going looking like that? I almost didn't recognise you for a sec.' He stood in front of me, cupping his chin and blocking the mirror. 'Shit, Maureen,' he said finally, 'have you joined a theatrical group or something?' Then he grinned and patted my shoulder. 'But whatever you want to do, Mo, that's okay with me.'

I stiffened at the nickname that I usually only heard from Elspeth. When all this was over he and I needed to have a talk.

The van glowed dew wet from the dawning and, as I walked the two blocks from where I'd my parked my car, a plover set up staccato calls to his mate, obliterating the silence.

I put on some glasses that Dame Edna Everage would have been proud of, thanked the cosmos for the latest trend in dark rim and, glancing at my watch, slid the van's key into the lock. My heart was pounding, like I was one of the last contestants in a Master Chef Grand Final.

I swished open the door, burped up air and thanked the wisdom of not having breakfast. Then I switched off the alarm system, my mind working on the auto of routine. Sylvia was not due for another half hour. Plenty of time to check out the machine and get the computer going.

With this latest full-field digital mammography, the picture can be magnified and looked at in different ways, straight from the computer screen. I'd learned this, and other stuff, last week when the radiographer had called me in to help support an elderly woman with balance problems. While we waited for the woman to undress, I chatted, watched and asked how it all worked. The day had been a long one and I welcomed anything new. Thank god now, for curiosity.

I slipped on a white coat, which was hanging behind the door in the x-ray room, and had everything humming beautifully by the time Sylvia arrived. When I saw her, I felt a momentary pinch of guilt. Then I recalled poor Elspeth's face and guilt fizzed away like a drop of water on a hotplate.

I half scanned Sylvia's consent form and asked her date of birth and whether she had noticed anything unusual on her breasts lately. *Like a stray man, or two, hanging from them, perhaps?* I almost smiled at my thoughts, but pulled my face into what I hoped looked professional.

I served Sylvia up like proverbial lamb (or should that be mutton?) to the slaughter. Prodding and pushing what appeared to be a superb example of breast-hood under the x-ray. 'Plating Up' had just taken on a whole new meaning.

Botox faced, it was difficult to see if Sylvia had any emotion. But then she frowned and I realised there had been no Botox all along. She was just one cold, hard, frozen bitch. Naturally.

I tightened my jaw and took up my position behind the machine's computer screen. Everything came into focus. I gasped at what I saw. Then I nodded slowly, and pushed the button I'd seen pushed when Elspeth had her mammogram all those weeks before. I kept my finger on it hard. The top plate slid silently down. To the lowest setting. Pancake, I thought, my mind gliding to Master Chef once more.

Sylvia's full bloodied curses were stifled as I shut the van's door. But I smiled a satisfied smile when I heard a compression-like pop and her sharp scream.

I may have been wrong about the Botox. But we'd *all* been fooled by one other thing as well. Or two, actually.

Sylvia's breasts were as false as she was. And what was left of one of them was pretty well cactus by now.

Like I said, I don't consider myself a murderer. I mean, what I killed was human, I'll concede that. But really only 'a bit of human'. If you get my drift.

No rendezvous for Sylvia and Jack tonight. She wasn't going anywhere. And with any luck, no one would find her until Monday morning. Thank the cosmos, it was my RDO.

And I still had plenty of time to convince Elspeth, who'd be feeling better, with an un-straying husband, to enter the Strathdurie Slam on Sunday.

I had one great poem in mind, all she had to do was put it into words.

The Murder House

I've bought the Murder House. My husband, Jack, would kill me if he wasn't already gone. Not departed 'gone' but 'gone' from our current home and from himself, most days. He now resides, I can't say, 'lives', at Peace Haven. 'A peaceful place for retired souls.' If you are to believe their brochures. Jack insisted on going there. He was still okay in the compos department back then. 'Anyway El,' he'd said, 'Peace Haven's got great rehabilitation care. And you can walk Bessy there too, instead of driving. You know how she hates going in the car.'

If I hadn't had so much trouble lifting him, I could have kept him at home longer, but as Lily Thomson, the care helper, said, I had no other choice.

The Murder House hasn't been rented since it happened. The triple murder. Triplet women actually. One local yokel called it The-Triple-By-Pass Murder, not because they were triplets, but because it was carried out with secateurs, those with the ratchet openings to larger trim. By-pass ones, even sharper than the yokel.

After it happened, the Murder House was rendered and painted a rose blush pink. Its yellow bricks had absorbed so much blood they were un-scrubbable, un-cleanable. And even though the pink is darker, in certain places, like shading, to me the house looks as fresh as a new beginning, which is what I hope it will be. I can't keep rattling around our old place. My and Jack's house. Too many memories and too much of me thinking that Jack is just in another room, ready to pop out asking if I want a cuppa or something, instead of lying abed in Peace Haven, sliding in and out of coherence and consciousness.

Mandy Billington, the murderess, kept insisting there was only one woman she'd done in, although she called it pruning. 'I only pruned one of em, took her off at the bud. Kept it on the slant,' Mandy told the judge, holding up her hand to show the angle.

It was no surprise to learn she'd been on Ice. Totally off her brain. At the killing and at her trial. I could kind of understand about the single woman bit though. The triplets are...were identical, like proverbial peas.

It turns out she'd used three pairs of secateurs and a bucket of Milton solution to clean them in between.

Lily the care helper was also the wife of the coroner and she filled me in on the grosser details. Even though Jack was now in Peace Haven, she still regularly visited him, along with other former patients who'd also gone there.

It was strange hearing all that stuff from Lily's lips. Lily is one of those people who looks like her name. Pale and ethereal and so thin it's amazing she didn't get blown away when anyone sneezed. Her voice was as soft as her skin but it didn't waver once as she sipped tea from her saucer and told me of her husband's findings.

'Should you be telling me this, Lil? I mean, isn't it confidential or something?'

She looked at me with pencilled eyebrow lifted. 'Not now Elspeth. Not now that the trial is over.'

The gruesome facts set my mind spinning with my teaspoon as I swirled sugar into my coffee.

I was pretty sure the things she'd told me were not open for public knowledge. I wished I could ask Jack, he'd been a cop before the accident, one who had to take pictures as the coroner worked. Not for Lily's husband though.

'So,' said Lily, drawing out the word. 'I suppose you want out now. Now that you know all about it. The cooling off period. Cooling off.' She blew down on her tea mid-cup, like underlining her point.

'Not at all, Lil. Not at all.' God, I was parroting too now. I gripped the table with my free hand. 'It's way too good a bargain, Lil, small farms like that go for twice the price. And it's been freshly painted inside and out. And re-carpeted.'

Lil looked at me with twitching lips. 'There's a reason for that, Elspeth. We all know there's a reason for that. And why it's sat on the market for five years. Five years.'

I thought of the real-estate guy, Hamilton Barker of Barker and Barker. The look on his face when I said I'd take it, subject to selling my place of course. But even that proviso didn't wipe his incredulity, or the creeping smile he tried to hide as he slunk back to his car.

He hadn't told me about the murders. He should have. By law, real-estate agencies have to disclose any 'material fact' which might prejudice the sale.

'It wasn't five years, Lil. That's how long since the murders. The owners moved back in themselves for two years, remember? Before even trying to sell. It's only been three.'

Bess chose this moment to push her head under my hand, leaving a little lick on my palm. I leaned over the table for a doggy biscuit, noticing with a short shock that Lil was eating one too. I pushed the dog biscuit bowl back and brought forward the people biscuits. 'Anyway,' I said, 'I can't let a bargain like that go. I've wanted to get back to the country for ages. Have some chooks and that Quarter horse I've had my eye on.'

Lil finished her biscuit, leant over and grabbed another dog one before I could stop her. She spluttered coarse crumbs through soft voice. 'Really Elspeth, at your age. Really. Your age.'

'Plenty of people still ride at my age,' I said.

'Not that, Elspeth. I meant you buying something out of town. And what about Bess. Her carsickness?'

'Actually it's close enough for us to walk in, to visit Jack.'

Lily sniffed and coughed up a crumb, it flew across the table, mixing in with the kosher biscuits. She hooked it out with a manicured nail, and placed it on her saucer.

'Anyway,' I said, 'Jack won't be in there forever.' Lil started cough-choking, and I realised how I'd sounded. I couldn't explain it, especially to someone as practical as Lil, but I just knew Jack would get out eventually. And not in an urn. Peace Haven has its own funeral home too, Lil's son and daughter-in-law run it.

After she'd gone I wrote a list of the things I needed to do with our current house. Clean the windows and gutters. Shampoo the carpets. Get rid of any junk. Buy some pot-plants to pretty up the veranda. Learn how to cook bread for the first opening. And most importantly, get in contact with some other agents, I didn't trust Barker and Barker.

The next few weeks slipped by like butter on a hot skillet.

As soon as she got wind of it, another friend, Maureen, Mo, dropped in to help pack. Lil's practicality didn't lean in that direction. Which was good, she'd been way too judgmental lately. And Mo bakes the best cakes, Master Chef worthy, also she'd been there for me when I'd had my cancer scare. And when I'd won the Grand Slam Poetry Slam in the city.

'You ought to write a poem about the Murder House, El,' she said, slapping down a huge double-layered chocolate slab cake on the table. 'Multi-versed with blood and gore, and ramp the suspense up into cadence like they do in those poems near the end.' She stared at her cake, mind god knows where and then knife-slashed it into six decent slices. I slid over my plate, nudging the biggest piece.

'Looks like you've got your appetite back then,' Mo said, a grin stretching her already wide face.

I swallowed a mouthful of chocolate heaven, closed my eyes, wiped my lips and swigged my tea to clear my voice. 'Actually, Mo, I've started writing a poem already. I'll show you when it's finished.'

I picked up her car-keys. 'You want to go out to the house, now? I know you're dying to take a look.'

Mo laughed, her body shaking like a walrus on a windy beach. 'Thought you'd never ask.'

That's the difference between her and Lily. Lil would have had a go at me for what she would have called 'My unfortunate choice of words.' And then, for good measure, would have added, 'Dying to take a look indeed. Dying.'

As we drove through the gates of the Murder House it was as if the engine had stalled, although the car was still moving. All the sound from the outside seemed compressed, like when you are ascending in a plane. Mo was still smiling and staring ahead, so I said nothing.

With a few deep breaths I flinched out of my growing uneasiness and started to unbuckle my seatbelt. My fingers jammed in the catch as Mo stomped on the brake. A huge white cat shot out from under the car unhurt, and ran across the drive in front of us.

'At least it wasn't a black one,' Mo said with a quick laugh.

In the glow of the late afternoon the house looked gorgeous, its rose pink softness, with its clipped green hedge (the owners would've had to get a new gardener of course) a living fence around it, made me wonder how it could have been the scene of such gruesome murders. I drew another deep breath and blew it onto the fingers which had been trapped in the seatbelt buckle. They were throbbing like my heartbeat.

'Bit of work there. Keeping that trimmed,' Mo said, sounding almost as practical as Lil. She glanced at me as she swung open the car door. 'You okay, El? You look as white as that cat.'

I nodded and forced a smile. 'Last time I was here Hamilton Barker put the key under that pot there,' I said, indicating a terracotta pot and stringy geranium which had seen better summers.

The door swung open without a squeak, no sign of sinister in its hinges, inside looked shiny fresh, like something out of 'Homes Beautiful'. I hadn't noticed much when I'd seen the Murder House before, with Hamilton. The land held my gaze then, the neat paddocks. The veggie patch running to pumpkins and zucchinis. The stables and the sheds where Jack could store his racing bikes.

Funny how the accident hadn't happened on one of his bikes. I mean careening down hills at 70ks an hour with only the lightness of Lycra between body and asphalt. Much more of a risk, I would have thought. But he'd fallen off a ladder while putting up smoke alarms. I had been on at him for months about those bloody things. If only I hadn't. I mean, they used to go off where they were on the dresser whenever I burnt anything on the stove, so they were working fine where they had been.

Jack was in hospital for four weeks with a fractured spine. When he came out I nursed him for as long as I could. Lily had been sent out to help me with his daily shower and with dressing him.

He could no longer work, but still kept in touch with the guys in the Force.

'Hey El,' Mo said, eyeing me, 'if you don't feel right, you don't have to buy it, you know. You could back out. Cooling off period's not up, is it?' Now she really did sound like Lily. I walked ahead of her into the kitchen, not trusting myself to speak. This was where the first murder had happened. The other two sisters had been killed upstairs, then dragged to the front of the house, 'spraying blood like fire hoses,' Lil's words.

One of the windows was open. The curtain had been blown through and was flapping outside like a truce flag. I could see paw-prints on the sink. Feline sized. A dish of water was half-full and nearby a grey mouse, mid-decomposition, gawped its internals like a tiny parody of the murder.

I shivered.

It was then I realised I was alone. Mo had scarpered. Not like her at all. She had always been my rock, granite tight and unwavering.

The toilet flushed and I breathed out as Mo came back into the kitchen. She pulled in the curtain, found a dustpan and scooped the mouse out of the window, firmly shutting it afterwards and dusting her hands together like summoning an encore.

It reminded me of the day I'd first met Lily, bustling in all starch and professional although she was casually dressed. She smelled of something my granny used to wear. Lily of the Valley?

My first impression was her wispiness, how would she be able to do anything? Jack could walk a little back then, but he still needed a lot of help.

Lil had flitted about, making coffee and tea for us, finding her way around the kitchen without asking where anything was. She'd even brought some biscuits. And as days counted into weeks she certainly proved much stronger than she looked, although in the end, even she had to admit defeat.

'Murder House visitor to crazy-friend-buyer of Murder House. Come in.'

I became aware of a hand flapping in front of my face. 'Sorry Mo, was just thinking about something.'

'I hope that something had second thoughts in it,' Mo said, without smiling. 'Let's get on with this, El. Upstairs now?'

The staircase didn't creak, no lighting or thunder rumbled overhead as we climbed, although the sky did darken. I shrugged up a new thought, one which comforted like a hug. That's what I'd felt earlier, a barometer adjustment in the air. An approaching thunderstorm. Nothing ominous at all.

Back in my own house, drinking coffee and finishing off the cake, I filled Mo in with everything Lil had told me. The bleach, the secateurs, the insistence by Mandy Billington that there was only one victim.

'She never denied it, did she though. I mean about the killing,' Mo said. It wasn't a question, lots had been written about it in the papers at the time.

I shook my head, bit into another large piece of cake. I'd skip dinner tonight, but then I hadn't been doing much cooking anyway since Jack had gone.

Over the first few weeks after he'd come home from hospital, he lost more and more feeling in his feet and legs. In the end I couldn't even get him into his wheelchair. He kept complaining about pins and needles and tiredness. His specialist talked about pinched nerves and neuropathy. Age factors and the accident. The way he fell.

Thunderstorm rain trampled the roof like a hundred Santas and their reindeer trying to get in. Mo began to speak but closed her mouth, nature's noise much greater than anything she could produce. Apart from the clatter we sat together in comfortable silence. Good friends can do that.

Two weeks later, surrounded in packing cases, wrapping paper and sticky thick brown tape, we were back in the Murder House's kitchen once again. I made a mental note to start calling it just 'The House,' then realised I'd spoken aloud.

'Has to be a girl's name,' Mo said, her mouth full of cake. This time it was Devil Angel's cake, a sort of combination which was more heavenly than devilish. It reminded me I wanted to learn how to bake bread. I'd made packet cake for my house's first opening. It'd worked, or something had. I had a buyer for it the next day. The house that is, the packet cake only smelled okay.

'Why so, Mo? Why a girl's name?'

'Stands to reason. Boats and planes and even hurricanes are named in the feminine.'

'Ships,' I said, ripping more tape off another box marked 'Kitchen'. 'Not boats. Ships.'

Mo rolled her eyes and sniffed. 'Anyway, it already has a name. I saw it last time we came. There's a plaque near the front door. Has some ivy growing over it.'

I lifted out a saucepan and put it on the countertop with its cousin. 'Okay. What is it?'

'Primrose Cottage. Lovely plaque, even has a little flower design. Must have had it specially made. It looks pretty old though, so I don't think the owners did it recently for effect, or to highlight the colour.'

'I think primrose is yellow, Mo. And *I* own the place now.'

'Gee, El, you've got bloody pedantic since you've become a landowner.'

I inhaled some cake and almost choked. 'Yeah, sure, a landowner of all of five acres.' We both laughed. It felt good and it felt normal and I had to admit I wasn't half as nervous as I thought I'd be on my first day in The House. But then Mo was still here. As if reading my thoughts, she said, 'Do you want me to stay the night?' Her fingers shook as she picked up her piece of cake and her eyes held the sort of wild of a trapped rabbit.

When I declined, she slumped back, her chair giving out a squeaky puff of relief. 'You can always ring me if you need me, El,' she said.

After Mo left, I surveyed the now neat kitchen then climbed upstairs to make my bed. I'd taken the room where a triplet hadn't been murdered, Merilee Jane's. The other two bedrooms I'd made up for guests to stay. That's if I ever got any guests. Maybe Jack's copper mates would visit.

I thought of the mouse that had been on the sink the last time Mo visited, and dread slipped down my back like ice on a draining board.

The light-bulb in the hallway blew out in fuse and glass, as I opened the linen cupboard for another pillow. Luckily it wasn't directly overhead, but I felt something cling in my hair and tug it down. 'Just a piece of glass,' I said out loud, as I scrabbled for the light switch. Of course it didn't work.

Now it was as dark as a blackout. No streetlights in the country and courtesy of the heavy cloud cover of another storm, the night sky was moonless and starless.

I hand-felt my way along the hall's walls like a drunk man trying to find his way back home, and slipped into the bedroom, clutching stupidly at the light switch again.

I could see a pulse of red behind my lids when I shut my eyes, but it was if I'd gone blind when I opened them. Crouching low I stretched out my hands until I found the bed, I flipped back the covers and slipped in, pulling them up to my chin. My breath was coming in gasps, I couldn't fill my lungs. It was as if I was drowning in my own air.

A gust of wind opened the window with a rip. It rushed in, played tug-o-war with the covers and almost won. The house creaked like the pylons of a jetty being battered by hurricane seas.

'Murder House,' I said, although I couldn't hear my voice, once again nature was far too loud. Then it was as if I'd hit the mute button on a noisy commercial. The wind stopped screaming and retreated. The house seemed to straighten up and tighten inwards. My mind went as numb as my frozen feet. I clenched fists of sheet and let out some of my breath through closed teeth. Then something hit the bed with a huge flop. It landed on my stomach, finishing off my breath in a whoosh. But this I did recognise. This I had felt before. My laughter bounded off the walls and filled the room. 'Oh, Bessy,' I said mid-laugh. I pulled back the Doona, and Bess snuggled her way to the bottom of the bed. I could feel her curl around my legs and her warmth prickled my feet back to life. I swallowed heavily as I thought of how Jack had complained about this very feeling. 'Pins and needles, but worse than that, El. It feels like something is burning into them as well.'

The next morning I woke to a bedroom which wasn't Merilee Jane's, it was Donna Gail's, the second murder victim. In the blindness of last night I'd gone into the wrong room. There was a fingernail as big as a man's tangled in my hair. It must have been stuck on the light bulb. I clenched my jaw and flung it to the floor.

Bess was still curled around my legs and sun was streaming lines of beams through curtain-less windows. The blind had spun upwards and the pull-cord had caught around the roller. Outside, in a lilac bush, a bird I knew no song for was whistling a fractured tune, the intervals being filled by another. I was pleased he wasn't alone.

Lily was coming this morning, now that I'd moved in properly. Her words. I told her I'd be baking bread, almost said, breaking bread. Isn't that what you do to appease? Could I appease The House? Why should I? I mean, Mandy Billington, shouldn't she be the one doing that? Although her grip on life was even more tenuous than Jack's. And he'd been drifting in and out of a coma for the last few days. The times he did speak it was as if I had a glimpse of Old Jack back, far too coherent for dementia. Terrible word. Sounds almost demonic. I hadn't told him about The House yet.

Lily puffed in, wispy as a cloud, dressed in white muslin reminiscent of hippy days and Woodstock. She carried a big bag of bread-mix.

I narrowed my eyes. 'Isn't that cheating, Lil?' I was surprised at the calmness of my voice. I was buzzing nerves down to my fingertips.

'Not at all, Elspeth. Not at all.' Lily looked through the window, where my five acres stretched across paddocks greening and sparkling from the rain.

'You know, I lived on a farm once, when I was a child,' she said. 'Going back a bit now, though. Back a bit.' When she turned, her facial lines were etched by deep shadows from the light. She was a lot older than I'd thought. Funny how I hadn't noticed before.

'Lots of rats on our farm. Nearly as big as that white cat over there,' she said, turning back to the window and pointing. When I came closer to look, the cat was slinking under the hedgerow that surrounded the house. Perhaps I'd put some milk out for it later.

I scanned the packet of bread-mix and switched on the oven. Lil was still at the window. She seemed to be talking to herself. 'Mama knew what to do to get rid of them. Those rats. Yes, Mama knew.

Better poison back in those days. Better poison.' Now she was freaking me out almost as much as The House.

When she started rummaging through the cupboards, I bit my lip. What did she hope to find in there, poison?

She brought out one of my large mixing bowls and set it on the bench. 'Let's get started, Elspeth,' she said, pulling out two matching aprons from her bag. 'I'll just put these other mixing bowls in the cupboard, nearer your workbench.' Same practical Lil. Although my skin prickled and certain words burned my throat as I swallowed them down.

An hour before the bread was ready The House lost power again. Lily swore loudly about bloody hick houses and faulty fuse boxes. Declared she had to go. Had other things more important to do.

After she'd left, I took out the barely cooked bread, broke it into gluey pieces and threw it to my chooks who were milling around the back door.

Then I found my notepad with my half written poem. I hadn't been able to bring myself to write about The House, just like I could no longer bring myself to put Murder in its title. My poem had begun dark though, and still held remnants of death and the dastardly stuff of homicide.

I knew from being a copper's wife women mostly resorted to poison to do the deed. Much cleaner and easier. I thought of Lil's rats in her childhood farm.

Blast the power being off. As if to oblige, the lights on the stove flickered briefly, The House creaked and cracked and the power resumed.

I booted up and Googled 'Olden Day Rat Poisons'.

Arsenic and strychnine seemed to be the poison of choice back then. Then Wiki flashed up another one, which caused my stomach to tighten and my mouth to go dry. In sympathy? Or something else?

Thallium: The Poisoner's Poison AKA Inheritance Powder. Whatever that meant.

A sudden loud tapping rushed me upstairs on legs of adrenaline. It was coming from Olive Rose's room, she was the third murder victim.

As I entered, Lily of the Valley enveloped me in its sickly fug. Lil's signature perfume. It wasn't there yesterday when I'd made up the guest bed. A Poe crow dashed its beak one last time on the windowpane and flew off in a flurry of black.

Now strangled squawking from outside made me run downstairs even faster than I'd run up them. Two chickens were scrabbling on the ground and another one was not moving. Most of the bread had been eaten. Clues slipped into slots like coins at the pokies and as fast as the sweat which was now sliding down my back.

I dialled Mo without even knowing I'd done it. Her voice was muffled as she said hello. My phone had only one bar.

I blurted out, 'Chooks dead. Poisoned bread.'

Mo interrupted, laughing. 'Hey, sounds punchy, El. This your new poem?' But she wasn't laughing by the time I'd finished. 'I'm on to it,' she said, her voice clear despite the lousy connection.

Driving into town, I joined symptoms like dots in a puzzle. Jack's hands and feet going numb and burning. Losing weight. And he'd got worse since he'd come home from hospital. When Lily came to help.

Thallium, in large amounts, produces death without time for symptoms. She must have used small doses. And the bread? Was I next on her list?

Motives? Well, she had a vested interest, her son and daughter-in-law ran the funeral home and her coroner husband could cover up the toxicology. My head was pounding so much I could hardly steer the car.

Mo met me at the entrance of Peace Haven, grabbing my arm, swirling me back and sitting me down on the outside bench. 'Don't go in there, El,' she said. 'They're questioning Lily now. But it's not what you think. Oh, and Jack's been taken to the hospital for tests, but not for what you think either.'

'Prussian Blue!' I screamed, 'I need to tell them. Prussian Blue. It's the antidote.' I made a dash for the door, almost crashing into it by beating the opening sensor. Mo, despite her size, was quick on her feet and caught me before I reached the Nurses' Station. She dragged me over to the coffee dispenser. 'Sit. I'm making you a drink. You were right about Lil being dodgy, but she's no murderer, just a thief. She's been on their radar for ages apparently. I must say you've got remarkable timing, El. It's all being wound up today.' She stared at me like she was seeing me for the first time.

'Whose radar, Mo? The police?'

Mo handed me a steaming cup and nodded. 'Yes, and the Board of Directors at Peace Haven.'

Twenty minutes later, Mo and I were at Jack's bedside. His copper mates, Trev and Gary, were there with him. 'Undercover,' he said, looking remarkably restored to Old Jack. I could have killed him. But then I had my own confession.

It turns out Jack doesn't mind at all that I've bought the Murder House. He loves living here. Adores having all that space for his bikes. I've got my Quarter horse, and we've bought some more chooks. I know better now, than to feed them half-cooked yeasty bread. Poor things.

I'm pissed off that Jack didn't tell me about the undercover stuff, or that his health was really improving, but Lily may have become suspicious if I'd acted differently. And I hadn't told him about The House so we're even.

Being in Peace Haven was a case of him being at the right place at the right time. The Board found out he'd been a cop and asked if he wanted to do a bit of PI work.

Lily Thomson got ten years for embezzlement and coercion. Stealing from the old folk. And befriending those without kin, to sign over their inheritance. Jack got the proof. All on hidden cam.

Him being 'comatose' convinced Lily she was safe to say and do anything to the 'old folk', retired policewomen, positioned in the beds either side of him. They all loved being part of it.

Jack's back in the Force. Only a desk job, but it's enough. For now.

I thought of what Thallium is also called: Inheritance Powder. And its meaning clicked into place. Poisoning people to get their inheritance. Lily's approach may not have been as final, but the premise was the just same.

Lily's lawyers weren't able to plead Reduced Culpability as Mandy Billington's had done. Even so, Mandy was incarcerated for life. Lily only got ten years. But then at her age, I guess, that was pretty much a life sentence too.

And the Murder House? We call it Primrose Cottage, its original name, now. Was it trying to tell me something about Lily? I'll never know. But one thing I do know for sure is Lily had never been in Olive Rose's room, and I've never smelt Lily of the Valley in there since.

Pet Fetishes and Pot Plants
published in An Eclectic Slice Of Life - Eclecticism AUS

The town had a carrot up its arse.

The streets were uniformly paved, the paths straight-edged with roses and prunus trees in alternate order. Tyler McClain is sure they're colour coordinated. Even with their winter undress he can tell.

He's not surprised when he passes a billboard with loud print declaring this to be one of Australia's tidiest towns since 1965. He smiles to see that a bird has slashed shit across *Tidiest,* making the word almost indecipherable.

Tyler uncrumples his long body, stretching the confines of his Mazda.

As a teacher without permanency his life has been one of beginnings and ends. The beginnings at caravan parks, living in one-roomed cabins; the ends before the Christmas hiatus with the packing up of the year. Then a new school and a *fresh* start.

Tyler snorts. Certainly this place is fresh. Fresh, clean *and* sterile.

One thing though, he will not be friendless. He feels relief as soothing as cold water to a burn. Jasper Lawrence, an old colleague, moved here two years ago.

As if on cue, Tyler's mobile summons him, vibrates a noise like breaking wind. Message from Jasper. He stops the car and reads: *Meet u at Maccas in 10.*

He's there first but only has to wait another five minutes before Jasper, clad in loose casual, flows in and orders, before dropping into a seat next to him.

'Hi, Tyler, long time no see. You ordered yet?'

Tyler lifts up an empty wrapper.

'Geez, Ty, you eaten already?' Jasper drops his tone when a female shop assistant approaches the table with a cloth and spray bottle. She wears her hair in brittle blond and makeup in faded memory.

Tyler tosses the wrapper back on the table, she scoops it and an empty cup onto the tray she is carrying.

'Sorry for this mess,' she says, flat voiced, 'the other customer just left. Your food should be here soon, sir.' The *sir* tacked on like a postscript.

Tyler watches the girl come back with both their orders. He grins at Jasper.

Jasper soft-punches Tyler in the shoulder. 'Same ole kidder. You haven't changed. Just like when we were children fooling around in Mandarra. Do you miss it, Ty? Our home town, I mean.'

Tyler sees Jasper's bun lose its lettuce, watches the burger flap like a wayward tongue.

He finishes his own mouthful, places his burger down and shakes his head.

Jasper raises his eyes, pushes back the burger but leaves lettuce on the table. His mouth-filled answer is barely coherent. 'I shure as damn miss it. Best grass this side of Nimbin. Can't get anything like it here. Bloody poncy place. How come you chose this town? I couldn't have been the only attraction. You gotta woman I don't know about?'

Tyler says nothing but thinks: I have a lot of things you don't know about. He finishes another bite has a suck of his vanilla shake. Tastes the sweet creaminess.

His mind jumps backwards, an eight-year leap.

When Stephanie Carmichael, his first, told him she was nursing, he'd thought conventional. Hospitals or old age care. But when they'd made love he'd found out the reality, and a baby's cry confirmed it.

A month later they'd all lost touch, moved on to different universities, different lives.

Only Jasper had taken up the same profession, albeit his was in the sports gym, while Tyler's was fronting grade fives and sixes with the three proverbials. He has no idea what Stephanie does now.

'Well Ty, this is bloody lovely. We haven't seen each other for... how long? Hell, it must be at least seven years. And there you sit, your head away in whatever. Come on, let's get out of here. Take your drink with you. I wanna show you something.'

'My car or yours?' Tyler holds up his keys.

'Nah, mate. I walked here. And, by the look of that paunch, you could do with some exercise. My place is only a couple of k's.'

Tyler takes a long draught, leaves the half empty cup on the table and picks up the rest of the Maccas' flotsam on the tray. Deposits it in the bin on their way out. Sees Miss Brittle-blond raise a tired smile.

Jasper takes off at a brisk pace. Tyler straining a step behind.

'Geez, you *are* unfit,' Jasper says, casting an over-the-shoulder glance at Tyler. 'Listen, Ty, have you ever wanted to get out of teaching? Don't answer that. I can see you would. Your job's worse than mine. And now they have those numeracy and literacy tests. Must be a bastard. Especially if you have some kid that's ten cents short in the dollar.'

Tyler nods, mid-puff. Jasper raises eyebrows.

He's not sure if I'm agreeing with him about getting out of teaching or if my job's a prick, Tyler thinks. He flips Jasper a Cheshire-cat grin.

The streets still look the same even when they get to the suburbs. Two kilometres turns out to be conservative. By Tyler's watch it's an hour before Jasper finally turns into the gateway of his house.

Two pot-plants, trailing grey stems like withered hands, adorn the front step. A hose in tangled green knots perishes beneath a rusted tap. The contrast is conspicuous. The houses on either side are as anal-retentive as fish.

Tyler notices a turbid bucket of overflow tilted under a cut-off downpipe, he tips some of its contents on the plants, watches as the water filters through them. Then he waves at the old lady pruning bushes next door. She smiles and flourishes her secateurs like a salute, her hands all parchment skin over knotted knuckles.

Jasper lowers his voice. 'That's Mrs Molly Edgeworth. Nosy old bitch. Come on, Ty.' He opens the door with a key attached to a plastic tag etched in blue: World's Best Dad, it says.

Tyler enters the gloom, his eyes can't focus but his nose picks up the aroma of stale prawns and something else, sweet and familiar as memory.

Jasper turns on a light, throws his keys on the table and opens the fridge. He takes out two cans of beer, opens one, tosses the other at Tyler.

Tyler catches it mid-air, puts it down on the table, and picks up the keys. 'What's this all about then, Jas?' he says, indicating the tag.

'Oh, the world's best dad, thing? Yeah, I'm a father. Little boy. Jeremy. Remember Patricia? Maybe you don't. A bit after your time. Never got hitched. In case you think I didn't invite you to the wedding. Nah, I had enough sense not to marry her. But even living together, the woman's entitled. Like the old joke goes, may as well find someone you hate and give them a house. Cut out the middle man.'

'Middle woman, you mean, don't you, Jas.'

Jasper laughs. 'You're a funny bugger, Ty,' he says. 'Dry as a ninety-year old's tits. Anyway, come with me. I didn't bring you here just to drink my piss. I want to show you something in the shed.'

Tyler trails behind like a faithful pup. They go through the laundry and then Jasper squeaks open the screen-door portal to the backyard.

The shed is wrought iron hung on stressed timber. It has an aviary attached. The only sign of birds are some windblown feathers in a corner, tangled to wire, trying to escape.

The shed reminds Tyler of his last lover, Janna Trewellen. She was the mother of one of his students and had come on to him, hot and melting, the first time she'd seen him.

'Just wanted to see the new teacher,' she'd said, her eyes flapping their impossible lashes - courtesy of Max Factor. He noticed the newborn in her arms.

It wasn't long before she was seeing much more of the new teacher, Tyler mused.

She had what she called this 'little bungalow,' but really it was nothing more than a glorified shed. It had an aviary attached too.

It had been several weeks before Tyler had been game enough to tell her what really turned him on. But she hadn't seemed at all perturbed when he'd asked.

He feels his face warming and wishes he could be normal.

Then he remembers the sweet-warm flow from Janna's breasts filling his mouth, soaking his chest, or pooling yellow haloed stains on either side of where they lay.

Jasper's voice as strident as a crow's: 'Are you coming in or not? Christ Ty, where are you? Not bloody here by that daft look on your ugly mug.'

Tyler sees that Jasper has the door to the shed open. As he enters he realises that inside is brighter than outdoors. He shuts the door behind him and looks around. Dozens of lights hum a static dance overhead. Rows of tables and benches, growing from the walls in sturdy timber, line the room. Plants in various stages of leaf fill all available space.

Pot plants. But these, Tyler thinks, are as far opposite in health, nature and name as you could get, from those poor geranium plants on Jasper's front porch.

'Bloody hell, Jas! What was all that talk then, at Maccas, about missing the home town? About not being able to get grass?'

'Yeah, well look what it's driven me to.' Jasper laughs as he adjusts a water pipe. 'Look at this, Ty, drip irrigation. Hydroponics. Climate control. Cost a fortune. Only the best for these babies.'

'Puts a whole new slant on your title,' says Tyler.

Jasper wipes a dripping tap, his face twisted. 'What do you mean?' he says.

'World's Best Dad.'

Jasper snorts. 'This is my passport outta teaching, Ty, and yours too, if you want in.'

Tyler looks up. 'How come you're willing to share, Jas? Seems to me you got it pretty much by the balls, or should I say roots?'

Jasper seems to ignore the pun. 'Not enough connections, Ty,' he says.

Tyler picks up one of many hose-connections nestled in a box, thinks better of the joke and places it back with its companions. 'What makes you think that *I've* got contacts?'

'Oh shit,' says Jasper, and strides to the other side of the shed. He fiddles with some wires. A light flickers to life, surges a short gasp then goes out. 'Hang on a tic, Ty. I need to get another tube.'

It's humid in the shed and Tyler is soon sweating. He feels thirsty, thinks of Janna and feels a part of himself pulsing to life.

The talent in every town since graduating had been different. For the most he likes this nomadic life, but these small places are the worst. Reputations are distorted to a growth of unbelievability. Loose-lipped talk from people with nothing better to do than spit fabrics of slander.

In big cities though, Tyler has found, one can be as anonymous as the Unknown Soldier. He has no intention of staying here for more than a year if he can help it.

Jasper returns and soon the lighting is fixed and shining. He shows Tyler the drying room where he cuts and packs.

'This place is like the Tardis,' Tyler says. 'It doesn't look this big from the outside. But I'd do something about your garden, Jas. A jungle like that could draw attention. That's the last thing you want.'

Jasper, sotto voce: 'That jungle, as you call it, is my camouflage. You know they have satellite surveillance now. I've stood on the house roof. This shed looks tiny. No one would suspect.'

Tyler rubs a hand over his mouth. 'I'm dying for a drink, Jas. You finished in here or what?'

On the walk back to Maccas to retrieve his car Tyler thinks of Jasper's last offer.

'Why don't you move in here, mate?' he'd said, as Tyler had got up to leave. 'I've got plenty of room.'

Tyler had answered: '*Not bloody likely*.' But he was having third thoughts about it now.

One of the things he misses about home is the fact he hasn't had one, not a house that is. Not since he'd started teaching eight years ago. He loves gardening too. Had a great veggie-patch at his parents' house. They certainly missed him for that.

He sits down at a bus shelter and rings Jas's mobile. 'You there Jas?' The call has run to message bank but Jasper quickly answers when Tyler starts talking.

'Hi, Ty. Sorry about that. I like to vet my calls. Never know.'

'No probs. About moving in with you. I reckon it might work. But some ground-rules. Okay?'

'Sure. Fire away.'

'Well, for a start, Jas, I don't want anything to do with your um... enterprise. And would you agree to a reduced rent if I do the garden? I'm a bit tight at the moment. I've only budgeted for a cabin at the caravan park.'

'Sounds great, mate. As long as you leave the bushes around the shed. You got your stuff with you? Come over when you're ready. Sorry I can't help you. Can't afford a car. Spent it all on... Well, you know.'

Tyler can almost see him tapping his nose. Hears the ruffle of the phone confirming his imagination. Thinks: God, he's carrying this cloak and dagger stuff a bit far. It's only goddam pot, after all. In the same thought he wonders why he doesn't take him up on his offer. He could do with the extra money.

That night he's booked into a hotel. He rings up the removalists, redirecting them to Jasper's house. By his calculations they should be there tomorrow, early afternoon. He doesn't have to start work until the new week.

The next morning, Tyler tries to ring Jasper to get the house-key, but his mobile is turned off. He curses that he didn't ask at which school Jasper is teaching. But he knows he has no time to search.

When he arrives at Jasper's house he checks out the carport and moves some loose planks of wood into position to use as pallets. He doesn't fancy putting his new lounge chair onto the oil-stained concrete. He pulls some hessian bags into shape, lining more of the floor and finds a balding broom to sweep out the rest. That will have to do, he thinks.

'Hi there.' Mrs Edgeworth's voice echoes in the carport and makes him jump. He notices she's still holding the same secateurs and wonders if she ever goes inside.

'Hi.' Seeing her this close, he realises she's not as old as first appearances led him to believe. Late fifties is his new calculation.

'Just call me Molly. And you?' Her eyes narrow, squinting the sun, but her mouth curves up.

'I'm Jasper's new housemate, Tyler. Tyler McClain. My furniture should be here soon. I forgot to arrange for a key so I was just cleaning up a bit.' Tyler sweeps his hand in an arc behind him. 'I'm putting it all in here until Jasper gets home.'

Molly shuts her eyes. A long blink. 'Mr Lawrence keeps a spare key under the geranium. The pot on the left, there,' she says, pointing with a twisted finger. Then her face glows like a stoplight. 'I've seen him get it. He had to use it the other day. Must have forgotten his keys.'

God, Jasper was right, Tyler thinks. She *is* nosy. But he's glad all the same.

After he retrieves the key he looks back and sees Molly hasn't moved. She's still standing at the fence. 'I'd help you unpack,' she says. 'But I can't lift anything heavy, I'm afraid. Rheumatoid arthritis, you know.' She holds up her hands in proof. Tyler wonders how she manages to do the garden. It's a flourishing tribute of azaleas, rhododendrons and laurustinus. Plus lots of other plants way beyond *his* horticulture.

'Thanks,' he says, holding the key aloft. But still she doesn't move.

'My husband will be home soon. He's just gone down the street to get the paper. He'll give you a hand.' She brushes away a fly and looks down the road. 'Oh, here he comes now.'

Tyler sees a stocky man of about the same vintage as Molly. He's carrying a newspaper and a green shopping bag. At the same time a large truck pulls into the kerb. A man dressed in blue shorts and matching tank-top jumps down.

He must be freezing, Tyler thinks. Then he remembers lots of truckies are fizzed up on drugs to keep them afloat on their schedule. He wouldn't be feeling the cold.

'Furniture delivery for a Mr McClain?'

Tyler nods. The man holds out a digital pad and hands Tyler a stick-like marker. 'Just sign here.' The sun is in Tyler's eyes but he makes a scrawl on the screen which he hopes looks like his signature.

'Could do with a hand, mate,' the man says, taking back his stick-pen.

When Tyler turns around he almost trips over Mr and Mrs Molly, who are standing behind him. He sees that Mr Molly is no longer carrying his shopping bag. Gee, thinks Tyler, for older people they sure move fast.

They both have that bursting-to-help-in-a-crisis, expectant look of volunteers.

An hour later, everything is unloaded into Jasper's house. The deliveryman declines Tyler's offer of a drink, but Molly and her husband, whose name, he's learned in the course of moving, is Max, agree with sugar-on-top.

Max picks up his drink and dunks a ginger-nut biscuit, then cradles it up to his mouth. 'So, Tyler, how long have you been teaching?'

Molly butts in: 'Hell, Max, he doesn't want to talk about his work. Do you, Ty?'

Tyler rubs his temple. 'No, that's okay. Just over eight years.'

'Well, that would make you around... let's see...' Molly taps her fingers. 'Finished school at eighteen... Four years for training...'

Tyler puts Molly out of her mathematical dilemma. 'I'm thirty-one,' he says. 'I deferred a year.'

'About the same age as our youngest daughter, Amy,' says Molly, smiling.

Max grabs Molly's arm and shakes it lightly. 'Now, Moll, don't you be thinking of matchmaking.'

This seems to have an instant effect on Molly, who suddenly declares they must be going. She has things to do. Her eyes are lit up like an evangelist's.

Tyler feels himself frowning as he sees them to the door, but he's soon engrossed in unpacking. He makes an attempt to meld his possessions to Jasper's without it looking as if he's trying to take over his house, but fails.

Jasper hasn't always been this neat, he thinks. But then Jasper doesn't appear to have much stuff. An old settee of dog-coat brown. An ancient desk with a green leather top and drawers down both sides. An outdated TV attached to a huge set-top box. Only the computer is new.

Jasper is furious when he learns about his neighbours' Good Samaritan act.

'Bloody hell, Ty. I have been keeping those two, well especially Molly, at arm's length for two years and then you're here two seconds and you're playing bloody tea-parties with them.'

'Well, Jas, they did help me move. My fridge and my bed are bastards of things to shift. It took the three of us and then we needed Moll to open the door.'

'Oh, *Moll,* is it now?' Jasper pulls a sarcastic face and then sighs. 'Just don't get too close to them, okay, Ty? You know what I've got out there.' He motions with a grim-reaper finger in the direction of the shed.

Tyler wakes the next morning with a cold worse than a hangover. He's glad that he's not rostered to work until next week. At lunchtime he gets up to make himself some coffee and finds that the electricity has gone on strike. He wonders if he should check the *enterprise* and looks out through the net curtains of the kitchen window. The weather has warmed and the shed shimmers beneath its greenery like a huge radiator.

Then he sees her. At first he's not sure if it's Molly but she seems to sense his presence and looks in his direction. He's pretty sure she can't see him and knows for certain that he's right, when she brings out a key from the front pocket of her apron and heads towards the shed. Galvanised into action, he rushes out of the house and calls her name.

'Oh, shit!' she says, turning to face him. Her hand has already turned the lock and she stands halfway in the door, he can see the greenery like jungle in the background.

Her face screws up like she has just been punched. Then she shrugs and hands Tyler the keys. 'Can we talk?'

'I think we need to, but not here.' Tyler turns around and Molly follows him into the kitchen.

He puts on the kettle and gets out two cups. 'Start talking,' he says.

'Well, you know how I've got this rheumatoid arthritis, well it's damn painful I can tell you.'

'Moll, cut to the chase. I'm feeling pretty crook myself. I've got the flu. I don't really need this. I trusted you and unless you can come up with...'

'What?' says Molly, her mouth twisting a little smile. 'You'll go to the police? I'm sorry, Ty. But I can explain.' She pulls out a chair. 'Here, you sit down. I'll make the tea.' She goes over to one of the cupboards and pulls out some biscuits.

'How did you know where they...?' Tyler shakes his head, nothing surprises him anymore.

Molly ignores the half question, pours the tea and opens the biscuit packet with her teeth.

'I knew something funny was going on not long after Jasper... er... Mr Lawrence, moved in. I'm not an idiot and I do know about gardening. All that stuff being taken into his shed, wiring, tubing, lights. Then those seedlings that look like tomato plants.'

'How...?'

This time she answers the unasked but has the grace to colour up. 'I have this little hole in my back fence. A knot hole.' Her hand pauses above the sugar basin. Tyler sees the spoon is steady. 'How many?'

He holds up two fingers. Doesn't trust his voice.

'Anyway, I thought, great. Just what I needed. I had been reading on the net that marijuana reduces inflammation. And I know it helps with pain.'

Tyler feels the cool air on his tongue and realises his mouth has dropped open.

Molly stares at him, her eyes as sharp as the edge of a knife. 'Don't look so surprised, Tyler. My generation invented non-conformity. Everyone smoked pot. A bit different now though. Stuff's more potent.'

She stirs their teas and glances at Tyler once more.

'So,' she says, 'I waited six months and then, when Jasper was at work. I broke in. Well... er... I mean I borrowed the key from under the geranium. It wasn't hard to find the one to the shed. I'd seen him

191

open it enough. Uses the bunch with the key-ring marked World's Best Dad. Couldn't miss that. It was hanging in the kitchen, behind the door.' Molly chuckles and takes a long sip of her tea cooling it through tight lips. 'Then, I got my own keys cut.'

'These ones,' says Tyler, holding up the two keys he had taken from her earlier.

Molly laughs again. 'You know, Ty, that key-ring of Jasper's reminds me of when Max and I were not long married. We went to lots of parties back then... When you got to the venue everyone put their car-keys in a bowl and at the end of the evening you were supposed to draw out someone else's. Then you swapped partners with them. They didn't call it the Swinging Sixties for nothing. But I had this key-ring with a bell in a silver chamber. Max wasn't game to grab anyone else's. He couldn't miss it by its size and the fact that it jingled.' Molly starts to shake and her sides heave.

Then she straightens up. 'Not that I'm a prude, though. Everyone has their pet fets.'

'Pet...whats?'

'Pet fetishes. I won't go into mine but it involves a certain fruit.'

Tyler laughs. 'Too much information, Moll.' But he feels lightness like a spray of sea-air. Perhaps he's normal after all. He makes a mental note to ask Molly more about her daughter.

'Anyway, getting back to the marijuana. I've only been taking little amounts so Jasper wouldn't notice.' Molly rubs her hands. 'It's been such a relief. I've been able to garden all day without stopping. No pain at night either.'

'Why didn't you just buy it off him?' Tyler says. He gets up and takes their cups to the sink.

Molly rolls her eyes. 'You really are a typical teacher, no idea about the real world.'

Tyler's voice rises. 'Hell, hang onto your insults, that's a bit harsh. I'm not the one here stealing pot.'

'Yeah, sorry. Actually I think teachers are doing it tough lately. My daughter Amy's a teacher so I know what it's like. I've told her about you, by the way,' says Molly, winking. Then she gets back on track. 'But, Ty, you're the one living with someone who's growing and dealing.' Her face softens. 'Seriously though, have you considered this? As pensioners we can hardly afford decent bloody toilet paper. There's not much money for other luxuries. I'm a member of this online arthritis help group. Hundreds of others in my situation. I'd love to be able to help them. But what can I do? If we could, Max and I would set up our own... what do you two call it? Enterprise?'

Tyler widens his eyes but doesn't answer. Then he knits his brows, feels the thumping of a headache tattooing his brain.

He slumps back in his chair. 'Leave it with me, Molly. I think I may have an idea, but I feel too crook to try and explain it at the moment. And I need to talk to Jasper.'

'Okay, you have to do what you have to do, I suppose.' Molly puts on a resigned face. Then she motions to the shed and mouths, 'Can I?'

Tyler half shrugs. 'Why not,' he says, and tosses her the keys.

When Jasper comes home late that evening, Tyler catches him at the door. 'I've got something I need to discuss with you, tonight, Jas, if we can?'

'I don't feel much like talking at the moment, Ty. Can it wait until morning? You don't mind, do you? Bloody teachers' meeting went on forever.'

'Suits me,' Tyler says, 'but I do want in on it now, Jas. And it looks like I might have those extra contacts that you need. But it all depends on you.' He sits down at the computer, rubs his chin, and casts a narrowed eyed look at Jasper. 'How'd you feel about doing a cut rate price for pensioners?'

Red Fox Rampant

Little Episodes Publishing - Florida USA

Damien Rouge is having his fifteen minutes of fame posthumously.

Hanging up in a tree like a primate.

The TV cameras are discreet, showing only the aesthetically acceptable aftermath of the plane crash, the squeamish stomachs of the six o'clock set have to digest their dinners after all.

I recognise Damien immediately from his ponytail dreadlock and distinctive tattoo; a red fox rampant.

I remember that because I was the one who did it for him, thirty years ago.

Do the tat up high will you Marcie. I need to be able to cover it when I go for interviews.

Damien's leg is cocked back, dog like, an angle denoting dislocation and fracture, held together by army pants, the type with reinforced utility pockets. Only God knows what they hold now.

I wonder if I should call my son. I wonder what I would say.

Hey Matt, your father, you know the one you've never seen? He's on telly. Yes, now. On the news.

It gives a whole new meaning to a public viewing.

I decide not to. It is better he remembers his father from the faded photo he left me.

Standing over a fresh kill, arm outstretched, fingers pointing to the lethal tusks of a huge boar. Mouth set in similar countenance.

Damien, the big game hunter.

Shit, Marcie, I thought you were taking something. I mean you did say you were on the pill. I don't want no screaming brat. Get rid of it.

I had been taking contraceptives, but what did I know? I'd had too much to drink, thrown up one day and missed a dose. And I was seventeen and fertile as the plains.

Hey, Marcie, one of the guys at work said if you run for an hour and then have a hot bath that will bring on your period.

I trusted him. He was twenty-seven years old and knew the world.

But nothing happened. My period was as stopped as its namesake.

I told Matt about his father the day he turned ten, not long after he learned about the facts of life. I figured he would understand it better then. Understand that the dad he'd known for the last eight years of his life was not his biological one.

All it did was to add fuel to fire, over the recent divorce.

Really, nothing I could do back then was right.

As the years passed he grew curious. Matt began to search, I began to search, his grandmother, who lives in the same city where I'd last seen his father, began to search.

We came up with names and addresses. But nothing matched.

Damien Rouge was as unlisted as his phone number.

Kids should be put in a sound proof room and hosed down once a week. And not taken out until they are fifteen and more interesting.

195

I laughed when Damien said this. It was pre-pregnancy and seemed funny.

I realise now how much he hadn't wanted kids. He was far too busy being one.

The plane crash has happened in France, the voice over sounds so nice, dulcet tones of French with lines of hysteria. You know, the sort the media manufacture. It sounds the same in every language.

The subtitles declare it the worst aviation disaster in twenty years. No survivors.

I remember the old joke: *If a plane crashes on a hill and one part falls to the North and the other part to the South, where do they bury the survivors?*

They don't of course, I answer myself, bury the survivors.

But *I* have been buried for years.

The camera pans back to Damien. His seat from the plane is still partly wedged in the fork of a tree, an oak I think: Quercus Robur.

His seat belt has worked, he is still strapped in.

He swings around and I am treated to a brief glimpse of his face, eyes squeezed shut as if peering into a letter box or just waking up. A brief mockery from the afterlife.

Look Marcie, you have found me but I still ain't going to acknowledge your bastard son.

His face reminds me of the death mask photo of Manfred Von Richthoven - the Red Baron. But this is no tri-plane.

Pieces of the aircraft are scattered widely over a landscape littered with clothes and body parts. I notice a water bottle and marvel at its completeness. It is still holding water.

Damien hated flying. I love it.

I remember the first time I went up about ten years ago.

Smiling like a child I gripped the hand rests and let the G forces push me down further into the seat as the plane jetted along the runway, faster and faster until we were airborne.

I wonder how I will find flying now.

I'd met Damien just before my seventeenth birthday, at the place where I worked, Body Artz.

Over six foot four, he stooped slightly to fit through the door. His presence filled the shop.

I had just finishing piercing some kid's ears and was telling the mother about the aftercare.

He waited until I was finished.

"Hi... Look... Marcie," he said, placing my nametag straight. "I'm after having a tattoo done."

He opened the portfolio he was carrying and unclipped a drawing. It was a picture of a red fox rearing. I didn't think it a probable pose. But the customer is always right.

And this one was brave. He didn't even wince as I dipped and pricked.

But sweat beaded like thaw and his voice was tight when he spoke.

"I didn't want none of that catalogue stuff. Bloody skulls entwined with snakes and I love mother. Bugger that. I got this friend who draws. I always wanted to have a fox done *una-cow-to-me-name.*"

I remember thinking he'd not seen what was available lately. But I was so mesmerised that I only managed to squeak "*Why, on account of your name?*"

"My last name is Rouge. That's French for Red." He moved in his seat, shuffling up his large frame to match his importance.

It was lucky I was not injecting, I would have blurred something.

"And I play rugby. They call me the fox, cause of me moves." A wink gave affirmation that rugby wasn't the only game he was talking about.

When I finished I wiped the bloody surface with some gauze. I wasn't wearing gloves. There was no such thing as Aids in the seventies.

He took my hand before I could drop the swab and I felt his fingers rubbing above my knuckle, acknowledging the bareness of my ring finger.

"So how about it, Mar-cie?" The way he drawls it out makes it *merci*. The only French I know apart from *oui*. Which is what I say.

"*What?*" he says, raising slivers of doubt. But youth and naivety win. And I answer yes to his please.

The news clip is going on and on. Now it's live – adding to the surrealism. Here I sit in my kitchen, watching my first lover, the father of my only child, the man whom I have not seen for over thirty years. Live. Except he is dead.

The paradox screams silent from the word beamed across the screen ad-infinitum.

I remember our first date - the beach at night, sand hills draped in silent purple, with *Imagine* playing on the radio.

I squeeze Damien's hand along with the words "...and no religion too."

"That's what I reckon, Marce. Religion is for bloody idiots! Opium of the masses."

Isn't it opiate? But I'm not sure.

Damien is never unsure. He has travelled abroad. And had amazing adventures. I sit entranced in the same way I listen when my dad recounts his escapades from World War Two. It is the only time my father gives me any attention. Attention that is positive. Now Damien fills the gap.

Osmosis like, his truth becomes my own until it is 'Opium' and how could I have been so stupid.

I ain't paying for no fucken kid I don't fucken want! You can't prove it's mine. If you keep it Marcie, you're on your own.

I am screaming and thumping the steel cabinet beside my hospital bed in time with the contractions. A nurse goes past then snatches back a step. She stands in the doorway and tells me to grow up. Childbirth is natural.

I think of that first night, of religion and opium and suddenly wish for both.

The only thing Damien didn't lie about is the fact he was French. He was born there. His father signed the birth certificate before he did a runner. One trait Damien had inherited.

His mother had skittered back to Australia, a reformed repatriate.

Finally the news is over. I switch off the TV and sit staring; the blankness of the screen reflects my mind.

Everything seems back to normal but nothing will be the same.

A brief knock to herald his appearance and my son enters the room. His cheery hello tells me he hasn't seen the news. I sit with the secret behind my eyes merging with his handsome face. Matt is so like his father. But in appearance only. And soon he will look nothing like him. I shiver despite the summer evening.

"Someone walked over your grave, Mum?' he says, unaware of how close he has stepped to the truth.

I smile and shake my head, a brief half turn. I hear his footsteps in the sitting room and a cork popped from a bottle.

"Want a drink? Sorry it's been awhile since I've called. But I've got some good news. Something to celebrate."

Matt's voice quavers slightly but I doubt that his news will counterbalance mine.

He comes back to the kitchen and hands me a glass. We clink the silence from the room.

"I've found my father," he says, and continues without halting from my shock. "Remember the phone call that Gran made when the woman sounded funny and hung up on her? Well, it turns out she was his wife. They were divorced last month and it was her way to get even. Giving me her husband's number."

My son gets up and hugs me, "It's okay, Mum, he didn't mind. I met him over the weekend. I was lucky. He is travelling to France today. He said he wanted to be back in the place he was born, wanted to die there. I told him I only wanted to meet him, nothing else, no strings." I see the stamp of completeness in his eyes.

I hold up my glass. "To Damien and Matt."

There is nothing left to say. They both already have their wish.

Covering the Moon
Fast Forward Press - USA

In the distance we hear a noise like tapping. I stop some feet short of the entrance to the graveyard, my brother Ben snuggled up on my back, his head buried in my parka hood.

"Look Ben," I say, "it's not the dead you have to be scared of."

Our mother tells us this all the time. We live close to the cemetery, actually only a glance away through our front door. Not that we knew instinctively to be frightened, but our friends soon let us know that it wasn't a normal thing. Aren't you afraid the ghosts will get you? How can you sleep? Stuff like that. But it's not the dead that do bad things. It's the living. Like Dad, he left us soon after Ben was born. And Ben, well he was a rape baby. Everyone knows this, even Ben, although he doesn't know what it means. And even though everyone always says, "Poor Mrs Anderson", that's our mother, I always think: Poor Ben. It's a lot worse for him.

Yeah, the dead can't hurt you, but that doesn't stop us from being scared.

We have done this: visit the graveyard at midnight on every Friday the 13th since Ben turned three. It was a dare set up by my friend Anica. After the first time she chickened out, but we kept it up like a tradition. This is our fourth year. I'm eleven now and Ben is seven but it's a good thing he's such a scrawny kid, he doesn't weigh much. I guess the rapist must have been a small guy 'cause our

201

mother is nearly five foot eleven and built like a rugby player. Sometimes I wonder how he managed it. There's this Australian spider called an Orb weaver. She's so much bigger than her mate who shares her web that he has to be very careful when mating. I think maybe the rapist would've had to be careful with Mum. I've seen her temper and how hard she uses the strap, especially on Ben, when she's been drinking. But maybe the rapist had a knife or a gun. Mum's never told me the details, and you can't ask about things like that, can you? I mean I'm not supposed to know, but my cousin, Daniela, heard her mum, my aunty, telling a neighbour. Daniela told me and then Ben heard me telling Anica. But we all haven't told Mum we know.

The tapping noise is getting louder. It sounds like someone with high heels but the paths are all gravel and sand so that can't be right. I don't know if it's coming closer to us, or if we are moving closer to it. The dare is to reach the middle, where the little buildings are. The mini-mansions I call them. They glow sort of in the night but I can't see that yet, we're still a way away.

I jump at Ben's voice, muffled by my parka. "I gotta pee, Sis. Now."

I lower him down and he goes behind a bush, even though we can't see anyone and the tapping is still ahead of us.

When he comes out he offers me his hand, which I take with outstretched fingers until I'm sure it's dry. Then we both walk on in silence. The tapping noise seems to be coming from where we are heading. But I still can't see the mini-mansions.

Ben pulls on my hand. "Sis," he says, "what does a rape baby look like?"

My mind can't find the words to answer him straight away. So he tugs at my hand again, almost pulling me sideways.

Up ahead is an angel statue, I've never seen her before, she's sitting in the centre of a huge plot divided into four, two at the front and two at the back. She looks like she's about to take off. For a moment I wish I could fly away too.

There's an iron seat across the path from her. I lead Ben across to it and sit down. He brushes leaves off the seat. He really is a tidy kid, especially for a boy. I have no idea where we are. Which way is home.

I'm gathering my thoughts like someone rounding up sparrows. They keep scattering.

"Well Ben," I say, "a rape baby isn't the baby's fault. It's still a baby, like any other."

I can feel Ben's eyes on me, staring, and when a cloud passes and the moon and stars light up his face, I see he's been crying.

"Oh, Ben, you're not *that* scared are you?"

Ben shakes his head and looks at the angel. "It's just that Jack said rape is a bad thing and that I was a bad thing, and that's why Mum hates me. And I was wondering, Sis... Will I go to hell?"

I can't answer him this time. The trouble is I don't know exactly how rape works. I know Jack is right, it's something bad and I know that it's something to do with mating. And also the girl doesn't want it. But does that mean the roosters are raping the hens? I see that all the time, the hens running away and the roosters jumping on them and pushing them into the dust. The hens certainly don't want it. The baby chickens are cute though.

Ben is sucking his thumb and leaning against me. Me and him against the odds.

I realise I can't hear the tapping anymore and I wonder when it actually stopped, how I missed the moment. I look around, back the way we came, and at the way I think we should be going. I don't know if I can find the strength to carry Ben much further.

The clouds are covering the moon again. I didn't think it was possible to get lost in a place we are both so familiar with. But everything looks so different in the dark.

Empty House

It sits still
on its hill of discontent
of abandoned lovers
Sitting room
with standing only

Outside gold-broom
sweeps the windows grime
and perfumed honey eaters
all things relative
silently scavenge

Tall walls marked
with rivulets
where
the roller stalled
on its way to the top
or from brushes
where momentarily
people forgot to care

Mortar and stone
always hard to warm

winner in UK's Global poetry competition

Opportunity to Knock

published as 'Small Town Murder' in That's Life Fast Fiction AUS. commended in The Rolf Boldrewood Award

I saw the child's abandoned bike long before the girl was reported missing.

There was nothing extraordinary about it. A pink bike carelessly thrown down mid pedal, by the way it was lying.

Kids have no respect for things, I remember thinking as I cycled past.

I should have taken more notice; they may have found her little body earlier and got onto the killer's trail before it cooled. But like I told the police, the bike didn't look abandoned, just waiting. It was on its side, one wheel twisted back, facing the pine break where I assumed the child had gone for a walk. The forest floor had recently been churned to waved ridges by log trucks and machinery for pine thinning. There was no way you could have ridden a bike in there.

I never believed it was a local who was responsible. And I was right.

My town boasts marginally more than one horse and it's a great place to bring up kids. Murders happen in different ways - premeditated or not, and opportunistic. I was talking to my friend Bobby about this several months later, after the killer was caught.

'That's it, Bobby,' I said. 'The murderer was passing by, saw the child, saw the pines, and took the opportunity to knock.'

'Yeah, Angie, but...'

Bobby always started his arguments in the same way. This day I was ready with a comeback.

Bobby and I had proven you could have a platonic friendship which didn't lead to sex or break-up. We had been mates all our lives.

He was a tiny kid. On our first day at kindergarten I carried him around on my back. (No way could I do that now- he was 6ft 3 and built to size.) We travelled together on the school bus, and sat at the back, and threw boogers at the other kids. Had swimming lessons and excelled in Drama. We were both hams.

He married my best friend, Sarah. I'm godmother to his kids, we are that close.

Now we even work together, at the town's only grocery store, where prices are marked up to a point which counter-balances desirability with necessity. Our town is 50km from the nearest supermarket.

Our boss is great, mainly because he isn't here a lot of the time and when he is, he's usually non-compos. He drinks most of the profits, giving a whole new meaning to liquid assets; I guess he's lucky business hasn't yet dried up.

This day was quiet, the Show was on in the city and lots of folks had gone, some for entertainment and some to enter their preserves, cakes, or flowers, or even the odd pig or two.

I'd made us a cup of coffee and had pilfered some donuts from the cake cabinet. For justification I'd argued they were past their use by date.

I sat there waiting for Bobby to collect his thoughts and scraped some of the pink icing from my donut, at the same time noticing my nails needed doing.

I'm a woman, I can multi-task.

He took a sip of his coffee, building suspense, before continuing.

It was hard to take him seriously with a cappuccino-froth moustache.

'But...the police didn't confirm that, Angie. The guy could have been stalking Cassie for all you know.'

It turned out we all knew the kid which, given the population, wasn't all that surprising.

'Well,' I said, 'no one had seen a stranger in town. And not many get past Queenie.'

Queenie was the postmistress, dubbed this because she was the Queen of all gossip. Having talked with others from small towns I think it's generic to the profession, that and reading their mail.

Bobby looked pensive, on the edge of giving in or starting anew.

I cut short his indecision with a poser: 'Do you think there's such a thing as the perfect murder?'

I knew he wouldn't answer straight away. I had plenty of time to drink my coffee. I thought about Queenie.

The thing I hated most about her and the Post Office was not the lack of postage privacy, but her collection.

I mean, a lot of us collect things, but hers were cherubs, the really cutesy twee sort, *and* she had them on display. Also, it seemed, whenever you went there to get your mail she'd bought a new one.

'Angie, look who's just arrived this morning. Miraculous Miranda. Isn't she gorgeous? I had to order her in. Limited edition, don't you know. I can't tell you what she cost.'

About flying babies, I reckon they could be dangerous, or at least a health hazard. I've never seen a cherub in a nappy. Just imagine the fallout! And they all look asexual to me.

I really found it hard to get excited, even for civility's sake.

Miranda was suspended on high –above the counter- by a golden cord. She had a golden halo, and carried a matching harp. The schmaltz was nauseating.

The trouble was Queenie wouldn't get your mail until you had made some comment. And I hate lying.

I must have been making a face because Bobby suddenly intruded on my reverie.

207

'What's up with you? Is that donut off? That's why they have use by dates, you know.'

He dragged his donut over, to slide it into the bin.

I tried to stop him and accidentally squashed it onto the counter. I let him carry through with his action. I knew what had been on there.

'Yeah,' I said, effectively cancelling the validity of my last thought about not lying.

'I don't think there could be,' Bobby said. 'A perfect murder I mean. I don't think there has ever been one. Only crooks getting away with it. That's different.'

I slumped forward onto the counter, careful to avoid the smear of icing. Bobby was off on a tangent, and when that happened all you could do was listen.

Sometime later as he drew breath, I cut in: 'I think I could come up with one.'

His breath caught in his throat like he'd been choked. 'Really?'

'Well, what's the main thing police always look for after a murder?'

'A motive?'

'Motives are overrated. I've read that some people get bumped off by those closest to them when they can no longer bear their annoying habits. No, before that?'

'I don't know, Angie.' The heat and lateness of the day were showing.

'The murder weapon! It tells a lot. You know, like finger prints or DNA. Not to mention its place of origin.'

'You really *have* thought about this.' Bobby looked a little incredulous before continuing, 'And you're right. If they can trace where the crim bought the weapon they might be able to find his identity.'

'So, it follows, if it can be eliminated you'll have the advantage.'

'Lots of murderers successfully get rid of their weapons.'

'Yeah, but if we're talking about the perfect murder, Bobby, there should be no way of finding them.'

'You mean come up with the perfect weapon? What about the hands? With gloves of course.'

'No good. You can't get rid of hands and they leave marks on the neck or wherever.'

At that moment a customer entered and walked to the back aisle. He came back with rat poison. I wasn't game to look at Bobby. And there was no way I could serve the guy. After he left, we both collapsed laughing. I know... we don't have much of a life.

When we finally calmed down, Bobby said. 'What about poison?' Then he quickly answered himself. 'Oh hang on, that can be traced.'

I looked him in the eye. 'There are some poisons which give symptoms mimicking other illnesses, like anaemia. Thallium has no taste or smell and leaves no detectable trace. It has to be used over a long time though, to be effective, and once again it can be tracked to its point of purchase.'

'So, Angie, by your definition not perfect.' His look held exasperation that quickly morphed to smugness. 'So, what would be the perfect weapon? There probably isn't anything.'

'Oh there is something all right. Something which self destructs but causes no damage. And the only residue it leaves is as harmless as air.'

I went out riding early the next day. A morning breeze with its promise of spring whispered warm on my face. The forest trees were dusted with pine pollen icing, and hazy yellow fog muted the horizon. A crow's maudlin cry echoed in the distance, and, before I could counteract, routine had me passing the place where Cassie's bike had been found.

I had deliberately avoided taking this familiar route before, because of the memories.

I knew the child well. She had been a friend of one of Bobby's kids. She used to come into the store all the time. A happy kid, hair like golden floss, and a zest for life which comes from the freedom of carefree country living. I didn't want to think of how Cassie died. Didn't want to remember her like that. But now my eyes were magnetically drawn to the spot.

Bunches of flowers were fading there.

Cassie's family had left soon after her murderer was caught. The memories and guilt were too raw to be constantly cut afresh by the nearness and familiarity of her haunts. There was the school she attended. Here was the hill slope where they had taught her to ride her bike. There was the tiny church where she had been baptized.

The murderer would get life. The family had lost theirs.

And yet here I was contemplating the perfect murder. I felt like some kind of monster.

But then, there were those who deserved to die and those who did not.

Really, it was that simple.

Sunday, I did what I had to do and went to bed early, wanting the morning to come quickly. I was like a kid before the holidays. I deliberately didn't watch TV. I wanted to keep my mind fresh.

The store was strangely silent that morning. And Bobby was late, which was not like him. There seemed to be fewer customers too. Just as well, given that I was on my own.

Bobby came in, an hour late, red in the face, and out of breath. He looked like I felt.

'Angie, there's been another murder... Queenie...'

'What about her?' I said dryly.

'No, you don't understand. Queenie, she was the one who was killed. Nigel found her when he delivered the newspapers to the Post Office this morning.'

My first thought was of poor Nigel, he was the quiet reserved type.

'Don't you want to know how she died?'

I nodded as I straightened the till.

'A blow to the head with a blunt object. And there is no sign of the murder weapon.'

Bobby looked at me strangely, I could see it peripherally. Suddenly I didn't feel like explaining anything. He certainly knew how to take the fun out of a day.

'I guess this means we won't be able to pick up our mail until later, then.'

I heard Bobby's shock intake of breath but really there was nothing else I could think of to say.

The Post Office was still cordoned off when I drove past it on my way home. There was a police car parked outside. I decided to stop.

I knocked on the locked door. The bell attached behind tinkled a muted rattle. It sounded so familiar I almost expected Queenie to arrive, grumping about how some people didn't come until after closing hours. Extra profit still ensured her opening for you though.

The officer let me in. She was the same one who'd interviewed me when Cassie was found.

'Well, Miss Airedale. Angela isn't it?' She extended her hand. Then remembered she still had hold of her pencil. She put it back in her pocket, alongside a small notebook 'Sorry.'

'That's okay, Detective Starrick.' I sat down in the chair reserved for the oldies. I remembered seeing poor old Elsie Spicer sitting here last week, patiently waiting while Queenie raved on and on about her latest acquisition.

'I suppose you've heard what happened?' Detective Starrick had grown up in a small town too.

'Yes, I have. It's terrible.'

All I kept thinking was I wouldn't have to look at all those damn cherubs anymore. The relief was as agreeable as a solid night's sleep.

'So why are you here?' Starrick's look held a mixture of exhaustion edged with hope. I guessed she'd had a long day.

'I'm not sure,' I answered honestly. 'I thought you might have a question I may be able to answer?'

'Like...?' I could see impatience beginning to resurface.

'Well, I rode past here on my bike yesterday.'

'And?'

'There was a van parked across the road.'

Detective Starrick nodded, and I continued. 'It wasn't a local.'

The detective resignedly retrieved her notepad.

I asked her where Queenie was found.

She indicated in the direction with her pencil. I got up and took a quick peak.

Of course the body was gone. But a large outline was painted there. Queenie was a very stout woman. And I'm being kind.

I also saw something else. Something which would have made me laugh out loud had the circumstance been different.

I wondered if I should tell Detective Starrick.

I wondered if she would figure it out herself. In a way I actually hoped she would.

Bobby had to go to Queenie's funeral. Apparently he was a nephew, twice removed or something. It didn't surprise me. A lot of us were related.

He came back to the store very subdued.

'What was it like?' It was a silly question and I didn't really want to know.

'Everyone was there,' Bobby said expansively, ignoring the fact I hadn't been. 'I didn't stay for the wake, Angie. I thought about you, here by yourself.'

'That's okay, Bobby, like you said everyone was there. I've only had one customer all afternoon.'

I wondered if it would be a good time to tell him about the perfect weapon. Really, I had been aching to tell him for almost a week now. It would never be a good time.

He took the decision from my mind.

'Angie...? You didn't have anything to do with it, did you?' Words ran from his mouth and stumbled to justify themselves. 'I mean...

you never liked Queenie... And you were talking about...' He stopped mid sentence, obviously fathoming the possibility.

He looked at me helplessly. I frowned as best I could. I'd had Botox the month before so it wasn't much of a deterrent.

'That's ok, Bobby,' I said, plucking him from his misery.

Then, tossing him back just as quickly, I added in dark tones: 'There is a perfect weapon, you know, like the one I said about. One that self destructs.'

His face became a blank page and almost as white.

Momentarily, I held the suspense before relenting, 'Bobby, it's ice! You can knock someone over the head with a block of it. And then it will melt away to nothing. I mean you could even drink the evidence if you wanted.'

Bobby looked slightly ill. Then he said softly: 'Is that what you did to Queenie?' He still sounded to be in a state of disbelief.

When I started laughing I honestly couldn't stop. You know how it goes. You keep seeing a picture in your head and the ludicrousness of it keeps it on replay.

I know it wasn't funny. A woman had died. But rationality does not enter into it when you get like this. After a time I stopped laughing, and tried to look serious; I was glad of the Botox then.

'Bobby, how long have you known me?' I talked fast, overlaying any answer he may have given. 'You must know I wouldn't be capable of anything like that? Surely?'

I was on the verge of hilarity again. I swallowed heavily and continued. Shock had rendered him mute so I had no competition.

After I had explained what had happened I saw his face crease into a grin.

'So you're telling me you think Queenie was killed by one of her cherubs?'

'Exactly. When I was at the Post Office with Detective Starrick, I looked up to where Miranda had been hanging. It was directly above where Queenie always stood. When I noticed the cherub was no longer there I naturally looked to the floor. You know, at first I dismissed it. After all, surely the police would have found it near the body. I thought for a second maybe Queenie might have moved it before she was killed.'

'Wouldn't it have smashed?'

'This one was different from her others, Bobby, it was made from a type of unbreakable china. She'd told me she'd had it on order for ages.'

'So, Angie, how come they didn't find it? I mean, it didn't fly off did it?' I knew then Bobby was feeling better. It was the sort of humour he was famous for.

'Miranda had dropped from the ceiling. When I saw where she was, I realised she must have bounced off Queenie's head.' I stifled a giggle. 'And then landed on the shelf. Her real-feathered wings would have cushioned her fall and prevented a rebound. She was lying on her back, legs in the air, and her elastic golden cord was shrivelled, umbilical like, but with the ceiling hook still attached. There's no way Queenie would have displayed her like this. I guess because of all the others the police didn't notice.'

'Sort of... sort... of... revenge of the cherubs.' Bobby's words were punctuated with snorts. He could see the rerun too.

As I said to Bobby later, it proved my point that the perfect weapon can often masquerade as something quite harmless.

Poor Queenie. I did feel sorry for her, I did, honestly.

First Flight

We float upon sea-air
miles stand beneath us
wings spread out
over nothing
while clouds run in teams
of streaky grey horses

I sit wide-eyed
my first flight bumps
beneath my feet
while you, white-knuckled
from many an intrepid flight
and two emergency landings
watch the Asian hostess
temple her hands
long sarong
drapes her fears
in prayers

when engines grumble and fade
as the plane rises
above the turbulence
I see the colour drain back
to your face

as fast as a dissipated dream

Unfasten your seat belts, says the pilot
his voice almost
as detached as this winged ship
we meet our differences, anchor hands
fingers entwine in truce
against any gravity heavier than air

published in Red River Review - Texas USA

Generations Lost

"Darkness cannot drive out darkness; only light can do that."
Martin Luther King Jr

The government of the day took
those words
it seemed
in literal sense
choose the half caste state,
the lighter ones,
they said
they will assimilate

They came
and then
we scattered
like hens
in their fowl yard
but never running fast enough
to beat them
to us

Our Dreaming
those things
best forgotten

they said
white religion
much better than darkness
they said
but I am lost now
in the lightness of my skin and
all the forgotten languages

'First Refuge' - Meusepress AUS

Dust to Water

winner Ballarat short story competition
published by Deakin University Press

The Great White Egret
scans the land locked lake and waits

I stand near the old pier, looking out over Lake Wendouree. There has been enough rain to make a difference - the lake is filling slowly and soon it will cover Edith Delaney's secret forever or for at least another lifetime. After all, the last time the lake dried up like this was in 1869 - fifty years before Edith was born.

My Aunt Beattie passed away early this year and she and Edith Delaney had been childhood friends, but I hadn't even known Edith existed until she phoned me soon after I posted the funeral notice. She couldn't make the service but when I told her I would be scattering Aunt Beattie's ashes on Lake Wendouree in several weeks time, she insisted on coming along. She'd heard about the Walk of a Lifetime event and how a safe path had been made across the lake. She agreed it would be a great time to carry out Beattie's last wish.

"We used to swim in the lake, you know, Andrea."

I lift my eyebrows. "Really?"

Edith takes a hanky from her sleeve and wipes her eyes.

"It was a lot cleaner then..." She surveys the 'Rocky Road' lake-scape around us. "I mean that was seventy years ago. *Everything* was cleaner then."

I smile and nod.

The lake-bed looks like Edith's face on a grand scale. Sunburned. Crosshatched dry from long years of drought. Crows' feet track the clotted mud, their owners with white wise eyes looking for easy pickings.

"Your Aunt Beattie was a great swimmer, lots better than I was." Edith's hand trembles as she replaces her handkerchief. "She could swim the length of the lake and stay underwater for ages. I could never do that. She would really scare me at times. I thought she had drowned."

Instantly I have an image of Edith pacing the lake's shore like a trapped animal. Sunlight gilds the ripples made by paddle steamers and bric-a-brac boats into knife edges of light. I hear the whistle sounds of the steamers and of people laughing.

The fecundity of youth.

I open my eyes to the present.

"Do you want to stop and have a rest before we start across, Edith?" The bus had been late and instead of waiting we had walked to the starting area.

I take her arm and lead her to the nearest bench.

"Everything changes doesn't it?' she says.

We aren't looking at each other, our eyes are following the lines of people meandering across the lake like errant ants.

I know what she means. As you get older mortality smacks you in the face with the number of people you have known who've died before their time. Before *your* time. Even those who die at ninety, like my Aunt Beattie, make you long for sameness or some sort of continuity.

She had lived a couple of blocks away and we'd been close all my life. I miss her terribly and it is only four weeks since she's been gone.

"Age is the great leveller, Andrea," she had once said. "Young people think we oldies were born old. But they find out. We all do." And then, laughing, she'd added "It's just a matter of time."

That's what I had loved most about her, her candidness. I guess that's why I was so surprised she hadn't told me about Edith Delaney.

We head out across the lake, people passing us quickly so those in front and those behind are never the same for more than a few moments.

"Did she ever marry, Andrea?"

I shake my head and look at the urn nestled in the crook of my arm. On my back I have a rucksack with bottles of water and a small foldaway stool just in case Edith needs another rest. It is two kilometres across and the going is not easy.

Edith stumbles on the soft turf and instinctively I grab her arm and hold her up.

"No one special then?" she says.

"No. She was in love with someone when she was young but she only told me his name. Eddie Montignac. And I only remember that because I asked her if the name was French. Montignac that is, not Eddie."

Edith breathes heavily; I stop, sling forward my rucksack, undo the zip and unfold the chair. With my bended elbow for support, Edith lowers herself onto it.

There is no break in the flow of people. We haven't reached the halfway point yet where a cameraman is taking photos. After that it is intermittent groups and stragglers.

I take the urn in both hands. Edith shakes her head. "No," she mouths, "not here." Her voice is barely a whisper and I am worried. I take out the water instead. Someone asks if everything is okay. My smile is twisted as I say yes.

"Let's head back."

221

Edith straightens. "No," she says, her voice much stronger. "I want to see it just one more time." She gets up from the stool and stands looking ahead.

"See what?"

She doesn't answer but keeps staring into the distance. I can see the other side more clearly now. Someone is handing out certificates. For no real reason I want one. A quote comes to mind; *Awards are like haemorrhoids, eventually every arsehole gets one.* Strangely I don't feel like laughing.

"Are you sure you'll be all right?" But already she is walking and by the time I pack away the stool and water bottles I have to run to catch up.

"You've been married, though Edith, haven't you? You said you had a daughter."

"Yes, she lives in Queensland. I go up every year to see her. Get away from the cold."

We pass a discarded sandal. We both glance at it. Post drought. Dropped there when the strap broke. No more use to its wearer. No historic worth. Funny how we value antique things but not antique people.

We reach the end. Stewards are giving out papers, they congratulate us. I look at Edith but she is not smiling. And I still have not done what I came for.

Irritation flickers a frown and Edith looks at me worriedly.

Now it is she who takes me by the arm and we stroll along the path until we are away from the throng.

"I want to show you something." The sun glances her face, smoothing the lines with light or perhaps the brightness blinds me as just for a moment she looks young.

"I know where Beattie would want to be. It's still here, I saw it the other day."

Now she strides ahead. She climbs down a small embankment. Willow trees encircle us. We can see no one through their low hanging branches.

"Be careful. The ground is slippery," I say as I skid down to join her.

She is pointing to a single pylon.

"The old pier. This is where your Aunt Beattie and I would go swimming. I was always too scared to put my head under water. I think that's why she was faster."

"Look." She points, grim reaper like. I follow the line of her thin finger and see, etched in the wood below the water line, a faint heart with initials. I move closer. "I never got to see it until the other day," she says. "Beattie scratched that there seventy years ago. Before I left for college. Before our friendship ended." Tears stream down her face. "The water kept it hidden. I mean it was unheard of in those days. Beattie was older than me. She was the one who ended it. I was only eighteen. And she knew I wanted to have children."

Edith slides forward; I grab for her and drop the urn. Some of Beattie's ashes mix with the small trickle of water flowing there. I pour out the rest and we watch as they float on the surface and swirl as gentle as a fingertip caress, around the bottom of the pylon.

"Edith...?"

"Some people call me Eddie," she says.

Hunting

His secret passion's within the bounds
which comes in leaps with hares and hounds
and horns a'blowing and stirrup cup
one sip of this is not enough

So to the hedges bogs and creeks
he rides his steed mid jeers and shrieks
For his fellow riders know as such
that his efforts never come to much

His secret passion a foxtail mounted
the only trophy for him that counted
the fact that it would never be
wasn't lost on they or he

For his horse it clips the top of fences
he's fallen off and lost his senses
he lags at back of field or less
never has he had success

And so for something else to do
he puts himself in Reynard's' shoe er... paw
who only wants to sleep and mate
and not have him to aggravate

And then he thinks of Foxy's den
of sleepy vixen and cubs within
and finds he really *can* relate
for he too, loves to sleep and mate

Man and fox are much the same
both are hunters
both are game
so part of him hopes all will fail
and Foxy gets to keep his tail!

Hospice Nurse

She sculptures tears
gathered from the curve of happiness
the crease of grief
the sharp points of loves lost
she rounds them smooth
wipes them away
but always she changes them
into something
more beautiful
the glint of hope
the grain of remembrance
the peace of acceptance
forever shared in her eyes
and shaped in this place of sometimes forgotten
souls.

Boston Literary Magazine - USA.
Nominated for a Pushcart prize

Wake Me At Five

published in Eclectic Flash

It's hard working on a production line. Mindless stuff. You start thinking, while the same object repeats itself in front of you ad nauseam, why did I go to school at all? I'd even got to tertiary level but my mates and their hotrods and independent living made any long term college dreams seem as distant and undesirable as nightmares.

My wife, Tanya, worked in a production line at a potato chip factory. Not the crispy packet sort, but the dinner table type, you know for workers feeding their kids on a budget. Meat and one veg. Sausage and chips. Cheap enough if you don't count the health cost.

She started in the days before noise control was understood. You were bloody soft if you wanted to wear earmuffs. The men at her factory would snigger at the mention of that word, earmuffs, and make the kind of crude jokes associated with blue collar workers. That sort of class. No class.

Not that I can talk. I was in construction, driving the commercial cement mixers. Big contracts and small, backyard and factory, the size of the job determined the size of the load. Or how many.

Tanya also worked shifts, graveyard mostly as there was more money in it and lack of education breeds the kind of desperation that makes you unworried about the toll it takes. What death knell it rings for marriage and body.

But she knew I loved her, didn't she? *Then why did she leave?* I've asked myself that so many times.

She was always on time. Early most times. It was a compulsion. She said to me once, 'Brady, it shows lack of respect if you're late for an appointment. Shows you don't care about the other person's time. That somehow your time is more important than theirs.' She was like that. Considerate. Punctuality was a huge deal to Tanya. Our daughters must have picked up on that too, both born on the day of their predicted births. No maternal leave but Tanya's mum came down from up north and stayed until the babies slept nights and then she disappeared back home to die a year later, when we had no funds or ability, to take any more time off work, for her funeral.

It got harder as the girls got older, but we made sure they didn't go without, although they say different now, like I guess most grown up children do. Not enough of our own time spent with them. Missed concerts and sports days, although I made the twilight ones.

Tanya never did, she worked double shifts and sometimes she wouldn't come home for two days running, taking lunches with her and buying her dinners at the factory canteen. Some husbands may have been suspicious, but I trusted her. And then there was always the extra money, the double pay-packet at the end of the fortnight, like proof.

I've taken up a hobby in my early retirement, working with wood. Lighter than concrete. With our daughters raised and our house paid for it's not too bad living on my super and with it being topped up by sickness benefit, I've even managed to buy a lathe and some other tools I need.

I don't blame Tanya for my condition. It wasn't her fault, not directly.

Wake me at five, she'd said. It was one of those days she'd come home between the shifts. She'd had an early dinner and put mine in the oven. I started at four in the morning so I was always home by three o'clock in the afternoon, unless we had a really big project on, like laying the floor for a factory.

I lay down on the bed next to her and stretched out. I could hear her breathing and I must have gone to dreamland because it seemed no time at all and then something must have disturbed me. Maybe my internal clock, although now I'm not so sure. I startled up and saw the bedside clock was five to five and it had been ten to four, last time I'd looked.

I waited and watched the clock like a worker wanting to leave. I remember feeling so relaxed thinking now I wouldn't miss Tanya's deadline. I shudder at that memory. When it was time, and when I shook her but she gave no response, I felt like I was in a dream. A doze where pictures flash your mind but no one moves. I touched her again, my fingers curling around her bare arm, it was damply clammy like someone who had just got out of the shower. Then I was awake, screaming her name, shaking her, watching for her eyes to open. Knowing, but not knowing how I knew, that they never would again. The next few hours were a blur of ambulance and paramedics. Blue and red and things I'd never known, like they couldn't take her to hospital, that I needed an undertaker. 'I', now not 'we'. That it had been a massive heart attack. That probably, and there is the word which haunts me still, *probably,* I could have done nothing for her, that it had been too late for CPR.

Wake me at five, Tanya had said. And I knew to be punctual, not a minute later. She would have worked it out to the last second. How to be back at work on time for her second shift. And with her so tired after standing on her feet all day, I knew not to wake her a minute sooner. God knew she needed the sleep.

Vegemite Whiskers

shortlisted Global Short Story; published in Best New Australian Writing UK

It feels as though someone is reading my thoughts.

Who am I? Can I hold your attention if I tell you I am no one important? Well, not to the masses and not even to my relatives, even though I have few left of those.

Strange to be sharing with you, someone I may never meet, someone I may never know.

I work for a synagogue bereavement committee. I am a *Shomer,* a body watcher.

Perhaps now you've decided I am male - not so. Although sometimes I feel as androgynous as humanity. It is no matter. I am well suited to this disassociation.

In days gone past a relative of the deceased would do my job, stay with the mortal remains of their departed (I do not say 'loved ones' as this is not always the case) to keep them safe from thieves and scavengers, until interment.

There are only a few of us left; around the clock staffing of most mortuaries has reduced our need. And our duties have become less direct, although we still prepare the body for burial.

It is a quiet time, this watching. Only reading of *Tehillim,* the psalms, is permissible.

This is a time of contemplation, a time of fasting. Time to relinquish the worldly pleasures along with the departed one, in reverence and respect - *k'vod hamet* - the honour due to the dead.

I am good at what I do, and for the most I felt content in my value, until three days ago, when the child came. Children are always the hardest, so much lost potential, and the relatives' grief weighs on my senses like lead.

A suicide. And at such a tender age, only nine winters had this girl seen.

It was by an old method, one where the body mass and rope length is a precise art, if it is to be carried out successfully and cleanly.

She got it right, unusual for someone so young.

In sharing with you perhaps now I'll be able to unravel my thoughts, for at the moment they are as tangled as the seaweed on the shore of a storm.

It was the vegemite whiskers which confused me. Little black wisps like half smiles, on either side of her top lip.

I used to get them when I was a child, after we moved here to Australia. Vegemite spread was unheard of in the country of my birth.

After a breakfast of vegemite on toast, Mama would say, "You can't go to school, Misha, wearing those vegemite whiskers." Then, amid my wriggling to free myself from her grasp, she would wipe away the marks with a spit-dampened hanky and give the rest of my face a swipe for good measure, like a cat cleaning a kitten.

I can still smell her saliva drying on my cheeks, stale like the air in our apartment.

I used to try and wash away the blue black numbers on the inside of her wrist. But my spit was not strong enough for that. She would watch me scrubbing with the determination of the young before wrenching away her arm and turning her face.

"It won't come off Mama," I would cry.

The lord is my shepherd, I shall not want...

231

The girl lies on the table that has the drain. She is covered with a cloth to keep her dignity. Face up to allow for respect. I can see her vegemite whiskers from where I stand ready with the basin of warm water, the comb and the file to clean her nails.

The water will flow back to *Gan-Eden*... so be it... and will return her soul with it, to its source.

I was born in the Camp, a week before the Russians came. I was the reason my mother missed out on the death march.

She should have sought medical advice for me sooner, after the Liberation, but she was only eighteen and terrified of doctors. When she did eventually take me, the hospital intern clenched his brows, covered the lower half of me quickly and muttered something about surgical reconstruction when, or rather if, resources became available.

I didn't go to school until we emigrated to Australia. I was seven years old by then and well used to the confused looks people gave me when I was introduced to them. It didn't help that my mother always dressed me in jeans and plain tops. And my name cast no light. It was as ambiguous as my clothes. In our homeland, Misha is short for Michael but it's sometimes used as a girl's name too.

Everyone assumed I was female, perhaps because of my slight build and fine features, and I gave no reason for them to think otherwise. It suited me for I found it was much easier to be anonymous. Female changing rooms and toilets offered me the privacy I craved.

The other children, with the insight of the young and without the inhibition of adults, soon let me know I was different. But I never gave them the opportunity to find out in what way.

He maketh me to lie down in green pastures...

This room I am in is like an operating theatre, high ceilinged and bright, but without the sterility of surgical bustle. It feels airtight and solid; nothing from the outside life, sound or sun, penetrates the thick walls. The linen shrouds are ready, they arrived the day after the girl was brought in, their pearl whiteness (they are the expensive ones) are draped over the back of my chair. I will clothe her in them after the cleansing is complete.

Her father has been fighting the authorities; it was desecration, he said, a violation of the body, to commit it to autopsy.

Our faith supports his belief. And I would have too, but with this child I am not so sure.

Somehow, a part of me cannot bind the normality of a sunny breakfast of vegemite on toast to the girl doing what she did soon after.

I was glad that I'd talked to other members of the *Cheva Kaddisha*, the burial society, about my doubts, and relieved when the coroner won the fight.

"What happened to you, Mama, in the Camp?" I used to ask my mother with the cadence of a child's innocence. The only camp I knew of back then was the one they had at school at the end of the term, where I was taken on a bus to the country. There I learned what I already knew, that cows gave milk and chickens supplied the egg for my breakfast.

"You do not want to know, Misha," she would say, which only made me ask all the more.

It is quiet here. I am quiet, the dead are noiseless, their time has been given, their bodies no longer needed.

The girl has pale brown hair, grown long. It is necessary for me to lift up her head to comb the back of it. I can see the marks on her neck, rough-red like the burns I got on my hands when I pulled on the rope at the school camp for the tug-o-war.

The other side did not win.

When my mother did talk, it was on my fifteenth birthday.

"You are old enough now, Misha. The same age I was when they came for me, and your aunt and uncles and my mama and papa, your grandparents."

I was not ignorant, I had learned about such things at school. I'd stopped asking Mama about the Camp five years before.

And when she told me, I sat, head bowed, listening to her truth until her words raised my eyes and my hands. I could not see her clearly through my tears but the outline was there of a woman sitting stiffly, eyes dry and hands clasped in front of her on the table. When she stopped talking I realised she'd been right when she'd said, *You do not want to know Misha.* But now I did know, and this knowing was heavier than anything my imagination could ever weigh. Afterwards she looked at me and shook her head. Then she hugged me hard without the usual back-patting and I knew there was something else. Something she was not saying.

When I left university I took an apprenticeship in a funeral home. My mother was not surprised. Death had always fascinated me. The burials for my deceased pets went way beyond the simple wooden cross affairs of most childhoods.

She was unsurprised too when eventually my faith took me to being a body watcher.

He leadeth me beside the still waters...

The skin of the child is softer than hope, I can feel the tiny hairs on her arm brushing my hand as the cleansing lifts them before the water sluices away down the drain.

I cover the girl's body with cloths. Only the parts I am washing I uncover, like a surgeon does when operating. I think of the forensic pathologist. He and I may be the last ones to see her. Our belief does not hold with public viewing.

I wash one arm, then the other, then the legs and the genitalia. But the latter I do not uncover. Female shall cleanse female and male will cleanse male, to keep their honour. Because of what I am I could do both.

My fingertips become as gentle as butterflies' feet as I trace over her chest and feel the tight lines of the stitches holding together her tiny body.

Mama came to my work once. She did not stay long. When I started the cleansing, the shiny table that curves to a drain reminded her of too much. "I have to go out for a while, Misha," she said, waving her hand in the direction of the stainless-steel bench and muttering, "butcher table," before scurrying out of the funeral home like a little dark mouse.

She didn't come back in.

I never knew my papa and even with her dying breath Mama did not disclose who he was. I did know that Mama had a twin sister, Natasha, who died at the Camp. The Angel of Death took her, she told me. Later I read about the experiments and I knew why I was like I was, without the telling.

About who fathered me - perhaps this was what Mama hadn't wanted to tell me on my fifteenth birthday - now this is a *something* I do not want to know.

Yea, though I walk through the valley of the shadow of death I will fear no evil...

"Misha, are you there?" It is the voice of my employer, Eli Feinstein.

As he enters, I do not answer (I want to keep the silence), he can see for himself that I am here.

I replace the cloth over the girl's chest and look up.

"No need to finish that now, Misha," he says. "There is to be an inquest." He looks at me with a slight incline of his head, and eyebrows raised. "You were right to be suspicious."

I scan the rows of shelves lining the far end of the room. Cold drawers of darkness. This is where she will be returning.

Eli stares at me, he expects a reply, I can see it in his eyes. I have nothing to say. And I'm not surprised at the pathologist's findings.

"The girl's father doesn't require your services anymore, Misha. It looks as if he may be implicated. He has more things to worry about now. And I will be here tonight to watch over her."

I hold out my hand, poised like a bird about to take flight, towards the child.

Eli nods at me.

I dip a corner of the cloth into the water, reach down to the girl's face and gently wipe away the tiny black marks from the top of her lip.

The Workingman's Pandora's Box

An Eclectic Slice Of Life - Eclecticism AUS

Today I have hit the trolley jackpot - as much luck as I can expect in my life at the moment - I am nearly through the supermarket and my trolley's still behaving itself like a new pram, not like a go-cart with three wheels.

Then my luck drains away as quickly as sump oil when you don't have the pan in the right spot. Just up ahead, in the chemist section, is Justin, an old friend of ours. 'Ours' being my wife, Sarah, and me when we were a pair. She walked out five months ago, leaving me to fend for myself.

Having to buy Sarah out, I will be, for the next ten years or so, living on instant noodles and sausages bought an hour's whisker before their use-by-date.

I try to slide past Justin before he sees me. At that moment my trolley decides to put its worst wheel forward and I steer into his leg. He spins around, holding up a box of condoms. To my disappointment he doesn't even look embarrassed.

'Oh, hi there, Kevin, I thought you were Carol. I was going to ask her if she wanted these. Look, they're special ones with vibrating rings attached. Bit more expensive, but what the heck, you only live once.' He throws the box into his trolley and winks at me. Then he looks serious.

'So, Kev, how'ya doing? Haven't seen you for ages. Sorry to hear about your break-up.' Justin rubs his nose, and then adds. 'We really must have you over for tea one night.'

I'm about to answer when Carol comes around the aisle, pushing another trolley. This one's loaded up with chocolate, white mud cake, oysters, and probably panda in aspic and tinned tongue of hummingbird. I try to push my sausage and noodle laden trolley out of view. The sausages are bleeding and I notice a vampire-like trail leading all the way back to the meat section, where some supermarket wag has written in bold texta: Sausages on Special 1$ a kg - hurry before they go off!

'Kids,' Carol says, waving her hand airily over her trolley, 'Always hungry.' Then, in unaware parody of her husband, 'You going okay, Kev? We'll have to have you over for tea one night.'

I mumble, 'That would be nice,' and turn away before they can set a date. They pass me in the next aisle, their trolleys humming two abreast and running as smooth as baby oil.

One more aisle and I head over to an empty checkout - I can't believe it, think that maybe my luck fairy has returned but I brush her dead from my shoulder when I see the girl closing up her till and putting across the chain. Justin and Carol are at the checkout opposite. Of course this one only has an old lady who drives her shopping trolley on Sundays and lives alone with a budgie. She's pulling away as I slip behind them and shrug into myself. They turn in unison, flash half smiles then go back to unloading.

When I place the slide thing behind Carol and Justin's big pack of salmon, a block of Dairy Milk nearly topples over onto my side. I put it back with their groceries. Feel mildly pleased that some of the sausage blood has stuck to the foil.

Some time later, the girl says to them, 'That's three-hundred and twenty seven dollars and thirty seven cents, thanks.'

'Cheaper than I thought it was going to be,' says Justin. 'Well done, Carol, I might have a little treat for you tonight.' He turns to me and gives a repeat performance of the wink he'd done earlier. I notice with a modicum of satisfaction that Carol doesn't seem to share his enthusiasm.

My EH Holden waits on an angle in its allotted space, away from the other cars. I'd been in a hurry this morning. It starts first time and I head out to Victoria Street to follow up on my hunch.

I run a second-hand shop in Fitzroy that deals in antiques and bric-a-brac. It means visiting lots of deceased estate auctions and rummaging around old peoples' farms for things they now know are worth a fortune. I liked it better when ignorance reigned, when my dad was in charge of the shop. Now he helps out part time. Sort of 'Steptoe and Son' we are. Only thing missing is the horse, and dad still has his teeth.

The hunch turns out to be a fizzler, like my morning, so I head home and divide the sausages into seven freezer bags. Then I notice my phone flashing a message.

I press the button and listen. A woman's voice says, 'Mr Harper, we have your test results. Dr Lewis wants you to come in as soon as possible, please.'

It must be something serious, I think. Dr Lewis told me I could just ring up for the results. I hadn't got around to it. Funnily enough I don't feel surprised but I'm not going to call back today.

I'd noticed this spot on my leg three weeks ago. At first I didn't think anything of it but as the days went by and it seemed to be growing, I made a doctor's appointment. Doctor Lewis had peered at the spot, then rubbed his chin and clicked something up on his computer. I was sitting behind it so I couldn't see what came up on the screen.

'Kevin, I think this should come off. I don't like the look of it. Do you use solariums by any chance?'

I unpack the rest of my shopping, which takes all of two minutes. Think at least I don't have to plan what I'm having for tea. Then I remember Dad's invited me over to his place tonight. He also wants to show me something he bought the other day. He wouldn't say what it was, but his words were running together and his voice was high.

I started collecting things when I was a kid, back then it was cigarette tins. I still have my first, a Lucky Strike tin, which I found in an old box of junk - up until Sarah walked out, I thought it was bringing me good luck.

At this morning's auction, I'd been hoping to buy an old mangle. People from the city will pay heaps for them. This one looked great in the catalogue but when I saw it in the metal, so to speak, I thought the reserve price was as optimistic as a blind man learning to drive. However, I did bid on a box of junk. At clearing sales there are always old boxes filled with such things as bottle openers, letter-wax sealers and odd spanners and bolts. A sort of workingman's Pandora's Box. You never know what you might find, like I did my first cigarette tin, hidden like hope, beneath the rust-dust and junk. I seldom go to an auction and come away empty-booted. These things to me are like a lucky dip to a kid.

I rub the spot, or where the spot used to be before it was excised out of existence. It feels itchy.

I take my box of hope into the shop and leave it on the counter. I'll look into it another day.

Eyes from a portrait of someone else's long dead relative stare accusingly at me. I wish someone would buy the damn thing; it gives me the creeps every time I come in here. The trouble is even if an item doesn't sell I can't bring myself to chuck it out.

When I get to Dad's place he's waiting outside, as happy as Christmas.

The place smells familiar as I enter the kitchen. 'Hope you don't mind bangers and mash, son. There was a special on,' he says.

I slump into the chair as Dad bustles around with plates and tomato sauce.

Over dinner, he keeps glancing up from his meal and grinning.

'Okay, Dad, what is it?'

He leaves a sausage gelling in sauce and disappears into the depths of his house. It must be good; he usually keeps things in The Shed.

He comes back carrying a box with a glass lid. It's half-wrapped in an old grey blanket. I can see copper coins lined up in rows. They all seem to be uniform, with no empty spaces.

'Pennies son. Early twentieth century.'

I take the box from him and peer into the contents with what I hope is a look that matches his enthusiasm.

I nod and make encouraging noises.

He taps the glass over the first row. 'Look at that, Kevin, a 1930 penny. Do you know how damn rare they are?'

I swallow my first thought. The thing is I'd been watching Antique Road Show or ARS as I call it, and the other day a lady brought in a 1933 English penny.

Even the antique dealer wasn't sure of its authenticity and told her it would be worth having it valued, as although fakes were common a real one could fetch between 20-25,000 pounds. It had got me thinking about the Australian equivalent.

The 1930 penny. I looked it up on the net and found that only six had been minted and all of those were accounted for.

I look into Dad's eyes. 'What are you going to do with it?'

'Keep it of course. You don't mind, son, if I don't sell it, do you? After all, you'll inherit it when I die. It's funny, I always thought if I got this lucky the first thing I'd do would be to flog it off at an auction and get as much as I could. But really I feel well off already. Anyway what would I do with all that money? I've got everything I need right here.'

I run a finger over the glass, circling the coin. 'Nah, keep it, Dad, if it means that much to you. I wouldn't tell anybody else about it though. People have been killed for less.'

I am wondering if I would be this generous if I thought it was real.

The next day, when I open the shop I see my box of hope sitting on the counter. I move it to the floor and several spanners fall out in a sprinkling of rust. I toss them back in without looking.

On Monday I make a doctor's appointment and feel mildly surprised that I can't get in until the end of the week. The receptionist is different from the one on my answering machine.

So on Friday I rock up at the clinic and as I'm getting out of my car I see Justin coming back to his BMW. He seems to be turning up - dare I think it - like a bad penny. He's on his own and looks worse than I feel.

'Oh, Hi, Kevin. Just had to pick up some...' His face crumples, reminds me of one of those dogs that look old when they're just a pup. Before I've had time to lock my car he's leaning, head in hands, on the bonnet and people are looking.

'Hop in,' I say. 'I'll take you for a drive.' I set off, feeling a mixture of relief and annoyance. God knows when I'll be able to make another appointment.

I stop at the Lookout. All the kids come here at night so it's deserted at the moment.

I look at Justin's face. 'Gee, Justin, what the hell's happened?'

'Carol's left me, Kevin, and taken the kids with her.' For the next few minutes I listen to a tune as familiar as breathing, at the same time I'm glad that Sarah and I didn't have any children.

I lean over and rub his shoulder. A car pulls up beside us, its back seat brimming teenagers. They glance in our direction, nudge each other, hoot and laugh then drive off, their back wheels spinning up dirt like spit. Justin doesn't seem to notice. When he lifts his head from his hands his eyes are red and he seems to be having trouble breathing.

'Geez, Jus. You okay? You look dreadful.'

He pulls a puffer from his pocket and inhales a few times. Starts to breathe more easily, leans back with a sigh.

'The thing is, Kev, I'm in debt. Carol doesn't know it yet but when we divide all our assets we'll each receive zip. In fact if we split everything down the middle we'll both owe over fifty grand.'

For a few moments I can't speak.

'God, Jus, I'm sorry. I had no idea.'

After I drop Justin back at the car-park I watch as his BMW slips out of view. I think of my dad and his modest life. I remember his smile as he waved me goodbye the other night. He doesn't even own a car. Justin and Carol had appeared to have it all but...

I can see an outline of a picture which seems to be coming into focus the more I think about it. I just can't put a caption to it yet.

I decide I may as well make another appointment while I'm here. Save the cost of the phone call.

The receptionist informs me that the doctor's running an hour late. So I'm just on time, I can go right through.

Dr Lewis tells me to sit down. He rolls up my pant leg.

'That looks pretty good. But those stitches need to come out. Why didn't you come earlier in the week?'

He ignores my grunt and begins to type something on his computer. It hums out a printed sheet.

After he's treated my leg I sit waiting like an expectant father.

He hands me the sheet and waves me out. 'It won't cost you anything today. I've bulk-billed you,' he says.

'What about the results?'

'Oh, sorry, I thought I'd said.' He pulls an apologetic face. 'It's been a rather long day. It was a basal cell lesion. A mild form of skin cancer. These things rarely spread. We caught it early. Nothing to worry about.'

As I leave the surgery, the luck fairy hovers around my head like a halo. She sprinkles dust that settles and I see the words to the picture materialising from a muted haze: you can't always change what life draws for you but you can choose how you'll colour in the lines.

Back in my shop I sit on the floor, place my box of hope in front of me and, piece by piece, begin to remove the layers of junk.

Swine Flu

Today has been snarling and snapping at me like it doesn't want me in it.

It all began when I arrived early at Pet Stop Pet Shop, which I manage. I like to get here way before my assistant, Carly, turns up. She's great with customers, but chattily distractive when I'm trying to balance the books.

The grey of dawn was lifting to another winter's day when I opened the shop's door and discovered bedlam. The place had been trashed.

I closed my eyes in disbelief and said aloud, 'Who the f... would want to do over a pet shop?'

I mean, what did they hope to get? Surely they didn't think there was much cash on the premises. We deal in fur and feathers, not gold and diamonds.

When I entered, wind gusting through a broken window slammed the door behind me with the finality of a gunshot. I switched on the main lights and all the mess was revealed in fluorescent glory. A snake-tank was shattered, dog baskets and pet toys were scattered clumsily on the floor, and feed and seed spilled a golden flood, where liberated rabbits nibbled at its edges. A parakeet flew over my head and disappeared through the broken window in a streak of screech. But thankfully, when I checked, I found most of the animals were still in their cages.

Then I noticed the door to the walk-in fridge-freezer, where we store our kangaroo meat, was gaping open and puffing mist like an icy steam train.

I'd managed to get an hour in yesterday, preparing one kilogram bags of pet mince and labelling them. I'd only got one box minced. I still had twenty-nine boxes left to do. You'd be surprised how many pampered pooches and coddled cats out there will only eat our national emblem. More spoilt than kids some pets are.

Anyway, all the meat from what had once been a large 'Jump', or whatever the collective is for kangaroos, was completely gone. The whole fridge had been cleaned out. And there'd been 300 kilos of meat, packed in cardboard and plastic. Closer examination revealed a trail of blood, in box-drag marks from freezer to window.

I jolted back as a two-metre carpet snake swirled past me and skimmed the perimeter of the room before skidding beneath some dog blankets.

The shop seemed quieter than usual though, as if the animals knew this wasn't a good day to be kicking up a ruckus. But the smell of spoiled straw and cabbage, and something I couldn't quite put an olfactory sense to, was stronger than ever.

After the police came I spent the next two hours picking up shattered glass, boarding up the broken window, getting loose animals into their enclosures and hooking the free-sliding reptile into a spare tank.

The books hadn't got a look in, although balancing them now would be as uneven as a one-sided seesaw. And I still had the morning cage cleaning to do.

I'd just started to empty the fish-tanks when Carly arrived. At first I didn't recognise her, thought it was an early customer, until I realised it was Carly's voice booming from beneath a head of hair that would've looked at home in a western film and not on the good guys' side either. Mohican, in iridescent pink.

'Shit, Sue,' she said, 'what the hell's happened?'

My eyes fixed on the top of her head. 'I was about to ask you the same thing, Carly.'

Carly shrugged out of her purple, plastic retro-coat and flinched it down onto the freshly washed counter. She grinned and flicked her hair. It didn't move. 'It's the latest thing. I had it done, like, last night. Before my date with Hamish.'

I swept my arm in half an arc. 'Well, we had a bloody break-in last night.'

Carly took her bag and coat out to the rear of the shop. She stopped at the broken window and traced her fingers around the masking tape holding the cardboard to the frame. She didn't say anything, so I lifted my voice to follow her. 'I told the police the only stuff that seems to be missing is the kangaroo meat.'

Carly looked back at me. One eyebrow lifted a row of silver studs in a lopsided facial salute. As she turned around to hang up her bag, she muttered, 'Why would anyone wanna steal that?'

I didn't have an answer. The police had asked if there was anyone I could think of with a grudge against the shop or myself. But really no-one came to mind. I run a good place. The animals are well fed; the cages are cleaned regularly and they're much larger than the legal requirement. Even the pet-meat comes from out of town road-kill, and kangaroos are truly free-range.

Jack Trewellen, a local pig farmer, collects the carcasses every day and sells me a truckload, cut up into manageable sizes, every month or sooner if I have extra orders. He'd only come a few days ago, so that meant I'd lost nine-hundred dollars worth of meat. And that's not including the profit. More importantly, although god knows I can't afford the loss, I don't like letting my customers down. As I said, lots of pets will only eat kangaroo.

Carly busied herself with the coffee machine and, like Pavlov's dogs salivating at the sound of a bell, I felt my stomach rumble in anticipation. I'd bought two triple-death-by-chocolate muffins from the bakery on my way in that morning. Mine and Carly's favourite.

'Sue, what are you going to do about Mrs Cavendish-Smyth? You know she always buys bulk on the last day of the month.'

'Hell, Carly, is it that time already?' I moved the mouse on the shop's computer, kicked the screen-saver into life and brought up the date.

'Sure is,' said Carly, without looking. She placed a steaming cup beside me. I heard her rummaging in the cupboard for paper plates.

While we had our morning coffee, Carly entertained me with the latest rendition of her date with Hamish, her current boyfriend.

Hamish was into greyhounds, owned nine of them, so every Wednesday night was race-night with Carly acting as strapper, or whatever the equivalent term was for dog-racing.

'Our Jack Trewellen was there, Sue. He didn't say hello, he was too busy ripping up his betting slips.'

'Not a good night for him, then?'

'Nah, like, I think he should stick to pig-farming and the road-kill business.'

'So what happened after the races?'

'Not much, Sue. Hamish dropped me home early.' Carly broke off a bit of muffin. I marvelled how its colour was almost as black as her nail polish. She continued in a small puff of crumbs: 'He had to go home and like, get some work done or something.'

'Maybe one of his bitches is whelping?' I said, wiping my mouth.

Carly shook her head and stared up at the ceiling. Then she pointed.

'Sue, did you know there's a budgie up there, sitting on the fan?'

After the bird was caught, the coffee drunk and the muffins reduced to a dark crumb or two, it was time to open the shop. The rest of the cage cleaning would have to wait till later.

As predicted, Mrs Cavendish-Smyth turned up as we were opening the door. She smiled at me then squinted at the boarded-up window.

'What happened, Sue? Did some naughty little boy throw a ball through it, then?'

When I explained about the break-in and what had been stolen she went quiet for a moment, then paled.

'Oh dear, Sue, what about my order? I do have enough meat for the weekend, but you know I only come in once a month. And I really need it today. Or tomorrow at the latest. I'm staying in town tonight with Clarissa, my eldest.' She stared at the freezer, as if by looking she could make the meat reappear. The door was still open, as I'd decided it was as good a time as any to defrost, but now the only things inside were buckets and absorbent towels.

'Oh dear,' she said again, this time clutching at the brown and cream cameo she always wore at her throat.

Carly pulled out a chair and Mrs Cavendish-Smyth slumped into it. I caught Carly's eye and held up the phone in a peace offering gesture. Carly nodded.

'Don't you worry. Like, Sue will ring Jack Trewellen, the farmer who sells us the roo-meat,' Carly said, placing her hand on Mrs Cavendish-Smyth's shoulder. 'Would you like a cup of coffee?'

Carly might look like Hell's reincarnate but she's damned good with the customers.

'Cup of tea, dear? If you could?'

Jack Trewellen told me on the phone that he couldn't make it in today, but he'd bring another truckload tomorrow.

Gee, I thought, the road-kill toll must be up lately. I'm in the wrong business.

I told Mrs Cavendish-Smyth what Jack had said. She immediately brightened, finished her tea, and left.

The afternoon passed in cage cleaning interrupted by customers, but then five minutes before we were due to shut, Mrs Digby, aka The Snake Lady, arrived.

Carly had seen her walking up from her car, which she'd parked down the road. The Snake Lady never bothered to lock it, but had never had anything stolen. We knew why: Sally, her four-metre anaconda, lived in the back seat on a crochet rug of multi colours.

'Quick, I'll like, pull down the blind before she gets here,' Carly hissed, grabbing at the string hanging in the front door.

'You can't do that, Carly. I know she's a bit eccentric but she's a good customer.'

'She's a bloody crazy old bag. I'd rather have a dozen Mrs Cavendish-Smyths than her. I'm not serving her. Last time I did she spat in my face.'

It was true that The Snake Lady could be a bit of a pain. And she had this speech impediment which had her spitting with every sibilant sound she made. And she was always talking about Sally or Sidney, or one of her other snakes. You were okay if you kept your distance.

She looks rather odd too: sort of large transvestite meets Barbara Cartland, except The Snake Lady prefers yellow crepe to pink.

She entered the shop trailing a faint air of something indiscernible, nodded at me as she passed and headed to the snake-tanks. Oddly enough, she made no mention of the broken window. Every other customer had asked about it.

I'd started to tidy a shelf, when a shuffling sound behind me made me jump. I turned around and saw The Snake Lady standing there.

Her face creased into a frown and she banged her fist on the counter. 'Sssue, do you realise you have one very ssssick sssnake?'

I stood back but she moved forward. 'He's ssssmashed his ssssweet little face on the glasssss. No doubt by people teasing him. They'll be sssssorry if I get hold of them.'

I pulled out a tissue and wiped my face.

'Well Mrs Sn... Mrs Digby, we had a break-in last night. He got out when his tank was smashed. Might have injured himself then.'

It was as if I hadn't spoken.

'His mouth is sssssooo sssswollen! He'll get canker if the broken teeth are not removed sssoon. I'll take him. No charge.' She strode back to the snake-tank, her filmy yellow dress streaming behind her like a comet's tail. I watched with my lips clamped. She'd meant 'no charge' to me. The damn cheek.

When I examined the snake through the glass I sucked in a long breath. His mouth *was* bruised. And badly.

I didn't feel like arguing. The Snake Lady was right, he would die the slow death of starvation if something wasn't done. And she was more qualified, in experience terms, than a herpetologist.

I got out the hook and snake bag.

As we were returning to the front of the shop, she stopped at the freezer. 'It's dissssgraceful,' The Snake Lady said, her mouth pouting a point towards the freezer's open door.

'What is, Mrs Digby?'

She sniffed loudly. 'All those poor little kangaroos.'

Before I could say anything, she snatched the bag with the snake and marched out of the shop.

Carly came up behind me, making me jump again. 'Like I told you, Sue,' she said, glancing into the empty freezer, 'batty as a fruit bat with rabies.'

Friday morning arrived as crisp as a freshly picked lettuce and I found myself in much better spirits.

Even though I was still trying to work out how I could cover the loss of so much meat, I realised things could have been much worse.

More animals could have been hurt, more goods damaged and Jack Trewellen may not have been able to refill my order so quickly.

Mrs Cavendish-Smyth was due at lunch time so I was pleased when Jack turned up soon after I opened the shop.

You know how they say people get to look like their pets? Well, Jack had become a lot like what he bred. His face was perpetually

251

pink and his eyes stared out between folds of flesh like BB gun pellets. He smelt like a sty, too.

'Hi there, Sue. Bit of bad luck for ya.' Jack sucked in his cheeks, making his eyes bulge, as he looked into the empty freezer.

'Yeah,' I said. 'I don't know how I'm going to make up for the loss.'

Jack shrugged. 'Well girlie, I know you hate leaving your customers in the lurch. So I gotta another lot for ya. Tell ya wot. I'll knock fifty off. Just make a cheque out for eight hundred and fifty dollars, instead of nine hundred. How's that sound?'

I was grateful for anything. And I was *really* surprised. Jack had never compromised on price. Everyone has a heart, I thought, even the ones you least suspect.

I gave him his cheque and he headed off in a hurry. I was busy too, I needed to mince and bag twenty kilos of kangaroo meat before Mrs Cavendish-Smyth came back for her order.

I got out the mincer, and the dry bread to help push the meat through if it got stuck. I seated myself on my canvas chair and pulled over the nearest cardboard box.

As I lifted the folded flaps I couldn't believe what I saw.

Bags of mince! And they bore labels, written in my handwriting, with the day before yesterday's date. Then everything fell into mind, even the extra funny smell in the shop after the break-in.

Carly rushed up, her voice as breathless as a long distance runner, 'I'm sorry Sue,' she said, 'Mrs Cavendish-Smyth is here, she's getting a bit upset and...'

Her mouth opened like a beached fish. 'Sue, I can't believe it. You've minced all that already... How...?'

I started putting the bags of mince back into the box. 'Give me a hand will you, Carly. We need to do another box-full. I'll explain everything after Mrs Cavendish-Smyth has left.'

When she'd gone, I called the police, fixed Carly a cup of coffee and began...

'So, Sue,' Carly said, after I'd finished, 'like, you're telling me you think Jack Trewellen broke in, stole the kangaroo meat he sold you earlier in the week, and then sold the same stuff back to you today?'

'I don't *think* he did Carly, I *know* he did. This is the exact truckload he brought last Monday. Look, this is my handwriting.' I held aloft a bag of mince, like evidence at a trial. 'Remember, I hadn't minced all of it, most was still untouched. Because it was only one box amongst many he didn't notice it.'

'Why, though? He has his piggery. Surely he makes enough money from that without resorting to stealing.'

I picked up the Weekly Times and pointed to the headlines in the Market section.

'I remember reading this the other day. The price of pork has taken a nosedive. Some people, it appears, are still worried about contracting swine flu.'

Carly sat up straight, her nose rings twitching. 'That's silly. Swine flu was years ago. Anyway, I thought everyone knew you can't catch it like that.'

I scrunched my shoulders. 'Seems not,' I said, folding the paper.

'Still, Sue, Jack Trewellen must have been really desperate to rip you off like this.'

I nodded. 'Yeah, he must have needed extra money in a hurry.' Immediately I recalled how he'd rushed off with my cheque. I also thought of what Carly told me about him losing so much money at the races. And what sort of people bookies can be.

'You know, Sue,' Carly said, lifting her cup to her lips, 'I'm glad it was like, Jack. I was worried about Hamish, you know, with nine greyhounds to feed and...'

'Yes,' I nodded. 'I wondered if it might have been him too. I even suspected poor Mrs Snake Lady, the way she was acting the other day.'

'Oh no, Sue. Like I said, she's just nuts.'

I lifted my mobile as if toasting a celebration. 'Well, Carly,' I said, while I rang a number, 'I don't know about that. But I do know one thing for sure. There's a certain cheque out there that's just about to bounce.'

Broad Sheet Music

or learning to sail

The clanging of the halyard,
like the ringing of a school bell
calls me to a classroom
its ceiling of summer blue
to lessons without walls

me a new chum to all things aquatic
where words are not what they are
on land
like sheets and painters
and the wind holds all the rules
nature made

The Norfolk Broads are not ladies
but their laps are wide
and on our yacht, Ondine
the water nymph, wind locked
we rock to gentle strains of luffing sails.

Along a Roman Road in Wales

I rode a horse along a Roman road in Wales
my mind-raising stories of Llandoobrey,
Brecon's tales
behind the windows
folk I could not see saw me
and so my trespass
riding on land of foe of friend
was grapevined and may be twining still

A woman from foreign lands
riding a chestnut cob - Keelan's Place
no right to be there

Travelling, and it's true for all
it's the people you recall
that ancient lady in the hotel with the lowest beams
telling how she always has the Scampi
because
it's something she knows
and how nine years before
on her eightieth birthday
a nasty man who should not have been there
was dying
uninvited
right here

she says
at this table,
she says
fallen face first into his Toad In The Hole, she says
a fitting end in irony
I think
and smile as many tales later I hug her good-bye
and then I recall
my own trespass
No horses on his land
my foe of friend, another nasty man,
even though he allows ramblers the right of way

Tattered Salvation, Store Bought Goods

Up The Staircase Quarterly - North Dakota USA

You'll never get the right answer if you ask the wrong question.

It starts with unexpected shopping from an open-all-hours store. You know the sort, every day, 7 days, all weather, all bleeding month or year. Neon lighting, red iridescent flashing. How many innuendos can I afford? They cost more than my tattered salvation.

The checkout girl says I am last in line. She is closing her counter.

He turns his head and looks at me, he of the long dark coat and rat tail behind. Good ole seventies rock 'n' roll boy. His fingers, stained from the daisies on his shaggin' wagon, make no peace sign.

This day they have the special but no discount and no returns.

"I just had to buy some peas," he says, holding up the tin as proof.

I have no answer to this. I sure as damn ain't going to show him the sanitary pads with wings and promised protection.

My car, waiting in the dark like a patient pet, flickers lights with a muted click as I point my keys. The heavens growl their discontent with spattered spit on its windscreen.

We climb into the back seat. The car park is deserted.

Mr Pea-Seventies man breathes sweet breath, new-mown grass on my face and earns his redwings.

Afterwards I tell him my name.

You know, you think you have it all worked out. Your cynical monitor is running low, chugging along smugly without missing a beat for years and years when suddenly bam, it comes crashing down around your shoulders and hangs there. A broken yoke of your disbelief.

My denial has no hindsight, hell, it has no foresight for that matter.

And up until recently my husband was making love to me with the regularity of the weekdays.

He went shopping before I did. That's why I've turned. But perhaps what I have become has always been there, like a pimple that refuses to come to a head but lingers beneath the surface. No one sees it but you sure as hell can feel it. No wonder they call it blind.

Infidelity. The one word track didn't play another tune no matter how it was switched on or off, or turned over with excuses of coincidence and paranoia. "Whaddya think," he'd said finally, "that you were the only one? It's like this my sweet, there are green apples and red apples and sometimes you want the green and sometimes you need the red."

I didn't ask him which colour I was. Peripherally I was rendered opaque.

I wouldn't have gone looking, if I hadn't had the need.

But the need has always had me twined around its fingers, probing and pushing to find the unreachable. Broken mirrored memories are scattered in the depths of my mind and it seems bad luck to retrieve them.

It is so far to the dawn, in this darkness I scratch up the walls of my reality, future cemented by hope, past layered in a particular order.

The joker laughs a belly full of cosmos and says, look, see what a bloody fool you have been and suffer the consequence. Ten fold, a hundred, a thousand, whatever it takes to crease you into admitting you were right and... wrong.

It is far worse for the knowing.

No one knows what they are capable of, isn't that what they always say? How anyone, even a god damn ninety year old nun, who has never had a fuck, has osteoporosis and is wheelchair ridden is capable of murder. So they say.

Actually I believe it.

Women tend to prefer clean methods of disposal.

I can understand that. I would be no different. We have always been belly button deep in muck: baby shit, menstruation, snot, spew, you name your brew. It's little wonder we women would want to do our killing tidily. I mean who always has to clean up the mess?

So it follows the aforesaid nun could easily (and, let's face it who would suspect) pop a little something into someone's Holy Communion. Maybe it'd be for that greasy priest who's always been trying to slip into her habit, or perhaps the parishioner who refused her years ago and that's why she ended up in this stinking school teaching for nothing.

Motives are overrated. One woman I visit on the inside even killed her husband for whistling. He was, and here's the funny part, peeling veggies for their dinner but, part of his passive resistance, because he didn't have the balls to say fuck off I've been working all day, peel your own god damn vegetables, was whistling. And none of that romantic Swanee River type shit, no, he does this monotone dirge over and over like some bloody song with no bloody ending. She asked him to stop, begged him to stop.

And in the end he did. It's pretty hard to whistle with your vocal cords severed.

I found out about becoming a volunteer prison visitor the first time I gave blood. There was this poster on the hospital wall, asking if you could spare a day or two, once a fortnight to visit inmates at Lantana Prison. Those with no one alive or willing. My house is within walking distance from there so, I thought, why not? I wasn't doing much else with my life, not if you don't count waiting on my husband like a wet nurse. I needed to keep busy. It was okay for him. In between his rutting he was building a yacht in the shed. His own secret project. He was always saying. "One day I'll just disappear, piss off and not tell nobody. You can all go to hell."

It was strange going through the ritual of being admitted to the prison. Sometimes I would pretend that I was being incarcerated and, you know, the sensation isn't half bad. There is a protective feel about prison walls, although, in this case, they are all wire and barb. Forget about that 'don't fence me in' bullshit. There is a sense of stability and safety in it. Everything laid out like a line. Never having to think for yourself. The security of institutional salvation.

My husband doesn't share my feelings about prison. He's been there and he says that was enough, never again. He says if I want to go there for real, why don't I commit an offence? Make it count though, he says, coz with all them bleeding hearts, if the crime isn't bad enough I could get off with good behaviour.

Perhaps that is what I am living now... I sure as shit try to be good. Somehow 'Good' is never enough. Words come out, twist in my mouth and turn into accusations I never make. He explains what I meant. For his defence I am never right, only trying to be.

Eventually I didn't want him anymore. He uses this for his excuse even though it is after the fact.

"A man has needs. Whaddya expect me to do?" I try to twist his words the way he does mine, try to roll them back on the truth or what I see as the truth. I am never sure lately.

The late nights become early mornings, the fractured excuses thin, the fumbled words charge like tension before thunderstorm.

"You fucken bitch. You've ruined my life." My husband's fist smashes the glass door. It shatters with hardly a tinkle. Blood trickles from between his knuckles and runs down the pane. His blood of my salvation. I thank god there is no white carpet and get the sponge from the kitchen. Then I go out to my car.

My husband has gone away. It is the one truth I do know.

It was a *starry, starry night* Elton John sang it so.

The memory is fuzzy, a nebulous moon waxing and waning.

"One day, I want to sail around the world, honey. Would you like to come too? Brave it out, tack the waters."

I'd laughed. I thought he'd said 'attack' the waters. Back then, before wife-hood, at 18, I was more naughty-gal than nautical.

I giggled at his pink socks and then gently touched his arm when nothing more happened.

Later, he told me it was one of the reasons he married me.

I doubt that anyone even knew about my husband's yacht but someone is sure to question when he stops showing up for work.

Now there is blood that is not mine in the trunk of my car. It smells of rust and impermanence. And so I wait for time to burst, to flood my lifescape, wait for the police to come and ask the wrong question. My institutional salvation only one right answer away.

Resurrect-a-pet

Vagabondage Press - Florida USA

Science mag: Cloned animals may have different spots to the original, due to varying environmental conditions in the womb.

I should have let sleeping dogs lie. Should have let Tilly sleep the gentle death of the innocent. I blame the internet. Somehow, when I emailed all my friends about my sad loss, it seemed to catch on, and 'pop ups' waving little flags covered in dog and cat paw prints kept appearing at the top of my pages. *Resurrect-a-pet will have your beloved pet back by your side quick as one dog gestation period*! it flashed, and just like its namesake, the site kept resurrecting itself as fast as I closed it.

In the end, just to shut it up, I opened it and then, like the site's owners had probably hoped, I was hooked. All they needed from me was a substantial, *but isn't your beloved pet worth it?* payment, and some of my pet's DNA.

For sentimental reasons, I had snipped off a bit of Tilly's beautiful fur on her death bed. She is/was a Saluki and her ear fur had/does hang around her face like a golden mane. I'm sorry to be mixing tenses like this but, as I type, she sits here perfectly still and staring. I can't say 'Tilly' because I know it's not her, well not entirely her at any rate.

At least she made me give up smoking, for that I should be grateful I guess.

Anyway, I sent away the sample of Tilly's fur and a cheque for 2,000 dollars, the other 2,000 to be paid on delivery.

A week later, I heard back from Resurrect-a-pet. The fur I'd sent was not enough, something to do with having no root follicles. Not enough DNA. I would have to exhume her and get more of what they needed.

There was no way I could do it myself; my stomach and heart were not ready for such confrontation. One of my friends did it for me in the end, making the short trip to the Pet Cemetery and returning with a plastic packet of what looked like not only hair with follicles, but also skin and something else of vaguely violet hue. As my innards were squirming I packed it off without further scrutiny.

In what seemed like a ridiculously short space of time, there she was: Tilly Mark II, with her DNA-certified certificate (not worth the paper it was written on as it turned out) and looking as cute as a backpack full of baby koalas.

I'd been held in a suspended sort of grief, alternating between crying and hoping, so my initial reaction was of pure joy and gratitude.

But this was not to last, there seemed to be this bluish aura about her that I had not noticed the first time round in puppyhood. And she was very twitchy.

Unfortunately, in this part of the Australian bush where we live, grows a beautiful tree, *pyranthus curlyfolii purpureus** of glorious purple hue and leaves like tiny feathers. Even though it's so gorgeous, it's also highly flammable because of its eucalyptus oil, so folk are discouraged from planting it in their backyards.

How flammable, you ask? Well it has been known to burst into flames (no harm comes to it from this, its leaves re sprout in days) when people have brushed against it while walking past and, after scientists realised its incendiary qualities, several people who were once believed to have spontaneously combusted, were found (with hindsight research) to have been within six feet of the tree. Their last words were probably along the lines of, "Oh, what a beautiful tr..." or something of equal gush.

Apparently, the gardener at the Pet Cemetery hadn't known this, as there are several wonderful specimens of *pyranthus curlyfolii purpureus** adorning the grounds, weeping their feathery purple leaves over the tiny graves.

I know Tilly Mark II can't help it; she can't know her running amok, as young pups are apt to do, can cause such problems.

I have to protect her from the authorities, but I feel so guilty. What if someone is killed next time? Of course I'm going to move back to the city, away from so much bushland just waiting to be ignited. Although will it be enough?

It's a shame really, her patches of purple, with filament hairs like tiny feathers, are so pretty.

Also known as the Lucifer Tree

Bloodline

The Valley Review - Massachusetts - USA

Celia Denim-Decourt's only claim to fame is her centenarian status, which she reached almost three years ago.

The lettercards from the Queen are framed and jostle for position on her bedside table, along with the photos from the paper and the DVDs of her appearance on National Television. She vows to watch them every anniversary but has only seen them once. The notoriety ladder does not stop at the one hundred year mark; every year she survives lifts her one rung higher.

The headlines boast: *Amazing Celia reaches 102. Reveals her secrets of longevity.* The journalists seem proud of their discovery, perhaps, Celia suspects, revelling in borrowed distinction. She doesn't mind, as the accolades and attention they bestow on her are greater than anything she's ever known before.

The last half century of her life has been happier. Certainly after she outlived her husband of thirty years. Andrew had died when she was only fifty. Half her life away.

She steers clear of answering any of those questions about her married life. Much prefers ones about how she's managed this feat of growing to such an age.

Celia doesn't know how she's done it. It just happened; time just happened and took her with it. Death has forgotten her, or maybe the scale is tipped in her favour. She's a great believer in balance. Enough other people must have filled the death slots and closed the grave gaps. But she tells the reporters what they want to hear: getting to bed at nine; a shot of red wine with her evening meal; her mile walk, which she still does albeit with a support walker of the human kind. All these things the truth.

And now it is approaching her one hundred and third birthday. Enough candles to burn the house down, she thinks, and recalls her earliest memory, of a cake with a bear and a little green pine tree. But that only had three candles.

Lately her reminiscences feel musty and cracked, like her old graduation picture she also keeps on the bedside table. She wants to live in the here and now, as the catchphrase of today tells her, not the here and after. The rest of her life is measured in days or hours, she doesn't want to live them in the past. How many has she left? Are they odds or evens? It's certainly odd she's got to this.

Celia feels victorious as she reads about someone younger than her dying (in the last few years they all are) and then instantly feels guilt at her triumph. She closes the newspaper, hiding the Hatch, Match and Dispatch within its folds.

She knows Margaret, her youngest and only surviving daughter, will be here soon. In fact she can hear the car pulling up in the drive as she thinks.

Margaret appears in a cloud of pink poly-nylon and green linen. 'Mum? Where's Mrs Ottoman? You shouldn't be alone. Here, I've bought some of that cake you love so much. I'll put the kettle on.'

Celia wonders if she was like this at sixty-eight. Can't remember, sinks back in her high-backed chair and waits for her morning tea.

When Margaret comes into the living room, Celia puts on her glasses and looks at her closely. She wonders where her daughter got her taste from but knows she doesn't have to strain the brain cells. Margaret's father had no idea of fashion.

'There you go Mum, a nice cuppa. And a piece of lumberjack cake on your favourite plate. I can't imagine where Mrs Ottoman has got to!'

Celia sits up and eyes her daughter over the rim of her glasses, finds her more acceptable in the blur and shakes her head.

'I may be old, Margaret, but you don't have to treat me like an invalid. I told Mrs Ottoman she could have the morning off. I made myself some tea an hour ago. Didn't you see the cup in the sink? I managed to put it there all by myself.'

'Gee, Mum, no need to be sarcastic.' Margaret pauses for a moment, and then wipes a strand of hair from Celia's face. 'Gosh though, you really are incredible.'

'So everyone keeps telling me. But honestly, I just don't know what all the fuss is about. It's not really of my doing, you know. And, as for living in my own home at this age, well that's providence isn't it? I was lucky enough to have married well, and have the funds to hire and fire.'

Marry well, the words stab her conscience with their mendacity.

And sometimes she feels as insignificant as dust. It's as if she's only now learning to grow. Why, she wonders, after all these years and with so little time left, is she feeling like this?

Margaret pours her another cup of tea without asking and Celia feels too tired or too despondent, she doesn't know which, to turn it down.

'Mum, I have a favour to ask.'

Here it comes, the real reason her daughter is here after so many months.

'You know Denise? Well, her daughter...'

'Yes, yes, my great-granddaughter, Amy.' Celia urges Margaret on with a queen-like gesture of her hand.

'Yes, Amy, she's doing a thesis on ageing, and she was wondering...'

Once again Celia cuts in.

'She wants to question me. What *I* would like to know *is* why I seldom see any of you all year, but when my birthday is approaching, I suddenly become more interesting?' Celia looks at her daughter's face. She sees only her long-dead husband, Andrew, in her. Andrew's

268

colouring, Andrew's eyes. She can't bring herself to feel ashamed of this outburst. And secretly she's glad Amy is coming. She hasn't seen her for so long and she loves her first great-granddaughter in a way she never did with any of her own children.

Amy reminds her of herself. When she was young of course, and pre-marriage.

'So it's all set then? I'll tell her it's okay?'

The next day Celia is waiting alone again. Mrs Ottoman has had another early minute, in this case, an early four hours.

She keeps hearing *the tune*, woke with it playing in her mind, an echo sounder from the depths of her past. The start of the confession Andrew made her listen to, furrowing out her wounds of guilt while salving his.

Hi there little bumble bee
I see you and you see me
Busy, busy little bee
Come along here follow me

If there had been surveillance cameras in those days, thinks Celia, they would have shown a man in a coat and hat, pulled closely over his appearance despite the warm weather, and, wearing a black and yellow striped jumper, a boy of three following close behind.

Celia doesn't hear Amy enter the house and she jumps when she begins to speak.

'Oh, there you are, Grangran.'

Amy has always called her this. As a toddler Great-grandmama tangled her tongue with too many syllables.

'Hello, Amy dear. Just resting my eyes.'

269

Celia looks at her great-granddaughter. Amy's face reflects certain belief that the future will be just as good as the past twenty-three years have been.

Her hair is fair-weathered and her skin holds the translucence of youth.

Just over five foot three, she's not as tall as Celia but her proportions are as perfect as the exquisite porcelain doll that Celia received on her third birthday.

With a shudder she realises that the doll, Christina, still en-glassed in a case her grandfather made for her at the time, will be turning one hundred years old in two weeks. And she's not so exquisite now.

Funny how she, Christina doll and the boy all share the same birthday. November the fifth.

'Sit down dear, and tell me all about your studies.' Celia indicates a chair set close enough for her to hear easily, but not too close for focus.

'Oh, you know Grangran, same old same old.'

That's what Celia loves about this girl; she treats her like one of her peers. Uses the same idiom as she does with them. This phrase Amy has said before, and Celia thought it quite clever of her great-granddaughter, until she discovered it wasn't original. But still, she appreciates not being talked to as if she was a senile child.

And Amy would never dream of telling her she looks *so good* for her age. What benchmark could people base that one on? she wonders.

'How are you getting on with the internet?' Amy says. 'I did get your email by the way. I just didn't get around to answering it.'

Celia smiles at her great granddaughter. 'That's okay, dear. It's fun. I have a webpage now, you know.'

It seems to Celia that Amy may be on the verge of saying 'You're wonderful'. If so, it would be the first time. She takes a deep breath.

'Guess what? Grangran, I'm in love. Real thing this time. Thomas Hart-Delaney. You were so right about Paul. Thomas is everything

Paul isn't. He's taking me out on his yacht over the long weekend. I'm going to learn how to sail.' Amy bounces excitement.

Celia lets out her breath. Relief floods her on both counts. Not being patronised and the fact Amy has *dumped (that's the right word isn't it?)* Paul.

In the same way that Amy reminds her of herself, Paul reminds her of her husband. Andrew had been blonde and tall, with a cyclist's backside, athletic build. Eyes too close-set though, and piggy. Her mother had always told her, *Celia, horses and men, look at their eyes and you will know how they'll behave.* Even now, she wishes she had taken her advice.

She finds herself wondering about the little boy she never knew. She could have done without the knowing. It has made her life more miserable than pain.

In the same moment of recall she realises why she is feeling happier lately. She is ready to confess. What can they do? Put her away for life? She laughs inwardly but shakes away the thought.

'Grangran, you all right?' Without waiting for an answer Amy continues, 'Thomas is into real estate. He was really interested when I told him about your holiday house in Toorak. Said he'd love to come and see it sometime. You'll really like Thomas, Grangran.'

Amy stoops over the coffee table and pours herself another cup of tea from the silver service. She holds up the other empty cup but Celia shakes her head then says, 'Anytime, dear. I'd love to meet him.'

Amy takes a long sip of her tea. 'I suppose I better get on with this interview thing. My questions are not very original, bit boring actually.'

She leans down to a briefcase from which she extracts a small digital recorder. She holds it up and makes a questioning face.

Celia nods. 'That's okay, Amy dear, I don't mind. I'm an old hand at this interview stuff now, you know. Television, Radio.'

'Okay, first question. Do you feel any differently now than you did when you were younger?'

Celia rubs a hand across her mouth. Feels the roughness of her skin, avoids looking down. 'Not at all,' she says. Then, knowing that Amy will expect more, she adds, 'Well of course you slow down in most things. Walking and...' She laughs. 'And thinking. Remembering takes longer. Have to go backwards in sequence. You know, to recall a name or a situation.'

She thinks to herself: Not *one* situation though. That stands her memory to attention without any salute.

Amy nods at her. 'Go on,' she says.

'You feel the same inside. Really, I still get a bit of a shock when I look into the mirror. One day I was looking at a photo someone had taken and I wondered who that old woman was. Luckily I realised before I asked.' Once again Celia laughs.

'Any regrets, Grangran? Things you didn't do? Opportunities missed?'

Celia takes a long breath. Starts to say yes but catches herself like a hooked fish and answers down pat.

'Of course there will always be regrets and missed opportunities. But none that stand out... Nothing... Not really.' Suddenly she drops forward and rocks her face in her hands.

Amy gets up and comes over to her. She tentatively touches her back. 'What's all this about, then? Was it something I said? You *do* have regrets, don't you? I've always known you've been holding onto something.' Amy reaches down and turns off the recorder.

Then she sits at Celia's feet, curls her legs beneath her, and looks up.

Celia is transported back twenty years to when Amy was three. *Read to me now, Grangran,* she had said, and then sat at her feet in just the same manner. Expectant and excited. But now there seems to be a sharpness to her look.

Celia sighs and leans back. The time has come and she knows it. What is the saying? A woman's time is when she gives birth and a man's time is when he faces death. Funny for that to be at the opposite sides of the spectrum. But always the balance, she thinks.

Andrew had balanced his conscience to tolerable by dumping his confession into the recesses of hers. Where she had choices - to tell or not to tell.

Sometimes good people do evil by doing nothing. Wasn't that another saying? Did that make her worse than her husband? And had she really believed what he had told her about the boy. That it was his.

Celia has her hand on top of Amy's. She can feel a pulse through her palm. Not sure if it is hers or Amy's. The fragility of life, the heartbeat thread of tenuous trust.

'I adored your great-grandfather once. He was so dashing. I know that's an old word but really it was him, in both senses. He was in the Tour. Tour de France, that is. He was the grandson of a friend of my grandfather's. You know, the one who made the glass box for my Christina doll.'

Celia is sure that Amy shivers at the mention of Christina doll. Thinks: Perhaps she's cold.

She doesn't ask, but continues talking. 'Andrew Denim-Decourt. I loved that name.

I spent so much time pairing it with mine. Rolling it off in voice and writing. Practised signing it.'

Amy leans down to her digital recorder. Looks up at Celia with eyebrows raised. Celia gives an almost imperceptible nod and Amy switches it on again.

'I do that,' Amy says. 'I mean, I sign my name with Thomas's last name. Don't you just love it when they are hyphenated?'

Celia frowns for a moment, raises a doubt. But it grows butterfly wings of denial and rises to the corners of her mind. Many of its companions flutter there.

'Do you still have Christina doll then, Grangran?'

'Yes, of course I do. Why do you ask?'

Amy sits back in her chair again. Celia sees her colour drain from her face like a faded photo.

273

'Oh, I don't know really, it's just that... I keep having this recurring dream. I'm about three or four. Very young anyway, and I climb the stairs and Christina is there in her glass box at the top of them. But she has her arms out to me and she is asking me something. Then she starts laughing but it's muted because of her being boxed in. It's just...really creepy. I wonder maybe if I saw her again it may stop it happening. In the last dream she broke through the glass and told me that I was going to be her mummy now...'

Perspiration is beading like thaw on Amy's forehead. Celia rubs her arm.

'That sounds like quite an ordeal, dear. Of course you can see her. It's funny, you know. You were always so fascinated with her when you were a child.' She hands Amy a handkerchief.

Amy takes it and presses it to her temple. 'I like horror movies too, but not when *I'm* in them.' She twists a smile which barely curls her lips.

Celia points at the recorder. 'Well, dear, switch that thing off and I will take you to her. When did you see her last? She's deteriorated a lot more in the last decade. A bit like me.' Celia chuckles but notices Amy doesn't join in.

Amy and Celia ascend the stairs. They are long and broad and curved. When Celia was young she used to play Gone with the Wind and flounce down them in her swirling dresses. Lovely fashions back then, she thinks.

Amy touches the carved wooden banister. 'This is such a beautiful house, Grangran. It would bring a fortune.' The last few words barely a whisper.

Well, Celia thinks, *it will all be yours, dear, one day soon.* But all she says is: 'Yes, it is. Did you know it's been in the family for four generations?'

She doesn't turn to see if Amy is nodding or not.

When Andrew had first started talking about the boy, he came to her drunk and almost incoherent. But his clarity had progressed with his confession.

'His mother doesn't mean anything to me, Sealy love. It happened after we had that big row about your birthday present.'

That flashed a memory of the Mercedes he had bought her. She had hated the colour - like gold flaked mustard it was - and insisted he take it back.

What a spoilt little cow I was back then, Celia muses, her lips thinning.

They reach the top of the stairs; Celia sees that Amy is shrinking back into herself. She's really scared, she thinks. 'It's okay, dear, Christina is in the pink room.' She leads the way across the polished boards to the far end of the corridor, opens the door to a pink-everything décor which gives the room its name. Celia walks slowly across the floor to a box three feet high, which is draped in a draw sheet.

She glances over her shoulder and beckons to Amy, who is still huddled against the door.

Celia whisks off the cloth cover like a magician to reveal an old glass box joined at the seams with a tar-like substance. Some of that has leaked to the floor and stained the carpet.

She takes the cloth and polishes the glass. Amy comes forward as if summoned from the dead. She stares at the doll.

'Oh, God, it's hideous, she looks worse than y...' Amy snaps her mouth shut like a flytrap.

Again, a doubt rises in Celia's mind, and again it retreats on gossamer wings. But only just.

She pulls herself away from the room and begins the descent downstairs. She doesn't stop and is surprised how strong she feels when she reaches the bottom.

She had always thought her confession would be to the police. After all, a child had been murdered. Seventy years ago. A cold case soon to be heated up.

When Amy comes into the room her face is whiter than the plaster walls. Her hand quivers as she switches on the recorder.

'I hope what you are going to tell me has got nothing to do with Christina doll.'

She looks intently into Celia's eyes.

'She wasn't always called Christina. When I got her she was wearing a name bracelet. Elizabeth Dolores. No hyphen.' Celia's voice sounds frosty even to herself. 'I called her Lizzy until about four years after my marriage. Then I changed it to Christina, an anagram of Christian. Well, I couldn't give her a boy's name.'

'Why would you want to?' Amy's voice flattens with the question.

Celia breathes in, holds her breath, then lets it out and begins her confession. So many years of not telling anyone add piquancy to her words. She gives reasons then erases them with her own arguments. Cannot deny Andrew's logic of it. Especially the inheritance. *Keeping the bloodline pure*, were his words. She never condoned it. But it was all too late to do anything, when she was told the boy was already dead.

She sings the song, the words a threaded tune sewing up her tongue. Guilt sticking it with dryness to the roof of all her years of indifference. Feels again the rawness of self flagellation. Tells her great-granddaughter the little boy's name was Christian. And it had seemed fitting to name her doll, who'd had never had a life beyond the glass coffin, in memory of him.

Afterwards Celia feels lighter than she has for many years. The seesaw of balance has dropped Amy's side down with a bang. Now she looks into Amy's eyes, holds them for a moment then looks down at the digital recorder in Amy's lap.

Amy glances at the recorder too. 'So, Gran, you are telling me that your late husband, my great-grandfather, is a murderer and you have been protecting him all these years? To keep up the good standing we have, I suppose. Makes sense but why tell *me* about it?'

'Oh God, Amy. You must understand what it has been like for me all these years...'

Amy cuts her off in a stab. 'Yes, Gran, I know exactly what it has been like for you. Housekeepers, chauffeurs. Trips abroad. Anything and everything you want. Have you any idea what it's like being a struggling student? My mother says it's character building. And you seem bent on my construction too. A lousy one hundred dollars for my birthday and Christmas, while you sit on millions.'

Celia sits staring, unfocused. Her mind is still retreating. But the butterflies have returned as wasps.

'Well, Gran,' Amy says, bringing her face closer to Celia's. 'You'll have to cough up now.' She pats the recorder. 'If you don't, you know what I'll do.'

Celia makes no move to grab the machine. *Good,* she thinks. *Take it to the police. Save me repeating myself.* But something stops her from bringing the thought to voice.

'Tomorrow, Gran, we are going to pay your solicitor a little visit. And then you'll pay after that.' Amy laughs softly, apparently enjoying her own pun.

She gets up, packs her recorder into her briefcase and then, over her shoulder, casts plain words, laced with sarcasm, 'See you tomorrow, *Grangran.*'

After she leaves, the room seems less quiet than before she'd come. It echoes the words Amy has spoken in the guilt-empty spaces of Celia's brain.

One thing Andrew was right about, Celia thinks. The bloodline has been kept. It's threaded all the way to her great-granddaughter. Not pure though. Never that. But she may be able to guarantee it will go no further.

She rummages through the rosewood dresser, finds her telephone book and dials a number.

Soon she is sharing pleasantries, business and left over lumberjack cake with her old friend, Damien Jack Trentworth QC.

A little while later she leans over and scans the documents. Brushes away a dropped crumb.

'Yes,' she says, 'that's right.' She indicates the long list of charities with her pen. 'And what's left over is to be held in trust until Amy Harrison my great-granddaughter turns fifty-five, on the proviso she has not had any children.' Celia pauses, holding the pen aloft.' Then her eyes narrow, 'And until that time I also bequeath to Amy Harrison, the care of the antique doll, known to all as Christina.'

Three Haiku

twin lambs
the ewe keeps watch
over the one not moving

Heron's Nest, New York USA

after bushfires
all her landscape paintings
koala grey

Notes From the Gean AUS

crooked path
an old man
bends against the wind

Notes From the Gean AUS

All published in Third Australian Haiku Anthology 2011

Where the Truth Lies

Highly commended in the JBWB short story competition UK
published as The Trousseau Box, Short Story America Vol. Two USA

When the gulls haunt the sea-cliffs, dipping and climbing the wind like rising kites, and all the children of the houses that cling like periwinkles to the ledges above are tucked into bed three-apiece because that is all the comfort poverty will buy, a mother may tell in quiet words of the sea. What it gives and what it takes and sometimes what it leaves behind.

'Hush now, my little ones and sleep will come to you. And Ellie, lie still too, while your father fights with the ocean to bring us back the fishy in the morning. We'll have work aplenty then with the salting and the pressing.'

Her voice is soft, like the waves which froth in muted tones, curling the edged bed of the sea before hissing back to tuck the hidden depths.

And then Ellie, her eldest, says in plaintive pitch, 'Tell us again, Maither, tell us the story of the trousseau box.'

'Yes, yes,' Tommy and Markey, her two boys, clamour. 'Tell us about the pretty lady.'

And the mother sighs away the truth gnawing at her like the wave-eroded cliffs and begins her tale.

'It was not unlike a night as this, your father had not long gone a-sea, two nights before. Chasing the haddock he were. He were to be gone for three days more. And me alone, except for Ellie. But she had only seen four winters. The same as you two boys be now.' The mother pauses briefly. 'And me heavy with babe.' There is another short silence before she continues. 'I got up to the privy and then I saw a light.'

Then Ellie asks, 'Was it like the one Uncle Caleb sets up to guide in the ships?'

The mother gasps back a breath and pulls her shawl tightly around, her arms almost crossing herself. She doesn't answer, and bites her lip until the pain takes away the thought stinging her conscience like a wasp. When she turns away her face, she finds her voice.

'The wind was so strong the grass was flattened like a mat and it blew me towards the cliffs. The shawl I had was not enough, I was in sore need of my coat. I hadn't got it on. The privy only being a little walk. So I came back for it.'

Suddenly the wind rattles the windows of shuttered wood then scurries up the cliff face to rustle the trees. The boys scrunch down in the bed until it seems that Ellie is its sole occupant but for the two little bumps merging to one.

The mother continues: 'The moon was high and washed like the rain had cleaned it. And I could see ahead without the use of a lamp. And the little light I had seen before was still a-twinkling. Then I heard a sound.'

'That were the pretty lady,' says Tommy, his voice blanket-muffled.

'Maither, tell Tommy to hush. Markey wants to hear it too.'

'Hush now,' says the mother. 'Or I won't be telling it to any of you tonight.'

And so they are quiet while the mother tells of the pretty lady dressed in her finery lying on the sand and she as wet as the sea, and how the mother gave her coat to keep her warm. And how the lady kept asking for her trousseau box, saying how it contained much value. But how the candle in its silver holder, with its matching flintbox, to light it, were the only things she took with her when the sailors came. And how she begged them to bring her trousseau box to the lifeboat, but they'd said it would mean they could save one soul less.

And when the mother draws a breath, Ellie slips from the bed, comes back holding a candle and lights it from the lamp. 'Look, Markey, this is not the candle but the holder is the very same, ain't it, Maither?' And the mother nods and stares into the flame and goes as silent as the children have been until Tommy tugs her sleeve. Then she finds her voice again.

'She was the most beautiful woman ever I'd seen. Hair she had like this flame.' The mother's breath makes the candle flicker until it almost goes out. 'And her skin was white and as fine as what they use at the courthouse to powder their wigs.'

'And the colour of her eyes, Maither, what about her eyes?' says Ellie, who does not let any of the story be forgotten.

'Ah, yes, the colour of her eyes.' The mother pauses again. 'They were green like the sea of a summer storm.'

Ellie jumps up again, the boys watch as she goes to the curtained cupboard below the stairs and comes back with a yellowing nightdress. There are threads hanging loose around its bodice and edges. 'This had real pearls on it, didn't it, Maither, until the sea took them?'

The mother takes the dress, lays it over her lap, strokes the silk. She doesn't raise her eyes to her children until many are the minutes that pass.

'Ellie, you be putting back that candle now, do you hear? We don't have enough of them candles to be wasting.' Her voice is sharp and the boys cover their heads once more with the old grey blanket, the one with the holes from the moths that let the cold in like tiny needles, and Ellie hurries the candle in its little silver holder back to the windowsill where it lives.

The mother keeps on stroking the nightdress, her fingers playing with the twisted knots, teasing up the threads and plucking at them like she would a chicken.

282

'I made to leave the lady then, because the cold was taking me. I was shivering so bad I said to her, I need to go now and can you walk a little way? Then we can shelter behind that crag over there. But the words she answered me tumbled about each other. Saying how she'd been married for but a year and her husband was waiting for her in their new home. Then she touched my arm and asked again about her trousseau box. Had I seen it and could I look for it. It were as if it were just a summer day and we'd mislaid a shoe on the way to the market. She said it in such a manner. Not panicked as she were but light and hopeful. I was scared then, as I'd seen others before her taken by a fever much less than hers.'

Markey stirs and gives a little cry, for the sleep that was teasing behind his lids with pictures of the pretty lady has vanished and all he has left is the hunger ache in his stomach and the cold tickling his toes like frost.

'She got to her feet and we walked towards shelter, where the wind was not as fierce. And she went to lie down before we were there so that I had to hold her up. But I got her there and put the coat over her. She could go no more. When I came back the next morning she were gone and we never did find that trousseau box,' says the mother.

The boys are sleeping but Ellie sits as still as a wall, until her mother nudges her and tells her to climb back a-bed. 'And no more talk now, it's late and there'll be work for us all in the morning.'

The sea is stirring and grumbling like a drunken lover. The mother stares at the nightdress, hears the wind whispering, turns the pictures of the story around in her mind until they sit up straight and beg for the truth. The pictures become words of the lies she told her husband when he returned. How she delivered herself of two babes, not one, twin boys, and all on her own. Then she tells him of the lady, shows him the nightdress. But she has already washed the death-blood from its neckline and the birth-blood from its hem.

283

The contents of the trousseau box had bought them food and clothes for a year.

Later, the mother drapes the nightdress over a chair and goes to her own bed but she is not long there before she feels the blankets lift and Ellie slips in beside her like a fish. She pulls the girl close and feels her arms encircle her.

'What is it, Ellie, can't you sleep, girl?'

'Maither,' says Ellie, her voice a notch above a whisper. 'I remember that night.'

'What do you remember?'

'You were not with babe when you went to the pretty lady, cause our Tommy had already come. Don't you remember, Maither? I got you the cloths and the knife to cut the cord. And Tommy had blood on him and he was screaming. But you said the screaming were good to made his lungs strong.'

'Why have you not told me all this before?'

Ellie shivers and turns over, stares at the ceiling. The stars are flickering light through the cracks in the roof.

'I seen other things that night that I don't understand, Maither. I need you to tell me.'

The mother sits up in bed. 'Tell me first what you saw.'

'When you came back for your coat I followed you. But I kept back. I was scared then of the ghosts Uncle Caleb told me of. But now I know the ghosts is just a lie to scare people from finding the truth.'

'And what truth may that be, Ellie?'

'Uncle Caleb is a Wrecker. Aint he, Maither? He murders people and takes what's theirs. I know that he puts out the lamps for the ships to come up on the reefs.' Ellie's voice is loud and the mother snatches a glance at her two boys but they do not stir and for this she is glad.

The mother finds a memory of her own childhood, an awakening not unlike this night, but there was no pretty lady and all that she knew then was what her father and brother told her. It's the law, they'd said, if no one is found alive then the owners of the shipwrecks will have no claim. They did not tell her of the part they played to make sure of no survivors, be they man or beast. They made a thin line between salvage and plunder, she thinks.

'Hush now, Ellie, or you'll be waking the boys. And don't tell your father any of this. He's a fisherman and proud of it. As most of the men in this village are. He knows of it all. And I do not visit with my family or my brother now.'

'You lie.' Ellie spits the words like a snake.

The mother raises her hand but then her arm falls limp to the bed.

'Oh Ellie, I cannot abide this, what did you see?'

'I seen you and Uncle Caleb. But that were later. Earlier you came back for the knife, the same knife I had brought to you only a few sleeps before that day. When our Tommy was born.'

The mother takes Ellie into her arms, and whispers. 'Oh, my poor lamb, you should not have seen it.'

She sits up in bed and pulls her shawl around her shoulders. 'The pretty lady was with babe and it was coming and would wait for no one. That is why she could not walk. She was brave and I helped as I could. She was torn between this world and the other.'

Ellie is snuggling into her mother's side. The mother brushes away a strand of Ellie's hair.

'I kept thinking this is what my Ellie saw when Tommy came. Oh, and it is so beautiful, such a wonder. I took the babe to the pretty lady's breast. And how strong the babe were, Ellie. How it suckled. And its maither, her face were so soft it were like the silk of her nightdress. And her smile it were sunshine. I wrapped the babe in this shawl.' The mother touches her shawl with a fingertip caress. 'So I had only my dress. But I did not feel cold. The wind went away and the night went still. And that's no lie Ellie. I swear. Then the pretty lady were thanking me. Thanking me Ellie! Me, a lowly fisherman's wife and she so highborn. Oh, that moment I wished would never go.'

'But then Uncle Caleb came, didn't he Maither? Why was he angry? I got so scared, I ran home.'

The mother sighs a long breath. She hugs Ellie and lies back on the pillow.

She feels relieved that the child did not see what happened next.

Before she could stop him with word or action her brother had taken the knife and run the blade across the pretty lady's throat. A thin line. She had not made a sound and her eyes staring, green like the sea of a summer storm, were the last thing the mother remembers of her before snatching up the babe.

She told her brother that if he tried to take the babe from her she would tell her husband, when he returned from the sea. 'Not if you're dead, you won't,' her brother had said. But then laughter followed in her wake as she fled, and the words. 'You'll both stay safe enough if you keep quiet.'

Ellie says, 'Maither, Markey belongs to the pretty lady doesn't he?'

'No, Ellie child, not now, he doesn't. He is mine, and he is your brother and Tommy's twin. You must remember this truth and say no other.'

Ellie is silent and lays back to sleep.

The mother thinks of the trousseau box, carved oak, how she found it the next day, wedged in a cove, seaweed like sirens' tresses wrapping it hidden. She kept it secret from her husband. And what it held saved them all the following year when the fish did not come and when the winter was so harsh the boats could not go out even if they had.

The mother climbs from the bed, takes the nightdress from the chair and draws back the tattered curtain where an open wooden box, without its lid, stands on its side for a cupboard. She stares at the square oak plates, their backs ornately carved but their edges roughly cut, the knife pared by years of sharpening to a thin line.

A draught flutters the curtain and she thinks she needs to be putting more tallow between the cracks once again, come a pleasanter day.

Brown Cased Bakelite

Age flees backwards
like pre tsunami tide
entices you to walk on
golden sands of childhood

before reality
flooded your innocence
Poseidon had been given
all the waters
both fresh and salt.

Echoes of the radio
brown-cased-bakelite
His Master's Voice
Radio ABC
the dulcet tones
of past colonial rulers.

Your mother listened to *Blue Hills*
while you dreamed
a future riding
across brown ranges
round your home.

Jason and the Argonauts
anyone could join
but you never did.
Their tale of The Golden Fleece
spoken larger than history
but coloured different from
your mind-read book
of Greek gods and myths.

In your real light Apollo was less bright
and Hercules much more
the warrior.

Serial story of *A Taste For Blue Ribbons*,
your ears were pricked.
An equine religion
every night before dinner
no entrée more delicious.

The words sketched their spell
drew you out of grey
so you paid your fifty cents
for a half an hour of living
something truly live.

You learned to rise
to the trot
lifted to
connected to
days gone by
when Poseidon
was also the god of horses.

Melbourne Poets Union AUS

When Horses Fly
Eclecticism AUS

The nasal tones of a teenage check-out chick echo again above our heads: 'Security to Cosmetics... Security to Cosmetics.'

The look I cast my daughter is returned, doubled. What is taking them so long?

No one has dropped a facelift, or spilt vanishing cream. What is happening is a full pitched argument which, by the sound of it, could soon escalate to bloodletting.

'At least I got brains 'n' that!' screams one young woman. She is wrapped in a high cut skirt and low cut top, with bulges of fat for garnish. Her nose sports more silver than a trophy cabinet. She and her girlfriend, similarly attired, are definitely in the running for the world's worst dressed.

Two men crowd into the girls' personal space, chests puffed like obese pigeons.

We are waiting here because I need some hair dye and this is the only store which has my shade.

If only they would move to another part of the store. I have an important date tonight and I really need that dye. My roots make me look like a skunk in relief.

I glance at my daughter, Jasmine, who is unashamedly watching. I remind myself that she has three more years before turning twenty-five, the age when a brain is fully developed, so she's in no way responsible for her actions.

'Come on Jazz, I'll try Priceline.'

'Mum, they don't have your number 96 there, you know that.'

I grab her arm and soon we are trading the cool confines of the shopping complex for the hot tar fragrance of the main road.

Cars honk on passing; I know their tune is not for me. Jasmine is gorgeous. Long blonde hair and a figure trimmed to perfection, she glides confidently one stride ahead.

As we approach the crossing the fighting foursome appear behind us, but I'm not surprised that trouble seems to be following me. Not with what's been happening this week.

I work for an art gallery-cum-gift shop, have done so for the past ten years. Trisha, my boss, owns the place and hires me part time, seven days a week during school holidays.

I love meeting people; ninety-nine percent of the visitors are fun, friendly and out to have a good time.

I also act as tourist information. I've lived in the district all my life and know about most of the attractions and where they are. Maybe not the best way to get to them, I have a lousy sense of direction - I always joke that women are good at everything else so we have to have one failing.

As I said, most people are nice.

Last Monday it was hot and humid. You probably think we'd have lots of visitors but the beach beckons with weather such as this. We do much better on rainy days, as people come into the gallery for shelter. They look at souvenirs and gifts and sometimes I can do my spiel and get them to actually buy something.

Really, I don't know how Trisha can afford me. She always says the gallery's a labour of love and I believe her. I've seen the books.

Anyway, on Monday I was on my own, placing and pricing new stock in the gift shop when I noticed a man in the gallery.

He was walking far too quickly to be looking at anything and he kept glancing furtively in my direction. Intuition raised hairs of apprehension but I approached him confidently when he entered the shop.

A whiff of stale clothes and alcohol matched his appearance. He looked and sounded to be in his mid forties.

He didn't answer my 'Can I help you?' but walked quickly through, barely glancing around.

Just before leaving he turned to me and asked, 'Your husband work here too?'

'I'm divorced.' My response was automatic. Inner alarm bells clanged louder.

He turned on heel, Nazi-like, and left.

I put the incident on the back burner when an unexpected busload of tourists arrived. I was flat out meeting and greeting for the next hour; they were from Broken Hill and it's true what they say about country people being friendlier.

My unease re-ignited when the man came back early on Tuesday. Once again he walked through without looking but this time grabbed a small gift pack of perfume and approached the counter.

'For my wife.'

I could tell he was lying.

'Are you from around here?' My voice sounded strained even to me.

'Yes. I'll have to bring my wife here soon. She would like this.'

So, he was promoting the 'I'm married so no threat' theme. But I wasn't buying. Not with the look he was giving me.

As he was driving off I wrote down his number plate.

The police got back to me within the hour.

'Mrs. Megan Shelley? The car belongs to a Mr. Thomas Duran. He is known to us and, excuse the pun, but he's a bad customer. In fact he's currently awaiting trial on serious charges. Oh, and there's no wife.'

So much for my ex-husband saying women's intuition is crap.

The police told me to be careful, whatever that was supposed to mean, but there was nothing they could do as he was in his rights, visiting a public place.

'Look, Mrs. Shelley, he may not even come back. Just stay alert. We can only act if he does something.'

I was stung speechless. Would I have to be raped or assaulted before the police could do anything?

Jazz was almost as non-committal: 'What does he want with *you*, Mum?'

Gee, did I have to spell it out? I hadn't skipped the birds and bees lesson had I? (Although I did have a vague memory of buck passing, along the lines of '*Ask your father*').

Thankfully the police seemed to be right. Wednesday came and went and the man hadn't returned. Also, Trisha had introduced me to a guy who'd asked me out on a date for Thursday night, so things were looking up. Or at least they were until Trish said 'Meg, you really have to do something about your hair.' Trisha's not big on tact.

Jazz goes off to work and I return to the department store. I get my hair colour and still arrive at the gallery in time to start work. The tourist industry is not an early riser; most places don't open until late morning.

I load the till and put out the decoy, a gigantic stuffed rat which usually takes the two of us to move, but Trisha's late and I have to shuffle it to its place by myself.

Set up to impede foot traffic, Ratty catches people's eyes with his cheeky grin. The large 'Open' sign he holds entices them in - well, that's the theory.

I am daydreaming, looking at the roses lining the sides of the road and thinking how ours could do with some light pruning when a familiar car pulls up.

I stare at the number plate but fear has etched it to memory and I know without checking whose it is. My stomach tightens. I catch a glint of something pointing in my direction through the windscreen. Binoculars? Camera? A firearm?

What should I do? Ring the police? But they've already told me there's nothing they can do. He has every right to be here. For a moment I feel hysteria rising. Perhaps I should run out and fling myself on his bonnet, ask him what he wants, maybe a mad woman will be a turnoff.

The car crouches like a waiting predator then slowly pulls out to merge with the increasing traffic. It's going to be a busy day.

Trisha arrives at last.

'Lots of tourists in town today, Meg.'

Years ago before PC we jokingly referred to them as 'terrorists'. Today it would be apt.

I don't answer.

She keeps talking: 'Heaps of number plates from interstate.'

Panic at last breaks my silence. 'Trish, there's something I have to tell you.'

An hour and several vanilla squares later (maybe added weight will make me less desirable) I am feeling a little better but Trisha is furious.

'I can't believe the police won't do anything, Meg. At least they could put you under surveillance or something? What if he finds out where you live?'

I pick up the last vanilla square and stuff it down.

The trouble is I own a hobby farm fifteen kilometres from town with no neighbours in view. And I live on my own; Jazz left home years ago.

Trisha touches my arm. 'Meg, look, don't think about it. You have that date tonight. Why don't you knock off a bit early?'

'It's not that the police *won't* do anything, Trish, they *can't* do anything. The guy hasn't been convicted yet, and even if he had he's still allowed to enter public premises.' I sound far calmer than I feel.

Trisha clears away the plates and cups and wipes the bench, concentrating hard on a stubborn bit of drying custard. She looks up mid-rub. 'Come back to my place tonight and stay for a few days. It will save you travelling in. It's going to be a busy weekend.'

As if in confirmation a group of tourists stop to take photos of Ratty and then crowd into the shop, laughing and joking. They had lifted the plush fur hiding Ratty's nether regions and discovered his anatomical correctness.

Some time later I answer Trisha's questions.

'I think I'll cancel that date. I won't be good company tonight, anyway. But I will take you up on your offer of a bed, Trish. If I can leave now I'll have time to bulk feed the budgies and ponies before dark, and make sure everything's ok at home.'

The countryside unravels as the kilometres tick by. The paddocks are crisscrossed with alternate blocks of brown and green, the contrast complete beneath a solid blue sky. Some of the irrigators are going and my car narrowly misses being sprayed as one overshoots the road in a huge rainbow arc.

I cross the bridge that spans the river, note the power of water surging below; despite hot weather recent rain is making it flow freely again.

I thank God I have air-conditioning and safety locks. I'm feeling as spooky and jittery as a race horse on speed.

I keep checking my rear-vision mirror but no one is following me. I watch out for the white ribbon I tied to a bush when I first moved here to mark my right turn off. All these side roads look the same and it's really easy to get lost. The ribbon is fluttering like a truce flag and I spot it easily.

I tend the animals and drive back to town, by then my heart rate has returned to normal.

Every parking space is taken up in front of the gallery. I note all the number plates of the interstate travellers. Trisha will have been flat out. I feel a little guilty for not being there. Ratty is still in-situ and I wonder if I should stop and help bring him in. Then I see the familiar car parked in the side-street and, worst of all, no driver. I pull over and with shaking hands and quickening breath retrieve my mobile from my bag.

My heart is throbbing staccato as I dial the gallery. Trisha answers on the fourth ring. I hear a clunk as she puts down the phone, scrunching of wrapping, and her saying 'See you later' to someone in the distance.

When she picks it up she is breathing heavily too.

'He's there isn't he, Trish?'

'Yes.' The voice doesn't sound like hers.

'Ok, just answer yes or no. Are you all right?'

'Yes.'

'Is he the only one in the shop?'

'No.'

'Do you want me to come back?'

'No! We definitely don't have any of that range left.' She sounds decidedly unfriendly. I wonder what the other customers will be thinking of her phone-side manner.

'Ok. Bye.' It feels like I am talking to a stranger.

Anyway I'm still going back; surely he won't try anything with two of us.

I needn't have worried; by the time I get there he has gone.

Trisha is struggling with Ratty as I rush up. She changes positions so I can help.

'I thought it was him from your description, Meg. Then, when he asked about you, I knew I was right.'

At that moment Ratty gets stuck on the entrance threshold and all I can do is grunt with the effort it takes to dislodge him.

Trisha locks the doors and pulls down the blind with the 'Closed' sign.

'What did he want, Trish?'

'He wanted to know where the other woman who worked here was. He gave me some half-arsed excuse that you were holding something for him. Then he hung around. Creeped me out.'

'I know the feeling.'

'You shouldn't have come back. You would've been safer going to my place.'

'What! And leave you here alone?'

I look out through the gallery's window but the street is hard to see from that angle.

'I think he's gone.'

I pray he isn't hiding somewhere, waiting for us to leave.

The warmth of the evening lifts the aroma of honeysuckle and hyacinths, making me feel at home as we climb the steps to Trisha's cottage. Set on a small rise, it is a jigsaw of sandstone, bluestone and slate shingles, looking every bit what it is - an artist's abode.

Trisha fusses around like a mother, putting on the kettle and rummaging in the freezer.

'I know I've got some herb bread in here. It will go down really nice with that pâté I bought at the market this morning.'

I go over to the wine rack and retrieve a bottle of Cabernet Sauvignon. I am pleased to see it has many companions.

After dinner we sit out in the cool inner patio with our second bottle of wine.

I feel safe here. Trisha owns two mastiffs, Bonnie and Clyde; they live up to the notoriety of their names by size and demeanour.

I trace a finger absentmindedly around the rim of my glass.

Trisha stares at an open magazine on the coffee table, set to the crossword pages.

She smiles and pens something in.

'I don't know how you do those cryptic ones, Trish. I can't work out how to do them even when I look at the answers.'

'Yeah, they can be tricky. You have to think laterally, then they are great fun like...'

Trisha suddenly closes the magazine and looks serious.

'That's it Meg. We have to look at this thing from another angle.'

'By *this thing* you mean my stalker problem?'

'Well... if the police can't do anything because he has legitimacy visiting a public place like the gallery, what if we lure him to a private place like your home?'

I stare at her like she's gone mad. I put on my sarcastic voice.

'Oh, ok, you mean we lure him to my place, wait for him to arrive and then call the police?'

Trisha nods vigorously.

'Not bloody likely, Trish. What if they don't get there on time and-'

She cuts me off. 'No, listen, we wouldn't be at your place, we could set up security cameras and watch from Joe Furner's house.'

Joe is my nearest neighbour; he is retired, lives on his own and keeps to himself.

I've met him only twice, once when Jemmy, my pony, escaped and ended up on his front lawn and another time when one of his geese flew into my chook run. I don't know what he'll make of this. He was friendly enough those times, although he seemed a little conservative.

'I don't know, Trish, I hardly know the guy.'

But whether it's through drink or desperation, Trisha's idea sounds more appealing by the glassful.

'So how do we get the man to my place?'

Trisha's face clouds; obviously she has not thought that far.

'Mm, that *is* tricky.' She pours another drink, hands the glass to me and fills her own.

I am feeling better – a coupling of relief from a possible solution and the mellowness of the wine.

We sit for several minutes in a silence interspersed with 'what ifs...'

Finally Trisha sits forward with her hands on her thighs.

'Look, just hear me out, Meg. This guy doesn't know we are onto him does he? I mean, the police didn't give him a warning or anything?'

I shake my head.

'Good. Then it should be easy. We get someone asking directions to your place while he's in the gallery.'

'You're forgetting one thing Trish. He may already know how to get there.'

'I don't think so, Meg, otherwise he probably would have had you already.'

In the morning Trisha tees up a plan with her daughter, Kelly, who coincidently, is friends with Jazz. They grew up together and now work with each other at the Library. Kelly is also a member of the local drama company. Trisha tells me she jumped at the idea of doing some acting for real.

The man arrives later in the day. Apparently bolder with impunity, he parks right in front of the gallery and enters the shop.

I unpack a box of small statuettes and try to look nonchalant while Trisha ducks out the back to text her daughter.

Kelly is there within minutes. The library is only a block away.

I see the man's shoulders slump. He must have realised that getting me on my own was going to be a lot harder than he thought.

'Hi, are you Megan?' Kelly says. 'I saw your ad saying you had a horse for sale?'

Good line, I think.

'Yes. I do. He's a great horse. He's done pony club and show jumping. What are you looking for?'

'I'm just getting into the show scene. How many hands is he?'

'Sixteen Two. Look, you should come out to the property and see him. Go for a trial ride. I'll be finishing here at five tonight. You can follow me home.'

Kelly looks genuinely disappointed 'No, I can't, I'm working late. If you could give me directions I could come over this weekend.'

Her performance deserves an academy award.

From the corner of my vision I see the man pause in front of a painting then slink closer.

'Head out along Highway Seven, turn...'

'Can we write this down?'

This girl is smart; perhaps her brain is maturing earlier than Jazz's.

I write it down as I am saying it. '...and then turn down the side road, the one with a white ribbon tied to a bush.'

Kelly reads back my directions aloud. 'So,' she says. 'I take the first left past the old cemetery, follow the road for five kilometres and then start watching out for the white ribbon.' If the guy doesn't know the way now he is thicker than he looks.

He leaves soon after without acknowledgment from us or him.

'Gee, Meg,' Trisha says, shivering despite the heat, 'I hope we're doing the right thing. Now he knows what time you'll be leaving and the way to your house, too. And what if he doesn't go there tonight? Or if he decides to follow you out?'

'I'll leave earlier then.'

I hold none of Trisha's fears. It probably seems strange but I am actually feeling very positive about it all.

This morning I went to see Joe Furner, my neighbour. It turns out he is a retired copper and knows all about red tape. He doesn't condone what we are doing but does understand why we need to do something.

I leave work before Trisha and detour past my place to Joe's farm. Even though the sky is clear, distant rumblings and the odd flash give portent of the storm to come.

I know it won't deter the guy from coming; he looked like a man on a mission when he strode from the shop.

Joe helps me set up the surveillance camera Trisha has loaned us from the gallery. The picture we receive is grainy but then we aren't after great photography, just a warning.

It is all going to plan.

Trisha arrives an hour later. We take it in turns to watch. It is tedious work staring at a static picture. I keep losing concentration and looking over at Trisha every time she speaks to me.

'You don't seem too worried, Meg.'

She is right, I'm not so concerned anymore.

Joe lets us stay overnight. He volunteers to sit up for the rest of what now is early morning. So far the man has been a no-show. The others put it down to the storm but I'm not so sure.

All the late nights gain me a deep sleep and I don't wake until 9 am. At first, the unfamiliar room and the fact Jazz is standing over me make me think I am dreaming.

'Mum, Mum! Guess what? They pulled a car from the river this morning, and get this. It was your man. You know - the one who was stalking you. The police haven't reported it yet but I saw the car at the wreckers, after it was towed in. It was his number plate. You know - when horses fly, two and four is six.'

'Jazz, Jazz, slow down honey. You're not making any sense.'

'You know, Mum, an acronym. I made one up so I could remember. When Horses Fly - WHF246. His number plate.'

I slump back onto the bed. Clever girl, this late brain maturing thing must only be for guys.

At breakfast, Joe makes a phone call and then sits down with us at the table.

He doesn't seem to mind four females (Kelly is there too) in his house all talking at once.

He puts up his hand as a brake and addresses me.

'I got hold of one of my mates on the Force. It *was* Thomas Duran, your guy, who drowned.'

My guy, like we had a relationship or something. But I smile and then wonder if smiling is appropriate. After all, a man has died.

'He must have taken the wrong road,' Trisha says, looking at me strangely. I realise I am still smiling. But I feel as relieved as a condemned man given a pardon. Really, this was the only way I could ever feel safe again.

'It may be my fault.' I try to look contrite. 'You know I'm not good with my sense of direction. Remember that tourist bus that time, Trish, ended somewhere out in the pines?'

The others are quick to defend me. Jazz even gets the directions I'd written for Kelly. 'See Mum, this is right. He just got confused. Those dirt tracks are treacherous. Steep all the way down to the river, and with that heavy rain, visibility would have been zilch.'

'Plus the river flooded again,' Joe adds.

I put my hand in my pocket and scrunch down the white ribbon. I'll tie it back later today.

Air Locked

Spelk Fiction magazine - UK. Shortlisted for the Global Flash Fiction prize UK

This is seared forever in my mind. Picking up a little blue sneaker, with its happy yellow Sesame Street characters playing down its untied shoelace.

Our much awaited move to the country. The new old house with its backyard of junk.

I was always so careful in the city. A child is at risk from predators of the human kind, and fast cars, trucks, and buses. Urban-noisy and dangerous. The city.

Here in the rural, I sit in silence. Peace and quiet.

I have the quiet.

I look out of my backdoor to a backyard backdrop that still seems incapable of such tragedy.

He was three-years-old, golden haired, red-lipped pout. My little Sammy. My Sam.

It was the longed for, dreamed about, much needed move to the country. All that fresh air. Isn't that what they say about the country, fresh air, so good for kids?

Those words crowd my mind in capitals, silently screaming until I can bear it no longer and I take a pill and then another. I huddle in a blanket, Sammy's favourite blanket, and fail to sleep.

I relive it in slow-mo, moment by moment. Wish I could stop, skip it to fast-forward but it's always on pause and rerun.

Now, in my hand, the little blue sneaker with the yellow characters happy as Sesame Street, full of Sammy's first words: Big Bird, and Bert and Ernie. *Then,* that day, spinning my whole world, again in my mind.

Mummy, come and play. Come and play with me, Mummy. I'm bored. When will you finish?

Go out in the backyard, Sammy. Find Mummy a feather.

The tiredness hanging on me, from the loading, the travelling, the endless unpacking.

Sammy is back, holding a feather. He hands it to me like a peace offering. I'm up to my elbows in packing paper and cardboard boxes, with their black penned titles: For the Kitchen. For the Sitting Room. For Sammy's Bedroom.

Can we play hide and seek, Mummy? Can we? Can we please, Mummy? I hardly hear him *then.*

Now I hear him as loud as a shout and my mind shouts back: Go, and I will look for you right this minute. This unpacking, these things, these bloody things are not important. I'll watch you looking for somewhere to hide in the backyard.

You, my Sammy, thinking *Mummy will never find me in here* as you pull back a hessian mat, patched with rot and mildew, to uncover a grimy, ancient fridge. There's a handle-like lever but being a boy you know all about handles and discovering things. The joy of hiding and being found.

Then as you lower the heavy lid and snap-lock it dark, your realisation that one of your sneakers has come off.

And I know you so well. *Oh, my Sammy.* Know you hope it won't give you away. That I won't see it. Won't find you too quickly.

Dog Daze

I've always been a dog lover, but lately I've had to question this premise.

If I think about it though, I still *do* love dogs. It's just some dog owners that I hate.

My mother always told me to be careful what you ask for, and, if you are to believe the latest hype you have to be careful not to ask for what you *don't* want.

My husband and I didn't want to live in a noisy neighbourhood. I distinctly remember saying, 'Gerald, whatever we do, don't let's buy a place next to people who have yappy little dogs.' The universe must have only heard the last part of this sentence and the word 'do', from the first part.

Funny though, I don't remember asking not to buy a house next door to drug runners.

Our neighbours' daily (and nightly) car trips are of fifteen to twenty minutes duration. Their Nissan Turbo car is bad enough. But worst of all are their dogs, Tibby and Fibula (or some such names). These dogs, both of the hairy vociferous type, set up a continual howling as soon as the neighbours leave.

In some ways I blame my mum. She's the one who told us about this *Delightful little house for sale only two blocks away from me with a garden to die for!*

Don't get me wrong, I love my mother but let's just say she doesn't always think things through. Even when I was growing up Mum had her senior moments. And she had me in her early twenties.

Most of what she did was harmless but one dire stuff up was the poisoning from mushrooms which turned out to be toadstools. Picking them with mum had been fun. Stomach pumping, as we found out subsequently, was not. But the staff at the hospital were so caring and understanding. It'd sparked my fascination with all things medical and I found I had no trouble deciding what I wanted to do when I finished school. Becoming a nurse was for me, the most natural of choices.

I shouldn't really blame my mother for us buying this house. We should've checked out the place more thoroughly. But Mum *knew* about the dogs and how noisy they were, she'd walked past this house every day on her way to the shops.

When the land-agent brought us here for an inspection, it was as quiet as an abandoned church. Later we found out he was friends with our neighbours. In fact we saw him there for a few minutes just the other day, before he left with a small package and a smile as wide as a farmhouse veranda.

'Oh yes, the dogs, Katy,' says Mum, when I mention how sick of them Gerald and I are. 'They're noisy little beggars, aren't they? Poor old Betty. She doesn't know what to make of them.'

I look at Betty, a black cocker, lying head on paws at Mum's feet, and wish the dogs next door could be more like her. And why couldn't the neighbours be more like the ones we had across the road, old Mr and Mrs Franco? Early seventies and always on hand with pasta and spaghetti, when anyone in the neighbourhood was ill. Mrs Franco was often trundling off to the shop with her canvas shopping cart to buy stuff from Woolies.

'More tea, Mum?' I say, holding up the pot. It's wearing - in a lopsided way - the cosy Mum made for it when she was in her knitting phase.

'I will have another cuppa, Katy dear,' says Mum, bending down to pat Betty's wrinkle-knotted brow. Then without looking up, she adds, 'Have you thought of talking to them about their little dogs? Or would you like me to?'

'That's okay, Mum,' I say, my words tumbling like cross-lotto numbers, 'we're planning to, just waiting for the right time.'

I shake the Bushell's animal tea caddy, feel its lightness. 'Oh, damn,' I say. 'I should've bought more tea. Do you mind a teabag, Mum?'

'No, no, not at all, dear,' she says, with a screwed up nose.

Then a minute later, she says, 'Maybe I won't have another one, Katy.'

'Hell, Mum. It's too late now.' I hold up the cups and put hers down in front of her with a thud, like the final word.

'Okay, Kate,' Mum sniffs. 'But then I must get going, I promised to visit Maria today.'

I crease my brows. 'Who?'

Mum indicates across the road, to the Franco's place.

'Maria Franco. We got chatting last week on the way back from seeing you. She's a lovely lady. And her sons adore her. Very close family, that.' I can almost hear Mum thinking: she would never give *her* mother teabags.

On night shift, in a quiet moment between the Knifing (requiring twenty stitches) and the Heart Attack, which turns out to be indigestion, I think of what Mum had said about talking to the neighbours. The trouble was both Gerald and I are non confrontationists. We prefer people to see the error of their ways themselves. Surely they heard their dogs barking? Gerald reckoned they may be dipping into their own merchandise, in which case they'd be too zonked out to hear anything.

Carol comes up and leans over my shoulder. 'What's up, Katy, love?' Carol is four foot wide and has a personality to match. She has a way of making me feel better and wanting to confess all at the same time. Sort of a mother/padre personality.

'Oh, not much really. It's just these bloody neighbours' dogs.'

'Still having problems? Have you talked to them yet?' And then, as if she's reading my mind: 'Look, if you don't want to confront them, write them a letter. It's the first part of the process, you know.'

I knew *that*. I'd read on the Council website about what you had to do with problem dogs.

Carol goes off for a few minutes then comes back with a box of chocolates.

'Here, have one of these, a patient left them for me. Make you feel better.'

'Me, not my thighs, though,' I say, taking one. Carol nudges the box closer and I take another.

'Yeah, Carol, we have written to them,' I say, my words a mumble of chocolate caramel. 'Actually I feel quite sorry for their dogs. They never take them for walks or have them inside.'

'Probably not allowed to. Have them inside, that is. Part of their contract,' Carol says, thrusting the box at me again. 'They're renting aren't they?'

I take a foil-covered chocolate and begin to peel it.

'Yeah, they are. Really, though, Carol, I don't know why some people have dogs if they don't care about them.'

The phone rings. I hold it away from my ear. Carol mouths 'Your mum?' and I turn the shake into a nod. She picks up the chocolates and heads off.

I sort out another of my mum's little dilemmas, this time involving her forgetting her pin number. Luckily I keep a copy of it in my mind.

When I finally finish my shift a wet dawn is cracking the horizon from black to grey, and cars with sleepy-eyed commuters are making their way along highways as slick as our real estate agent.

After getting the kids off to school and seeing Gerald off to work, I try and sleep but Tibby and Fibula are yapping fit to burst blood vessels so I've no hope of drifting off.

I get up, do some housework, and two hours later slip into bed once more.

The phone cuts into my fortieth wink, it's my mother again. I almost don't answer it but know that I won't be able to sleep if I don't.

'Hi, Katy. I'm just calling to say sorry for last night. I waited till this afternoon to ring. I knew you would be tired this morning, after last night's shift.'

I prop myself up onto one elbow. Tibby barks in staccato, punctuating my sighs.

'That's okay, Mum. Can you hear that? I'll take the phone to the bedroom window.'

'I can hear them. Katy, were you still in bed? Oh no. I've mucked up again? I probably woke you, didn't I?'

'That's all right, Mum. I don't have another shift today'.

'Listen Katy, about the dogs. I was talking to Maria and she said her son, Antonio, could deal with your neighbours. I'm not sure exactly what she meant. But I said I'd talk it over with you.'

Intuition prickles the hairs at the nape of my neck. I've seen Mrs Franco's son. He reminds me of one of those actors in Underbelly. I never thought much of it at the time. But now...

'Mum, please don't get involved. And I don't think you should be seeing Maria.'

The line goes quiet then Mum puts on a voice I've never heard her use before. 'Look, I'll see who I like. I know you think I'm a silly old fool, but I do know when people are genuine. Maria is a lovely woman. Anyway, I'll let you get back to sleep. I can tell you're tired. We'll catch up tomorrow.'

I roll back onto the bed, still holding the phone, and close my eyes.

That night I sleep like I'm in a coma, I wake at seven am, feeling refreshed. I lie still for several minutes wondering what's missing.

Then I know what it is. No dogs barking.

I nudge Gerald. 'Darling, listen!'

Gerald stirs and groans.

'What is it, Katy? I don't hear anything.'

'That's just it,' I say.

Gerald sits up, rubbing his eyes; he puts his head to one side.

'Bloody hell, the dogs must be sleeping in, or something.'

I think of Maria Franco's son and hope it's not the something.

Gerald heads off to work and the kids leave in a flurry of consent forms and sports bags. The rest of the morning's quiet. Even next-door's Nissan seems to be missing.

Instead of enjoying the peace, I feel my stomach increase its churning with each silent passing hour.

Mum's usual visiting time comes and goes. She's not at home and seems to have her mobile turned off.

I start pacing the floor like one of those bears you see at the zoo. And I'm beginning to feel just as grumpy.

I look out of the window and feel my anger dissipating with relief. Mum is walking up our drive, with Betty in tow.

I open the door and Betty leads Mum over to her favourite chair.

'Mum, thank goodness you're okay. I was so worried. You know, the dogs next door are missing. And I haven't seen the neighbours or their car since yesterday.'

Mum looks at me, her eyes flashing like a surgeon's scalpel.

'I know,' she says, folding her hands in her lap but not dropping her gaze.

My stomach clenches.

'Oh god, Mum. What have you done this time? You didn't get Maria's son involved, did you? Please tell me you didn't.'

Mum shakes her head.

My stomach subsides once again.

310

For a moment we both sit quietly and then begin talking at the same time.

I close my words and let her speak.

'Katy, dear, after I got off the phone to you yesterday I started to feel awful for being a bit short. So, I decided to come over and apologise. I didn't want to ring you again in case you were in bed. When I got here I noticed your blind was still pulled so I decided to leave you a note.'

'I haven't found any...' I start to say.

Mum puts up her hand. 'I didn't have any paper so I went over to Maria's to borrow some. I swear that's all I was going to do. But we got talking.'

Betty comes over to me, her claws tip-scratching across the tiled floor. She places her head in my lap like a peace offering.

'Go on,' I say.

'Then we saw your neighbours.'

I nod.

Mum takes a sip of her tea and squeezes her lips. 'They were just getting into their car so we took our chance. I remember you telling me they go off for at least fifteen minutes. So we figured we had time.'

I raise my eyebrows. 'Time for what?'

'First we went to your place and Maria hid behind your shed.'

I begin to say something, and again Mum raises her hand.

'I went next door. I wanted to make sure there wasn't anyone else at home so I knocked on their door. No one answered. Then I went around the back. Funny thing, Katy, the dogs stopped barking soon as I started talking to them. They seemed to love the attention and I think they might've smelt Betty, too.'

At the mention of her name Betty presses her head onto my lap and wags her tail. I scratch behind her ears and she wiggles her body like a seal.

'I tucked a dog under each arm, went to the side fence and handed them over to Maria, who was still behind your shed. Then I got out of there. We heard their car coming back. I think they must have forgotten something.'

'God, Mum, did they see you?'

'No, not at all. That's one thing about that noisy car, you can hear it blocks away. I was hiding behind the shed with Maria and the dogs before they pulled up in their driveway.'

'Hell, what were you thinking? You stole the neighbours' dogs?' For a moment I sit just shaking my head.

Mum ignores my questions. 'I was hoping they wouldn't realise the dogs were missing, Katy. But they did straight away. I'd left the gate open in my rush to get out.'

'Well, that's good. They probably think they've run away then.'

'Yeah, that's what we were hoping. The trouble was the man went off to look for them while his wife stayed at home. In case the dogs came back, we heard her say.'

'How the heck did you keep the dogs quiet?'

'Oh, that was easy. Maria had brought some of her spaghetti bolognaise. They loved it. Didn't even lift their heads when their names were being called.'

For a second I feel guilt like a hollow log but I fill it with the memory of those two little dogs huddled on their back doorstep in the rain. Mum seems to read my mind. 'They are really skinny under all that fur, you know Katy. Maria was so angry when she felt them. She kept saying stuff in Italian. But the only word I could understand was her son's name, Antonio.'

I feel my eyes widening and the cool air in my mouth.

'So, how did you get away from here with them?'

Mum smiles. 'That was no problem either. You know Maria's shopping cart? The canvas one on wheels?'

I nod.

'Well, they fitted in there like twins. No worries. Maria wheeled them out of here and over to her place. They didn't make a sound. I came over a while later.'

I slump back in my chair. Words are forming in my mind but I can't find a sentence.

'Katy, we found really good homes for them. These two nice gentlemen bought them.'

This time I have no trouble bringing thought to voice. 'Bought them. Do you mean you sold them? Hell, Mum, you only took the dogs yesterday. How did you manage that? And what if they've been micro-chipped?'

Mum waves her hand. 'Well, I doubt it. They hadn't even had a bath or had their nails clipped for ages. I don't think your neighbours knew what a vet was. We put an ad in the paper for today. Tim and Nigel rang this morning. Such lovely boys. They own a hair salon in Melbourne, you know.'

'Oh,' I say in lowered tones. But Mum doesn't miss a beat.

'We donated the money to the rescue greyhound place. Over five hundred dollars. It was Maria's idea to ask for that much. Antonio has a dog like them. Cost him a packet.' Mum pulls over a corner of kitchen curtain. 'There he is, that's Antonio, there. He's been out for a while,' she says, through thinning lips. A black BMW roars into Maria's drive. Fire spews from its exhaust, and smoke rises from its tyres like it's zoomed in from hell. Maria emerges and the garage door ascends with the click of her remote. I glance over to our next-door neighbours' drive, still no sign of them or their Nissan. I swallow heavily and take a deep breath.

Mum goes over to the kettle and switches it on. Then she turns around and looks unblinking into my eyes.

'I didn't stuff up this time did I, Katy? I did good, didn't I?'

'Yeah, Mum,' I say. 'You did good.' I give her a hug and take the teabags down from the cupboard.

This time she smiles as she hands over her cup.

A Walk in the Park

Have you ever noticed
how a father's arm
is always long
enough to reach
his child's hand,
and a bumble bee
is softer and
more impossible
than any of
our imaginings

Trees in the beginning
of spring's promise
breathe in
silent growth
And stirrings of earth's heart
beat in time with
every living thing

Illya's Honey Journal - Dallas USA

Life's Living

I have galloped a brumby bare
beneath my thighs
dust deep ingrain from his
up north beginning
staining my conscience red.
In full flight I gave him the freedom
of the wind
while we pushed the earth away
with every hoof beat travelled.

I have ridden my bike
sitting on my hands
to prove my balanced trust
freewheeling down a slope
I would never dare to climb.
Then on the flat, swerving
side to side
to expose my nerve
while finding it hard
to bring it back to straight.

I have swum the ocean
above chasms of coral
A fish bluer than despair came to brush

my fingertips, while my flippered feet played
dolphin to the sea.

I have laboured all through
the hours
to finish the day
and longer night
being the first eyes my baby
would ever meet
while my body still
shared life
with its mother's milk.

I have faced flares
dotted like camp fires
across a sky
dark with the smoke of
many fractured fronts.
A fickle change had taken a family
minutes before
their souls numbered ours
while I resisted the pull of god's help
to choose my own.

Orbis International Literary Journal - UK

How It Ends

Radio Adelaide podcast

I was named after an island. Not the Virgin Islands, although I am twenty-five and still a virgin, but a tiny island called Iona.

When I was old enough to reach, I scrambled up on Papa's desk and turned the ancient blue globe to look for my namesake. I found the island only after using a magnifying glass over all the flaking oceans, and rotating the world by degrees. The island of Iona, off the western coast of Scotland. The letters naming it were curved in old script, fainter than the glow that struggled through the vine-covered window of Papa's study.

Iona. An island, a faction of unrest, I learned its history well.

My main companion as I was growing up was Holly, a border collie. A puff-ball puppy of black and white, she was a gift for my seventh birthday, a year before the accident which changed my face and life forever. After that, while my sister and brother's lives swirled around me, I stayed at home, was schooled by my mother, *Better for you my dear, away from all the stares,* and after Holly died, I didn't even venture as far as the bricked-in courtyard that walled off our house.

Papa used to say, 'My children are my happiness.' But he stopped saying that after the accident happened.

There was comfort in isolation. And, most importantly, I learned to laugh at myself. Not at what I looked like. I avoided mirrors, although windows have their own reflection and cannot be ignored.

But at my situation. At the dreams I'd had, which seemed more ludicrous the older I grew, and with the realisation that nothing more could be done for my appearance.

I had wanted to be an actress. I especially loved all the classic films, *A Wonderful Life*, *Breakfast at Tiffany's*, my favourites. And every silent movie. Even when I was a kid they held me in their celluloid spell. Papa loved movies too and I remember us watching Jules Verne's *Twenty Thousand Leagues Under the Sea* together. Papa said he would take me on a cruise ship one day and we would visit my island.

The first film Vivian Leigh made after *Gone With The Wind* was featuring today on Channel Five, the Classics station. The movie was called *Waterloo Bridge*. My neighbour was coming over, Jeremy, the sight-impaired guy. Mother used to say: Isn't it good Jeremy can't see you my dear, no pre-judgement.

That afternoon when Jeremy knocked on the door, he was holding a bunch of chrysanthemums and his gorgeous face was split with a grin. He'd never let his blindness stop him; when he was younger he went tandem riding and swimming with his brother and travelled all over the world. But he also loved films and, since he'd bought the house next door three years ago, found a sympathetic companion in me. In the action moments, the parts without words of the film, I'd explain what was happening. Not the plot though.

'Hey Jeremy,' I said, letting him in, 'I Googled Waterloo Bridge. It was a play in 1931. MGM bought the rights in 1940. They had to change it a bit for the film. Apparently it was too raunchy.'

Jeremy went into the kitchen and pulled down one of mother's vases. I remembered how she use to pronounce vase with a drawn out 'a'.

I saw him trace his fingers around the design. His hands were beautiful, long and tapered. I'd never let him touch my face.

'This is the one with the blue irises.' It was not a question. 'Should look good with the yellow chrysanthemums.' He deftly placed the flowers and filled the vase with tap water.

'Okay, Island Girl. Get seated. I'll make the coffee. Movie starts in ten. And don't tell me any more. Spoils it if you know too much.'

When the movie was over, Jeremy stretched out then leaned forward to push down the footrest of the armchair. It made a heavy metallic clunk.

'So, what did you think of that?' He had his serious voice on, the one which said I want more than a one-word answer.

'Well,' I said, 'the name says it all, really. Doesn't it? I mean, Waterloo Bridge.'

I put an emphasis on Waterloo.

Jeremy nodded and raised his eyebrows. His eyes looked far away. Unfocused. I averted mine and continued, 'I don't feel there was any judgement for the female lead being a prostitute. Seeing she was sort of forced to become one really. Although it was a bit of a lousy ending, her topping herself like that.'

Jeremy steepled his fingers and turned his face in my direction. He wanted more.

I rose and strode over to the TV. The adverts had come on and were screaming a half-price sale, for goods I'd never want, at me. I switched the room into semi-silence. I could hear the tin roof catapulting the heat in loud cracking noises.

'You know, Jeremy,' I said. 'In the 1931 play, the woman doesn't do the *honourable* thing. It's an accident that kills her.'

Jeremy gave a short laugh. 'Oh God, Island Girl, do you mean to say you knew the plot and the original plot all the time we were watching the film? I'm just glad you didn't say anything. Doesn't it take away the fun? Knowing what's going to happen? How it ends?'

'Well, you did ask me not to. Tell you, that is. And to your last question, no, it doesn't. Not for me.'

Jeremy said, 'Anyway, I thought it was a bloody good movie. Ahead of its time.' He took the cups out to the kitchen.

I raised my voice, 'I love the way they hint at things in these old movies. Not once was the word prostitute used. No sex scenes. And even when she throws herself under the truck, no graphic shots. Still powerful though.'

'Yes, in some ways more powerful, I think,' Jeremy said, coming back into the lounge room.

'How so?' It was my turn to lift my eyebrows.

'Well, the imagination is stronger.'

I went silent for a minute. I thought, Yes, that's how you have to live your life, Jeremy. In your mind's eye. What did *I* look like in it, I wondered?

And the thing was, to him, those scenes were once removed, so to speak. I'd described them the best I could, but they were only words. Words painting a picture, I guess. Once again I wondered.

I sat and thought about the film, the actors now all dead, their only living roles were these scenes, and not even the truth of themselves. They were characters of design, written by others and remembered as such. Not their own stories but forever and now, only screenplay.

The next day Jeremy came over again.

I opened the door wide. 'This is getting to be a habit. Haven't you got a home?' I hoped he could hear the smile in my voice.

The thing is, I only saw him once a week, for the feature movie. He was always too busy working. Jeremy was a consultant at Travel Tight, the local discount travel agency.

He strode into the house. 'I just thought I'd come over and see my Island Girl again.' He sounded cheerful, but I noticed today there were no flowers.

I'd never known Jeremy to take time off work.

I made coffee in silence and saw him twirling patterns on the kitchen table. He scratched at a piece of something stuck to its surface. It was immutable. A tiny patch of hardness in a sea of green melamine.

'Iona,' he said slowly. 'Are you happy? I mean, really happy. I know you haven't left this house for, how many years?' He opened his hands, palms out in my direction.

Thoughts somersaulted but I spun them around and countered. 'What about your life, Jeremy? You're always working.' I turned my back on him and went to get the milk from the fridge, even though I knew it was sitting on the sideboard.

'I mean, Jeremy, have you ever even had sex? I suppose you have.' The words escaped before I could catch them.

Jeremy's intake of air was audible.

'Christ, Iona, what sort of statement's that? What do you want me to say? Blindness has its advantages? The sympathy factor. Give the blind guy a fuck? Is that what you think?'

I swallowed. 'God, I'm sorry. I don't know why I said that.'

Jeremy took a long swig of coffee and screwed up his face. 'If we are both going to get all deep and meaningful, I bloody well want something stronger than this.' He got up, swilled his coffee down the sink, and headed for the door. 'Back in a minute,' he said, gesturing over his shoulder. I watched him stride over to his place. How could he be so confident when he couldn't see what was ahead of him?

He took about an hour to get back, but didn't offer any explanation. I had left the front door open, so he let himself in.

Without speaking, Jeremy got out two glasses and poured some whisky and coke. I took a swig, but couldn't taste the cola. I felt it flow through me like lava.

He held his glass aloft, slightly to the left of where I was sitting. When he heard me speak, he straightened up towards me. Touched my glass. I clinked back, and a tiny drop of drink slivered down his fingers. They were so beautiful, his hands.

'I'm really sorry I said what I did, Jeremy. I had no right. I was angry because you were having a go at me. Well, I thought you were. I mean, I've told you why I don't go out.'

Jeremy drained his glass and poured a refill. He held out the bottle. I shook my head and then realised what I was doing. It was easy to forget Jeremy couldn't see.

'It's okay, Iona, I'm the one who should be sorry. I was out of line. I should have asked myself the same question. Am *I* happy? But I'd been thinking about your need to find out everything in advance. I mean, how you always research the movie. Have to know about it all. Even the ending.'

'No surprises that way.' I finished my drink and put down the glass. It sounded as hollow as I did. Jeremy leaned over and refilled it before I could protest.

He laughed again, softer this time. 'You know, Island Girl, it's only recently occurred to me we're always talking of lighter things. Movies. My work. All you've told me about yourself is of when you were a child. All those stories of you and your papa. And Holly of course. But I don't even know how you live.'

'Papa died in a car crash when I was nine and Mother got an insurance payout. When she died, I inherited what was left. It's enough.'

'That's not what I meant. Why don't you let me see *you*?'

I'd moved across the room, Jeremy was facing away again, focusing his voice in the wrong direction like an actor on his first day, not sure of where the camera was.

When I answered he turned towards me, his look serious.

'Jeremy, I've told you. I was in an accident. A party at my uncle's farm. A bonfire and some lighter fluid. Do I need to draw a picture?' Instantly I regretted my words. I knew he hadn't meant my appearance. But he didn't flinch.

He came over to me. I closed my eyes, seeing what he saw. The darkness, but mine was tinged with red. He led me back to the table. Poured me another drink and sat down next to me. The silence brought in the outside. I could hear the birds in the magnolia tree. Somewhere down the road a car tooted its horn. A lumbering sound of a garbage truck, the whoosh of its brakes and lifting arms, discharging all the rubbish into its depths, seemed like it was in the room with us.

Jeremy ignored my outburst. 'I'm sorry, Iona, I should have visited more often after your mother died. But I was so busy with my job.' He paused. 'No bloody excuse really.'

I stared up at the ceiling, noting a long thin thread of web descending but no spider.

'Let's stop apologising.' My words sounded more level than I felt. 'There's an old movie on right now, called Jezebel, stars Henry Fonda and Bette Davis. We've missed the start, but we can easily catch up.'

Jeremy got up, scraping his chair across the floorboards. 'I bet you know what's going to happen anyway.'

I picked up both glasses, dunked them down heavily on the sink, and sat back in my chair, not bothering to switch on the TV.

'I don't really,' I said, being obtuse on purpose. 'I mean, you come over here all high and mighty. Asking if I'm happy. What do you actually want from me, Jeremy?'

He was standing behind me now, his hands swept my hair from my forehead. I shrank into myself.

'It's okay, Island Girl, I don't need to see your face. I know you're beautiful. Oh God, if you could only see how I do see you.'

I turned halfway and he dropped his hands.

When he spoke it was like a slow dance. 'You must know how I feel, Iona? I've been coming here for three years, hardly missed a week. I was wondering if they'd run out of classics before I got up the nerve to make the first move. And yes, I have gone out with girls before. But you, Iona. You're different. Oh shit, that sounds like a line. So lame. And I don't want it to be.'

I spun around, my breath quickening. How dare he. Was I that fragile to him? Unapproachable? A fragile useless young woman too frightened to step out of her own house. Agoraphobia. That's what it was called, wasn't it?

My hands found his face and I drew him to me. I had watched enough movies to get this right, surely. Our lips met and Jeremy crushed me to his chest, his voice husky. 'God, Island Girl, do you realise what you're doing?' I could feel his hardness and gasped. More warmth flooded me like the whisky.

He released me and pushed me back. I nearly stumbled and would have, but the kitchen bench stopped me.

His voice was barely raised. 'No, this is not right. You've had too much to drink. I've said some stupid things.'

'We both have,' I whispered.

I didn't try and stop him as he left the house. 'I'll be back tomorrow, Iona. I'm finishing work early, for the rest of the week.'

After he'd gone, I felt embarrassment rising in equal degrees as the effects of alcohol diminished. What the hell had possessed me?

And yet I was strangely pleased with myself. An unknown feeling. I felt as if I could do anything. I'd only needed to take that first step.

I hesitated at the back door, then thrust it open and walked out into the garden. The breeze caught my breath like a newborn. Leaves, blown across the yard, huddled a heap in the corner as if they were trying to escape the walls. Colours merged like a Monet.

It was so bright my eyes ached. Mown lawn and garden perfumes tagged my mind to fonder times. Holly, her mouth full of her favourite toy. Dropping it at my feet and bounding away, happy expectation on her widely grinning face. Life had been so full back then, so full of possibilities.

I knelt beside Holly's grave, brushed away the clippings, remembered Jeremy's hands brushing the hair from my face.

And then I heard my mother and papa. Shadow voices from the gusts of wind which played eerily on the overhead wires.

You can't take her, Henry. I mean for god's sake look at her.

Well, she can't stay here can she? Not with you. You've never been a mother to her even before...

Why don't you say it, Henry, my dear? Before the accident that you insist was my fault for not watching her. But it wasn't. It was you and your brother arguing why the damn fire wouldn't light.

That was the day before Papa left us and, less than a year later, we received the news of the car crash. There had not been time for a divorce.

'Iona.' This voice was real. I spun around and there was Jeremy. 'God,' he said, 'I didn't expect to see you out here.' He was grinning, this time in the right direction, and holding out some brochures. I took one from him and read *Discovering Scotland in Spring*. There was another, outlining the itinerary. Stuck along the tops of each were strips of Braille. I realised they were some of the leaflets he kept for reference at the travel agency. I started to give them back, but stopped. Nearby a bird flicked itself free from the magnolia and disappeared into an impossibly blue sky. Two butterflies joined in a flutter of colour.

When Jeremy spoke again, his tone was crisp and clear, like bubbles of champagne. 'Iona, I've left my job. I phoned in my notice yesterday, when I went home to get the drinks. Instead of selling it to others, I'm going to do it myself. What I love. Travel.' He must have felt my hand pressing the brochures into his, but when he pushed them back to me I took them. Wasn't travel like life, a series of steps?

And, although I knew he couldn't see it, I smiled, nodded as he asked, 'You wanna tag along, too. Island Girl?'

www.ingramcontent.com/pod-product-compliance
Lightning Source LLC
Chambersburg PA
CBHW021457110726
47899CB00001BA/198